THE

INK

RUN *A NOVEL VIGILANTE*

Published by GMGA Publishing

ISBN: **9798594923362**

First Printed and bound in Great Britain by Clays Ltd, St Ives plc.

Published by GMGA Publishing (www.inkyourlegacy.com)

Design & Illustration by James Ryan Foreman www.jamesryanforeman.com.

Front cover image: The tranquilizing chair of Benjamin Rush, derived from a wood engraving originally published in 1811.

THE AUTHOR ...

DALE BRENDAN HYDE was born in Salford in 1974 yet has lived most of his life in the City of Wakefield West Yorkshire.

A troubled life throughout his teens crescendo into a lengthy prison sentence for robbery. Upon release a mixture of attending college to retake failed schooling & continued trouble with the police & high courts until a university place seemingly became the catalyst to a more determined path of making his occupation that of a Writer.

He published his first poetry book by Route at the Yorkshire Art circus for the TS Elliot prize. Contributions to other writers books followed & magazine articles on his passion of bare knuckle boxing reveal his extensive repertoire in his writing styles.

Trouble free now for over a decade, his debut novel THE INK RUN finally shows the true depth of his talent.

His first Poetry, published by ROUTE, is now available in paperback & kindle for the first time to the public under the title, THE GODS R WATCHING.

His first short story, titled, THE WHISKEY POOL, is like all his books, available to purchase in paperback & kindle on AMAZON.

His second full length novel titled STITCHED, is an autobiographical account of his early years in trouble, dealing with a potential Decade behind bars for a miscarriage of justice & his ultimate Acquittal. Available on Amazon in paperback & kindle, published by GMGA.

His third novel currently under construction will be available via GMGA Publishing. THE DEATH ROW THRIFT SHOP. A crime fiction serial killA thriller.

IT'S SO PEACEFULL IN THE NIGHT

BUT OUTSIDE CREEPING IS A FRIGHT

TOO SCARED TO SEE WHOS THERE

YOUNG OTISS DOES NOT CARE

A VILLAGE VIGILANTE BY THE MOON

BY DAY HE WAITS & QUIETLY FUMES

IF YOU GO ON THE LIST

THEN JUST TOO BAD

HE MUST HATE YOU LIKE HIS DAD

IF YOU'RE A FRIEND THEN RELAX YOURE SAFE

BUT FOR THE OTHERS

THE RAFT AWAITS

RECOMMENDED TO BE READ BY CANDLELIGHT

'What some people find in religion a writer may find in his craft....a kind of breaking through to glory' Steinbeck.

Persons attempting to find a motive in this narrative will be prosecuted; persons attempting to find a moral in it will be banished; persons attempting to find a plot in it will be shot. Mark Twain 1835-1910

Attention all lizards, THE INK RUN has begun.

(Nod to Castaneda)

They are able. Who think they are able

Virgil 70-19bc

CAVEAT EMPTOR!!!!

You know what my Art was to me, the great primal note by which I had revealed, first myself to myself, and then myself to the world.

Oscar Wilde

{SANCTUARY chapter 1} *In the reflection of my distorted face, the small pebble dropped away, swirling to the depths where the water darkened it from my view. That plonk when you drop it into the water, that's the sound barrier breaking.*

Circular ripples now in the stream slowly ebbing away from me until the last ring vanishes. The smoothness of the surface returns again bringing me back to the serenity of the rafts enclosure.

Every so often you could hear the rumble of trafik on the village lane above. I was staring hard now into the cool waters. You didn't make out the colours here. Blinking caused the bruising to nip at my skin. I knew the colours were there, they always were, like the permanent chrome yellow in Van Gogh's sunflower.

This didn't feel like love though, tear stained eyes, blackened you could say, but they never came close enough to see the damage. A darker yellow should be on its way soon, or at least that is how it happened last time, purple for the weak end.

I could still hear them arguing. Strange how you can carry drama & shouting around in your head, even though you fled the scene. The stillness of my handmade raft held some comfort. It had been my secret getaway now for quite awhile.

I'd lose track of time down here, with the gentle bobbing of the raft lulling me with the stirred up current this far down stream. It gurgled & boiled angry up near the arches entrance, the man made waterfall from the rag mill crashed violently down. From my far back safety spot the sheer wet curtains hid me nicely from everything.

The last slap round my head before I fled out the door from the house had set the horrid ringing off again inside my ears. All my other friends, well really there was only Johnny Sand who spoke to me about it, never came to school beat up.

"Why you would never understand" they my parents would yell at me inbetween Da locking mum down the cold cellar & smoking what she called his funny fags.

I couldn't switch the abusive dialogue off in my ears.

"Otiss, get your scrawny little body here now, do you hear me boy!"
"Otiss you fuckin little dummy"!!!!

That's all I remember of youth. Thirteen years had passed. Mum &
Da had always had problems, I was no dumb kid. I knew deep down
what they were doing to me was wrong, but they were my parents &
they drummed it into me with violent repetition that it was for my
own good.

Today's fun & games had started at the lekimeter door. Stan had
noticed in his stoned existence that the emergency was on £1.80.

I knew what was coming when I hear the Bullseye TV show theme
tune whistling up the stairs through Stan's cracked lips.

I had been reading up in my room a book Johnny had lent me.

The war blanket swept aside. Stan threw the dart. I wiped the blood
trickle from my calf. He was probably aiming at my head. He
dumped a bowl of copper coins upon my bed & went back downstairs
to his shaman chair to smoke some more.

Limpin down the lane, my mission to return with fifty pence pieces
that fed the meter. My embarrassing jingling pockets, my teeth
chattering, I was a sad one man band alright.

All these thoughts flashed with quick succession as I stared back into
the water n watched in my mind how Stan had attacked me because
Mr Longbottom at the shop had said he couldn't possibly take all the
old pennies.

Stan had flipped out n I bobbed about on the swaying undercurrent
once again.

I usually waited a few hours on the raft n then trudged back as if the
hangman's trap waited. To Coventry first, as Da played his
multitude of games in different order to keep me off balance.

Tish, my mother, would be glad his fists were now upon me, giving her a small break from his torment. Stan's silence wouldn't last long. Yeah I'd been called a genius before many a time. It always left Stan's mouth in this vile leering spitting mock sneer, usually as I left every morning for skool.

Build me up, knock me down with the knocking a regular rhythm like the quiet background ticking of the hall clock.

I recalled once late in the night, I had been asleep, not long though as my stomach had ached for food, keeping my retreating bliss interrupted with moments of waking. Hunger pains stabbing at my ribs, right under the fresh bruises Stan had leathered into me earlier in the day. Da had come in from the city centre, he had left ten hours ago slamming the door on his way out. "I'll be back in an hour or so, just off to meet the boys".

Back then in that time mum would open up a little once he was safely on his way up the lane. I could see she hated him with the amounts of whiskey she drowned the glass with each time it dared to nearly empty. When you've lived with someone for so long they start to control a certain part of the others mind she would explain.

Stan had certainly got inside mums brain for sure. A lobotomy of love she would often say. She would yell at the door after he had been gone a few minutes, Screaming that he was a lousy no good bastard n he would not be back until the sun dropped out of the sky. Mum was usually right and that day had been no exception.

I must have slipped off a little, yet now awoken from dreams that seemed impossible to imitate into my shit day to day life.

Stan rattled the whole house when he brought reality crashing home. I could hear him grabbing at the rail on the steep stone stairs, pulling his heavy drunken frame to its pit.

Dragging the odd assortment of rag tag covers over my head; I'd held my breath and listened intently for him to hopefully just pass oblivious by my wrecked door frame. He had shoved me through it the summer before and all that hung there now protecting me was an old war blanket.

Thankfully stumbling on and into the bathroom next door, I heard Da gip, then the splash of his poisoned vomit hitting the pan. Id wanted to shout out to him, like any normal kid, goodnight Da, I love you.

But I'd smiled at his discomfort, thinking as I buried my head into my pillow, Goodnight wanker.

{SOCIAL MAN KNOCKS chapter 2} That next morning had been breezy as I'd watched from my bedroom window my washing dance on the line, like a tramp lambada. The tree branches seemed to clap in time to the swaying limbs that were powered by the force of the oncoming winters freeze.

Dad had not risen yet, which was no different from any other morning except today's Fate or destiny, which ever force pulls the man stronger through life had decided to come a knocking.

"Otiss can you come down here a minute sweetheart"

I knew then that there was someone important at the door; she never ever called me sweetheart any other time. I hurried to pull on my other set of clothes that I had worn all week. I had been in the bathroom trying to wash off some of the stains when I heard her call. Running down the darkened hall, slowing to navigate the steep stone stairs that always spread such coldness along the floor into my room, I now half way down, caught the tone of a voice that was very unfamiliar. I had no recollection of the owner of such a shrill tone.

"We have received a number of complaints Mrs Kites"

As I entered the scene, mum was holding the door ajar and I could see this shiny black shoe pocking through the gap and through the distorted glass panel a be speckled suited man, poking his beak into our family life. The voice sounded more like a young girl than a man, but I suppose I was a little biased living with a cave man for a father.

"I must insist Mrs Kites"

Mum heard my movement and turned her head to look at me, her face held an expression that I had seen many times before, a painted on smile beneath a scared yet angry face. "Otiss sweetheart, go wake your father please, NOW".

I stood rooted to the spot for a moment, my mind spinning. There was definitely trouble at the door, even if it wasn't my trouble, I was going to get some, I had to go wake dad.

"Otiss now please I said"! "Yes Mum"

I hit the stairs like being led to the gallows, Pierrepoint gripping my young hand, telling me it was going to be ok. Which after each step rising and thinking of the alternative, seemed a blissful drop.

I turned onto the landing, Bentleys bend. Outside Dad's door I could hear the snores. My hand hovered over the handle, I tried to open the door quietly, and stupid really as I knew I had to wake him. But if I woke him the wrong way, or as Stan would put it in his clichéd way, you made me get out of bed the wrong side this morning. There was a clip coming round the head either way.

He laid there still dressed from the night before. As I looked over him, he looked worried in his slumber, like he knew the new dawn would only remind him of his short comings in life, which he totally blamed on me and Tish. I gently shook him, my little pale hand pushing against his massive hairy arm. I always read dads tattoos when he was asleep as they fascinated me still, no matter how many times I'd studied them. I pressed my finger into the dragons face and thought as Da stirred that the monster actually came to life. One of Dads bleary eyes opened and as it glared straight through me. It reached deep boring right down into my soul.

"What you in this room for BOY"? "Sorry Da but mum says" "I don't give two shits if the judge said! You get the fuck OUT".

Retreating with a stumble I headed back to the top of the stairway.

"Mum" The silence was lost Air shrilled from her reply with anger, "WHAT "All the electrodes in my brain screamed dilemma. Fearing both parents at times, which as I grew older only seemed to intensify caused me so much internal pain and anguish. I never seemed to be able to please them both at the same time. Usually it was Stan whose mark I failed to measure up to the most. I got ready to enter again.

Heading back down the hall got me thinking of Granddad Pedley's tales of the mineshafts. Dark tunnels filled with haunting visions of paranoia, danger lurking above.

I loved Granddad Pedley. I had only recently started to get to know him. Mum n Da had told me when I inquired one day about why all the other kids at my skool had Granddads n I appeared to have none. I certainly remember how believable they made it sound. Granddad was dead. Killed years back in a bare knuckle fight nr a small village outside of the city called Hemsworth.

That was my mum's side. With Stan's, the info was zilch, a wall of silence. I wasn't even entirely sure if my last name was my true birth right, like some mystery man with no blood line to trace. Now if it had not been for my one true friend Johnny Sand I would never have unravelled their lies.

Johnny had told me one day that his Granddad n my own had been friends years back. A friendship created by a certain bare knuckle booth man. Mr Topliffe ran the fairground booths of their day. The infamous terror booth was no place for the faint hearted. And it was on this famous pitch where Johnny n my Granddad Pedley became stable mates n firm friends.

When me and Johnny had next visited his old Granddad he had given me my Granddads address, telling me to give ol Poleaxe Pedley his best. He wrote the addy down on the back of an old tattered photo and as I turned it over thanking him Isa three tough grainy faces staring hard back at the camera.

On the left there was no doubt Johnny's Granddad. He still had the jet black swept back slick hair style. To the right I stared strangely into a mirror, ol Poleaxe Pedley looked the business alright. I certainly wouldn't have fancied going around in the booth with that man. And holding the photo together, the glue in the centre was the one and only infamous Mr Topliffe, the terror booth in the background as a stark reminder of a bygone era of the glorious days of men and bare knuckle fashion.

I had only waited till the next evening to sneak out up the lane to his close by addy. As I first visited him he seemed happy to see me, yet a little reluctant to open up about anything period.

"Did your Mother finally let you see your ol Granddad then?"

He would sit me down on his battered leather red settee n the tales finally began over time. The tales of the mines fascinated my young mind. The dark tunnels where the constant danger, dreadful deaths and special friendships were made for life

He would switch stories and they all seemed to just mingle into one great tale of adventure. The stoker job he had held in the navy, the submarine he had served on and the most amazing for me, the booths on the fair where he had been champion.

He had taken the photo Johnny's Granddad had given me and led me to his elegant table that held pure silver picture frames. Pride of place in the centre was the same photo.

The only sad thing that bothered me while listening to these wonderful tales was the long painful coughs that abruptly stopped him like a sudden clout to the solar plexus. A sudden clout that I sure expected to be heading my way as I focused back on my predicament at hand, as I held my hand hovering near to Stan's door handle; Granddads battered old mitt flashing a candle light way down in the shaft below.

Time seemed to stop for a moment and the silence of the landing only seemed to intensify the knock as bone connected with old worn wood. No answer came and I deliberated for a moment whether to take the punishment off Stan or go back down and take what Mum would dish out. Stan would go to town. He had already told me to get out once, plus I'd woken him and he was hung over bad. Mum on the other hand would not touch me straight away, not with the specki man at the door. She would feel shown up though, undermined. She always felt embarrassed easily and once the door shut tight she would double lock it and come find me. Then again, Stan only teased me anyway when Mum hit me. "You little sissy boy", he would yell, giving me the manly clout on top of Mums punishment. To toughen me up he would say as he claimed his breath back from the exertion.

I knocked again, the punishments weighed up. Tensed, for the mind was already reacting to what lay in store. Still no answer so I entered warily into Stan's domain.

As dark as the landing, so no adjustment for my eyes, I could just make out he had moved a little since I last entered. One arm hung heavily over his eyes as if the dark was not enough for him to retreat into. He must have woken from my knocking, just ignorant as to what I wanted. He spoke to me without moving the arm away, my eyes now fully transfixed on his mouth.

"Otiss how many more fucking times, get out of this room"

I stared at his teeth, they were not real. Knocked out he had once told me. "You should have seen the other guys" I recalled the braggin. Mum had told me that it had been ol Poleaxe that had smashed them out in the early years of their doomed marriage.

"Otis" for a minute I'd lost my hearing, mesmerised by the false teeth that hid the true state of my Fathers mouth.

Now he took them out, which he always did when he was trying to scare the living daylights out of me, all I could see was a gaping hole in between two sharp fangs.

I decided to turn n run for the door. Maybe just keep on running, jump through the window and run on broken ankles to catch the man from the door, tell him everything. Just blurt out my hell on earth existence. Hope for a rescue. The grip was instantly numbing, blood supply goodbye.

He pulled me effortlessly towards him, my eyeball now lined up with his fanged mouth. I smelt the previous evenings drink turned sour with the dry mouthed night he had slept with.

I tried to breathe it in through my mouth, my nostrils not content to give in to such a stink, so powerful though it was creeping n swirling up my mouth and into my nostrils the opposite way, inflamed with a stench so foul is how they felt. Stan just kept pulling me closer, my eye now just been robbed of the dim light, the dry saliva lips starting to suck. I thought this time that he would succeed in sucking the eyeball right out of my skull, he held back just only letting go at the last moment before it ripped out of my socket, the red swell stinging. Blinded, for he made up for not going the distance with a straight ram rod jab to the other eye. His rasping drunken laff now accompanied the assault.

The knockout blow I never saw coming, but come it must have. From the lumps throbbing on the back of my skull it was painfully clear that I'd been dragged down the staircase.

My eyes flicking consciousness quickly back into my vision. Lurking in the kitchen they found focus on Stan, his paisley shirt striking a balance against the flock paper on the wall.

Ma was busy burning holes into her useless evening gowns; the ironing board set up was an old towel on the breakfast bar.

The specki man at the door was gone and not the topic on Stan's agenda. Firstly he wanted me n mums opinion on the 2.30 at Epsom, [silver by nature] was mentioned with a long deliberation on whoever we believed a straight sum to win on the nose was a better idea than going with[don't push it]each way.

None of it mattered what we thought or cared, He would wonder off n do what the hell he liked. He would do the spot the ball, a hundred X's for ten bob. He always drew his pattern of x, s into either a picture of a spiff or a gun. But he would screw that into a ball n throw it in the bin, redoing a spare sheet with some shape more respectful to his bullshit persona he liked to keep up around the village. He must have known what he was doing at the bookies cos he always came home with some Winnings, or what was not drunk out of them in the village pubs.

{THE RAFT chapter 3} A large truck that usually didn't use the small village lane rumbled loudly above. It brought my drifting mind back to the surrounding water of my raft. It was the usual routine down here. I would drift off with horrible scenarios from my home life.

Going under the road where to my young tormented mind the falls were Niagara and all the Angels flowing together. I make my way down past the Manchester stamped iron turning wheels, still standing solid for 170 years and now I have my foot upon it, tying a lace that a bramble wanted while hacking my way here with a snapped off branch through the undergrowth. Even my trodden path was a little wild still and for good reason, it hid the way to my sanctuary. On the way this time a humanitarian asks from inside my mind as to whether I should cover the fresh dead frog? He seems so vulnerable to hungry prey, lying on his back on the large stone slab. I gently nudge him off and into the verge, rip up some nearby long grass and cover the loss. The dandelion I leave on top makes me look skyward and I nearly ruin the good deed by hoping God noticed that kindness of a free burial. Throw a red and white rose for me please, for this Mancunian is the Yorkshire boy on the other side of the Pennines. The first time I trod the path, dense was the forest of nature. It held back hidden from my sight the gush of white noise, this new path I dragged my scrawny body through with the bracken trying its best to bar my way from its huge angry bubbling call.

I hacked and slowly followed the path, like a new found Buddhist finding the scent of the josh stick swirl inside his nostril helping him towards seeking nirvana.

The crashing curtain of water came into view, my eyes trying to take in its power, distracted as a dislodged log from upstream lost its battle and submerged out of sight, the cool surface not the only witness. It had taken like most things when as a kid the whole long lazy school summer break, to finally finish my much needed sanctuary. The working men's club next door to our house, and you can note if you will that I did not say home, had put some new doors on the garage at the bottom of the large car park, where it kept the bowling team bus. One half of the old pair that had come off had been lugged by yours truly like Jesus struggling with that cross under the cover of darkness to the roadside, where there was a small in length iron railing.

From a pedestrian point of view you could see through the gaps far down to where the stream gathered force, but you couldn't see the waterfalls curtained entrance. For that you had to go where no one bothered to tread. The old mill had been shut a few years now, but out of loyalty to ol man {cemetery name} they had kept him on as security. There might have been some valuable lead or machinery knocking about the place, but no one went the quarter mile through all the brambles to the river edge. I had thrown from the roadside barrier the garage door over the side one early morning. It wasn't ideal, for it risked from that height breaking, but there was no way of sneaking past ol man {cemetery name} with it on my aching back through all that hidden tangled path. I'd retrieved it well and luckily intact and spent the next few days fitting with stolen rope from Mrs Burnley's garden these large plastic containers that I'd found in the mill grounds. They had great potential as floats, filling them a little to pull the raft nice and level to the waterline. It was steady enough and it wasn't long before I started retreating out of Stan's way to its bobbing, lulling peace. I always had to head back to the house though.

I was completely shit scared of what they would do if I stayed away too long. I think they allowed me a few hours, probably glad I wasn't around, but I liked and needed to think that it was because they were sorry and allowed me a bit of recovery time.

{DIRTY POTS chapter 4} *As soon as I entered the long ginnel that brought me warily to the back door of the house, the fear level hit its familiar high. Going in and seeing Stan in the kitchen made me freeze to the spot. He motioned me forward to where he stood by the sink, his slow bending index finger calling me silently, his eyes dead fixed with hate. "Get that fuckin washing up done you little girl's blouse".*

The water was filthy, much darker than the stream under the road. Dad stood rigid and silent next to me, breaking the moment with a loud mocking laff as soon as my hands disappeared into the gloom of the sink. When I felt the first stab of pain I realised Stan had caused his own sick amusement again. He was still laughing as he pulled the metal strung plug. Tears had now formed in my eyes, both our eyes in fact, yet Dads were just tears of laughter.

Through the watery glaze of my sight, the well placed knives and broken glasses revealed their danger, lurking, waiting to cut me. What really hurt though was Stan clouting me round the noggin for being soft, barking orders that I had better get this mess cleaned up before mum got in. The task seemed to take forever, trying to finish at the end by clearing and wiping down the side. My wounds still spilling claret and clean worktops would again be dirtied with my young dripping blood. It wasn't long before he was down to inspect. Timing it as usual, just a few minutes before Tish came wearily through the door from work. His last act before she did was to go fetch his ice cube tray from the booze fridge. He held it steady under my crying eyes n filled the little squares up to the brim for his whiskey later.

He had been busy up stairs getting shaved n splashing on his strongest manly aftershave. I watched him check the leki meter door. Over his shoulder I could see it was on £6.66

He turned back to face me, a devilish grin spreading across his jowls. This time I didn't have to walk the lane to Mr Longbottom's. Stan was heading out for the night, going to meet the boys at the liberal club. All the info coming by way of this chat to Mum, she was to iron quickly his best shirt to match the suit he fancied wearing. As a good will gesture he told me to get out of his sight n that he would do my chore of grabbing the top up for the leki as he past the shop to the pints he was going to sink. As for Ma, he always asked if she wanted a fish supper bringing back. She would dutifully smile and say that would be lovely. He never once brought it home.

{MRS BURNLEY chapter 5} I spent the next few days off school, sitting in my room listening to the rows and getting the odd punch in the gut instead of a kiss goodnight. From my cluttered window I would occasionally see Mrs Burnley from next door. She was a strange creature for sure. Probably around the seventy years of age mark, quite a small woman with a bad limp. Her bottle glasses were always shoved high into her grey hair, holding the mop of unruly strands back from off her face. We had her brick shit house in our part of the shared garden, our house in the block of four cottages was the only one with an inside privy. She would occasionally wear flamboyant wigs, which I knew cos mum had told me were from her days as a showgirl in the thirties.

A heavy drinker, the reason Stan had declared she would be a grand neighbour. The backdoor to her home would only open a few inches due to the mountain of empty Guinness bottles climbing her walls. Mum had also told me once that the coal man had started delivering her pile of black heat inside the front door. Not in the bunker, like normal folk, but at her request right there in a sooty pile on the living room floor.

Stan would call her a nosy curtain twitchin ol hag, the funny fag's paranoia swirling heavy in his rotten brain. I'd seen her the night I had started my seclusion up in my bedroom from after the washing up incident. The rains dull sprinkle against my window had been soothing my head from the throbbing pains in my slashed hands. The security light snapped on and caused me to look down towards the patio area of the gardens. The Beethoven wig I caught sight of first and then a pink swirl of her favourite gown, the faded name of some late forties cabaret club on the back as she then went out of sight into the shithouse. I would always come away from the postage stamp window, give the old doll a bit of privacy! I could hear sirens over the wind, passing cars splashing their way down the lane, it was back to school in the morning and my only friend Johnny sands would want to hear all about my fresh scars.

{CACTUS COMB chapter 6} Stan cornered me early the next day in the tight confines of the bathroom. He had risen to release last night's almighty intake of the clubs finest tipples. I was brushing my teeth, spitting blood onto the white porcelain basin. Suddenly he grabbed me by the hated school tie and stupidly in what I thought was a rare fatherly tone of concern said. "Let me comb that mop of yours lad, you can't go off to school with your hair all over the bloody place "Then like a flash of lightning, he pulled the cactus plant off the back of the toilet cistern n dragged it up n down my scalp

"You need to be able to fit that dunce's cap on your head boy", his final words of encouragement as he booted me up the arse n out the door. The postman on the way up the ginnel said, "Morning young man", but I stayed mute, the blood trickling down the nape of my scrawny neck. I'd have a lot to explain when I arrived at school, but I had my strict instructions from Stan as to what a clumsy kid I was. Always getting into scrapes, always falling down, you get the drift. I ambled up the lane, fresh graffiti on the walls I noticed.

Thatcher Thatcher milk snatcher.

One to ask Johnny about for he seemed the smartest kid I knew, smarter than all the adults to be fair. He gave me great books to read. I had to hide them from my parents though because the last book when Stan threw the dart into my shin had gone straight on the garden fire. The last thing they wanted was me becoming informative. So I read under the road in peace, learning about the world. I'd read the bit where the fabulous author had put down the bones of the plot, but I had not been able to resist bringing it smuggled back into the house. My torch hadn't quite run out of batteries and I had not been able to stop licking my finger, turning new pages. From under my bed I reached and read how the writer had fleshed out his bones and further. Fascinating scars and tattoos and sunburnt pigments had me speeding late through the night to its twisting, turning clever end.

But like a shit book, where you skip a bit and flick through looking for a sign of brilliance, the next day's school lessons had me drifting my eye to the clock every five minutes, wanting and needing to get back to my room to read it from the start again.

As I approached the house, I could see the black smoke from the lane, snaking out of our ginnel. I had dilly dallied on the walk home, trying to time it so Stan would be out at the bookies, the school bus passed like clockwork with the usual jeers from the school bullies, who didn't realise I did my best to miss the ride home due to the fact my parents wouldn't give me the fare.

As the cruel laughs faded I hit the ginnel entrance and a mouth full of ashes welcomed me home. As I viewed the scene it was obvious Stan had been busy searching my room for fuel again. He was stood there next to a small fire, pitch fork in hand, poking the flames as they danced like a demon. My favourite book nestled on top the small wood pile. He had heard me click the gates latch and looked up at me with his sooty face, winking and glugging from his beer can. "Come n get a warm boy", I moved slowly nearer and caught the book title disappear into a twisted melting moment. From that day on if I ever had a book from Johnny it would have to be read with discipline under the road. It had not been the end I remembered, the one I had wanted all day to get back to. Hoping to relive the thrill of the great twists of the plot inside its pages, to see if could see it unfold in the plot this time, now I knew the outcome of its clever end.

I then noticed as some wood burnt through and gave way. My favourite football shirt screwed up near the fires edge. It had scorched from the heat; Stan seeing my distress hooked it like a duck at the fair and plonked it where the flames were raging. He then emptied back his can, throwing it at my feet and leaning the fork against the fence. "Clear and level those ashes", the clip around the head, his final passing shot, his usual habitual way of passing me, especially when he was stomping about looking for more grog. I waited two hours, mesmerised by the dying flames. The pages of my book catching some heat that made it disappear for good. I held onto its contents so precious inside my memory. I wasn't going to let him rob me of that.

{FLOWER TEA LEAF chapter 7} There was on occasion a small glimmer of hope. The next day I'd got home from skool I found him ripping this small white message card from its wrapping. His real big mistake was not reading it. He just struck a match like an ol cowboy, striking the flame to life from his boot and headed out the back door and threw it lit into Mrs B's bog.

"Not a word to your Mother" he pointlessly stated, going on to reveal like the braggart that he always was that on his way out to the bookies he had spotted a ponce flower delivery lad knocking without reply on a street, on a door, on lives that Stan knew nor cared fuck all about. He had looked for a sign of impression on my face as I stood there listening to him go on about how he had stashed down a ginnel and watched the lad write out n leave a note along with the flowers on the doorstep. Stan had clocked the van disappear and casually snatched them to his empty heart zipped up the crime under his bomber jacket and headed home.

Mum not long after I had gotten home came in through the door from her shift of cleaning the offices at the local slaughter bungalow. I like an idiot tried to blank out the shame of Stan's soppy gesture, trying to convince myself that maybe we were normal happy flower givers.

Dad looked uneasy when Mum started to search for a water vase. I looked away as the same white card he had earlier sent up in smoke reappeared like some sick trick. Mum was beaming for a change at Stan's face as her workers hands pulled the card from the little white envelope. The atmosphere soon changed, she didn't need to read it all, the war dead members family were probably wondering too where this year's kind offering of remembrance was. Mum didn't shout or anything. She just left the room with a quiet sentence, "get rid of them Stanley, take them back to where ever you stole them from". Click, the door latch now left me with Dad on its bad side."Boy go throw them smelly weeds somewhere out a my sight "He banged out through the door, swearing blue murder, his voice booming in the confines of the ginnel, I scarpered for the non-safeness of my room, his shouting had stopped. He liked to keep up a front to the village that he was a decent sort. He would wait till me and Mum got locked in later, then the torment for his rebuff would commence.

{BROWN BRUSH chapter 8} *I'm sure Da had poisoned the dinner as I felt the sick keep rising with an annoying gip. A painful cough brought the inevitable bile rushing into my sore throat, which I reluctantly swallowed back down into my gut. I hit the stone steps n slowly climbed upwards towards my room, digging out my hidden toothbrush.*

I'd stashed a spare a while back when I had accidently come home early from school one day. I had been bursting for the loo and headed directly into the house. I had contemplated using Mrs B s brick shithouse but I noticed her pink night gown trailing from under the door so I'd sprinted in and up the stairs. It was just my look that our bathroom was occupied too. I knew it was Stan, I could smell him as I turned onto the landing, steadily plonked on the crapper with the pages of the daily rag definitely turned to the nags form. The door was a jar n I watched him through the crack finish without flushing away his dirty ol bastard turd. I stepped back a foot into the dark landing holding my piss swelling cock, thinking how lazy Stan was not even bothering to get rid of his stench. A new surprise awaited me though.

I could see him now, his face in the mirror mumbling something dirty unwashed hands picking dead food from dead teeth, then a burst of laughter that scared the hell out of me. His actions now were busy fumbling in the cup that held our three toothbrushes, when he lifted mine I dreaded the thought that he had been using it to brush his rancid mouth, bad enough that contemplation, but I never for one minute figured his next dirty move. Now I knew why he had left the shit in the pan, his back to me reflected enough to know what he was doing, using my toothbrush as a bog brush, then his horrible laughing face in the mirror again, replacement of my brush, a satisfied look for his latest little piece of cruelty. I back peddled the long shady landing and went back down half the stairs quiet, then so he could hear me, a bit of mock marching back up. "is that you BOY" "Yes Dad" , as I hit the last step n turned onto the landing he was in front of me , blocking me , daring me to try make a move past him. "I've just flushed Scargill down the pan and that page three bird n all, now MOVE" Never gave me the half second to try to obey the order, wind knocked out of me as sudden as he crushed me into the wall . From that day on I had to try to outthink the sick fucka, which was always hard to do as he could drop to new depths of depravity that stopped prevention. I crept out of breath to the other side of my blanket, all I could hear was him thunderin about down in the kitchen, spewin hatred, abusing the chosen stars that he wiped his arse upon from out the paper. I think it made him feel good. Mum had her soft roll, but that was off limits, she kept it on top of her wardrobe. My inside leg was wet through.

{POSTAGE STAMP WINDOW chapter 9} The scene through the decrepit window cast bleak thoughts back into my mind. A hint of sunlight encased by groups of bullying clouds wouldn't break through to brighten my day. Damp like the cellar, my feet froze to the spot. Bare floors of old stone that if restored could hold beauty. A lack of birds

in the air I notice. Huddled in their nests they had the right idea, too cold to soar for them today. The old well at the bottom of the garden had swollen to its lip, heavy rain fall that had outstayed its welcome throughout the day. The dog shit from the local strays freshly served on our lawns bed of grass, steamed away, up into the fresh mill smoking sky.

It was unusual for either of them to pop their heads into my war blanket and tell me it was time for skool, usually a screech from below would be my wake up call. This skool morning Ma stuck her rumpled bed head into my room, "come on skool time Otiss." She must have sensed my dejection and entered to sit at the foot of my bed. Rarely did she open up about Stan, but she just started spilling words from her cake hole. Stan had been born on mischief's night, bad enough I thought, but there was more, lots more. He had been born at the exact time as a celebrated hanging that had took place. The local man had murdered his entire family, roaming the house first smearing blood upon the walls then moving up the streets dabbing bright red blood prints upon his neighbour's doors. It was a local bit of Gallowthorpe history. Maybe the spirit of the executed murderer had taken over a new soul. Stan certainly held all the characteristics.

Mum certainly believed in the spirit world, she had a gypsy friend called Dolly Blue who came to our house every now n again. Mum was on a roll with her tales and I stayed still letting her continue to spill the beans. She told me that the first time she had found out about Dads messing about with other women, she had taken the route over the back fields up to the common where she told me of the old women who could cast spells n shit. Now to be honest I wondered off a little, mesmerised by the clouds outside the postage stamp size window. She carried on, a tale to fascinate young minds, or so I believed once upon a time.

I was still none the wiser how ol Dolly Blue went about her old spell shit. I knew it involved her n Mum convincing Stan to drink this peculiar kind of black tea. Dolly referred to it as oolong. I had once though seen Stan out the back of the working men's club with this young slag from the village she was rumoured to have a beaver like a wizard cuff. He never saw me spying him; mind you it wasn't as though he was trying to hide the fact. He was probably hoping his pisshead mates would stumble upon the village stud. He was certainly risking his reputation that he had falsely built up over the years. The thing that I remember that surprised me most was the snippets of conversation I was picking up, "get it ard then", silence then some more fumbling "must av had (hiccup) too much ale lass", then frantic rubbing down below from the slag, she wanted action. Stan's zip ripping up the chilly night air, more snatches of despairing convo, the tart making off back into the club desperate now for a filling. Stan didn't move for some time, almost from my view point like he was frozen static, his mind so busy trying to find the words in his drunken brain to mumble dejectedly at his shrivelled punctured tool.

Mum finished her tale as I drifted back from the window and into her sentence. Skool Otiss, now hurry up. I wondered aloud why she never had the old witch put one on Stan to stop him from being such a bastard, but Mum said as I started to put on my skool blazer that there was no such spell that could ever stop that horror. The impotence spell was cock on though, pardon the pun.

Skool passed in a dream as usual, walking home most of the way safely until Johnny turned off at his exit point with a wink n a cheery, "see ya tomoro mate"

I decided to call in and see ol Poleaxe. He answered the door coughing, but soon led me to the leather battered settee that was as creased as his old big fists. He told me on this occasion how he had once lost two large fields in a card game, laughing out loudly when he added the so what they would only be worth a couple of million quid in this day n age. He told me a little tale about his own Ma. She had driven him n his brother Wilfred crazy over the placement of a certain desk in her home. "She had it put in every part of every different room and it was never quite right. The last time she had asked him to move it, Wilf had gone to the upstairs window, pulled the twist n prized down the pane. Granddad lost in anger then threw it out the window into the yard below, where it laid in the rain. Great Grandma said when she had cooled down that it looked at its best just there.

He clocked me staring at his battered mitts, telling me that when he was a bairn, his Ma would empty the tin bath that they bathed in front of the coal fire with a couple of scoops of her cupped hands. As I left that day to head home he guided me again to his table of silver framed photos, picking up one so I could closely inspect his Mums Polaroid credentials to the biggest fists I'd ever seen on a man or woman.

Back home the house was fairly quiet, Ma was out cleaning the slaughter bungalow, just the faint sounds of Johnny Cash at San Quentin hollering away in the living room from where Stan sprawled stoned in his shaman chair. At his feet laid vinyl. I'd popped my head round the door to announce my return. His red eye clocked me and he commanded me to go clean out the bath before Tish got home. Stan's eye shone in the firelight like his homemade lamp, a salvaged deep diver helmet with a wired up bulb. It sat in the corner of our bathroom, dangerously, electrifyingly, close to the metal tub. He was certainly in one of his weird stoned moods. As I'd trod up the stairs to do his bidding, I saw the hanging plug chain had sea weed left wrapped round from where he had taken his hot strange bath. Sometimes, but not on this occasion he would submerge buckets of old pennies and foreign coins like a poor king soaking up all his wealth. The bath looked like a coal man's horse had rolled around its confines. Stan was such a scruffy bleeda. After much elbow grease I was nearly there to see it sparkle again, noting there was nothing wrong with his timing as he stuck his head round the door as I bent double over the final wipe.

"Mums home boy so hurry up n finish it" As if on Q I heard her come in the back door, Stan gone, sucking up to her now. The sly bastard from the top of the stairs I heard saying, "Just had a lovely bath girl, spent bloody ages cleaning it as well". Probably after shag I thought as I swilled away the last visible stains from the lying filthy pig.

{BLOWBACK chapter 10} Stan's index finger and thumb were black at the tips, like old tattoo ink dipped into elder's skin. He had crumbled so much of his resin into the stoned night that he had run out and was now as I came across him in the room building what he liked to call his bajanga spliff. The room was in near darkness, the heavy drape curtains pulled almost shut. The street lamps orange glow showed the blossom trees over the road were bare, a good indication to the season. Raking through the cinders of dead love, Stan had the poker in hand, while Ma who had been commanded from his shout to the kitchen was on her sooty knees, removing the pile up of smoked spliff ends, steadily building them into a neat heap. Pa liked this monthly ritual. All the bits from the fire grate would crumble from the pile, torn dirty rizla all over the glued Marley jigsaw board that he used for this task. The fresh clean rizla's did a white swan lake ballet, a lizards tongue to follow such elegance, dry n crusty, mushing them into a long white strip, where done twisting them around into his preferred cone shape. A click from the flint n the shits burning good. It would result in a horrid cloud of ganja, coal and stale tobacco, Mum getting the first exhaled blast of shit when he blew a steady stream of pure hatred in her direction. The hash tray flowing over like a spilt urn, lights turned down again, the lamp larverin away with a red swirl. Stan's Triffid excelled in strength and growth with every lung full of weed he blew over its giant leaves. The eerie bulb that shone such a strange light behind its branches made it seem even odder. Ma would switch off the plug whenever Stan was out, but he would automatically flick it back to its surreal best as soon as he entered the room, then it would be straight to the booze fridge, n then a smack for me. Not always in that order but usually that way.

I stupidly got the mood all wrong tonight. I thought he must be pretty chilled, his hand reaching for the lighter again, his favourite shaped like a shotgun. Mam had finally nagged enough this winter month. He levelled it to his ear, and flicked it alive. The gross hairs that protruded like a hundred year old professor whooshed into thin air, just the scents of scorched earlobe skin drifting towards Tish's thin victorious smile. He laid back, eyes shut, moulded to the shaman chair, quiet for minutes, then mumbling on about 1977 been a great year, for king size rolling papers had been launched, inspiring him to concoct super lengths to his funny fags. He was still for a moment while he inhaled deeply, then suddenly bursting forward to grab the poker that had its white hot tip just enough in the fire to brand. He declared in a slow drawl, "Colonel Mustard, in the library with a candelabra", shouting the last part, "al give ya clue its MURDER"

Stan was well zonked out tonight for sure, almost as sudden sinking back into his shaman chair and a stoned unconsciousness. The hash tray getting clattered to the floor, the bajanga spliff still lit in his sleeping hand.

Twenty seven spliff's of nugget flavoured skins later, he came a lookin. By the TV was his big hammer, the one with the loose end, making it unpredictable as to when you might cop for it as he waved it recklessly around his head. As I fled the scene of what was going to unravel into a severe mellow beating for yours truly, noticed as I raced out and past Mrs Bs garden that Stan had earlier ripped up her not so long ago planted pansies and thrown them scattered all over her famous rhubarb bush. When he was stoned I always took the option to flee. When it was the grog he became fast n sly, always trapping me.

As usual I never seemed to recall much of the journey down the lane, I knew of some of the nasty characters that dwelled in the area. Stan wouldn't hold back in our household when it came to either slaggin or braggin bout his Fellow residents of Gallowthorpe.

Luckily on this occasion I bumped into no one, even ol man {cemetery name} was dozing on his chair as I crept passed quietly anyway n headed off the edge of the yard to the start of the brambles and my path beyond. The noise of the water fall didn't seem as loud now to me after all these meetings. Certainly nothing like it had boomed when I first encountered it at close quarters. When you got through the quarter mile of snaking twisting turns, there were a few levels of earth to jump down before getting to the large stone arch way where the heavy curtain of water rained down in a sheet of power. The corner, if you squeezed tight against the stone would just about enable one to pass through without getting drenched. Cat like I disappeared through to the other side. Once through I always heaved a heavy sigh of relief. I had my sanctuary for a while and my heart beat gradually started to return to normal.

The source of the water ran from a large lake at the far end of the village, the local kids had nick named it the lake of stars. The river flowed a few miles through the side of an old golf course and into a large dam that was located at the back of the rag mill. From there it came down a manmade weir and levelled off again for a run through some large boulder rapids. From prying eyes it lost itself there to woodland that was thick n heavy with sharp bramble, so dense that nobody attempted to tread through to its edge. No one really had much need, as for miles you could enjoy its banks n views at easier points. But for me, I had a need to go beyond. From the other side, the front entrance to the disused rag mill was where I had curiously followed my fear, looking for a place to hide from home. The river, everyone knew ran under the road and further over some abandoned land showing itself again through another archway that had collapsed many a year ago. It was perfect for me because no one could enter from this side. The collapse leaving a tangled stone wreckage where the water powered through n on to where the river again quietened and snaked its way out of Gallowthorpe and onto the next village which was Scroftune. There was only Johnny who had seen my way to the other side of the curtained water. I had shown him a few months after I had got the raft set up. He had promised to never reveal or come again to my spot. Telling me it was my own sanctuary, which every man needed. Before he had left that one day he had spent twenty minutes or so scratching something on the wall just near the entrance on the secret side. He had left me on the raft, curiously wondering what he was putting. As I had left that day I had read on the arches wall

GOD GAVE HIS HARDEST BATTLES TO HIS TOUGHEST SOLDIERS

On this late night, I squinted to read the scratched words a few more times, trying to gain courage from what he had intended them to mean. Stan scared me so much I hardly felt like a soldier. The battle part I could relate to. Again the journey up the lane hardly noticeable in my mind as I kind of woke up from the sleepy walk back, my mind jolting back to my horrible reality as I passed brick street and caught sight of the stone gabled end to our small row of cottages. I hit the ginnel, listening for signs of the atmosphere. As I entered the back porch, the lekimeter door was open, 1066 blinked back from the reading. Yep, the battle was still raging.

Stan had wedged the front room door wide open with his old battered truncheon. The flies would at least escape the beatings. I couldn't hear mum anywhere close by, Stan on the other hand could be hiding, quiet, waiting to make the assault for disappearing come out of the blue.

As I turned to head up the stairs to my room, he appeared as a giant silhouette at the top. "I'd not bother speaking to me for the foreseeable future understood?" I didn't know whether to answer and disobey him, or stay quiet and receive a belt for ignoring him. I got one just the same as he thundered down the stairs, flying into me, a square shot to the abdomen his choice of blow. Then still trying to get me to play his one sided game again, hanging over me, his mouth close to my face. I would have gladly taken any air offered at the time, except his disgusting bog rat breath. I just turned my head to the cramped space of the wall and shuddered from the pain of not being able to breathe. Thankfully he left me alone n headed back up.

"OTISS", it was unmistakable, his voice booming down the stairs. I knew what he wanted, I just didn't know in what shape or form the release for him of violence towards me would come. He had always caught me off guard, but it was his game, his rules, so the advantages he held were always considerable.

The hoot from the train startled my heart. It was letting the few that crossed the point at the back of our house know it was on time. Usually solitary dog walkers or the odd gypsy cutting over the common, taking a short cut back to the jolly sailor camp.

Then his voice loud again, stopping for a moment my heartbeat, "OTISS." "Yes Daa", no answer. I was familiar with this methods scenario. Then he was there, legs astride, arms folded. All I could make out in the tight confines of the stair well.

"Are you fuckin deaf boy". No time to smartly answer that it would have been bliss to be defected in that fashion. His shirt that was unbuttoned, lightly scraping the walls as he headed for me. The next time I remembered anything, I was still at the foot of the stairs, the house eerily quiet, only the faint sound of mum getting ready for work upstairs n the hum of traffic from the lane. I didn't expect too much sympathy as Ma came down the stairs, but I felt hurt and very alone as she just stepped over me, the click of her small heels echoing in the ginnel as she disappeared away from the chaos towards the slaughter bungalow. Stan left me alone for a while. I just did my tasks, starting with the fire grate. Threats over with for now, I swept the broken remaining shards into the dustpan. It had been a present from Granddad Pedley that I had to lie about. Stan had threatened the day I got it to smash it to smithereens. I had said my mate Johnny had given it me for my birthday. It had been in a nice cherry frame, which now lay broken in a pile where Stan kept his fire wood. The picture, crumpled into a loose ball amongst his smoked spliff ends from last night's session. Suddenly the click of a lighter behind me, turning startled I clocked Stan. He was good at creeping for a big fella. He scooped up the picture from the grate and unfolded its creased former scene. He clicked the lighter again, catching the pictures corner. The whoosh now caught the Winning legs of Henry, as the burning shrunk Ali away from the 5th round canvas and into just blackness and flames. He held it in his hand long enough to show me how pathetically tuff he was, then let it sail spiralling down to the sooty hearth.

{PLUNDERED LUNCHBOX chapter 11} The next day as I woke for skool, the first thing I heard was "HAG" Oh Stan was certainly wooing Ma today. The word that he knew she hated the most bellowed down the stairs. "Where is my fuckin breakfast" came next, followed by the

club that he kept at the side of his pit banging and hammering relentlessly on the wooden carpet less floor. The window in my room, which I had left open slightly, to rid the rooms oily odours slammed, shut with the wind, as if in cahoots with his racket. Totally awake now, I slipped out of bed onto the floor, like a fish with a surprise hook in its neck landing onto the deck of a boat. In the kitchen Mum was busy making cheese n onion sarnies, which always became just onion sarnies once Stan came down, plundering the fillings away into his greedy bastardo mouth.

He was here now beside me, as if on Q, reading my mind. Half the cheese gone already as he flung a used t bag into any old mug to hand, slight hot water from the sinks red tap. Washed down, dribbled down, not really felt at all.

I was good to go, rushed through the door n alone again at the end of the ginnel, waiting till the skool bus passed n then walking through the village lane, Nelly Ball on the steps of her sweet shop as I passed the half way to skool mark gave a wink, as if she sensed I needed a friendly gesture.

My day brightened, as always when I saw my mate Johnny heading across the playground towards me. The first time I met him, I had a bruise on my neck that looked like someone, or something had painted a pair of strangling hands around it in bright purple paint. I'd tried to hide it from the 400 pairs of eyes at our skool. Mum buttoning my jacket tight, the top collar of my shirt already done up. But he had seen it, noticed it, even without coming too close to me at first, as if he had the knack to just read my mind as I tried to act all cool in the rising summer heat. I had begged him not to inform the staff or worse still tell any of his decent family. It was agreed that even though he disapproved of the silence he would just be there for me when I needed a chat. After the school bell had become a distant clang, we were on our way down the lane home, well he was on his way home. I on the other hand was on my way back to a house of horrors. Just before we parted, he lifted up the back of my wool skool jumper and spun me around, looking me in the eye now with concern. The foot long black bruise was ugly. It was Stan stamping his authority again for no one to clearly see.

{THREE MINUTES chapter 12} I called in on ol Poleaxe. I certainly needed support. He went through the usual routine of sweeping me through the house n getting me comfy on the big settee. I sipped at the freshly made lemonade as he looked towards the window lost in thought and said. "Three minutes, oh it could feel like an hour, an hour where the head has been cut off from its oxygen supply. The crowd in the booth as you swirl through your footwork a blur, the sweat upon your brow cascading into your stinging eyes, a hell of an effort to breathe for three minutes under the onslaught of bad intention attacks. Vinegar soaked hard fists, smashing away your skin, blood mixing with the scuffed marks of your feet on the apron floor. A lovely sound, the bell, ending all your fear"

Granddad Pedley stopped the chat and lit his pipe. He placed the box of England's glory next to his glass of lambs navy rum and I knew where he had been and where he was coming from.

The fear was back though as I left and got closer to Stan's territory. A moment of inside laughter as I noticed on the goggle box video store wall some fresh graffiti, the football hooligans who Stan mocked n called weekend offenders had been busy at the weak end. MAN U SCUM dripped down in large strokes. The Leeds lads had been busy with the brush, but there must have been a trip to town from the ICJ at some point.

Another not so fresh, but certainly quite new bit of paint read by the side of where the Leeds had written a reply.

YOUR GOING HOME IN A FUCKIN AMBULANCE

CHANT PINCHING BASTARDS

I smiled inside at the banter, but it soon vanished as I thought of Stan waiting at the house. This wasn't banter; it was a fuckin real statement. He had certainly been horrid even for his standards this past week. Mum had dropped the odd hint here n there that I had overheard about his cheating. She knew the spell from old Dolly Blue had worked. She also knew Stan didn't understand how. Even so I thought she was taking his attempts at screwing the village bike lightly. But as usual I was wrong and didn't know how either of my parent's minds worked.

{KETTLES ON LOVE chapter 13} They had rowed again, Stan brooding quietly on the front room settee. Tumbler of cheap whiskey filled to the top in his grip. Mum had stayed in the kitchen, also quietly seething.

I stood like a spare part, leaning against the battered piano that was rammed tight against the back kitchen wall.

Mum had crossed the room and I never thought much about her innocent action. She must have decided a nice cup of cha would do justice to the situation, rather than going Stan's method and drinking darker, much heavier thoughts.

She told me without looking in my direction, to go see what my Father was up to, moving away from the mugs she had just stuck T bags into after flicking on the kettle.

I pulled off slow from the maple instrument and moved through the door that led to the small landing below the stairs, gently closing its door behind me.

I noticed Dad had slammed the front room door hard enough to pull it nearly clean of its already loose hinges. I held my breath for a moment in the quiet space then pushed the wonky door into my own private hell. It looked like it too, as I noticed the fire burning in the darkness. There was a chink of lamp light from the street, where Stan had yanked the curtains shut in a fashion. I stared at his devil silhouette.

 He looked towards where I stood, probably ready to shout if it had been Mum, but he took one look at the size of the figure and just knocked back the whole glass of liquid in one go. Cracking glass I heard next, his off white coloured teeth chomping the tumblers rim. "OUT", the only heavy word he muttered. So I went up to my room and watched the normal kids play ball on the clubs car park out of my tiny blocked window. Another set of his ladders that I suspected came into use in one of his many scams taking up most of the view.

The screaming was a strange sound, not a scream of pain, not a scream of a woman scared. It was more the scream of a tortured demon that I connected with in nightmares about my Father. I had not heard Mum climb the stairs and with my war blanket hanging heavy not seen her neither. She had boiled away alright.

I had gotten her method of calming tea all wrong. I didn't hear her faintly popping open the front room door and asking Stan in a pleasant, forgiving way to come into the dark confines of the landing. Now from earlier unintended interruptions, I knew that the whiskey made Stan frisky, the bottom of the stairs landing with both doors shut was one of their make out spots. So I figured Stan must have thought they were sorting things out. I guess only has he reached the landing space, pulling the door shut behind him, Mother was not there. She had stood at the top of the stairs I figured, confident that she had coaxed him into hitting the first stair with sexual intention. The fully boiled kettle, which she had held out of sight to him, just crashed down. All of this I now concluded as the scream had me flying through my smelly war blanket and into this very sly and calculated attack by my Mother. Stan it turned out later had been pretty lucky. Only half his chest and forearm scolded. The smells of bubbling, burning flesh that were already rotten to the bone stank the house out for hours. There was no instant retaliation. He was certainly wary for a few days, but it was on the cards for sure. I just didn't know whether he was planning on including me in his almighty pay back.

{THE JUG chapter 14} *I think the worst thing that caused me ongoing pain, was every time I took a piss I reluctantly remembered every time I went to the bog, the day when even for him, Stan had been particularly horrid and sadistic.*

He must have had it all planned out, but I never imagined the bitterness of this particular operation. It started with Mum safely busy up at the slaughter bungalow. Stan cornering me in the living room as I unusually got to watch a bit of the Sweeney. "Let me teach you some self-defence" he had on this crumpled judo outfit. "Coslet's face it boy, you're as soft as curry shit"

He let me, well I say let me, I had no choice, take up my best defensive pose. He took up the sleeper hold position, Stan breathing heavy n vile down my neck. "Ready"

"DAD"

Blackness like a winter Derry night hit my eyes. Breathe gone, just now waking back up, pain instant upon waking to such a horrible bursting feeling. My arms were tied I realised in a panic as I struggled to move. Trying to raise from my own bed an impossible mission the way he had me secured. I could see large jugs filled to the brim with water next to the windowsill. Stan stood leaning against the door frame, looking, waiting there laughing to himself.

I needed a piss badly; my cock felt like it was tied in a knot. He moved I remember at this point, pulling back the covers as he ventured towards me. My cock looked like a kids water balloon, only this was my skin, not some brightly coloured balloon to fill from the tap n have fun in the summer with. The untidy thread, where he had finished with a snip of bravado completed the disturbing scene. Dr Stan seemed pleased, so pleased he showed mercy. His hand gripped my mouth roughly, while his other mitt emptied the contents of another jug. Even though it spilled heavily down my front, I had no option but to swallow most of it, as if I was drowning. What I also remembered was him punching me a terrific blow to the face. My cock did look unnaturally big, the jealous bastard hated nature's way, hated his small gift. Damaged goods were what Mum had been yelling at him since the spell from Dolly Blue had zapped him. The pain can't really be written. My jap's eye looked ready to burst. The fucka only cut the thread with his Stanley blade when he heard mum announce her return by shouting up the stairs in a tired voice, "any one there?" The release of the white cotton thread, instantly piss soaking my rag tag blankets. The next moment he was at the top of the stairs shouting down to her. "Tish, Tish, the dirty little bastard you shit into this world has pissed all over his bed again."I heard her come up the stairs slow and look over his shoulder, peering in at the scene. She was too scared of him to question the assortment of jugs n cotton threaded needle that didn't belong in the picture. He even went back to leaning against the door less frame after removing his big brown belt from around his jeans, supervising now the instructed belt I was about to receive from my Mother. Not that she needed much encouragement or advice when it came to swishing the leather against my stinging raw legs. Every time now I needed to pee, he would get me with dull pain to start, then stinging sharp slashing pain. And every time I flushed the chain and wiped the cold sweat from my brow I vowed one day, to kill the son of a bitch.

{UNDER THE ROAD chapter 15} There were so many incidents that occurred that they just all spilled into years of my teens. There was no point trying to remember them all. Some were not worth mentioning, some were so horrific that I couldn't drag them up from the deep locked space in my mind.

 The point was years of my childhood just seemed to fly past me. I didn't get the logistics of time, just the odd birthday card from Johnny that hinted at the growing age of my soul.

I think it was around the age of fifteen that Stan started his alibi bullshit. It came around the same time I had called him an Irish bog rat. He had smacked the shit out of me and smeared all the bloodiness from his hands all over my bedroom walls. I had said it to him with a bit of venom in my voice, for he had waited a while but had eventually beaten Tish very badly for throwin the kettle over him. She had looked a real bad mess, shockin me enough to foolishly call *him a name. I remember that I had spent a lot of time bobbing about on the raft that high skool summer. Which in turn, meant that the shit at home was turned up high like the misery index? As a reference, this time I found myself under the safety of the road, because I'd earlier like most kids bored of the long hols, stuck my head into Stan's paper. He had been lounging in the front room on the sofa quietly studying the form in the rag, certainly ignoring the skeel.*

I had been knelt at his feet, nervously waiting to pluck up the courage to ask him if I could go with Johnny to the fair that had set up on the heath. I had spent the last few nights laid still in my bed hearing the faint sounds, screams of horror and delight mingling within my dreams of late. In the distance the bass line rumbled and I could taste the candy floss in the blowing breeze. The twinkling lights mesmerising me in the not so far off darkness of the common, with the moon a show mans torch beaming down above the giddy proceedings.

I'd sneak there if I had to, but I had got this crazy idea in my head that I couldn't shake, to get Stan's blessing. I was still the optimist, still thinking that the past could freeze and the ideal parents would emerge to love n protect me. All I wanted was to spin until I was sick on the carneys bright swirling waltzer car. To lose my money on a scam that was obvious, but you gave it a go just for the fun of distraction, for that moment in your life where you were happy at the fair.

Johnny n I would take his metal detector up to the fields when the fair packed up n left town. We would scour the fields looking for where we thought the rides had been wild, where you were certain to lose your spare change. Sometimes we struck pay dirt, the Carney kids missing the odd coin.

My nerve held. "The fairs set up on the common Da".

Stan folded the paper down into his lap n said "do you know what Anoxia means." The fear started riding up my nerve endings, knees shaking as I held on to my legs to stop the big rattle. He bunched both fists tight out in front of him. Just holding the pose ramrod straight right in front of my knelt figure. "So you want the white knuckle ride boy eh"

He reached out n nipped the rizla packet that was laid beside him on the sofa into his fingers.

"What's Anoxia mean?"

This was my usual homework assignment, the thrilling info from the back of his spliff papers. I knew the Seven Wonders of the World, Stan adding on that particular days test, the eighth.

Today I was unsure where he was heading. He got up n left me feeling small on the floor while he headed to the kitchen. As he quickly returned, he hovered at the door with the polish n a dusting rag in his hands. He then kind of sung in a fashion, a limerick he had concocted in his sick mind.

"The rag lived under the sink, Stan has a wicked wink, a headache like no other, when I finally come too, n I still have the polishing to do." And with that he winked n flew at me. The rag he had already soaked, my blackout came quick, like the gas mask at the old dentist.

I'd gone to the raft this time because as usual when I had come around, Tish who had been upstairs getting ready to scrub the slaughter bungalow had just stepped over my crumpled body again, as I must have blocked her feet from descending the stairs. Casual little side step, practice makes perfect. Then the slam of the door, silence, then clicking heals in the ginnel as she passed, then silence as she hit the lane. My legs had felt hollow. I would not have been surprised if Stan had drained me of my blood. The bite marks were certainly there and I heard him upstairs laughing to his self, so I'd gathered what little strength I had n here I was again, bobbing gently on the safety of my raft.

It was a good distance under the road. I had it anchored with a large boulder that I had wrapped in some old blue fishing net. As you came under n past the sheer wet curtain, on the left hand side there was a narrow like tow path that went thirty metres. It had gone all the way to the other side of the roads other entrance, but at the twenty metre mark I had spent a few long days in the summer, when I had brought the raft down this far, smashing the tow path away. The light was quite dim down this far end.

I had smashed the concrete n stone until it looked to any one that ventured under the waterfalls curtain as if the path just disappeared for good. Not that anyone was coming down here, but I was certainly taking no chances. I had crumbled the stone, which sank without trace for about seven metres. I had then put the raft at the end of this dead end nicely out of sight. My safety was complete. For me to get to the raft I had after the twenty metres of good path, hammered a steel rope cable that I had found in the mill yard two foot down into the waterside. I had a towel on the raft, which I used to dry myself. I would get to where the path had gone then take off my socks n put them in my coat pocket, roll up my jeans to the knee, sling my trainers around my neck by the laces and carefully sink my foot into the cool water until it found balance on the thick steel cable. I would then place both my palms steady on the wall and inch my way down to where I had left the path intact. From there I had only to pull the rope that I had attached to the raft, its boulder anchor deep in the water only there to stop the low currents moving it too far out of reach. Yet I could pull it the five metres from the centre of the water to the side n step on. I would then use another rope that I had nailed to the other side of the raft n the other side of the wall to pull the raft back to the centre. It was a chore, but I felt it was necessary for in order for me to feel cut off n safe.

From that view looking down the stream, I could see the sheer white curtain of water because of the outside light illuminating it from behind. But if anyone ever found the step through the curtain of water, to the dark side of the stream, I was nowhere to be seen. Not even from the edge of the towpath if you followed it down into the depths. I always sat with my back to the curtain when reading by my snake torch. Not willing to be given away by artificial light. I had Granddads photo glued to the rafts wood in the centre. My small collection of books that Johnny fed my mind with stacked in a neat *little pile. There was the towel to dry my feet and a large army jacket to keep out the chill. In its pocket I had my favourite marble, the one that shone in the light as you held it aloft in awe, twirlin it in your fingers as the sunlight gleamed through. Not mere glass, a jewel that had been blown well. It was the same if you looked deep into my eye. A lot like a sunflower. That was my lot, n it was bliss to be away from that house with my meagre belongings, my peace of mind more valuable than any amount of materialism.*

Maybe at that age I should have said something. Told the local beat bobby or told the headmaster at skool. But I just sucked up the punishment and torture and kept schtum.

{TWISTED DIAMONDS chapter 16} *Sunday dinners were cold n stodgy on account that they materialised at all. My only indication from upstairs would be the burnt cabbage smells rising like autumns burning leaves out on Stan's compost heap in the garden.*

Confronting my already dead to the touch toes against the bitterness that only stone in winter time can hold. I trod a cautious path without conscience thought. The in bedded cobwebs shivered their way across my forehead, a practised quick glance down the corridor, the old war blanket falling back into place in my shattered door way. My small cluttered window light shut off now, mine shaft gaps in the stairs I trod with ease, creeping on my hunched legs, listening for them, scared witless of them. Mum had been as keen as Stan these past few days. As if his latest beatings were putting him too far out in front when it came to the scores I thought they kept.

As I had entered home from my last blissful retreat to the raft, after Stan had spring cleaned my head with his polish soaked rag, she had cornered me by the door to the cellar head. A crazy look on her drunken face, probably stoned too from Stan's unwanted blowbacks. She was now turning her rings, twirling the stones out of sight. Angled now in her palms how she wanted them she gave me no time to move as she quickly swiped me round the back of the head. The trickle of blood I felt soaking into my collar. She then cuffed my ears several more times for good measure, the blood now running free like a non tranquil flow.

Her torment came in sections. She would then leave me alone and blank me. Days later, my ears she would grab. Wrestling me into a chair or the corner, it didn't matter as long as she had me trapped. Long nails, grown to spiked points she would use, soothing me in a mocking tone while scab scratching. Never stopping till the congealed blood blocked space down her cuticle. Most women wore nail polish; my Mother wore my dried blood proudly upon her hands. Even Stan would comment, telling her the red was a lovely colour. God when Ma took on Stan's behaviour to please him I dreamed long and hard into the night about patricide.

{TRIP TO QUACKS chapter 17} *I had come awake with knife in hand. I had come to the dawn wiping the crusty sleep from my eyes, to stare in wonder at the scissors wedged between my toes. One morning it would be a normal wake from disturbed sleep, the next a rolling pin, or a jam jar, even once a dead rat lying by the end of my bed. Stan would always be there to shake a slow head in disgust and remove the object, always tuttin n saying that it was weird behaviour all this sleep walking. Not normal behaviour, which coming from his warped mind was like boasting that the shadow was full of blood. The few months that I had started to believe sleep walking had taken over my nocturnal body, had seemed to delight Stan in some way. He revelled in its weirdness and used its happenings to mock my brain even more so, for even though he had a variety of abuse, something like this seemingly coming out the blue, had potential to be manipulated to tantalize his sickness. There had been the odd time late in the night, more the early moments of the dawn, when I had fuzzily remembered upon waking, seeing Stan in my room, that feeling of not quite being able to remember your whole dreams, putting the image to the back of my mind in the mornings. The night wanderings were apparently getting worse. My body was travelling further in the dark passages of the night. The one recurring thing of late was that I would wake at the top of the cellar stairs. Stan not a usual* *early riser was now always a presence as I woke in my strange spots, constantly standing witness.*

It had been decided that a trip to the doc, a local gent named Dr Tree booker was on the agenda. Stan had been keen to stress that this behaviour must be written into my youth file. I had taken no notice of his insistency. Why the hell would it have occurred to me that he was concocting such a strange plan? Mother had just gone along with Stan's request, telling me to get ready in my best clothes, which were ceremoniously delivered from out of their wardrobe for the occasion.

A little blazer to jazz my appearance up a bit was the ticket. Stan was already down the end of the garden when Mum kicked me out the door. As I descended the steps to the lawn, Stan headed round the corner to the garage. I stood waiting for him to back the car out, firstly getting a mouth full of fumes as he revved the arse of it with his foot on the brake, then standing for an eternity as he manually wound down the driver's window. The old four track player that he would not update blasted out Johnny cash live at Folsom. He ejected it n fiddled about in his dashboard, searching, then putting back in the Cash with a clunk n the car zoomed back nearly flattening my foot. As he braked hard, I headed to the passenger seat. He screamed from out the window. "OH no you don't "I then went to pull the backdoor open n he shouted again. "What the fuck boy" He climbed out and headed towards the boot. He popped it up n motioned me over with the index finger. "Get in" "But Dad", he grabbed me by the hair n slung me up off the ground n into the confined space. His eyes bored into me as he took one arm down from holding the boot open n smoothed down my blazer lapels. "Keep Quiet" and with that word came next the darkness. Not even a slit of light to hold some comfort. He wheel spun out from the car park, but drove slower as we turned out onto the roads. His horrible tuneless voice now accompanied Johnny as we made the trip to the quack. I guessed we were there as he pulled the car over abruptly banging my head into the confined metal roof, but I was wrong. He had parked a few blocks away from Dr Treebooker's surgery which was situated in his old family home. The sunlight expanded now my pupil size as I rose from the boots tomb. Stan had popped the lid n I saw him while I just sat there dazed, dash across the verge to this monkey puzzle tree n turn his back to it. He then went up n down in this swaying motion like the grizzly ol fucker he was. This was nothing new. Mum had a clipping from where she had ripped it out of the local paper. The edition always had a (one day in America) section, where this story had occurred of a woman shooting dead her husband because she had mistaken him for a bear. It was stuck to our fridge door with the horseshoe magnet, a gift from Dolly blue. Stan had as usual taken no notice of this n continued to relive his itch in the best fashion he knew. He had even planted a small tree of the same seed in our garden, hoping that it would one day grow taller than it was now, which was about the height to relieve an itch on your shin.

After five minutes he collected me roughly from the boot. I had just sat there waiting him, scared to move. After dragging me out, he locked up the motor n we headed down the street to my appointment. It did not take long for my name to pop up in digital light on the doctor's wall, Stan now pulling me by the blazered arm to my feet, in my ear all the way along the corridor his raspy voice coaching me on what to say. At the door as he knocked he clipped me hard round the head. "Let me do the talking dip shit" I entered the calm office, Dr Treebooker's friendly face there to greet. I sat mute on the chair, then over to the couch then back to the chair. The tests that could be done were done. Stan lead the conversation, filling in the gaps for the good Dr. Scribbled notes on a pad, typed keys on the computer. My file GREW. Dr Treebooker soothingly asked me a few questions, which Stan interrupted with his own prognosis, adding that I appeared to be also getting rather aggressive towards my darling Mother. It was news to me but I stayed mute n let him ramble on with his bullshit. I was given a prescription for some Prosom, Klonopin and some Trazadone, Stan telling Treebooker as he took the prescription from his hand that he would be sure to see I got my correct dose. The chemist dealt with in the building next to the Drs, I was walked quickly back to the car, Stan clocking the street for people before bundling me back into the boot for the journey home. A backhand to the mouth my treat for being a good boy before he slammed the boot lid down hard!!

*Even as we turned into the familiar car park, Stan doing a few circles
to dizzy me at speed now we were off the main road, the torment did
not end. He would slow the car back into the garage n I would hear
all the noises, the voice of Cash shutting off, the car door open n
close, Stan banging his fist onto the lid of the boot with the "Good
Riddance" the last I heard as the garage door crashed down shut. I
just about made out the sound of the gravel under his foot as he
wandered back up the garden path. My Mother would be informed of
the Dr's prognosis n what had been arranged, prescription wise.
Stan would tell her he had let me out to play for a bit. Hours later the
door would crash back up n he would pop the trunk telling me to get
the hell in for some scraps from their tea time plates. I would head the
opposite way. The raft was calling.*

*The dripping from the over flowing drains up by the roadside had a
calming effect under the road. I had the anchor dropped n the snake
torch light lit up the new book Johnny had given to me the other day
on the way home from skool. It was something he had written with
his own hand. The torch shone on the black cover. The silver title
sparkled back at me.*

The Spirit of Morality, a collection of poetry by Johnny Sands.

*I flipped through the pages stopping random n blazed the torch beam
down into Johnny's soul.*

Picture hung up there with the stars

Smile like the shining without tell tale scars

Naked eye of mine burns in the orange bottles glow

Lost inspiration never stems this inks flow

Flooding back this vessel soon

Brain a wash with thoughts consumed

Waves of wise words I flow

Drowning out any hidden blue

Mellow colours splash my walls

Scattered memories evenly scored

Ringing ringing drowned out calls

Found a float for this drastic world

Bottomless empty oceans

Vocabulary as vast as poison

Kill you doubters in one swift motion

Floating bubbled words

Cool surface the only witness

Clinging then free

Icy chill contemplates

Fate or fast fatality

Compromising never

Water in the lakes

Rivers running free to the sea

Inside your dead eyes already

Shelter from the cruel storm

Step forth the playful moon

New and old it still lights my path

Village wanderer to the lake of stars

Reflections glow in ripples

As my stone of thought

Skim those dangerous shores

I'm sure as I read it over and over again that he had had me firmly in his mind as he wrote this one. I closed the book and placed it on the small pile of others. My army jacket I would use whenever I left to cover and protect my collection. I stayed an hour, the current lulling me as I tried to recall what Dr Treebooker had spoken about.

As I reluctantly returned home, the first thing I noticed, as I opened the garden gate to the back door entrance, was Mrs B's middle finger to Stan. She had on her kitchen windowsill an emptied Guinness bottle full of the pansies that Stan had ripped up the other day. It made me smile for a moment, but it soon disappeared as I entered the door. Mum and Stan both just seemed to come out of the kitchen walls at me. It was medication time.

{OBSERVATION TIME chapter 18} *After the beating they both gave me I scarpered up to my room. Stan had wandered past on the other side of my war blanket, touching it, making it move, but not coming through it. He loved to fuck with my nerves. He now had reverted to whispering the word, somnambulism through the gap. Dr Treebooker had given him a new word for my sleep walking problem.*

It wasn't just me who got the benefit of Stan's mind games. He had different ways for Tish. He loved to subvert Ma's mind. He would leave notes, the yellow sticky ones, around the house, usually where she would easily find them, like stuck to the oven door, or the iron. I would cringe as I got older and realised that as a kid, what I stupidly thought were love notes were actually sexual orders for that day. Blowjob 1pm shed. Strip tease 9pm shaman chair, etc...

Every now and again Stan would take Ma out in the car for a drive. Before I had found my spot under the road n built the raft I'd had another little place to get away to sooth my mind. Everyone was out, about two hours they had barked, Stan slamming the door on his way. One day he would take it completely off its already loose hinges. I loved it, being alone in the house, a nice chance to gather around me thoughts to please. Every fucker needs their inner voices calming presence. The attic was calling, I loved the house empty, but best of all it allowed me the chance to explore. I was already on the second floor, so I fetched the ladders that Stan kept behind my wardrobe. My room was Stan's junk room, he never cared that my room was like a crowded cell already, without all his useless shit everywhere. Throw it in the boys room was all I heard, he won't mind!!!!

Scrap, magazines, tools, the ladders came out easy. Practise makes perfect. Under the spot on the dark landing where the entrance lid to the attic was, I placed the ladders up against the high wall. I climbed steady n struggled with the lid. It fitted uneven into the grooves but after a stubborn twist it lifted off. I pushed it upwards n let it rest just inside of the darkened space. I moved up a few more rungs n hoisted my body up onto the dusty old floor board. I just crouched for a while, soaking up the atmosphere. There were a few chinks of light from chipped or loose slate tiles. Not enough light to see the other end of the room though. Alit with Stan's shotgun lighter a candle that I'd stuffed into my back pocket earlier. The flame took hold of the wick n showed in front of me a zig zag pattern of random floorboards. At the far end of the attic laid a hole made from the collapsing brick wall. Here was where I was headed. Special attention with the candle held low as I now slowly crossed the floor. It was Mrs Burnley's observation time.

It was early afternoon, so she would have had a few by now of the bottles of the black stuff. She really had taken to heart the advertising bullshit that the stuff was good for you. I climbed the low wall through the gap n lifted quietly her attic lid. Peeping through, she was nowhere to be seen, her room more cluttered than mine, making the descent difficult. One foot on her old hover handle, the other stuck wedged into a cardboard box full of cabaret trophies, I steadily got down.

I never stayed long too. I crept down the stairs to see her zonked by the fire. She had a sooty rug wrapped around her legs n a Guinness in both hands. She was snoring away peacefully, the fire still burning in the grate. I was going to look about in the kitchen for a bit of grub, but as I went to the door I caught sight of her lekimeter. She must have not so long ago put a tenner on it. The receipt I read stood in front of the illuminated digits for a moment, it clicked down to £9.99 and I felt the emergency to leg it n get back to the other side of her walls. She can't have fallen asleep too long ago. Not a great big adventure, but back in my bedroom waiting anxiously for my parents return I felt a little calmer for heading over to Mrs B's

I didn't get many opportunities to scale the ladders n check out the attic, but whenever they were both out I would. It always helped, made me feel like I had a bit of control over something, even if it only was viewing a lonely ol alki.

{SHAMAN CHAIR chapter 19} *Dad would sometimes get flung back into his chair. He would rise up so far, like in slow motion, then at speed, arms all array fall back to where he had started from. He had been of late, busy choking on his hulk weed. The super strength shit that his mate Poidge Barrett cultivated.*

All the fireworks from the council estates had died down, the new rich estates were still exploding in multi coloured tricks of light, conjured by the darkness into dazzling spectacles. Green shards, blowing red stars, boring yellow flashes. Stan had refused earlier in the evening to take me to see Guy wrongfully burn. He had a few principles that I strangely agreed with. So I had made do with watching the other people's fireworks from out the window later.

"Rolling since 1796" Stan proudly announced. He did the swan lake with the rizlas. His hulk weed was a special strain, which in turn got the special treatment. He kept it in what he referred to as his special ops tin. It had an SAS sticker on it that read **who dares**

skins.

The special event?, my double black eyes, for not moving out of his way quick enough when he had managed to get out of his shaman chair. He had gone to grab the poker to stoke up the fire. That done, he left the poker end in the heat, glaring at me, grinning like a stoned maniac. "I think I should brand you boy, make sure if you ever get lost they know where to send you back". I just stayed quiet, shrinking back away from him. I cringed as he rose again from the chair again, but he revelled in my obvious fear n passed me without striking out this time. In the kitchen now I heard the cupboards bang. He was searching for concoctions to add to his already super strength joint.

He kept his stash of different substances in everyday household tins. But he rarely when smashed could remember what was where. I'd gone to the kitchen door, ready to flee as I didn't want to stay in the room, waiting for the poker to burn my flesh. He opened one kitchen cupboard n a single white rizla flew out to announce its presence. He smashed the door clean off shouting "Fucking ones no good". I couldn't risk trying to get passed him to take the safe option n flee to the lane n the raft, so I crept half way up the dark stairs n waited to see or hear what he would do next. I heard him crash open the back door. A strange sound came next, a kind of whoosh of air n then a moment's silence n then a thud. My bravery, along with my curiosity, held me firm, as I crept back down n poked my head around the kitchen door.

I caught Stan driving through with a seven iron golf club that he kept outside by the back door. The poor frog sailed through the darkened evening air, hitting with a thud the shed at the far end of the lawn. He wasn't really hiding the fact. He clocked me as he turned slightly to nudge the other poor frog into place. He had it trapped loosely under his boot heel. The maniac smile he delivered to me, fangless. Then without a care in the world, turned his back n got ready for his next big shot. I shot as well, straight back up the stairs, not that there was going to be anywhere of safety to be found. It would only delay for a moment the torture that was coming my way.

I heard his voice from below in the garden, "Fooooooorrr"; the sick bastard was having fun. I thought about the attic, but there was no time to drag out the ladders. Mum was only the other side of her bedroom door to where I needed to rise up to a bit of safety. It was too late anyway, the distinct stench of hulk weed drifted through my war blanket. Stan was here to play another game.

Usually I could escape his clutches when he was stoned, but the resin that slowed him had been put to one side of a late. This hulk weed was like trying to outrun a juggernaut that had mounted the pavement as you strolled in the summer sun blinded to its approach. The rain drop slid down my opened bedroom window. It matched the speed of my tears running down to the dent now in my cheek. The frogs were not the only ones to get used for swing practise. Stan was back down stairs, I could hear him, the volume on the TV high. He flicked through from the news that he hated, to some wildlife programme, the commentator loud in my head as he described the hunting methods of the great white. Next Ma was summoned by the poker that he banged on the living room roof. Their bedroom was directly above. I heard her pass my room not long after. I followed her down five minutes later. I needed to steal some grub from the fridge, which they kept locked most of the time, except from when Da had the evening munchies and got too stoned to bother messing about with the key.

I could hear him whistling his blowbacks into Mums head, and then telling her to put the hot water boiler on so they could soak up there ache's n pains. My pockets full of looted cheese I popped my head carefully around the door, trying to assess the scene before I jumped back up the stairs into bed. Mum was coma like laid out before the fire on her back, just staring at the ceiling with dead eyes. Stan's face, from the side I saw light up as the shark on the telly drew blood.

Goodnight wanker I thought in my head as I headed up to nightmare land. I could hear as I went Stan telling Ma to put the hot water on so he could soak up his aches n pains. Too stoned to realise he had only told her two minutes ago.

In the morning I caught sight of mum's legs. Bitten from the thigh to the knee as Stan had found his prey last night.

{IT'S SHOWTIME chapter 20} *I was now n then allowed to watch a bit of t.v. The professionals were my favourite, right up there with the Sweeney. Benny hill I had liked right up until Stan had started copying the end of the show in what he thought was a funny way. The theme tune music wasn't funny anymore. The bit where the music speeded up n Benny, bless him, chased all the saucy tarts about now for me turned into Stan chasing me around the house in quick bursts. The volume of the t v up full blast so that even up stairs I felt I was in some horrible remake. I had once craved my five minutes of fame. Jim L fix it was a popular show. Mostly rubbish, like a kid jumping through a hoop of fire n Jim getting some out of work stunt man to come in n make the kid look like the fall guy for two minutes. I had written in with my own letter. One of my favourite cartoons was the road runner, this annoying bird that the Wiley coyote could never catch no matter what trap he set. The bird always used his amazing speed to get free. My idea that I penned to Jim had been for me to get fixed to go to a studio where they make cartoons, design with the illustrators a small length cartoon where for once the bird got caught n killed by the Wile E. Coyote. I was going to show the letter to Johnny n post it on the way to skool.*

After telling Da of my great idea, Stan being Stan had ripped up the envelope in disgust, shoving it into the grate to use to light the living room fire later on. He had laughed at me while shaking his head. It wasn't an angry look, more bemused as he had walked past me, his voice deadly serious as he turned to level his mouth with my ear, "That old bastard is a fucking NONCE"

The reverse of Benny hill happened when he had been stoned n allowed me stay up late to watch the hammer house of horror. Frankenstein was slowly crashing about in black n white. Stan would rise from his shaman chair n do the same, arms fully stretched out, thumping about, robotic looking, always just missing me on purpose as I shuffled through his legs. The capture would come eventually, squeezing me into breathlessness. Mums words, somewhere dreamy in the room, "Stan you'll break his ribs, put him down." The concern not for my welfare, she was just a little worried for the knock on the door again from social services.

{INNOVATE chapter 21} I wasn't too far off reaching the end of skool, one more term after this soon to begin long summer holiday would see me out of there. I had started cutting through the pear orchard on the way. It killed two birds with one stone. I stuffed my face with fresh fruit, making up for the lack of breakfast n also it stopped any contact with the jeering bullies on the bus on the way. I called in every now n again at ol Granddads.

He never questioned my bruises. Probably assuming wrongly that it was just kids rough n tumble stuff. He never questioned my early years of absence from his life. He just took me as he found me on his door step n always cheerfully invited me in. I loved his tales of adventure. They were like missing pieces of my DNA. I mentioned as he got me sat comfy, the miners scab graffiti that was popping up all over the village. A bad business he had said but turned the conversation to some graffiti he had noticed on the way to the shops.

Innovate

Some sprayer was using this cool tag. I had seen it myself n liked its optimism. I never for one moment in my young mind thought how, or what the older end of the community would make of it. Granddad liked it too. He said it gave him a feeling of when he had just finished the war and England was great.

I had asked him if he had noticed another graffiti sprayer who was always of late spraying nr to where innovate had left his mark, the slogan, Class War? He said he had, said he understood, without telling me why. On that day though we mainly talked about the old bridge gym, it had been I was informed owned by my late Great

Grandfather, who the locals affectionately called Faver. Some said that the White rose had been the first boxing club in the city, but if you asked the great fighters of the city like Ernie Fields they would tell you different. The bridge was the first, end of story. It wasn't there now, Knocked down long ago. The building was the Bridge hotel. The gym like many in the olden days was upstairs above the bar. The front of the pub had lovely green & gold tiles. On its demolishment they had carefully taken off the tiles n transported them to London, where they were now splendid on some villainous East End local.

ol Poleaxe spun his magic tale."I remember young man the first time I ventured up those bridge stairs. My Father was not about, but one of his trainers who I later found out to be in the Guinness book of records as the fastest skipper in the world was. He pointed me to a box full of sweaty mixed up leather gloves n told me to lace up. I got one nearly done up, then he marched over n finished both hands with a fancy loop to each lace. I remember young lad him pointing me then to the ropes n telling me to warm up, shadow box, let's see what you got young Faver. I can tell you lad my nerves were steel as I climbed through. I felt my destiny there n then as soon as my bare foot touched the apron". He stood up straight, pulled a classic John L Sullivan pose n winked at me. "Fancy some lemonade" I nodded at my hero as he went off whistling softly n singing, when life gives you lemons.

 When he came back n we were settled again sipping real fresh homemade lemon pop .He carried on the tale of the bridge. "With the joining age being ten, they had spotted straight away my keenness. Your Great Granddad had been trained in the martial art of Jiu-jitsu. He trained the local ruffians, keeping them off the streets n out of trouble. He would take them to the point where they could with his help fill out the forms n get the pro boxing licence, many a score of lads, owed him for a better path in life. The odd few for a championship career too. With me he had noticed I preferred the style of the bare knuckle man n taught me the difference between boxing gloved n boxing proper. He broke off from his tale, a terrible retching cough rumbled up through his chest, turning away from me to kill the racket in a hanky. I noticed as he took it away from his mouth the dark congealed blood. I tried to act as though I had not seen it, but he knew I had. He cut my visit short, saying I should give the boxing a try. "It's in your blood young man" and with that I was out the door n back on the lane heading to Stan n probably another one sided scrap.

{A QUICK FRAME chapter 22} The kitchen was crowded as I stepped in through the back door. Stan's dodgy pals, Poidge Barrett n Bricky Arsom were huddled together, whispering. Stan shot me a look that spelled out my orders to quickly disappear upstairs to my room. I didn't need telling twice. I hated these two characters. Whenever they spent time around my Da, he would when they pissed off turn even more nasty than usual.

I sat on the edge of my bed n thought about living permanent on the raft. Why I didn't just tell Granddad I never figured out. Even in his twilight years I would have put my life on him beating Stan to a pulp for what he was doing to me. After about half an hour I heard Stan shout cheerio to his pals. I moved to the small part of the window that had a view n clocked them walk the length of the garden n then drive off in this large black van which looked like the one I had seen on the telly when they had caught the ripper n taken him to Dewsbury magistrates.

I was tense. Stan was on the stairs, heading no doubt my way. He popped his head through my war blanket. "Fancy a quick game of snooker at the club?"Now I was confused. Every so often he would do this. Pretend to be fatherly. If I refused or looked disinterested I would get a crack, so I played along. "Yeah sure Dad, cheers". "Hurry the feck up then". I quickly pulled on my coat. I didn't bother changing out of my skool uniform. I didn't have much to change into anyway.

Even though Stan was a bullying demon behind closed doors, he had been clever when it came to his rep in the village. He especially arsed licked the vicar, always filling the begging bowl with a big show of a note instead of a few coins. Sinking steady sipped pints in the local bobby frequented pubs. Never getting wrecked, just having a few, showing his restraint. He was well in with the club next door to our houses committee men. He had laid the foundations for his false profile alright.

I on the other hand got to see the real Stanley Kites. We headed into the hop filled air. There were not many patrons in. The landlord Ted, who had been in the local papers for fiddling the books, but had been found not guilty when a fall guy committee man had taken the rap, nodded over at Stan. Pa shoved me towards the door to where the three snooker tables lived. "Get in there while I sort the drink".

I got busy racking up the balls. When I had all the reds in the wooden triangle, I realised the blue n black were missing. Stan came banging through the double doors. He had a half supped pint in one hand n a pair of the behind the bar cues in the other. He never mentioned the two missing balls, he just said, "My break". After a few shots got a lucky red that he had left hanging over the pocket. He wandered over to a row of cues that hung on the far wall in leather n metal cases. He fiddled in his pockets, his back to me, so I couldn't see what he withdrew from his pocket, but when he turned back to me for his shot he had now in his hand a brand new Jimmy White cue. A few scores for Stan later, he headed back to the bar for a refill. He would tell Ted that I was not thirsty, or that my bladder was weak so he didn't have to buy me a small pop.

I moved to the double doors where you could see the bandit through the glass panels. Stan on his wait for his pint to be pulled, nipped over, fed a quid in, whacked the start button, n after a quick check of the reels turned n disappeared through the Gents toilet door.

I strolled over to the big bay window that swept the front of the snooker room. I leaned on the ledge n day dreamed out the window. The lane was fairly quiet of trafik. A tractor rumbled by to remind you that it was a rural village, the abattoir wagon full of cow skins right behind it with a stink that penetrated the double glazing.

Stan announced his return by smashing with his hand all the remaining balls left to play in the frame. "Game over"

I mentioned I needed the loo, n he rolled his eyes as if it was a strange demand. "Hurry the fuck up I'm hungry n the chippy just opened". I walked quickly to the toilets. I noticed straight away that the floor was soaking, Stan had pissed everywhere except for in the trough. Even as I zipped up my pants n went to wash my paws, I caught sight of the cubicle. The lowered toilet seat was soaked, he had even finished with an obvious blast at the soggy roll of bog paper that hung now limp on the wall.

As I came out Stan was spinning the cherries again, banging his fist now on the start button, looking for bars. He won nothing, blamed me for giving him bad luck, shouted tara to Ted n out on the lane we now stood.

The chippy was just up the road. As we walked, Stan suddenly looked up n down the lane n after noticing it was deserted pushed me hard into the wall and from out his pocket pulled the snooker cue chalk n twisted its blue dust all over the end of my nose. He thought this was hilarious, laughing the rest of the way to the chip shop door. He sent me in with the money n order. The full works for him, a bag of scraps n a sachet of sauce for me. As I came out I noticed the fish n chip sign on the black board had received Stan's chalk as well. I cringed inwardly as I looked at where fish had once upon a time been written. Now swan n chips were apparently on the menu. Stan chuckled n we set off back home, quality time with my Father as always. The fun time was not over yet. Stan was really rolling out the red carpet for me today. When we were back in, he called me from the kitchen into the living room, where he had found on the TV a kung fu film that had flying ninja's n old masters with long beards n eye brows that were even longer. I was ordered to watch. After half hour he got bored n pulled out from the side of his shaman chair a homemade weapon, his nun chuka. Two chopped up broom handle pieces, with a small chain nailing them together. After whacking me on the shins a few times, he threw them onto the floor by my feet. He was no Bruce Lee. "You can have these." Wandering what the catch might be, he rolled out next from the floor at the side of his chair, two snooker balls. "There's a clue in the colour boy" I stared at the clubs missing black n blue.

The colours were his wicked sense of humour. He pulled off his shoes n removed a sock, plonking the clinking balls into it. He tied the end in a tight knot n started swinging them about in a loop, getting faster with the twirl as he got up towards me. "Let me show you break building" My skull replaced the slate bed of the table. The crack of noise was the last I knew of the game. I came around out the back. He had slung me into the nettles at the bottom of the garden, my trousers legs n jumper sleeves rolled up as far as they would go. My body was covered in stinging red blotches. My head, as I gingerly touched to feel the lumps must have looked like the snooker balls were sewed under my skin, massive lumps that surely had internal bleeding. There would be no x ray to confirm though just a wet cold cloth on my napper and a day off skool.

{STONED IMMACULATE chapter 23} I was still sleep walking, only now I was always waking at the door to the cellar. Stan had left it a few weeks n returned me to Dr Treebooker's office the same way as last time. The only difference was that he had left me in the boot most of the weak end. He had come down to the garage and opened the boot for a minute every now n then to make sure I didn't completely suffocate and die. He watered my dry to the bone mouth, spitting a stream of Tetley bitter from, his gob into my face. He had it appeared, cut short his afternoon pint to come n check on my welfare. I had reluctantly licked the fluid from my face, swallowing a now bit of moving saliva that just about trickled its way down my throat.

The hulk weed had now mostly replaced any sign of the resin block he had usually burnt n crumbled into his spliffs over the years. The stench of it overpowered the whole house. He, if at all possible, was getting worse. The paranoia was ripe, the anger no longer bubbled away just under the surface. Ma was getting abused as bad as me these days. I had caught him strangling her unconscious just the other day as I'd arrived home a little early from skool. Slumping *against the flock wallpaper, Tish was out cold, Stan holding her up by her hair, screaming into her face. He had turned and screamed at me to get the fuck up the stairs. I hesitated just that second too long. His karate chop to the back of my neck felling me straight onto the kitchen floor.*

I tried to scramble to my feet, hoping to leg it passed him n up the stairs, but he had let Mum crash to the floor now n his attention was fixed on me. "You need some self-defence lessons boy"

Next he was yelling at me to run at him with my head down. I did like an idiot, to which he just rabbit chopped my neck into a blackness that I had started to like. He made me, on coming around, run a hundred times at him n straight again into oblivion, finally leaving me in a state that I could no longer rise from. I just laid, dazed staring at Mum besides me, who was still completely unconscious, maybe I thought, even dead. He left the pair of us like that on the floor while he headed down the cellar stairs. It wasn't long before the stench of hulk weed drifted up, its fumes so strong that I blacked out into a long dreamy sleep from its fumes. When I awoke from my welcome home from skool, Mum was sat by the fire on her knees, staring deep into the burning woods flames. I was also still on the floor but I was now wedged up against the wall in the darkened front room, directly opposite my view sat Stan. He was still smoking joints of hulk weed, lounging back into the shaman chair. The hash tray was spilling over as usual. It looked like a spilt urn, his premature death hopefully building up. I noticed briefly out the window Fag ash Lill passing by. Stan had given her this nick name for every time she passed our window on the way to the club for bingo, she had a cig in her mouth that had a long ash end. Stan noticed my glance at the window. "Pull them fuckin curtains too" I shuffled over n yanked the heavy drapes together. The room was now more violent. The tension in the air was like waiting under a tree for the lightning bolt to piss off. "Where was the last resting place of King Arthur?"

"You learn anything at that skool you go to?" I was about to say Avalon, I had heard the tale in history lessons, when he then said, "Never mind dummy" He crushed the smoked joint into the palm of

his hand n started rolling another one, speaking to the wall as he looked over the rizla packet again. I was informed that the sun was 330,330 times larger than the Earth.

He looked at the state of the fire in the grate when he had finished wrapping the rizlas around his smelly weed. "Sort it". It had always been my job to chop the logs, clean the hearth and kindle the grate. It was Stan's job to stick the poker in until it was glowing, then pull it out n leave it leaning against the hearth, staring from my eye, then back to the wicked heat, fucking with my nerves as always. When I got back from fetching some chopped logs in a wicker basket, Stan had Mum waltzing around the room as if there was some party in full swing. They were clinking stouts together n shouting "HERES MUD IN YER EYE" He let me rest the basket down n feed the dying flames with fresh fuel, telling me to get to bed when I'd stuck the last stick of wood onto the blazing hearth.

It was obvious as I leaned on the ladders by my window looking out. Stan was building up into a monster of proportions that I could never comprehend. His behaviour was so distorted that I feared now for my very life. As bad as he had been to me over the years, I had never contemplated him stopping my heart beat for good. Only now I was not so sure, this hulk weed was sending him spiralling out of control.

The desire to continue wanes at times. Life with Stan was not really a life, merely an existence. He would often bawl at me about not knowing his own Father. Yelling, "you've got it feckin easy BOY."Jesus the luck of the Irish really had missed me out if that was where my blood line lay.

{KETCHUP chapter 24} I rubbed my aching head, seven fingers n two thumbs kneaded at my damaged skull. I was trying to practise what I had read from a book Johnny had given me on Indian head massage. It was I hoped the way forward to relieving the constant throb. The missing finger had occurred last year. I had been ordered to the end

of the clubs car park at the back of the house, to chub some fuel for Stan's fire.

I had collected most of the branches from around the large trees. There had been a wild wind a few nights before, which had left a fair bit of wood scattered at the base of the trunks. I was just about to gather up the pile I had collected when I had noticed Stan striding across the tarmac towards me, axe in hand. He had been watching me from the back door with his binoculars. "What about those large branches that aint quite snapped" I looked towards where he was staring, there were a few branches hanging down that still held onto the trunk. Stan half dragged me over to the one he had in mind. I pulled on them with all my strength to try n get it snapped off. After a few minutes of pulling n twisting, Stan just came out of thin air behind me n whistled the axe blade straight into the cut off point. "That's how to do it boy"

It certainly had been. My little finger on my right hand was now redundant on the floor along with the pile of wood. Bright blood red splatter across its diameter mesmerized me away from the pain. I remember him making a shrug, as if to say it wasn't that big a deal. He had thrown a grubby hanky at me n told me to stop been a baby n wipe away the tears, which had started after the initial shock turned to horror and tremendous pain.

We had headed back to the house, me carrying the bundle of sticks. Stan had helped me a little to ready the fire grate for lighting, spoiling the gesture by throwing when it had got going my severed finger into the flames. The stink of flesh was strong, then the hulk weed joint that he had picked out of the hash tray, half smoked, lit up n the scents mingled into the living room air.

Mum, later in the day had asked about the finger, but said to stop lying when I had started saying what he had done. For skool it was reported as an accident with the car door. Clumsy Otiss was always getting into scrapes. There was no hospital or doctors. I was given the odd pain killer n it was left to heal in a fresh bandage that Johnny had applied.

The lumps from a few weeks back, where he had clobbered me with the snooker balls were still sore. They had gone down, but the area was constantly throbbing with the most violent of headaches.

My last week of skool had started as usual. Cleaning out the mess from around the fire grate I had pulled this screwed up piece of paper n read in Stan's spider hand writing,

Cannabis Cannibis Cannibas cannabbis

He was so stoned he didn't even know which was the right way to spell it. At the bottom of the note of paper he had written in bold strokes **HULK**

I had left the house hungry as usual, after finishing my morning chores. I went the way of the orchard, grabbing a few pears that were free of maggots, thinking that after the last bell I would call in on ol Poleaxe, for I wanted to ask him if there had been many deaths in the bare knuckle game. But after skool that day had finished, my skull was so in pain I passed Granddads door, didn't cut through the orchard, took the jeers from the bullies on the bus n hit the ginnel with relief to be just getting hopefully up to my bed to sink into my pillow for a little relief.

The door was shaking as I entered. Evil Woman by E L O was blasting out from the kitchen stereo unit. One good thing, Stan was out. Mum wouldn't be playing this if he was around. Our house d j only spun the Cash on the turntable. Anything else n he would rip it straight off with a horrible scratching noise of the needle. I headed out of the kitchen, Mum must have been upstairs somewhere. I'd hit the silver volume dial on the stereo as I passed, hoping she wouldn't notice if I knocked it down a notch or two. I got passed my war blanket n fell onto my bed, burying my head in the pillow, looking for any reduction in pain. I must have slept, cos I woke from a dream where I had been this large crow in the turrets at the tower of London, to my bedroom now filled with darkness, faint sounds from downstairs, chatter between Stan n Ma. It wasn't long before I was summoned with a horrid screech from below. The lekimeter needed feeding its dinner of fifty pence pieces. I had to go change a fiver note at the shop.

As I left the house I clocked the meter. It was on £18.33, strange really that Stan seemed keen for me to get to the shop to top it up. I thought no more about it, except the skool history lesson again paying off, but I was sure they had said it had been abolished, for some maybe, but certainly not in this house.

Mr Longbottom greeted me with relief when he saw I wanted change n not to pour over his counter a mountain of pennies. As I headed back I came nr the part of road where only myself & Johnny knew below its tarmac sat my raft. It gave me a feeling of comfort that unfortunately steadily disappeared as I edged closer to the back door of the house. A big crack of thunder deafened my ears, like as if on cue on a film set the director had ordered the special effects to ramp up the scenes gloomy tension. Looking back it was a sign from the Gods itself, warning me of my doomed fate?

When I entered the gate I noticed in Mrs Burnley's garden a buoy. Like the ones at the side of a lake, in case you fell in and started to drown. It was black n white n tattered. Shining in the moon yet going to save no one. The back door was locked. I knocked n waited, getting steadily soaked. The rain had started to drop down in buckets, so I moved to the kitchen window to see if I could see anyone. The lights were off, so I went back to the door n knocked a bit louder. I then heard through the door a moaning sound. As the rain trickled down my neck I shuddered as I thought that I had stumbled upon them shaggin. Then it went silent n the light popped on. After waiting again, no body still came to open the door, so I went back to the window n got the shock of my life.

Mum was laid out on the stone floor of the kitchen, not moving, blood all over her neck. Stan stood a stride over her listless body. A toothless wet grin fixed onto his fizog.

He saw me at the window, but ignored my beady eye. He just next grabbed one of Mums lifeless looking legs n dragged her out of sight through the door towards the living room. My head was blank, like the now kitchen scene. I didn't know what the feck to do, so Iran to Mrs B's and stood soaking for five minutes, my finger held constantly on her door buzzer. After what seemed like an age I heard her behind the door, fucking about with different keys n door chains before I finally saw it open.

I could hardly speak with fright n on top of that Mrs B had drunk a shit load of stout going off her stinkin billowing breath. She didn't seem to be able to hear me too well when I finally blurted out a sentence. She in turn started off saying something about needing to head out to the shops in town cos she needed some, "Mrs B my Mum looks dead." Still not registered with the old love, "Mrs BURNLEY, come help my Mum" After about ten hick ups in succession I'd got the pissed up reply, "why does she need a cup of sugar little boy""Oh for Ffff sake"

That's about the moment I dragged her off her porch n into the rainy yard. "Just look through the window please" She nearly stuck her head through the pane, but it jolted her out of her stupor long enough for her to get the gist on what I was going on about. "My Mums hurt bad Mrs B!! Dads bit her neck or something."

I could tell by the change in her expression that she had clocked with her own eyes the blood red streak marks, where Stan had dragged Mum out a sight.

"Right I'm off to call the police young man", n with a swish of her sodden pink gown she disappeared back through her own door, the sound of a few Guinness empties smashing from behind it as she busted it wide open in her hurry . I moved away from the window n towards the safety of her door. A minute later I heard the key in our door lock turn, n the heavy black bolt slide open. Then silence, only the rain spitting down on the puddles. I had it seemed, been invited back in.

My nerves were shot to shit as I cautiously stepped over the thresh hold. The mop had been busy. It was lent up against the freshly washed out bucket. Mum was I could see lying upon on the sofa, the door to the front room wide open. She was trying her best at playing the actress, lounging without a care in the world behind the local weeks paper, the one I knew was her prop, so as to not have to look at me. She certainly wasn't reading the latest stories. Her quickly rising breast indicated that she had rushed very recently to clear up the mess. I could still smell what I thought to be a ketchup scent that the mops bleach hadn't quite swallowed. Stan on the other hand, stood motionless by the door that led to the cellar head. His stillness unnerved me to the point where my brain was yelling inside my head to just run, but my feet were rooted to the kitchen floor, the thought of hopefully the police arriving soon held my nerve a little as I faced him.

"How was school Boy"

He on the other hand didn't turn to face me. But he wasn't using any prop to hide behind either. The words just came out from the back of his head. "But Dad, I thought Mum was hurt her neck, you" No more of the sentence came out, the breath did, but in a gush, he had moved quickly like a panther, slamming a heavy fist into my gut. "So you called the pigs eh?"

He had to wait for the answer. I could not breath n as I nearly made a vowel sound he cracked me again a tremendous wallop to the guts for the second time. About three agonising chocking minutes later I finally told him that I'd gone for Mrs B, who I thought had gone to call them. His grin was manic, his words stoned and strange. "Good, good, goody-goody gum drops.

I was sent to my room, relieved to be out of there way for a while. I heard the distinct coppers knock on the back door. BANG BANG BANG BANG, walkie talkies beeping n crackling. Stan now talking, Mum then talking, a snippet that I made out where they mentioned Mrs B's name, then surprisingly laughter from them all. They eventually came to my room. I was made to sit n listen while in very serious tones they explained to me the implications of lying to the police. I tried to interrupt to say it had been Mrs B who had seen as well what I had and that it was she who had called them, but it was no use. The look I got was enough to realise that they thought I was a crank. Stan had obviously got to their ear downstairs. As I was been told by another of the coppers bunch, the story of the boy who cried wolf, Stan passed my war blanket, which was being held aside by the mighty blue arm of the law. "Excuse me gents, can I just squeeze past, I need the loo"

The boys in blue crowded my room even more, as a few moved into the door way to clear the landing so he could pass. Stan didn't miss the opportunity to add on the way back from pulling the chain that it hadn't been the first time I had lied. That of a late my behaviour had become quite strange, what with all the sleep walking, coming around with knives in my hands, even telling them that he had caught me smoking marijuana, which with this bit of news he added the mighty shake of his fatherly head.

A few of the cops left, saying they were just going to go n double check the neighbour's story. The ones that remained just stared hard at me, not speaking. After ten minutes of intimidation the ones that had gone to see Mrs B were back. I waited for some response to indicate that they now believed what I had tried to say from the start, but there was just silly looks upon their faces. They then went on to explain to Stan that they were sorry for wasting his time. The poor old dear was now unsure as to what she had seen and in their view confused n not really able to make a statement. Stan n the cops laughed. "She has a very serious problem with alcoholism officers" They all burst out laffin again. One of the ones that looked more or less in charge said" You getting up to the rotary club this Friday Stan, there is a great turn on?" The fuckers were tight, I had no chance, zero.

Before Stan led them off down the stairs, shouting see you Friday at the door, I was made to sign a small statement stating that I understood the seriousness of wasting police time n lying to a senior officer. When it was all over and the house was just filled with a cow, a bull n no pigs, my little lamb to the slaughter brain whirled with confusion. Stan not finished yet though, strolling into my room, statement in hand. "You need to stop this silly lying boy" There was no point trying to say anything. He just glared at me for a moment n turned n shot through the war blanket. A split second later popping his head back through, "I'd check under that pillow if I were you" n with that he was gone, whistling a cash song clear n loud down the steep stone stairs.

I lifted the corner of the pillow to see the big red sauce bottle staring back. What the fuck was all this about? It was obvious that they had wanted me to see what I believed to be blood n the dragging part. See the big act, nothing really happened. Stan made sure I was seen to be a liar to the police, no one believed old Mrs B, she was after all an eccentric pisshead, which makes you a liar right? Fuckers, head games, I was on my way to the raft. I needed its peace and quiet, its solitude. I needed to get a grip, needed to get my head round whatever the fuck was going on.

{FUNNEL KILLER chapter 25} I nearly doubled back from heading to the raft. A horrible premonition came shivering all over me that I should change direction and head to ol Poleaxe n spill the whole of my guts. But like a man upon his death bed, looking back at the paths trod, I ignored my intuition n took a direction that was going to cost me dearly. I never saw my Granddad alive ever again.

The way to the raft passed as usual in a dream. It was as if every time I headed to its sanctuary, I switched off n just floated there without taking in the journey. I got warm under the army jacket, the night not cold, but I felt I needed to cover myself. I pulled its large hood over my head n drifted off on the light swaying current beneath me. I had always returned to the house a few hours later, but this night I stayed till the dawn. I woke cold n confused, a wet foot on my left leg where it had dipped into the stream, due to me tossing n turning. I had been in the strangest, yet most vivid and believable dream. It must have been down to the swaying rhythm of the raft. I had been afloat in the vast pacific ocean stranded on my under the road raft. Everything was the same except the location. Then I had witnessed what I thought was the sky crashing upwards n away from my vision. Only realising when I began to see the rusting masts that now jutted out all around me that it was actually the Pacific Ocean emptying up its lost treasures to man. It had all happened in such a *peaceful way that as I tried to shake the dreams n sleep from my mind, I nearly forgot the dead awful reality of heading back towards Stan. I had become so robotic that even though I knew the best thing to do was run away, or stay on the raft forever, it just was not possible.*

I got up n stretched, worked my way back out of my sanctuary, n as if the night had never happened, found myself back at the ginnel, ready to face the music, or so I thought.

The house was eerily quiet. I knew Mum was out. She had a few times throughout the week, early shifts cleaning the slaughter bungalow before the killing of the animals began.

I headed through the kitchen to see if Stan was in his shaman chair. The living room was empty. The usual mess was there, his spliff papers everywhere, bogart ends in the hearth. On top of the mantelpiece, dozens of empty lager cans. His betting slips pierced through the silver Scorton arrow, Something I knew only a little about. It being a trophy for an archery event in Yorkshire that was believed to be the oldest sporting event. The winner, which Stan certainly wasn't, received a replica of the silver arrow. The original, that use to be kept in the Royal armouries at Leeds, had turned up one day at our back door. Poidge Stone received a nod n a wink n this fat envelope full of cash, while Stan received something he shouldn't, for which he used from that day on to pierce his betting slips for safe keeping. It had been quite a story in the local and national papers. Another thing Stan had cut out n pierced proudly through its stolen ancient tip.

I headed up the cold stairs, hoping he was in one of his strange baths or unconscious from the booze, snoring away in his pit. But as I listened, stood before my war blanket, the only sound I heard was a small squeak from up in the ceiling. Then another louder creak right above my head. That's when I noticed in the dim light of the long landing, Stan's ladder leaning up into the open attic space. I already felt uneasy. I had stupidly believed that he didn't know of my trips up into the roof space. I didn't dare climb the ladders out of curiosity to see what he was doing. I was just relieved he wasn't in front of me.

I slipped into the war blanket n came out the other side into my cluttered room. A lay on the bed was the next thing on my mind. My brain was so confused of a late trying to take in the strange head games that had been going on, trying to deal with the constant pain from my regular injuries, hoping to God for a miracle that I knew wasn't coming no matter how hard I prayed.

I was just drifting off with my feet up on the bed with my head nestled into my ketchup smelling pillow. I had tried to piece together the Pacific dream, its peaceful descent through its fathoms, but just as I was dropping my chin onto my chest, eyes drooping shut, the water in my brain creating vast oceans in a repeated dream, I woke with a start. The attic hatch had slammed shut. Stan was not so gracefully descending the ladders. I waited, holding my breath, hoping he would pass without realising I was back. But a moment later he stuck his head through the war blanket. "Fuckin grass."

He had a huge cone of hulk weed tucked behind one ear, another ready to light twirling in his left hand and a strange thing that I didn't think much about at the time. His right hand had held a funnel, like the one you use in making home grown beer.

He left it at that, let the blanket fall back into place n headed off down the stairs. I waited tense for a few minutes, thinking that at any moment he was going to rush through n attack me, but it never came. I remained laid on my bed, staring at the junk. I knew the exact spot where the funnel had laid gathering layers of dust, its empty space now revealing behind where it had been, a battered old tin cup full of old darts and other useless shite.

Mum came home and I smelt the burning come rise up the stairs from her attempts at dinner. Not that I was offered any. I heard Stan shouting n plates smashing, nothing unusual in that, then silence for a long while. Dusk now creeping in my postage stamp window, a full moon up in the sky, my stomach growling at it.

It had I thought been safe to nip down n try to find some grub to eat. I had stayed in my room all day n night. No one had bothered me, which was a relief. I had heard the TV click off its racket. I thought also that I had heard them both pass my room without saying goodnight n get into their pit.

As I crept down the stairs n into the kitchen, the first thing I noticed was the cellar door a jar. A faint light shone through. It was hard these days to pin point Stan in the house from just the stench of his hulk weed. The whole house seemed to wreak of it. I felt like a couple of large buds were constantly living up my nostrils. I thought the light in the cellar had maybe been left on by accident, but as I went to turn it off I choked back on the rising smoke. Stan was down there, stoned out of his mind, dangerous.

I was just about to forget my rumbling tummy n scarper back up to bed when I heard him talking to himself. His slow stoned drawl floated up from below to my lug hole. "You won't be grassing any more now will ya ye old crow." I really started to strain my ear to listen now. I waited while he rose other sounds up towards me. I heard him again dragging hard n long on his cone, blowing out the poisoned breath then, "enjoy the free drink you nosey old bitch." He was laffin now, chocking n laffin at his stoned words. It was all stoned crap to me. I grabbed a block of cheese that had been left out on the side. It had a toothless fanged chunk bitten out of it. I fled back up to my room, Stan's lighter now clicking frantic down below, he was lighting up another large cone. In the morning I was told that I didn't need skool for the next few days. Stan locked all the doors n windows n more or less ignored me and Mum for the whole of the first part of the week.

He gave me the odd clip round the ear if we happened to pass each other on the stairs or if I was coming out the bathroom, but apart from that he had pretty much ignored me. I just put it down to him getting better at the Coventry game he liked to play. Nothing more, n I was glad of the peace. Skool would be informed of a small break to the Dales National park or some other fantasy destination that I could only ever dream about.

He did now and again make me aware though of just how much he hated me. I was cleaning out the fire when he started spouting from his chair around the third day of silence. "Don't you realise you little fucka that if I'd flushed you down the pan when I had the bleedin chance I could go out n have a pint or two without having to worry about coming home to all this crap" Yeah Dad was such a sweet talker.

I'm sure Mum knew her fate as well, living with such a sick twisted bully. All I ever seemed to be was a burden to him financially. He had often over the years gotten right in my face to ball at me about his lack of money. He never spent it on me so I kept quiet as usual n just wondered what the hell he was raging on about cos he always seemed to have a wad when he needed it.

After that outburst, he went back to silence. The whole house was like death. Then out of the blue, a massive banging on the door. Not the pigs rat a tat tat, something more urgent.

I had finished sorting the fire n had been sat at the top of the stairs when it happened. I heard Mum open the door, then the coalman who delivered to Mrs B next door, blurt out his worry.

"I think there's a problem wiyer neighbour love"

I felt a connection with Mrs B. I slid down the stairs n sat listening on the bottom step.

"Yeah love I was trying to deliver coal like n she erm"

Mum started to close the door on him.

"LISTEN LOVE, I tried to get her to answer door, n I had a quick shufti through winda n she looks DEAD in chair"

My Mum turned to look at me n said, "GO GET YER DAD NOW." I slipped through to the living room to find Stan fiddling with the curtains, looking out onto the lane. "Dad?" He spun round n looked a little worried, "WHAT." "Mum wants you the coalman is at the back door, I think some things happened to Mrs B" He walked towards me, pointing a finger that soon turned into a clenched fist.

Snarling as he pushed past me, heading to the kitchen. I waited at the door, wondering what now.

I heard him say calmly to the coal man that she was probably just pissed n asleep, yet the coal man repeated his concern n said he was going over the road to use the red phone box. Dad shut the door hard on him shouting through the glass panel that she was a fucking piss head.

I headed quickly out of the way back up the stairs. I looked out the small postage stamp window, scared for Mrs B's welfare. I knew Stan too well to realise he had got to her, hurt her in some way. But surely she was not dead.

Twenty minutes later I heard a terrible din, the police, as I looked out the window n down onto the yard were everywhere. They had smashed down the back door n were disappearing single file into her home n out of my sight. They seemed to be in there a good hour. When I finally caught site of them again they were all huddled together quietly talking, one on his walkie talkie, speaking to someone.

Quarter of an hour later, I heard Mum say in the house to no one in particular that there was a coroners van out front.

I didn't dare go down nr Stan. But I was so shocked I ventured up the landing n into their bedroom. Looking down from the window I saw the gurney come trundling out. I just stared down in disbelief as these two men in black got ready to lift her covered body into the back of the dark smart van. I shuddered for I noticed her pink gown slightly hanging down, garish looking against the crisp white death sheet.

The cops came later when she had been driven off for her last drink, the embalming fluid. It was all routine, nothing to worry about. Stan looked like it was another he knew from his drinking dens. They chatted easy at the kitchen table, even laughing a little, which I heard Stan explain was a side effect to shock. The copper who was at the breakfast bar was explaining that it looked like an accidental death.

Too much drinking over the years was what Stan had come back with smartly for a reply.

Mum n I had each separately been summoned to the kitchen n gently asked if we had noticed anything suspicious going on.

I noticed the glare coming from Stan. I knew then what he had done, her overdose hadn't been an accident, that funnel from my room had killed the poor ol dear.

After Stan had seen the police out, he locked all the doors. There was going to be no escape to the raft this time. I was sent to bed with an almighty kick up the arse. I waited on my bed, staring again at where the funnel had once lived. Tea time n supper time came n went without any food touching my insides. In the darkness of what I thought was about midnight, Stan crept in to my bedroom. I could smell without knowing how he intended to aid my kip. The furniture polish knockout sent me crashing deep into the land of nod.

{UXORICIDE chapter 26} The morning that my life went from bad to worse started with me waking unable to catch my breath. Raising my aching face from off my pillow I felt the cold chill from the opened window bite into my neck. I felt so tired even though I had been sent to bed at tea time. I then recalled the helping hand I had received knocking me into the oblivion of my lumpy pillow.

I had tried before the polish knock out to drift away to sleep n back into the ocean emptying dream, but it had just not appeared. I had though been treated to Stan's frequent toothless manic grin. It seemed to come in my dreams just before the dawns rising sun. It would always be there to be remembered in the mornings when I woke, after my other nightmares had faded into nonsense's analytical stream. It would be centred in blackness, coaxing me towards its broken fanged hole.

As I heard Mum pass my broken door frame, I had shouted out in desperation to her. She popped her rumpled bed head through my blanket to stare at me. But when I had started to blurt out why Dad had dragged her, the ketchup, Mrs B's death, she just spat at me n and disappeared off down the stairs. It didn't take long for the pair of them to start arguing. This heated row penetrating straight through the kitchen ceiling. I couldn't make out exactly what it was that was fuelling the war. I didn't care after years of listening to them. It was raging on though, Stan every now n again roaring his dominant part in the proceedings.

I don't know if my Mum ever thought Stan would take his sick games too far. I was unsure if she was aware of Stan's descent into murder. She might have been a little more wary around him these last few days, but he had pretty much ignored the pair of us.

Just as I thought Mum was raising the stakes, her screams piercing into the argued points she was trying to make, there came a crash from below. The words now had escalated into Stan pushing her around. It carried on for a minute. Mum crashing into cupboards or the door, a scream of abuse back from her as she gathered herself back up for more shit, then a long drawn out scream that made me run through the war blanket in panic. It had been straight out of a hammer house horror. The almighty crashing sickening thud at its end, spelled only tragedy.

My bravery surfaced from out of nowhere n I headed down the steep stone stairs to see what the fuck had happened. As I ventured warily into the kitchen, Stan looked at me in a daze n said, "What you done boy". He was leaning against the cellar door frame like an old gunslinger. The pair of shorts he had on, the only thing he had on, made the image of the western soon disappear though. The ferry man that took you across the river stix to the other side was more fitting.

Besides his dragon tattoo, he had a full bottom leg piece. The 3d galleon ship was his masterpiece. The crow's nest was needled in dark ink around his knee cap. A carved wooden head of the lucky lady wrapped its way around his Achilles heel the fine detail of the rigging up the sides of the calf. On the top of the foot the boat's deck inked with shaded splatters of the dark blue sea. The cannons n slave rowers detailed careful by the gun. For him as he looked down his leg, *the crow's nest gave the boat deck a 3d effect. And up all over the bottom of the feet, the crashing waves of the sea. As I thought of the word crashing, I dared to ask him, "where's Mum Dad?" Walking towards me in a dream, the dragon getting closer, he just, without looking at me said, "All the doors and windows are locked, yer going the same way as that dumb bitch"*

I made a dash for the back door handle, hoping he was bluffin, but it was shut tight. I expected him to launch himself at me, but he just sauntered into the living room without a care in the world. Gathering my shattered nerves I moved towards the cellar head, needing to see if he had done what he had said. I stepped through the doorway n looked down the dim lit stairs. She was there alright.

Like some dolly that little girls leave with limbs all a stray after they finished playing, my Mum was mangled n distorted at the very bottom of the cellar stairs. She had her head twisted strange against the wall, her neck broken for sure. Her legs were folded up underneath her, making her look like she was trying to do a low limbo dance move. But this was no party. The bright blood was still clearly seeping from out the back of her head. Like the steep stone steps, I just froze to the spot staring, transfixed on her face that looked shocked at its final resting place. I then snapped out of looking. I could hear Stan shouting in the front room, shouting that I was going to be next for the ferry man.

I shot up the stairs like a whippet after the hare. I didn't bother with my room where the war blanket was hanging nearly off where I had fled through it minutes earlier, its junk a blur as I now sped past heading for the ladders.

Lucky for me, Stan had left them out at the end of the landing instead of shoving them back into my bedroom. I quickly flew up them, taking the attic hatch cover out of the way with my hardened head. I had no torch or matches in my back pocket so I tried as best I could to remember the zig zag lay out n get as far away from the opening as I could. I was trapped whatever I did. I thought about getting into Mrs B's house through the gap, but realised with fear that he hadn't been ignoring us for no reason these past few days. I could just make out from the shards of light that streamed down from some cracked tile, the hole that had led to next door was now fixed. So I waited in the dark, my only hope I thought at that time, was if he came up to get at me and I could maybe get past him n try to break out of a window downstairs n flee.

It seemed like an eternity before I knew he was up on the landing. My mind was running at a thousand miles per hour thinking that he would appear soon, strangle me and burn the property to the ground or something sinister like that. But his next move was as calculated as you could get for a sly dominating murdering bastard. He was directly below the hatch now, his voice very clear now, shrinking me back into the cobwebbed shadows from its tone. "Otiss I'm calling the police".

Thankfully I thought he had realised his descent into madness n was ready to confess. My nightmare may be at an end. But shouting out his next words, just blew me truly away. "YOU FUCKING MURDERIN LITTLE BASTARD". I let the words sink in for a moment. They then crashed into my brain with a terrible force as he shouted even louder again through the hatch. "YOUVE FUCKIN KILLED HER".

I stayed silent, unable to comprehend this twisted distorted fact. He started to climb the ladder, his heavy feet straining the metal rungs. He was closing the hatch. The darkness became total. He dragged the bolt across and locked me up. "I'm calling the police Otiss".

I heard the thud as he jumped back onto the landing from the bottom rung of the ladders. Moments later I faintly heard the back door bolts slide open n seconds later his echoing footsteps in the ginnel. He was crossing the road to the red phone box. He was actually calling the police. I closed my eyes, even though I was surrounded by the dark, my head hurt from trying to take in the sequence of events that were occurring since waking this morning. Mum was dead at the very bottom part of the house n I was trapped n as confused as ever at the very top. And as usual, Stan was somewhere in the middle playing his sick fuckin games. I don't think he worried about trying to pull it off. Probably in his private moments of planning, enjoying its complexities. He didn't know a bishop from a knight, but planning to set your Son up for murdering his own Mother was different. To him it was anyhow. Pushing her down the steps wouldn't be hard for him, n plausible in his plans for me to act out. He also knew with me in the attic he would have time to steady his nerves. Getting the story straight had been practised. Knowing I would be off guard, in shock, angry at what he had done, giving just the right combination for him to make the police presence look to me as the guilty party, instead of focusing on the real monster right there in their midst.

{ARREST FROM ATTIC chapter 27} *The sudden impact of the lid hitting back against the inner stone wall, crouched me instinctively into a low stance. So here, so close to the itching underlay, I dimly viewed this tit head protruding through the gap, his fat body in blue slowly followed. With a click, he shines some high powered torch beam up into some cobwebbed mass. The dozing spider now scurried to his larder n laid still.*

The creak in the haphazardly spaced floor boards kept me informed of the pursuit. Knowing that I was to be the hunted had come to my early attention by way of Stan's shouting, from the foot of the ladder. His chatter consisted of information that he wanted to place in the cops head. "That little bastard's been building up to this for ages." A louder squeak of the floorboard, the pursuit was getting closer. More lies floating up from Stan's big gob.

"If I was not a law abiding citizen, then I could easily take this countries fine laws into my own hands." I heard him smack his clenched fist into his other palm.

Mums life had slipped through his murderous hands with much methodical calculation. Stan now sobbing loudly, the Oscar was his.

As I stayed low, ignoring the commands of the tit head to come out n show myself. I held my nerve crouching behind the pile of unused bricks n half bags of cement where he had botched up the old collapsed gap in the wall. I nursed the thoughts of Mums death as I prayed silent to the rafters that the end had come quickly. Thinking of her broken looking neck, I was sure it had. I couldn't dislodge the image of her fragile bones, crashing hard into those steep solid stones of the damp cellar.

These thoughts soon cleared as the body in blue seemed to reach through the gloom to collect me. The long arm of the law had arrived. The fibres from the floor scratching my face as he uncouthly bundled me towards the ladders.

Shoving me down, my eyes came to rest on Stan's scowling face. He wiped away his crocodile tears n made a lunge for me. This other copper on the landing grabbed him n held him back saying, "he isn't worth it mate."I caught a glimpse of a samurai severed moon as I was shoved the length of the landing, n past the postage stamp window of my bedroom.

Down in the kitchen, there was a group of blue bodies hovering around the top of the cellar. The radios were on fire crackling info along the airways of the murder n the successful capture of the young heartless killa. Stan still behind me, scaring me more than the fresh cuffs that were tight, n fastened way beyond regulation. My blood supply restricted, my dizziness stumbling me along n out the door to the ginnel.

Noting the situation though, no one was going to start listening to me if I protested. Stan had weaved a considerable amount of fictional bullshit. Mum had never stood a chance either. So I just retreated inside myself, staying mute as they shoved me up the ginnel towards the Black Maria that was parked up on the kerb at the front of the house. Stan's parting shot was to throw his boot at me. Not a bad shot I agreed as it whistled up in a straight line through the narrow ginnel n caught me like a fouled rabbit punch to the back of my neck.

I was now out on the street front.

A few curtains were twitching over the road and I was glad in a way when the van doors slammed on me. I was in this little seated cage, my hands were still cuffed, windows reflected out onto the lamp lit lane. The couple of coppers that had brought me down from upstairs were chatting away, pointing towards the working men's club doors n checking their watches. The one who I took to be more senior then went back down the ginnel. I seemed to be seated for about half an hour when I noticed the last bus of the night coming down the lane. As it levelled past the Maria I still felt the jeers that didn't come, penetrate into the van n my brain.

Suddenly the van rocked a little at the other end. Bodies had seated themselves in the front n the driver's seat. The engine roared to life.

{*BLUE MARIAH* chapter 28} Another car took some other cops away first, the lights still flashing on top from where they had initially pulled up in hot pursuit. I was going the other way, down the lane towards the city centre n the cop shop. Just as I heard the grind of the gear lever Stan appeared on the pavement. He was staring through the glass panels of the vans two side windows, our eyes, with or without knowing were glaring at each other. Then as if on Q, the under takers dark van pulled up n parked a few feet away, from my numb cuffed body.

As the solemn figures climbed out, Stan once again got the consoling that I so badly needed. The crocodile tears were swamping his face again, clean white hankies been offered from more than one direction. The writing on the back doors in a very fancy swirling letter stated that Mr Jack Slack was to be the man responsible for the safe n dignified removal of my Mother's body from the scene of death. I didn't get to see her again. The van had started to pull out into the empty lane. My head bowed now as it hit me seemingly all at that moment the situation n its severity.

It wasn't until the van was opposite Asquith's butchers at the end of the lane that I raised my head to stare out the window. His not so fresh rabbits were hanging in his window, behind his counter I could just make out the blood stains on his white apron that he had hung up on closing. Straight away the vision of the back of Mums head slammed to the forefront of my mind. The van was picking up speed now as it left the end of the lane n turned onto a busier rd. The blur hit the window for a moment, then stopping as we slowed to now level my gaze with a house n its blue plaque on the wall. It had been the childhood home of the sculptor Barbara Hepworth, who had died in a terrible accident when her studio had burnt down in her later years. I had often passed it when out with Johnny. She certainly wasn't the only one trying to mould and sculpt their dreams from this small village. Johnny certainly was though but we couldn't have had more parallel lives. This was the strangest evening journey I had ever taken. As the van trundled on I knew without looking that we had just turned left onto Bunker Street. At the end of here, the next turn would bring my innocent young bones onto Stormy lane, the cop shop just up at the end with a last sharp turn into Harrap Street. I stared out the vans window, the speed to get me to the cells making all the view distorted n blurry. I thought back to all the times I had seen Stan acting oddly near the cellar. It all made some sick sense now. I, without knowing it at the time had been witness to his preparations for the murder.

He had needed some effective method. One that firstly without question would cause Tish certain death and secondly could be attributed to me in a plausible scenario when revealed to the police.

The reality of the situation came back to me. The bouncing wheel arch of the van flung me there. Pulling myself back up to the window I thought how much of the scenery I was noticing. Every fine detail when your free you take for granted. This black sports car suddenly in view, looking down from the raised van I noticed a young exotic executive at the wheel. Her black tight pencil skirt riding high with the quick high gear change as she flew past. Those black lacy stocking tops robbing me of any youthful passion. The whizzing images blurred, suddenly in focus for a fraction of a second as the traffic slowed. We were near the cop shop, the van now stood at a traffic light waiting, opposite on the other side of the road a small mechanics garage that had a large reflective glass window to its front. I stared through my window, looking back on myself. I noticed the lights change n the van crawl forward. The P and O from the word police not visibly reflected in the garage window now, but the word lice clearly there. We shot through the grinding van gears n slowly did a sharp turn n we were at the dreaded destination. The last thing I noticed in the gutter was a babies dirty bid and some rotting red roses.

The heavy gates to the stations inner yard whirred open from some secret button n we were in. Out the van n inside, every cop turned to glare at me. Nobody ever told me there was going to be a day like this, captured from Hell, passed over from a singular devil to a corrupt bunch that pretended to be the symbol of upstanding civilian order. All this came to my mind from Stan's Sunday cabbage dinner rants. As a young boy I knew very little about the ways of the system. Quickly though it started, the finding out.

{SOUNDER OF SWINE chapter 29} Here goes another wasted journey. This wasn't the right path for sure. The pig station was busy, yet not at all how I had imagined it. Not that I had spent considerable time dwelling on the shit hole.

Stan filling me in now and again on some of his finer moments of bullshit glorified incarceration. Tales of his old lag pals like Bricky & Poidge, tales that he seemed super proud of.

The sergeant, yes I know I should use a capital, but I have no respect and it filters through to my unorthodox style of writing. Anyway, the wanker in charge behind his scruffy self important desk inquired with arrogant tongue as to if I would be requiring legal eagles to fly me from this cage?

Some other plod pulled down a contraption that looked like a blackboard, but it was dull white, n scribbled with a marker pen the

word *MURDER*

My surname, date, time of arrest etcetera was written below. The usual mundane crap that got a suspect processed. Screaming men, pounding with heavy bare fists and feet on their steel doors gave the sight added dread. Other blatant bent fuckers on duty, trying on *working men's foot wear that had been removed n left outside the cell doors selecting pairs here n there for home time the Cheeky fuquas. My shit ypo pumps would be heading straight for the bin. The two cops who had brought me from the van had stood silent behind me while the desk serg booked me in. They now put their ugly heads together, n very important this, selected me a cell. Left right, left, left, left down the maze of corridors. The cuffs were still in place as I was shoved in the back and sent flying onto my chin into the selected grubby cell floor.*

Alone now with the indignity of the situation, my minds thought settled on the sergeant's desk and the info he had tapped away into his type writer. The worry in my body got worse when I thought to the red marker pen smudging the word murder as it had shot back up out of sight. Whispers that I was meant to hear about the tactics for extraction. My admittance in the heated interview room was to follow quickly they hoped.

A blandishment first as the good cops on duty get ready to deliver, then the bad cop ripping up the rule book n hitting me hard to avow. But they would let me stew a bit first.

Late into the night, the silence still had not got to me. The peace was welcome. The only real sounds came from down the maze of corridors, faint mixtures of steel doors closing with ruff attitude. From what I could gather, crime if guilty of it, could be a long drawn out affair. But if you were like me, innocent, then the time could hang like a glue covered clock that held no batteries. I had never been in control of my movements really at home, but I'd always had my sanctuary under the road. But here the normal man had to take a piss under the ever watching eye of the cells peep hole. Wait till the bastards remembered to feed you, take a walk that made you turn after every fifth pace. After the search the pigs had missed my old school pen that had been in my back pocket. They say the pen is mightier than the sword, but you wouldn't think that if you viewed my worn out nib. I had tried to add with a faint scratch my name to the others who had persevered in adding their mark to the crumbling wall.

I had only got as far as the O and T before giving up.

When you are the suspect, the funeral is in your mind. A total blockage it seemed from any other thought but doom. But it was my Mother who the cold dirt would hit. Covering the wooden box n any trace of her from the walking world, hollow footsteps as the dead to walk again. My concrete tomb seemed so wasted. All this space would need tons of earth to fill it. My thoughts interrupted as some kind of sound from the cell area come flooding through. It was pleasing at least I wasn't like Mum, totally alone. Maybe I hoped visitors to Mums grave would comfort her from above. Maybe she wasn't there. The lights just go out forever. No dreams, no other place, just a switch that clicks goodbye, forget me.

Stan the bastard should have been the one laying twisted at the bottom of the cellar stairs. As I stared up into the only window in the ceiling, distorted glass reflected nothing but the dark night n its horror.

Mum had looked like a broken necked young chick that had been blown from the gutter nest to the hard floor, the cruel wind taking another victim. My back aching from the slab bed made me angry. Mum would have given anything to feel these discomforts. Although I had hated the way she had reared me, she was still the one who had breathed life into me. The tiredness of stress laying me now to a fit full sleep as I pulled the itchy green blanket over my head, covering my eyes from the cell light that burned twenty four seven, my clock for now the ever changing block of glass above reflecting its dark or light moods. Sleep hit me like Stan's big old hammer.

Just as I was snoring away, I was awoken by n introduced to Superintendent Clout. He drearily informed me through the now lowered hatch in the centre of the cell door, to my extension of stay in said police station, plus the informing of a few of my rights. Not that many had been adhered to up to now. And as quickly as he appeared, he sodded off again, closing the flap as he departed.

Over the high walls of the cop shop I hear sirens reach my ears. I had thought again of Mum. Fresh spade dug soil in a heap, ready for the empty body. Everyone I supposed was going to lay down for the Lord n let him take your boots with your heel now heavy with clay at the mysterious grave side. No names now, just whispers in the cemetery trees of who you had been.

FUCK THE LAW

It's keyed somehow deep into the wall, nearest to where my head laid crooked. A webbed foot hopped into the skylights white light. No chirp from the skies. More cell block fidgeting throughout the early dawn for me. I had pulled my school jumper cuff over my face because the thinness of the itchy blanket just wasn't blocking out enough light to retreat into.

I crept back to my waking nightmare dream. The comprehension of a Mother lost. At least she was well away from the grip of Stanley's hand. He would be alright at home, pleased with himself and his conquest, probably wrapped up all snug in the sheepskin rugs that he made Mum pinch from out the slaughter bungalow. His voice in my head, "More than bones o meat come out o a slaughter ous Boy" My shivering frame, now wrapped up the best it could in the smelly tramp blanket of the station didn't need reminding.

The waiting seemed to be all that was left now. My eyes had cleared now from the fabrics of the attic. My life it seemed had become the Q that never moved. The wheel of justice, a dinosaur that had hidden until all of that era had become extinct. Then it had reared up and pounded the earth. Small specks like me just caught up in its passing crushing might.

Cramp now had crept into every part of my bored body. The sleeve of my jumper having to be re angled over my eyes, my Tired arms no good to hold it there. Slipping out my arm for the cold to bite was the price to pay to fold it and carefully balance it, so I could stay in the retreats of the dark. Wiggling my toes was the entertainment. My age had been taken into consideration from one of the humans that had slipped into the force. The steel plate in my door now lowered. Every now and again a half face would appear as curiosity getting the better of the tit heads became apparent. Comments overheard, such a young scrawny boy, such a shame that he had the heart of a coward, a killer of his own blood.

Over the period of the last twenty four hours I had got to pick up on some of the pig's names. At the hatch now I heard officer Dick sigh n say, "so the police still live at 999 lets be avenue." Oh how inspector Brassfooler spat out his kenco at that one, half of it spraying straight through the hatch and onto my stocking feet. There was a few more who I had overheard their names in the corridor being spoken or ordered about. Pc Squirrel seemed to have as much clout as officer Dick. Sgt Gip stye and inspector Brassfooler seemed the ones running the show. And whoever those upstairs were that I kept hearing about. Well they seemed to be running the whole fucking world. My world or what was left of it for sure.

It seemed in the plush offices upstairs tonight, common sense prevailed at times. But the instructions filtering down to these tit heads caused me to be concerned for my welfare. I didn't deal with any of it for a while, sleep drugged me.

A flash of a dream that steadily distorted into a full blown nightmare which thankfully didn't last too long as pc Squirrel enjoying his little exertion of power over me woke me with a start. His small paper cup of water he had sent flying through the hatch just before his keys hit the lock to open me up.

"INTERVIEW KITES" The command sounding weak and feeble, why the double put down?

Whack goes the metal of the heavy door against the wall, making sure I was awake. He sensed his own limits of power, stamping now his foot as though he had some senior experience, a silly move that confirmed he was nothing.

Outside the cell the narrow corridor was deserted. The metal panic strips that ran down each side were set off when pc Squirrel shoved me into them, trying to make up for his pathetic attempt at vocal authority. They were ripping up the rule book today or at least its blank pages. Straight in front of my eyes the piss take commences. They never bothered writing the bastard in the first place. After the beating they dished out in the confines of the alarm filled corridor, I came too in the hush of the interview suite. It had only been Squirrel n pc Dick, fuck all after the years at the hands of Stan. The heels of my now bare feet were badly scratched I noticed. Probably from where they had dragged me from my unconsciousness on the floor to prop me in the chair that I now found myself coming round in. Besides the carpeted floor n walls, the statement sheets and pen on the table were the objects to be focused on. The pool of dripping blood that was running from my nose to my feet was to be ignored.

{WHEN THE RED LIGHTS ON chapter 30} *Florescent bluish lights popped on in the ceiling like the colour of Stan's old poker end. A final quick gut punch from the boys in blue before they flicked on the record button gave me no voice at the start. Frail, my eyes focused on the whirling spool as a very weak yawn betrayed the extent of my fatigue. When the red tape lights on yer knackered, they had me right where they wanted me. By my reckoning with the town hall bells, the time was either four or five in the morning. Cold tea in front of me on the desk, there to loosen tongues, Bobbies the other side reading from their dummy cards as my rights, as the folk before me ignored. I at least knew I should have a solicitor present.*

Gripping pens like daggers poised to stab the info out of me. A large bulk of files filled one side of the grey desk which happened to be theirs. Controlling conditions should have zoomed in on me, but they had switched off the cameras way before the first attack.

officer Dick had now stretched n wandered off to doze lightly against the carpeted wall. inspector Brassfooler, who acquainted his name to me by way of polishing very slowly, for what seemed like ten minutes, the proud brass badge he wore for id, got straight as the gorton arrow to the point.

"We are charging you with the MURDER of Tish Kites, your Mother. You have the right to counsel, but not at the present time."I

stare as the red light flickers. The spool lazily revolves. pc Squirrel starts off the dumb questions. I'm not listening.

officer Dick peels himself away from the wall n tries a different tactic, which isn't working. After an hour or so I start to feel the irritation that there squeezing out of me. I get a little hot under my school jumper. There trained like shrinks to pounce when they notice more weakness. The inspector had left the room for coffee over half hour ago, leaving me to the mercy of these fuckin trained monkeys. "So you want to attack us eh" officer Dick chimed in with. Straight after him Squirrel says, "So you want to do the law" I couldn't help myself at taking the piss because even fatigued I was sharper than these two prats would ever be. "What like at University" It went way sailing over their heads. Just confused looks n, "answer the feckin question BOY" The word boy just sent my arm flying out, all the files papers were now scattered on the floor.

Just as it seemed I was about to get another dig, Superintendent Clout stuck his big nose round the interviews suite door. "His solicitor just got here, so wrap it up n get him back to the cell".

{LIBERTY chapter 31} Liberty's entrance to the station house was like a tonic to my poisoned soul. As soon as I came out from the interview suite n clapped eyes on him, I felt that the sun was shining again outside the tough walls. Though in reality, outside the north winds and dark thunder were prevailing. But his sheer presence felt for a moment like a surprise summer day. He was leaning strong against inspector Brassfooler's desk. Turning as I passed by behind him on my way back to my cell, he spoke in a most reassuring tone to me. "Everything ok young man?" I nodded a weary head.

Back in the cell I felt a little better. I had held as far as I was concerned, my own against Dick n Squirrel. And thankfully now it seemed I had someone on my side.

A while later, a monotone voice hissed through the flap, "Kites, lawyer to see you" The palava with the keys, holding back this *innocent killa, dealt with. The inwards swinging door groaned, giving me my first full on scale view of my counsel. Mr Liberace Kerty stepped forward. I shook his offered hand, feeling it swallow up my tiny paw. "Break bread with the enemy" he spoke, jerking his head back, indicating bang on where officer Dick's frame hovered pensively against the wall. The tears that had fallen through the night held now. He knew and started with more inquiries that changed through subjects even quicker than Johnny had ever done.*

He held my gaze, his sea blue eyes steady, yet ready to look away, so my own aversion for contact didn't seem obvious. I moved towards the back of the cell n lent against the tea stained wall. One long stride n he was leaning there with me.

"Close the door officer Dick, I need a private consultation with my client, to see first of all if he has been treated professionally" My mouth twitched in the direction of a smile. I felt comfortable for a moment, even in my shit predicament.

Once the door shut, I blurted out all at once, the scenes that had played out the evening before. Liberty never tried to interrupt, wanted to, but he knew that important details needed fresh airing. I speeded along, my jaws going a thousand miles per hour.

His clenched fist holding his cross pen, the thumb reaching up to the clicker every now and again. Turning on the nib, the ink running, a flurry of notes into his red leather bound pad. He clicked the nib off again n just held both hands in tight large fists. My own clenching fist was just as tight behind my back as I relayed verbally Stan's betrayal. I cried a tear or three, when we went over the cellar part. Even though Mum had been bad to me, I felt and wanted to believe in my heart that she had done it only to please Stan.

A few hours later he was ready to leave me n head to his chambers to think what could be done. There was already a lot of damning evidence against me. Stan's statement had already been written up n looked damning towards me. Liberty mentioned something about the police checking some doctor report of me having violent episodes of sleep walking and carrying weapons? My mind as if not in enough turmoil just couldn't comprehend any more of the bullshit. He made sure officer Dick had given me another blanket n a cup of sweet tea before he was gone. I liked the serious intimidating stare at officer Dick as he went.

After all the activity, the cell now seemed very quiet. I layed a little more comfy, the extra blanket most welcome. Outside the cell door I overheard the conversation. Sgt Gip Stye wanted the dragon light fetching. The lazy legs of officer Dick ordered to the task. They wrongly assumed I was fast on. How the hell was I deep on within this pickle of lies being spoken. The slow thump of officer Dick's clunky boots trailed off down the corridor. The plan that they had childishly discussed in between slurping sweet tea had me informed. A very powerful mobile torch was on its way to rudely awaken me, dazzle me they hoped to a startled standstill.

They were actual curious if it was powerful enough to blind me. But after more eaves dropping at my cell door, I sighed and went and slept at last. The daft bastards couldn't find any batteries to power it after all.

{THRUTH n ELUSION chapter 32} *"Not everybody takes sugar sarge" Liberty had declined the pre packed liquid. The fatty who stood behind the main desk dipped into his sugary sludge and licked the custard from the cream. A small crowd of tit heads surrounded the all important lump of teak. The old desks were probably chopped up for reserve truncheons. I'm sure plenty had been snapped around the noggins of the poor men before me.*

The gates that brought you from outside to the stations heart beat clattered and pc Squirrel scurried in. "Broken the little murdering bastard yet serge" Even in this shithole, buttons, pips n lapels spoke. Did the Squirrel expect a man who has spent ten years longer than him, kissing arse to reply. Liberty got things moving. He didn't toss about. The paper work swiftly covered, with a magician's speed of hand. He had signed the relevant paper work to take the case.

At least I had Liberty in the interview suite this time. But they were good these bastards. The red light was clearly on. Everything above board, the video was capturing the procedure in all its text book standards.

I swilled the remains of the cold sugary coffee around in the bitten Styrofoam cup. My eyes were looking to the floor. The bits of white from my nervous chewing, like little teeth scattered. Stan's fangs sprung to mind. ol Poleaxe had the right idea when it came to the bullying beast. Liberty had been careful not to chew the end of his sharp pencil, yet a steady tapping on his brilliant white teeth he allowed. The statements that had been made from my Fathers detailed oral bullshit were on the table. A neat bundle tied with a blood red ribbon, so fresh looking in the middle of all this internal mess. Liberty would look towards them every now and again, placing a manicured flat palm on the top, as if trying to feel the heart beat of the words.

The pigs left us alone for a consultation. Liberty knocked the pause button into stopping the recording. His blue eyes lit up like Balzac's cane, flashing magnifique. "This is all out of order", I blurted, my need of help so desperate in my voice that he reached out to pat my hand in reassurance. "The spokes are turning young man"

I melted back into the chair, while he did a shadow box move over in the corner. Navigation of the mind through exertion he explained smiling at me. He was studying the neat nail on his well manicured hand. "No blades allowed", he said confusing me for a moment. He then pulled from his shoe, its heel out to one side. He was care full to have his back to the camera. A small hidden compartment appeared, that he now withdrew from a wickedly sharp small blade and with a flick of his knife upwards, the ribbon fell apart. The blade now gone and the heel back in place, the smile still in place. A sly fox, my appointed saviour it seemed.

But I think we both knew after looking over the evidence that it was going to be an uphill battle. There was never going to be any question from the pigs about the credibility of Stan's testimony. They even went as far as saying to me when the interview resumed, that the Inspector was going to speak personally to the crown prosecution about Stan's good character.

Like any miss carriage, you just couldn't make it up.

The interview went nowhere. They tried a little subtle pressure, but Liberty didn't allow them to take the piss like they had done earlier. They cut the interview short, stating they had to go out and look at further evidence from the case.

Liberty told me before he left to keep calm n try to rest. Easier said than done, but I got back to the cell and thought about food for the first time in days. Even the slamming of the cell door didn't seem to make my heart jump as much now.

Tonight for your entertainment only, the cell walls, RAAAAAAAAAAAAAAAHHHHHHHH, pause, applause.

You a door me. The scratched words on the back of the steel cell door took me a while to get. My skylight above containing now pieces of the early morning light. Not much movement or noise from the maze of corridors. The other cells seemingly full of sleeping men. pc Squirrel ignored the flashing control panel at the main desk. My emergency buzzer manned by the walking dead. All those questions he had asked in the interview suite must have tired his little brain. The fat bastard was probably snoring away in the inspector's chair. I pressed with every finger the button inside my cell. Then sat for two hours, I think, going off the town hall bells, wanting to shit myself. In the end the charge sheet came in use full. There was still a flash of my spirits defiance somewhere deep inside my innocent crim bones.

{LAY DOWN chapter 33} I was for the beak in the morn.

Liberty said he would try to be there for support, but not to worry too much. It was all routine n with the charge being murder it would be a simple bail hearing, which would be refused n remanded back to the police station on what was called a lay down.

It was pc husbandman who collected me for the short trip to court. I had been looking forward to seeing the free outside. But no I was cuffed and informed of a passage way that tunnelled from the cop shop under the main road outside. It popped you back up on the other side of the road where the magistrate's court was situated.

Time held like the spinning Venus going against the system.

officer Dick smirked as I was led passed the main desk and on towards this little door in the floor. The hatch reminded me straight away of the attic at home. The descent, which was awkward with the cuffs on dealt with, I found myself now down in a dim lit arched roof tunnel. The raft obviously came to my sad trapped mind as we trundled along towards the darker end.

Two minutes later n I was climbing another set of metal ladders, catching my first view of the beaks domain.

It was only what I could describe as a dungeon view. The hatch had led me to a small desk where they looked over your paper work. Even though I had gone no more than a thousand yards, I was still classed as been moved n in the jurisdiction of other officials as well now. After sitting on this concrete slab bench for half an hour, I was finally called n led by pc husbandman up some wooden worn green steps and into the beaks court.

On the climb up, I had not known what to expect. A small crowd of people I hardly knew greeted me with hostile looks.

That didn't bother me too much, but when my eyes came to rest on Stan, my whole world fell apart again. He was going for another Oscar gain.

Sat with what I believed to be a member of the Church and a uniformed pc, his sobs could be heard all around the room. The vicar's hands busy, making the sign of the cross against his body when the charge was read out.

Like the journeys to and from the raft. The stress of the situation had me drifting off. A court appointed solicitor took care of the prompts for when I was needed to speak or nod n stand at the appropriate time. I had hoped to see Liberty, but he was absent. In the back of my mind, I could only hope he was busy in his chambers trying to free me from this terrible miss carriage.

The hearing led by his lordship Tusk, like Liberty told me, didn't last long. I was soon on my way back down the green steps, the fresh knowledge in my ears as to my Three week lay down. I had been informed off the duty solicitor that three weeks was an unusual length of time to be remanded to the police cells, but then my charge was murder, so it could have been down to that. He left me with the info that probably on my next hearing I would be remanded to a youth prison to await my trial.

The only good thing about the morning was a couple of cheese sandwiches the guard from the beak tunnel offered me. His wife after twenty years of marriage still put him them up even though he had told her he hated cheese. He told me all this in a cheerful way n it gave my soul a bit of nourishment as well knowing that there were still a few good eggs about.

Back under the road and up into the cop shop I was greeted with mock friendliness by pc Dick n Squirrel. They slapped me on the back saying welcome home son. I was glad when the bastards settled me back into my cell n buggered off for lunch.

It was around nine at night when I finally got a bit more grub. It had been left on the hatch I noticed after opening my eyes to read the names on the wall n door again. I had tried to sleep since around the afternoon, hoping to sink back deep into the pacific dream. But I'd got nowhere n just had to content myself with keeping my eyes shut tight. The grub was cold but I wolfed it down anyway. The moon could just be made out through the glass block window in the ceiling. As I had a wander up n down the grubby floor, pacing my strides long, then one foot behind the other, just to shake off the boredom, one of ol Dolly Blues mad chants popped into the forefront of my

*mind. I had heard her say it to Mum one winter night when the
moon had been like a brand new shilling.*

*Ancient moons, lend your power. Bring me peace, this very hour. I
call upon your strength n might. Bless your child this secret night.*

*It had done fuck all to my predicament as I woke in the early
morning, freezing. I felt as if I had lived the week as a tramp on his
personal bench, day by day punching in my time.*

{PRESSURE CONFESSION chapter 34} *They had worked me over a bit
more each day. When Liberty left the station house they would
pounce. You could never imagine the depth of the barrel. They were
deep, scraping away, making sure I was going to be convinced myself
of the guilt. Whispered threats that I knew were real. They were
ready to fucking do anything to make me cough up the confession.
"What's your profession" they would yell, over n over, turning the
word to confession now n again. Silly word games to confuse my
tired mind. The red light was off. That's if they even bothered to drag
me to the interview room. Mostly I would be crushed into the floor of
my cell as Superintendent clout dished out the orders to his minions.
"Soften him up boys, the little murdering mother fucka"*

*Other days, Liberty would be in on the interview. They played it all
professional then with cups of sweet tea n gentle cajoling. Other
times they just left me alone to rot, working on breaking down my
spirit. There is no noise, except my groans of discomfort. All the
tricks to get to you have been set into motion. Isolation, one of the
worst when shit aint good in your world. How long had I been here?
You got to the point of not really caring. The block of cells, the maze
of corridors, the interview suites, the little exercise yard, the
reception. The fucking mind bending fools. It all resulted in the same
glued time.*

*I hoped I'd get the chance to stretch my legs today. I shouted through
the block, no answer. I shouted through the silence again, just for the
hell of it. Yesterday I think I shouted to the man next door, the day*

*before he answered me. Confused? So we were. So you see. And so
another L-----ong day unfolds.*

*The need to move me to the cell next door was trifled with. The
pointlessness was beyond me. Officer Squirrel buried his head in
some mundane paperwork. officer Dick ignored the desk phone. They
had me for three weeks. The iron tooth brush I was given helped me
rinse my mouth with blood every morning. Last year's newspaper
didn't help the twenty three hours behind the door. Not that I got to
read it. They left it on a shelf just outside my door, just to wind me
up. The only little blessing came from my barbed wire fresh air. That
is when they decided to let me out into the little exercise yard. I
wondered whenever they did let me out to trot round in a tiny
circular path, just what Stan would be doing back at the house. No
doubt using Mums best plant filled pots as hash trays. Burnt already
Imagined her best Sunday frocks. A slag he would yell at her if she
showed a little ankle.*

*Exercise never lasted long, my thoughts sporadic back in the cell, the
lonely names on the scratched iron door my friends of mystery who I
doubted were in the same shit as me. Liberty had his wife send me
one morning out of the blue, a lovely card with handwritten words
inside telling me to stay strong. It had the poem IF by Kipling also
printed upon its inner pages.*

*Liberty came n strode his polished heels into my drab day every
weekend, clearing his calendar for the entire month for me. Burnt
candle wicks he would hand over to me on his departure with a wry
smile. The words Doing my very best scratched alongside the
convicts name on the door, he had done it while they reluctantly let
me take a shower after a week. When he would leave the station, I
would chill out the best I could while his protective presence
lingered. Back to lying on my slab looking up at the pigeon's feet in
the transparent skylight, amusing myself with their webbed shapes
hopping about.*

*Surprised that they let me out today into the tiny yard for exercise,
the weather permitting rules not applicable to a young murderer. The
heavy gate released me into a small area that they monitored, the rain*

bouncing down so hard that the floor seemed to resemble a large sheet of Braille that spelled out the gloom. The regulation hour that I should have been allowed was ignored again. They kept me out just long enough to get a good soaking, shoving me back into the dark pit of a cell. Naked from my own doing, I curled feral into the tightest part of the corner n slept fitfully. Later the evening having sneaked upon me, I dressed into my damp clobber. The night had dragged uncomfortably on and I had spent most of it awake freezing away the early hours of dawn with this cold chill deep inside my bones, sneezing my way now through the clap cold breki that had been balanced on the flap in the centre of the door. The grub, if it came at all, was always mixed up. Mind games being played out again. The breki would be a curry or Shepherd's pie in the morning. Tea would be beans or eggs late at night. They didn't realise that I'd been hunting for scraps all my life.

Boredom had a contract out on my soul. Thirty three gaps I counted in the grate on the floor. Various pictures of the imagination, lurking in the paint bobbled walls. My head in my hands most of the morning was how I would have been viewed through the flap. I couldn't now control my shaking legs. The same start of another wonderful, wasted day. Something different this morning as I was shoved and measured up against the wall. Back in the cell I rubbed the white chalk out of my hair where the sarge had sliced through with his mark.

After the dinner didn't show up at the flap I struggled through some exercise, a little attempt at gaining back some lost strength. ol Poleaxe in my mind as I pressed out on the blood stained floor a few reps. I gave up quick on the press up. Twenty sit ups later n I was sure they had me. I was a mess, a physical n mental disaster.

And as if on Q, they came for me for another interview. The big guns were out. Inspector Brassfooler, Superintendent Clout and sgt Gip Stye all ready to tag team the confession out of me today. They let officer Dick Culprits read out his statement first. The one he had typed up on arrival back at the station on the first day of my arrest.

The red light was on, interview resumed, another serving of my crim bones. No time for thought or reason. No thought or reason to time.

Who invented the question mark? Stan's homework rizzla questions popping random into my head again unwanted.

Dali swirls as the tape reel ferrised out again, three red lights, two of them behind my bloodshot tired eyes. Pc Dick cleared his throat n looked to the tape.

"I attended the residence of the deceased, who I now know to be a Mrs Tish Kites. Also at the scene of the crime, her visibly distraught and badly shaken Husband, now widow, Mr Stanley Kites. Upon confirming with Mr Kites that it was he who had contacted the police, I had, once entered the property, been brought to the attention by Mr Kites that there was a third party in residence, who he certainly believed was responsible for the killing. I was given details, indicating the Son had carried out well sworn threats to shove his Mother down the cellar steps of the property. Moving to the second floor of the residence, it was again brought to my attention by Mr Kites the said where about of the suspected culprit. Upon using some ladders I reached the, locked I may add, door/hatch of the attic. After repeated commands to come down and show himself I broke through using my truncheon. After a while of searching with my torch, my beam came to rest in my opinion on a cool and very calculated killer. I apprehended the suspect without much trouble and removed him from the property and placed him in the back of my police van and brought him back to the station".

I heard the gate outside the interview suite door squeak open. Please let it be Liberty my mind thought. But he never appeared. The policeman named luger, brooded in the background. His job was to scare the shit out of me, which he managed most when he yanked his brown tie up around his neck. His bulging eyes staring straight through me. A few years earlier n they would have been after the noose from the courts for my neck.

They took it in turns to scare me, to pressure me. All the while the constant normal questioning with the red tape light on would *continue. Then the tape n light would be off. I would be marched out the room, then as if I was back in my cell. They would turn the cameras off in the interview room n drag me back in for a grilling. As they entered for the hunt, Liberty and his advice to stay cool melted. These hot heads wanted a trophy, my head on a stick, and if that wasn't possible then my lame scrawled signature on the confession sheet. Whenever I tried to plead my innocence, sgt Gip Stye would yell. "I've never heard such sanctimonious crap in all my life" I had no chance.*

They knew when I was ready to spill. Knew I had no resistance left. Even that sure that they called Liberty n said he needed to get his arse to the station pronto, because I had confessed n was willing to confess again in his legal presence.

I had confessed orally. But the red light was off. I thought stupidly that if I told them what they wanted to hear then I might get out of the clutches of these scary deranged bastards.

They had me all set up n ready for when Liberty barged in. He got the request to speak to me in private back in my cell for a while. For a laugh n to try to lighten the situation he pulled out of his attaché case a pair of old boxing gloves. They were straight out of a 1910 fight scene. "I'm here to fight your case" I smiled weakly, but broke down very quickly. I was so scared of the police, that I told him I just wanted to confess on tape n get it all over with. I just wanted to get out of this police station.

Liberty quoted me something from a man named Gerry Conlon.

"If there is a hell on earth, it's been in prison and been innocent"

I tried on the gloves, thinking that ol Poleaxe had never liked them. They killed your clout he used to say. Liberty sat staring hard at the wall, trying to get to grips with the developments. Over the past few weeks we had understood that they had a very strong case, even without my now fresh confession on the horizon. The doctor, Treebooker, had worded a quite alarming statement about my unstable sleep walking episodes. The coming too in the mornings with knife in hand had all been documented and now sounded very worrying, considering the implications of the charge. Then there was Stan's horrid lie riddled statement. Yes a close relative, but an actual witness to the killing. He had made a very long and detailed account with his chummy drinking buddies. The ongoing threats to harm my Mother, the weed smoking that Stan and the Doctor believed to be a cause of my aggression. The cruelty to animals that Stan had added to make out I was a sadistic pig. Mostly the stuff he was, yet now here it was written as an official statement attributed to me to try to send me down.

When Liberty and I finally got back into the interview, they started the red light n the news just got worse. Now they threw into the mix another statement from a serving police officer, who I knew to be a pal of Stan's. They were deep into the weed situation. I didn't know all the details but I knew this pig had dealt with Poidge Stone & Bricky Barret, n that meant only one thing. He was dealing in the skunk big time, the hulk strain.

In the statement though, the only mention was a brief chat now n again at the respectable liberal club that he n Stan were lifelong members of. He detailed in his bullshit that he had participated in numerous chats with Mr Kites about the concerns Mr Kites was having about the unstable growing nature of his young son. It went on to state that Stan had on a few occasions divulged to him about the boy threatening to kill his wife and also to once trying to push him down the cellar stairs. When they went for gold and brought out officer Dick's third party threats to kill statement, I just broke down n grabbed the pen from off the desk. Dick had gone on record to say that on my first night in the cells he had been threatened through the hatch by yours truly. Apparently I had said menacingly that if I ever got out of here I would do the same to him as I had my Mother. Of course there was no witness to this, but there didn't have to be. He was a serving police officer, Respected in the community. Why would he lie? Liberty got a quick consultation before I signed the confession. With my head so far up my arse, the words he used went sailing right over my head. Automatism was a theory he had been working on. There had it seems been a few cases over the years of people committing murder under the influence of sleep walking. He tried hard while explaining all this to talk me out of signing anything, but I was adamant that I'd had enough n just wanted all this madness to come to an end. Oh how little I realised at that point that the descent into madness was only just beginning.

{DIMINISHED RESPONSIBILTY chapter 35} They made sure I was still going to sign the confession. I think they would have liked to have kept me in the little ease, popping me next door for a bit of gentle persuasion in the dreaded old tower of London. Johnny had once told me of the little ease. It was the name given to the cell they made you wait in before getting taken for a go on rack.

Inside the interview suite my cold coffee I stare into, mesmerised with the liquid, peering over the rim of the Styrofoam cup, lost for a moment, back to the safety of the raft. The heavy hand of inspector Brassfooler bringing me back to my senses as it smashed down on the desk. He knocked half the bulk of folders to the floor, leaving them there as he stared at me with disgust. I was sooo tired the coffee bounced up n out the cup n just seemed to freeze in the mid air for a while before soaking my side of the desk. The Dali swirl of the tape recorder came back into my vision, while just for clarity he questioned me again about why I killed my Mother. I said no more, only that I had not meant to kill her. That I had not known what I was doing, that for God sake I had been asleep when it had apparently happened.

They had what they wanted. Superintendent Clout entered at this point n said, "Do you need the other statement?"I knew what it was. I didn't need the braggin bastards smile as he was dismissed by the inspector with a wave of his hand.

Brassfooler handed me the necessary paperwork to sign. The other statement he went on to tell me had been the false claims I had made to the police about my own Father trying to kill my Mum. Along with everything else, it just sounded the death knell.

Liberty assured me that he would do everything he could to help me at the court. He led me back to the cells with officer Dick in tow. The briefcase settled on my bunk, the clasps expensive click, clashing with the crash of the door as Dick tried again to show his power. The bastard didn't need to, for he had stitched me up well n proper. The only way a piece of scum could do, with lies.

I could hear pc Squirrel disperse some local noisy drunk who thought he was in some karaoke bar. The group of bullying boys in blue soon joined Squirrel to knock the fucka into quiet oblivion.

Liberty looked at me as if he had let me down badly. I reassured him the best I could at the time that it was not his fault, that the evidence was stacked. Even though I hardly knew the man I felt a great sense of affection towards him. He had wanted to help, had helped within the limited space of hope I had given him to deal inside this stinkin case. We shook hands. He told me I would be taken to the beak again in the morning to be committed to crown.

Alone in the silence, the tears came. They swamped my face, nearly drowning me. And in that fashion I closed out the dark of the skylight, turning my head away to the wall to block out the cell light n fell into a deep horrid sleep.

{NOT QUILTY, NO GUILT chapter 36} I signed my life away on the condition that I was pleading diminished responsibility on the grounds of automatism. Liberty said that if the doctor's statement was strong one way for the police, then it was also strong now our way for the use of defence.

There would be another quick trip under the pig station road for the beak to commit me to crown as his magistrate powers only allowing him to sentence me to a max eighteen month. They wanted to ring a lot more time out of my scrawny neck than that.

The next morning I was cuffed again to pc Husbandman. The familiar raft once again came to mind as I was led back through the *dungeon tunnel. There was little difference to the last appearance. The district judge wiped his hands of my case. In the language of the law he sent me on to crown for me to put in my plea. The cheese sandwich screw wasn't on that day, just this nasty old bastard that had served a life sentence under the road. He shoved me about n growled every word. Strangely I was glad when I made the trip back to the cop shop n finally after a long morning got settled back in my cell. I was now to wait out the days until I was taken to crown. Normally you would be months waiting and taken to a youth prison on remand. I had, I was informed struck lucky, as some lengthy large trial at the Wakefield crown had collapsed due to jury tampering n I had been offered a slot in front of the Judge to enter my plea at the end of the week. Naively I thought this was good news. The sooner I was dealt with the sooner I could make my way back to freedom. Surely they wouldn't give me long as I had done jack shit after all. I wondered how many other poor souls had been dragged through a miss carriage.*

One of the humans on today, officer Trailblazer plonked down gently on the flap, a nice cup of tea without sugar n half a ripped book called the Hobbit. With my blanket wrapped round my legs n my hands warming on the boiled liquid I read a strange tale n drifted away from my cell for a while, surprised with myself feeling rather content with my meagre treasures.

It all changed in the evening. I had read until my eyelids had drooped n awoke with the book open still on my chest. It had been the other cell doors crashing open to deliver food that had stirred me from my slumber. Nothing appeared at my flap. The scent of beans n even butter wafted through the hatch n up into my snout.

When they had finished feeding the row, I thought that they had brought me the last supper. The cell door opened n pc Squirrel dived on me, cuffing my hands behind my back. Luger stepped from the shadows, with some clippers in his hand the type that a farmer would shear the flock in spring time with. As Squirrel held me down with a painful bony knee into the small of my back, Luger got to work cutting my hair for my big day. I think they were hoping that the short skin head I now half sported would make me look all moody n dangerous. But if anything, I believed I would only look like the orphan I had seemingly become, straight out of a dickens tattered manuscript, more a small boy with an empty begging bowl than a cold hearted killa.

officer Dick had stayed away from my cell. I believed I had overheard correctly that he had actually been transferred to other duties because he was fearful of his wellbeing around such a brute as yours truly. He was certainly playing his part in sticking one of the nails into my coffin well. Stan had banged away with a hammer in each hand, n Dr Treebooker had held the nails steady for him. About five days later I was rudely informed that my cell was needed for some local crims. I was going to be moved, because technically I resided on remand. I would have to wait the last few days before the plea at crown in the beaks dungeon cells. At that moment in time I cared for nothing.

On the morning of the move rain had hammered down all night on the cells sky light. As I was led away from the horrid bent bastards of the station house, I climbed down the hatch ladder n straight into a foot of water. pc Husbandman took me again, the raft so clear down here, its watery floor before me, as I trod along. My chains length of confinement held me close to Husbandman who was leading the way at a fast pace towards the dim centre of the tunnel. The cuffs tightness not an issue anymore, I had been relieved of any feelings when I had signed the statement confessing to the crime Stan had carried out.

After all the transfer paper work was over n done with, I was led to the end of the dungeon row of six court cells n told to make myself at home. The way the cell door slammed had the effect of Stan's heavy handed clips to the back of my skull. A large iron bolt shot across the already solid barrier of a door, making the claustrophobic air even heavier. Just like when Mum had turned the stolen diamond rings on her hand inwards, ready to cuff me hard to the ear lobe n crush me into the floor. I fall to my praying knees n then without hesitation fall some more, all the way to the cold floor, there is no salvation in holding my palms together. From this view I look up all alone n recall Liberty's advice that had floated through the space in between the flap of the other cell I had spent my time in. It didn't help much, but I tried to stay upbeat. A piece of chewed Styrofoam cup lies looking at me in the corner. I don't rise off the floor, but stretch out towards it, poking two eyes in it and ripping with my ever growing dirty fingernails a smile to reflect back to me some much needed hope. The companions of my lonely fate, talking to the cups face was I figured no more crazy than talking to the scratched names of old that nestled blunt n chiselled into the dungeons four walls.

I wide awake realised in the early morning hours that I didn't have the required knowledge at this relatively young age to comprehend the seriousness of my situation. Soul searching by trying to stupidly look for answers in song, the clashing n banging background of Stan's Folsom prison vinyl all too real now, Mums, I can't explain by the Who going over n over in my mind. Every now n again I would slap my palms on my trouser legs, drumming a bit of a crazy beat like moon the loon. Eventually with the first light of the new dawn I closed my eyes for a fit full rest. I didn't have the half hobbit book no more to read. Inspector Brassfooler made sure of that. I had tried to stash it down my skool pants but the old time bastard had sussed the bulge n got Squirrel to throw it into a nearby bin with a howling laff. I had hoped that now I was over this side of the road that the guard who had kindly given me the cheese butties would be looking after my custody. I was not lucky. He had taken two weeks off to cruise the Caribbean oceans with his wife. I was left with the gnarly ol so n so who hated spending his life down here with what he called the dregs of society. Luckily he was like most of em, a lazy twat who spent the majority of his days at the other end of the corridor, away from my cell, dozing n moaning to anyone who could stand to listen, sprawled in his thread bear armchair. It was only meal times when I had to put up with his shit. One thing decent, over this side of the road, at least the meals arrived like clockwork n were hot enough to look at for a while before wolfing down.

It must have been Monday morning. The court was busy with its agenda. The reason I had been shoved all the way out to the end cell was so I stayed separate from the day to day dealings of the beak. It had been that busy though, the sounds of cells filling n other solicitors arriving to try to outwit the boundaries of the law for their clients. The dungeon cell directly next to mine eventually had its door bang open. After a few minutes I heard a voice coming through to me, via the high up in the walls barred window. I plucked up eventually the nerve n bravado to shout back n have a natter. The burglar it turned out was not giving himself too much hope for the outcome of his sentencing. He wasn't heading upstairs he was being taken in the van across the city to the crown. He had heard that the judge on today's circuit at the crown was Pickles. He went on to inform me that if it had been a kilo of weed he would have walked with a nod n a wink n a slap on the wrist. But burglary was a touchy subject for his honour. When he later in the afternoon came back down from his day out up in the crown court, it didn't take long to hear his sobs so loud with my ear resting against my side of our shared dungeon wall. When he had got to his feet later n shared his voice up at the window again, he told me of the six years he had just been given by pickles. The reason for the severity had been explained. Pickles had a daughter who had been the victim of a burglary. But as if having your home ransacked wasn't bad enough, the dirty bastards had shit on her bed n wiped their arses on her curtains. Any one from that day on who copped for him on the crowns circuit with a charge for the same would be dealt with severe. But yet the lad next door went on to say before leaving on the bus for gaol that pickles loved a pot smoker n would be lenient as could be for that offense. Apparently he was a big campaigner for its legalisation. Maybe I thought I should mention I knew as a family friend Poidge Stone? Maybe he and Pickles were tight.

Then again I thought I best just keep my mouth shut from now on, I was in enough trouble. From next doors cell I now smelt the familiar stink of cannabis rising through the breeze. I guess with a six for burglary, he needed to drift off away from reality. I just closed my eyes and didn't escape there from mine.

{TRIALS & FIBULATIONS chapter 37} *"The trial a cometh," Liberty announced. The last few nights I hadn't slept a wink. It was Wednesday morning, around seven am. The first strange thing I thought was what time Liberty must have woken to look so immaculately groomed n dressed. My own clothes were shit to start with but after nearly a moon in the cells I looked a sight for sore eyes. My head was lent against its rough stone wall for support. I felt dead on my feet. All the files were brought by Liberties junior, who would under his guidance make a good silk himself one day. He was dismissed, in a civil fashion. Liberty placed a large hand upon the files n patted its bulk.*

Bulk, lies, it was all the same. A smug bastard's signature held its importance at the bottom of every sheet, except my own forced scrawl.

"Picasso was a skin head as a boy"

That brought a little smile to my face. "I'm going to do my best young man" We went over the files in the dungeon.

You kind of hoped that every time you re read through the statements it would appear a little less damning, yet it never did. If anything it just looked worse. The five main bullets in the prosicutrix gun were full metal jackets. The sixth bullet with the name of yours truly on it was gonna be fired at the end of the day by the judge. The miss carriage slug was going straight into my head, blowing what was left of my poor confused brain to smithereens. There was no safety catch. Stan had made sure of that with his carefully laid plans to destroy me. It was like playing Russian roulette but having no empty chamber.

After a few hours Liberty got ready to leave. He needed he said to get to work back in his chambers. To make sure everything was covered to prepare for the automatism defence to work. Our best option now, with the Worst case scenario being they would not accept I had unintentionally killed my Mother n find me fit to be tried for Murder in the first degree.

As he was heading out the heavy cell door he gave me a few business cards of his. "Thought you might like something to read" I took a few n said cheerio. The glue clock was set back into motion.

After the supper had been dished out, the corridors again became ghost like. The old gnarly screw had gone home thank fuck n old Douglas the night guard seemed ok. He gave me a last hot drink before disappearing into his small office at the end. As I sipped at the hot brew I looked over the cards Liberty had given. The first one had on one side a pair of boxing gloves, the left side having his full name upon it. Mr Liberace Kerty QC. The right side had under the gloves in smaller print the statement I fight hard & dirty for your liberty.

I checked out the second card. Flicking the first one against the back of the cell wall like me n Johnny had done at skool with our treasured footy cards. A hand glider with a man with very red eyes stared back at me. The writing was on the flip side. Again Liberty's name, along with the slogan, hand gliding is more dangerous than pot smoking, with larger letters stating, Question Civil Liberties! Maybe I could flash it at Judge Pickles if I got him as my Judge. I flicked it towards the first card that rested tight against the wall. The second card landed almost on top of it.

The third card had no picture. The red card had black letters stating that, black eyes are sexy. On the reverse it was printed, domestic violence open up your peepers. I liked that one the best, as I sent it flying through the air to land next to the others. I played the game for a few hours trying to take my mind off the looming day at crown.

I slept a little, dreaming of the hobbits idyllic little home, unsure as to where he was heading because of the ripped out pages. But what are dreams for if you can't make up your own ending. In the early morning though, this nightmare would unfold to its own climax. The more important question was where the hell was I heading? Liberty was good, was going to give it his best shot, but he was no Gandalf to cast away this miss carriage that felt like an avalanche about to collapse on an igloo.

Because I was pleading guilty in front of the crown, If the defence I was putting forward was accepted then Liberty had told me that there was a chance that the same judge if applied to by him could very well sentence me on the day, instead of going on remand to be brought back later for sentencing. At this stage, even though Liberty had told me to obviously expect more than the eighteen moons the beak could have dished out, but not to worry. I could expect a couple of years, maybe three at tops, served within a hospital that would treat my somnambulism n give me counselling for dealing with my loss of a mother. Liberty said just to play the game. To go along with the treatments n let them see that I was fit for release at the earliest stage. Maybe I would do as little as a year behind the wall. I could return to the village n go live with ol Poleaxe. I hadn't heard anything from him. He never ventured out these days n didn't read or watch the news, so I was unsure if he even knew what had happened. Tish had stopped visiting years ago. I knew one damn thing Stan wouldn't have dared to go up the lane to tell him. He had always seen straight through young Stanley Kites. I hoped after the plea to get a letter out to him at Hunts man fold where he resided. Liberty told me that Johnny had wanted to put in a statement for me. Detailing all the times he had seen me come to skool bruised n battered. But Liberty said that the trial already stinking to high heaven of corruption stank even more when that idea had been whispered in the corridors of power. The rumour was that it was going to get ruled irrelevant to the case by the judge, as if it was all predestined to find me guilty of this bullshit charge.

{GREY GOOSE chapter 38} *The cons called it the grey goose in America. Over here in sunny England it sometimes got called that but it was usually called the sweat box.*

Its loud running engine had awoken me from a nightmare that had multiple Stan's torturing me for fun in this old basement. The van was here ready to take me on my unwanted date with the judge. Outside, the sunlight hurt my eyes, as if the fabrics from the attic were still scratching at the retina. The grey goose turned out to be a white van. I don't think the yanks are colour blind, probably the dust from the chain gang highways turning the goose grey over there side of the pond. My main concern at that point wasn't the colour spectrum of vehicles. Hells Angels were rocking the shit out of the van. Not that I knew, until I climbed up the metal ramp n into the back of a load of leather clad, hard faced gentlemen. I had heard of the blue angels MC. Stan had often spoken the name when he had his head together with Poidge n Bricky.

The old gnarly dungeon screw had put me into the adult van on purpose, to rattle me at least, or hopefully get me a beating. He slammed the sweat box door on me for my initiation. There were some hard sonny barger stares at first. Johnny had once told me of the most notorious of angels. Johnny had mentioned him when he had given me an early book written by Hunter S Thomson. Apparently they had given him unique access to their lives in the motorcycle club, but after a while had turned on Hunter n beat the shit out at him.

I was tense n ready for a crack when the biggest of the lot of em in the back of our van said, "Whay ya in fer kid?" I thought about lying n trying to say something cool or what I hoped they would think was cool but I just blurted out, "Murder"

The stares remained hard n levelled at me. But now the one who had asked me winked n said, "Tough guy" I knew with the size of his chest in his leather tunic that he was taking the piss. "I've been set up" "Welcome to the club kid"

Thankfully they seemed to believe me when I blurted out for five minutes the main points of the past month. I even curried favour with the big guy when he looked at me with a bit of respect when I asked him if he wanted out of his cuffs. I did it for him, as the old bastard screw had only cuffed me to the front. It had been a trick I had been shown from ol Poleaxe one time. He had picked it up from one of the fair workers when he had worked the TERROR fighting booth.

Just as I was about to undo another of the angels, the van door ripped open n I was told to get out n get to the youth van. They all wished me luck as I jumped down. The old screw not daring to mention the big Angels cheerful wave, cuffs dangling down from his huge hairy wrist. They started rocking the van even more crazy when the door re shut.

The old screw didn't speak again. He just shoved me in the back towards this other vehicle n I was now sat hunched up in this little cubicle inside the youth van. The engine soon got us going as the invisible eye opened the big gate n I saw the street again as we turned out from the cop shop into the road. A stray dog brought a grin to my chops as it skipped down the pavement smelling every doorway briefly before shooting off to the next. Everything seemed so fast paced after the slow glue clock time of the station house.

A beautiful young lady stepped to the back of a stationary car, waiting to cross the road. I crushed my face against the vans small window to see her freckles wiz past. I realised after waving at a few folk out shopping, that only I could see out n they could not see in through the glass. We swept quickly through the city, passing Faver's old Bridge Hotel, or the space where it had once stood proud. A lot of the elegant old buildings like Eastwoods stood empty. There was a lot of activity outside this new night spot that was just opening. Two men on ladders were hanging a large banner that I just managed to read as we swept by. Maybe when I got back home I would try a night out at Roof top gardens. While the distraction of buildings and ordinary people getting on with their day to day lives helped, the nearer we got to the cities Crown court the more I started to sweat, also now realising that it wasn't probably the heat of the weather that had given the van its nick name. The first I knew about arriving there came with an almighty smash against the window. I could see cameras pointing at the van where a small group that must have been from the papers stood in a group hoping to get a front page snap. Another group of what could only be described as total crack pots seemed eager to harass anything they could. Luckily a few cops holding them at bay but not able to stop the odd one sending some

Irish confetti in the direction of my window. The thud as rocks hit the van deafening me for a minute in the confined space.

The van flew past the chaos and into this court yard. Large wooden heavy gates closed slowly behind it. I was transferred through the reception n after the usual bollox of paperwork, I was placed in a white clean box of a cell to wait. I spent the time sat upon the floor trying to recall all the details of how I had arrived at this terrible place.

The trial I supposed had arrived without much delay. I was constantly informed that I had struck lucky with this large case collapsing due to jury tampering. I had not, fortunately, had to go to a youth remand prison. The cells, even though boring n staffed by mostly cruel bastards hadn't been that bad. With my home life I suppose you would have to place me somewhere like in the middle of a world war one trench to feel worse heat.

The evidence though seemed to have been decided to be clear cut. I was on occasion even wondering if I did kill her while I walked about the house a sleep. I wasn't sure if I did suffer from somnambulism or if Stan had made me believe it. Those haunting visions of him around in the shadows before I awoke from sleep making me unsure. With all the stress surrounding my head it wasn't clear at times just what had occurred. But on good days, I knew deep down I had nothing to confess to the Lord about. I had always known my Father was a horrid beast, but it was difficult to get the head around the situation he had created.

I had spent many an hour in the early rays of the morning light, looking skywards n asking why he had done it. The answer never came, yet I felt sure that whatever the outcome, one day I was going to beat the answer from his lying mouth. And then whack the bastard to death. There was the report from the police shrink who had arrived a few weeks into my laydown. He had spent the morning sat on a wooden chair just outside my cell door. It had been left open for him to observe my behaviour. Luger had prowled about in the corridor, just to let me know not to try to step foot over the thresh hold.

When he had tried to engage me in idle chat, n I had remained silent. His report had been drawn up with the conclusion that I was a cold calculated individual. He had added some fancy case reports, relating to others who had murdered while sleep walking. The intention was there even though I was asleep I had wanted subconsciously to kill my Ma. It was all fantasy, worded to make me sound like a deranged psycho. Plus attached to these were the faxed reports from my own doctor, who I believed had been sucked into Stan's plans as carefully as my good self.

In Stan's master plan, his own statement was the diamond in the rough. His bent buddy McDermott had written it all out for him. The lies to the police concerning Mrs B, the close proximity of the lies to the actual reality that now existed as far as Mum was concerned. I had tried to say that Stan had killed her, or attempted to, yet she had been found in perfectly good health. Now Stan was saying that I had murdered her and she was dead as a door nail when the pigs had arrived.

Inside Stan's statement, he had made sure to use everything to make it all look legit. There was collusion between him n Dr Treebooker, where he had gone alone to complain that I had stopped taking my meds and that Stan had caught me secretly spitting them out on several occasions. Included were mentions of Incidents where I had supposedly come around in the morning with a knife in hand. Also documented was where I was always being found near the top of the cellar stairs. Then the bent bastard coppers had done their bit to help Stanley. I didn't understand why they were doing this, but I knew there had to be a reason. I suspected it involved Poidge somehow, but it could have just been Stan that had something on some one. Someone was scared of something he knew. officer Dick's statement I could understand. It was nothing to do with the miss carriage set up. He had done it out of a sad pathetic attempt to show me who was boss. He knew I had no respect for his inferior position in the force. To me and any other soul who had ever had the unfortunate luck to meet him he would always be a pc who would never become more than just a Joey in uniform. For his weakness, I was going to pay the price. His statement on its own didn't seem too damning, but along with the rest of the bulk, it had the effect of making sure that the gravel was going down with a banging guilty whack.

{JUDGE YAMA chapter 39} It was around eleven am when Liberty got my cell door opened for a last minute consultation. I had been staring straight for an hour at this scratched rhyme on the back of the cell door.

My name is Dale Jail made me pale

His voice now broke the transfixion of my gaze on the wall. He was there to explain that he was ready to go back in to see Judge Yama. He told me he had been in the Judge's chambers since nine am. The slightly worried look on his face wasn't exactly filling me with confidence. He explained his anxiety. Judge Moizer had been scheduled to take our case, yet a last minute switch with no reason given had left us with the most feared Judge on the crowns books. Liberty had gone on to say that he had tried to speak with Lord Philips, the highest Judge in England, but had only had the phone slammed down on him. So we were stuck it seemed with Yama, a bastard judge from Hell. Liberty was convinced that Yama would, if we took the case in front of a jury, led them towards a guilty plea. To nod there twelve weary puppet heads in agreement that I was a killa. Liberty worrying me when he said he didn't like the sound of the scheduled list of juror's picked, the empanel already coached it seemed.

My mind was wired. The fate of a thousand cuts awaited me. We made the decision together; he held my small shaking hand in the claustrophobic tomb. Liberty told me that he knew I hadn't killed anyone, yet for reasons above him he had to just get me through this bullshit the best way he could. So we opted to swerve a jury.

After he had gone back to plead the facts to judge Yama I laid still n numb on the stained floor. An injection of heavy tranquilizers couldn't have kept me any more void of the reality of the situation. I was wide awake in a nightmare. From Liberty's earlier visit to see me

*I now had the knowledge that Stan, if made to, would take the stand
n speak through his glorious statement of lies. No way would I call
Stan to the stand. That adverse bastard would hold his head high, eye
contact direct at the jury. The please, you must believe me look on his
sweaty mopped face, swearing blind to affidavit. His previous crim
record, antecedents was the term Liberty used, would have been
buried conveniently by his bent bastard pig mate McDermott.*

*Liberty had already told me that the Attorney General was not likely
to step in to inquire why this charge seemed to be an open n shut case
from the start. A nolle prosequi from the leader of the English bar
didn't seem likely, too lazy propping the fucker up with the rest of the
silk stocking gentlemen, out of their wigs with drunken power.*

*I didn't have to wait very long, maybe two hours before the door
groaned open n the gnarly old screw told me it was time to go. At the
bottom of the stairs that led up to the court room, Liberty flew out of
a side door where he was getting changed into his silks. He had
bought me a Matisse patterned tie, placing it gently around my neck,
tying it like a patient Father, trying to not make it feel like the
dreaded hang man noose or worse Stan's strangling hands.*

*It's like these small crumbling steps, as you climb, you wonder where
the bejesus into the skies there taking you. This journey up was a
horrid reminder that not all steps lead to Heaven.*

*I will never ever forget the moment I left the dark confines of the
stairs n caught my first sight of the court. Its walls were the red of
Hell. Floor to ceiling bound volumes of law books in leather bound
covers. I was on a balcony of sorts. To my left n centre was a higher
podium with a large ornate carved chair in the centre. Below in a
kind of pit was Liberty, who nodded dignified up towards me. The
prosicutrix besides Liberty wouldn't have looked out of place in
Madame Tussauds. He was a dead wax looking individual. The
comfort from Liberty nodding soon disappeared when a deathly hush
fell over the entire room. Judge Yama had entered, and I knew
straight away, as soon as I looked him over that if he could have, he
would have had me swinging at the end of a rope by lunch time.*

The wig was way out. Fashion had hid the mirror. The gravel was in his hand, its fresh glue nearly making it come apart again from where he always slammed it down hard to start proceedings. He really went for it this time. I nearly jumped out of my skin. Out of sight to me, down in the pit somewhere, a dreary voice shouts, "All RISE" my weary puppet body gets told by the screw next to me to move to the front of the balcony. I get my first hard stare from Yama, his eyes a cold grey swirling fog.

I felt the ball n chain that he instantly wrapped around my leg. You couldn't actually see it, but it was there for sure, tightly secured. Writing steady n neat in a ledger, he proceeded with all the pomp of sherry drinkers. A quick flick through the mostly empty pages while eyeballing me, a show of strength, to let me know he would fill those clean white sheets with bullshit, erase the lot n sentence me how he felt fit.

The start like a two edged sword as had with Liberty's help of persuasion been granted this special court sitting. There was to be no trial of sorts. More an informative run through of the facts, with a sentence delivered at the end of the session. But I should never have been here at all.

For me it was hard to follow. I just listened the best I could n watched Liberty try his hardest to reason with Yama on some points of the law.

After the prosicutrix ran through the lies that made up his statements, Yama retired from his maple throne for a late lunch. I was told I would remain in the same spot to wait. I watched looking down as Liberty and the wax prosicutrix hurried after him, their black silk capes flapping behind, one hand on their heads to keep the ridiculous wigs from flying off. The three of them would thrash it out in his chambers. No doubt they would be sat their shaking, trying to reason with the devil himself. He returned forty minutes later. He spoke directly to me, stating the facts of the manslaughter charge he had agreed to sentence me under. To me it seemed crazy, even down to the label. Mum had been slaughtered alright, but by no man. Spineless coward slaughter, Oh look it up.

It was agreed by all parties that I was to be found guilty of manslaughter, under the ruling that I was temporally suffering from insanity, which had been brought on by bouts of somnambulism, where this fatal incident had occurred within. It was complicated. Hard to follow, yet I strangely felt relieved somehow. Liberty spoke up to Yama accepting that he was upon agreement to move to sentence, a nod from the wax dummy and here comes that decision. Yama spoke down towards the pit n Liberty.

"Occasionally and very unfortunately sleep walkers kill people, usually a member of the family. He emphasised the last part.

Judge Yama then turned his scrawny neck n looked down his be speckled nose at me. A nose that held a bone that was shaped like the slippery slope to Hell. The same one on which he was about to send me down on.

"Young man, from your silence throughout this hearing, it is clear to me that along with what I already agree with within the reports, you are a very cold individual. I do however accept, maybe a little reluctantly that you have committed this horrendous crime under the hypnotic state of somnambulism. And so regarding this fact, I agreed to refer you to be held in a state hospital where you will hopefully receive a cure for your involuntary conduct, which appears to have been brought on by some external factor. In this case the use of automatism is agreed by both defence and prosicutrix parties and I hear by sentence you to be detained under the mental health act for a period of no less than ten years. Take him down", and when he said down, I realised with horror tearing up through my gut as a feeling so intense, he meant to the depths of Hell for a decade.

{FABERON chapter 40} I wanted to run as fast as I could back down those steep stone steps with Yama's voice ringing in my ears, his words that meant the end of me non removable from the silent stairwell. The screw now nudged me in the back with force coaxing me to move my grounded feet to start the descent. I swear to God I

saw flames as I peered down the black yawning gap. Heavily I lifted my heel n trudged down into the dimly lit misery.

Once they had left me alone to wait for the transport, I sat in the centre of the dungeon cell. The silence was so great I spoke out, wandering if shock could relive a person of hearing. I had once on the outside witnessed hearing about the strange aspect of a man's jet black hair turning white overnight. It had happened to a cousin of my Mothers. His daughter had drowned in the river Calder while trying to retrieve a love poem that her lover had written before he went off to war. The wind had ripped it from her grasp and landed it near the water edge. My Ma's cousin had been summoned from work when his daughter had been seen to tumble in, but she was never found. The letter washed up later in the evening when her Father had been grieving at the spot. He had put it under his pillow that night and in the morning he had woke to look in the mirror at his hair now pure white.

The body could react in the strangest of ways. Luckily I heard my faint voice, funny how you start praying hard to the Lord when you're troubled deeply. It turned out that I didn't get chance to see Liberty before I left the court. He had another case to deal with and had told me before I had gone up in front of Yama that he would try to come down to the cell area before I left, n that if he didn't, not to worry n he would be in touch. I heard a roar of a voice through the corridors, "TRANSPORT". It wasn't the van though this time. I was unlocked quite quickly and led out to a waiting dark saloon car. Two burly attendants dressed head to toe in white handcuffed me to my front with this leather belt that held my hands out like I was praying. We set off and I soon was lost in the blurring hedges of the back lanes that led out of the city. I had overheard the driver mention a city called York. A place I had heard of from ol Granddad.

The drive was completed in silence except for when one of the guards said to the driver, "Hope they saved n stuck us a dinner in the hot plate" As he said this, the other nudged me from my day dreaming, "There it is"

On the horizon I clocked its foreboding chimneys spewing out black dusty clouds high into the sky. Minutes later we turned off the country road and into a long red gravelled drive that swept me towards some very dominating gates of metal. Strangely the plaque on the side of the stone pillars that held the heavy gates bolted stiff, read in small raised lettering, **FABERON.** *Yet in large swirling soldered iron work on the gates the words*

EX HOC METALLO VIRTUTEM

I knew it was Latin but didn't know the translation. The atmosphere in the car didn't have me inquiring either. The noise of far of dogs penetrated the vehicle windows. Even from a distance they sounded dangerous n hungry. The driver wound the window down n leaned his head out enough to be seen. Whirring security cameras perched on top of the gates pillars beeped with recognition, setting off the expensive mechanism that opened the gates in silence.

The apogee to the car journey abruptly ended with the brakes raking up a fine mist of dust all around the windows as the driver's clumsy heavy boot slammed on a little too hard. We had parked in a semicircular drive way that had in the middle of it a small stone weathered fountain. Its greenish looking water trickled slowly down what looked like a man's head that had been trapped in time, howling at some terrible demon. Probably some Latin poet or mythical God, but I had no time to dwell on the matter. I was dragged from the car and up a flight of beautifully carved steps and positioned in front of a grand black double door. The hungry screw spoke through a walkie talkie that he had fastened to his white tunic n we were instantly admitted. It was the smell that got my attention first, a clinical smell of death.

Mums hands before she bathed after a shift at the slaughter bungalow had the same sort of whiff. That bastard Stan's toothless grin penetrated a picture into my mind as soon as I remembered anything about her.

I was taken down a polished corridor, floor length mirrors were one side, old portraits the other. Strange looking men of importance, bearded with glasses, or curled wax tashes with monocles looked down on me as I passed, yet the mirrors on the other wall giving the effect of them looking at you from behind as well. One of the attendants, for I had been told to refer to him as this instead of screw or guard, pointed to a few as we passed n repeated the name of the figure that had sat for hours to capture from the portrait artist, the blazing intensity of his eyes, the serious reserved smile. "Sir William Charles Ellis" the attendant spoke as we passed the most blazing eyed portrait.

I was in a way starting to strangely relax, somewhat soothing were the mellow colours that a washed the walls. The polished floors beneath, had a gliding effect. There was chlorophome in the air, sucking away any lasting awakened feeling I had left.

But as we ended the row of portraits n started passing solid shut doors with brass plated handles, I started to hear faint screams. Moans that I was sure were seeping from under the door jams. We arrived at a door that was for my admittance. The attendant suddenly stopping in front of me, making me walk into his white starched back. He turned to say something but before he got out the words the door was opened from the inside. Dr Woo greeted me. He instantly offered a small feminine hand and spoke his name very softly, adding,

"Welcome to the Faberon Master Kites."

He motioned to a chair, which I gladly placed myself in. The attendant stood off to the back of the room, but Dr Woo told him it would be quite alright to wait just outside the door. He left the office with the parting words, "I'm right outside Dr if you need me" There was many a file on his desk, a family picture that had a beach hut in the background, a Japanese bonsai in an acid yellow pot. There were two clocks ticking, one upon the wall and another upon his desk, a carriage clock of sorts. They to my ear seemed to be ticking just a second behind each other. It gave me the sound of a trotting horses hoof. Dr Woo settled himself into a leather reclining chair and stared at me. Not a nasty stare. Just a stare that almost said out loud, who and what have we here then. I looked down at the floor. He cleared his throat.

"Of all the afflictions to which human beings are liable, the loss of reason is certainly the most severe. Deprived of this noble faculty, man is at once shut out from every social endearment and becomes a painful spectacle to all around him. The restoration then of the mind to its natural vigour must be to every feeling heart an object of the most anxious solicitude."

My eyes started to rise from the floor to meet his stare.

He didn't bother me with many details. Said there would be plenty of time to go through the files and the case. Of course getting me settled seemed to be his main concern. We ventured from the office and after a small trip through some more of the never ending corridors turned out through a door onto an enclosed large walled garden. In the corner a few old men, weather beaten ashen faced toiled with hoes at some flower beds. Hypnotic they performed.

Dr Woo sat me on a bench away from them and spoke a little about the hospital and its grounds. He firstly mentioned that the director's house where he had resided for thirteen years was about 3 acres away, closed off from the day to day running of the Faberon, his family life a private matter. He held a clenched fist to his throat n cleared it again.

"I like to walk in the early mornings and gather my thoughts for the day as I make my way through the wooded grounds to my office"

It all seemed very pleasant but I could not wipe from my body the feeling of being somewhere very disturbed.

There was obviously a front to the hospital. Maybe a side for the visiting folk who needed to come here, the ones who had a right to see that everything was above board.

I started to get nervous about what lay waiting in the background, the far off sound from the hungry dogs breaking the tranquillity as if on Q.

We moved on from the garden and went in at the other side through a different door. Here I now found myself in what Dr Woo said was the main part of the hospital. The institute was grey and brown, ceilings yellow. Dr Woo strolled down the corridor. At a door that read examination upon it, he stopped and stated that he would be leaving me at this point and that after a simple check up, a nurse would call for an attendee to take me over to one of the wards. The shock of the trial had left me numb, all I really wanted was to close my eyes and block it all out. I stared at his back until he disappeared like a ghost down the corridor. A blonde angelic vision opened the door he had left me outside and introduced her name to me in a velvet tone. "Hello Otiss, I'm Nurse Silk, please come in"

The examination that was obvious hospital regulation, consisted of nothing much, just the usual battery of tests. It passed without much notice, except the odd remark by the nurse's assistant that was over in the corner, twirling a pair of silver scissors on his index finger. "Going to behave now Kites?" and after my muted reply, "I'll stay in the room nurse, keep an eye on the mother murderer. I was too tired to react. Probably the same shit every one hears on admittance, digging for a reaction, hoping to give me a beating. I was going to try to keep calm n get the fuck outta hear ASAP. Liberty had repeated the keep cool mantra enough and I was sure as hell going to try to stick to it.

I found out the bastard nurse's assistant was actually one of the main attendee's called Gerard. Nurse silk had addressed him by that name when she had become annoyed with the scissor twirling, asking him firmly to put them back down on the instrument trolley. I smelt the faint rum fumes on his breath. He had tried to hide it with polo mints, which he had stuck out of a pocket in his tunic, but after Stan I could smell a drop at a thousand paces. From the moment we left the nurses' station and headed to another room where it was left up to this alki to decide where I would be spending my time, he was on my case. I was allowed to sit in a plastic orange chair while, with his back to me, munching n crunching mints he studied this large board full of names in red and yellow chalk. A quick knock on the door minutes later, followed by a nameless faceless arm that jutted into the room clutching a file with my name upon it. Gerard turned and snatched at it, the door closed again without an exchange of words. He pulled from the file a clean white sheet of paper. After studying its contents for a moment he added my name to the board. The chalk was red.

After this we left the office and a little further down another part of another corridor he spoke. "Dr Woo it seems deems you potentially a candidate for our Netherfield ward." I didn't quite know what reaction he was looking for. I certainly didn't do a jig on the corridor. My face remained impassive while my head just slightly nodded. Not in agreement but in acknowledgment of my hearing. The Netherfield ward, was it good news?

At this point I didn't care, all I wanted was to lie down and shut out all this drama. Maybe kill myself with a noose n go face the crowd, but the thought of never taking my revenge on Stan gave my legs a boost of energy and I followed Gerard's white stiff collar, his black neck for some reason conjuring Mrs B's favourite tipple into my mind.

There was no place now where silence dominated the air, even with the corridors empty of other patients being moved like myself to pointless zones. Certain distractions hung in the air, along with the cracking paint, strange tapping sounds on the pipes that were bolted up along the high ceilings, sounding like codes being sent. Gerard making my heart beat a little faster when out of the blue he screamed blue murder up at the roof. It oddly seemed to stop the tapping for a moment, yet as we glided along it started beating out its metallic rhythm once more.

As I lagged behind with fatigue, Gerard told me to get a move on, "Your new home awaits", he snarled. Christ I hated his rum guts already. He unlocked a door at the end of the last corridor we had ventured down. I was totally lost for direction now. Outside yet *again, we crossed a yard that had row upon row of old wooden wheel barrows n carts. Something like you would see on the old railways for moving goods about.*

The ward that they admitted me to was situated in one of what looked like the older parts of the hospital. It was isolated partly by the edge of the woods that I presumed if you went right to the other side held Dr Woo's home. As I first clapped eyes on my building it seemed very strange looking. The Netherfield was a Victorian looking Elizabethan, Tudor mishmash of styles. All manner of different periods portrayed its battered style. Obvious repairs from over the passing mad centuries held it together.

Stan's hammer house horror film started ominously creeping to mind.

We waited a good five minutes, Gerard impatient, his thumb held tight against the buzzer on the door that would admit us inside. I just turned my face away from his staring n focused on this scratched name that was level with my eye on the trunk of tree behind me.

Christopher taylor 23 nov 1818

I hoped he was still not here. A loud buzzer sounded n made me turn back towards Gerard, we were going in.

I was informed that I would be held overnight in an observation cell. Just a precaution I was appeased with when I went to try to ask why. There was a small row of cells against the left of the door we had just entered. A bit like the pig shop except now this was my permanent way of life. I was though led past these and into another room somewhat like the one nurse Silk had been in. Up until now things had been relatively calm. I soon realised the undercurrent of the mood had changed. Gerard grabbed my collar n moved me into the corner of the room where there was a chair with leather restraints upon its arms. He flung me into its seat aided now by another brute that roughly tied me in and pulled up my jumper's sleeve. They directed some medicine straight to the soul. "Settle you down buoy",

Gerard's voice floating above while my feet seemed to crash through the floor. They snapped the needle off in the crook of my arm for good measure. Not that they think you can see that little part. Further stings of pain as they decided to now dig it out n sooth the wound. Stemming the blood with a brillo pad, the last thing I remember seeing was the cotton wool swabs mocking me on the silver rusting trolley in the corner.

I came too, God knows how many hours later. I had been plonked in front of a large brown wooden t v. The volume was turned down, voices on faces in black n white trying to say something to my slavering brain. Gerard must have been monitoring me, for as soon as I woke he was over dragging me up and along to the row of cells. "They usually hose them" through the fog I saw the smirk on his fizog as he stepped back after turning the key. I got a shove in the back towards a horrid stench.

Writers block had obviously not barred the minds of the men who had sat before me, the wiff so over powering that I regained my senses for a minute. My new cell wall I guessed was once a dull off white. The artist had dug deep into his personal toolbox; the extent of the message, combined with the size of the lettering alone must have taken weeks of strain to spell out. Trawled thick with now hardened shit I stared in disbelief. Gerard banged the door hard, walking away laffin .The wind hadn't stirred much throughout the morning, yet now a gentle breeze wafted through the iron grill that was my only window. The stench was so overpowering that I moved towards this full piss pot that was in the corner for relief. The artist had been busy. In the dim light I hunched down hugging myself for comfort and read the wall.

`Art adorns our prison walls, keeps us`
`silent and diverted and indifferent.`

I read it a few times until the injection over took the shock of the stench n I just fell away back into the blackness.

There seemed times throughout the night when people came to my door. I registered it opening with its heavy creak, but didn't recall much. Some more talk I think, all very official no doubt. The grill shone through its tiny hole some light. It must have being the morning. I woke thinking I was still hugging myself but stiffened when I realised I had been put into a straight jacket. It seemed to be made of some kind of hardened hemp. I gave up the struggle, I was not quite Houdini.

Gerard came to the door, his key forever in the lock before it opened up. "Bowl of stir about?"I didn't get chance to say what, "Porridge, do you want a bowl Oliver?" I shook my head n he slammed back the door, encasing me again in the stinking atmospheric gloom. I dared to dream of a Costa Rican banana, a sip of Columbian coffee, even a good old boring cup of British tea. I'd always done the same at home.

Another request for dinner had me wondering where the hours had drifted away to. I thought I had stared at the shimmer of light coming through the bird shit caked grill, yet I must have slept. This time I think they had injected me in the neck. The sting faintly there whenever I tried awkwardly to turn in the jacket. Its heavy straps were strangling me to the point of having to measure my breathing or choke. After lying on the floor and trying to work out how far I would have to count silently in my head to keep a track on hours. The dose of meds that were up to my eyeballs, failed my brain. I gave up trying to times sixty seconds by sixty minutes. I knew it was a simple equation but not on this mad shit that they had pumped into my veins.

After the door had creaked opened for what I thought was the third time in the day. I noticed that I had been removed from the straight jacket and left to stare at the bruising along both my arms. There had been mention of food but I was to be moved to the proper long term cell on the Netherfield and would get some late scran up over there. I was weary now of the injections, yet strangely already addicted to its powers of blackness.

Gerard it seemed had gone off duty for the night and the other attendee that had helped inject me, took me on the short trip up to my new world. But just before that move, there was laughter from a group of brute guards, who with sleeves rolled up, dragged me over *to this side room where there was some clinical looking white baths. In the second one nearest the door they decided to drown me for a good few minutes.*

Dripping n gasping for breath I was now in their minds, baptised n ready for my new ward.

{CLOUDY POND chapter 41} *Above the door, the sign read in faded green, Netherfield. There was more waiting while fingers held buzzers to inform those on the other side that they had a new patient. It couldn't be any worse than the holding observation cell. When we finally swung through the doors, the same deathly smell hit me again. There were a few people in sight. Another white coat seemed to be in some animated exchange of words with a youngish long haired man on a wall phone. The white jacket that was with me ushered me along the polished floor towards them. As we passed the long hair turned to me and went, "Cocaine, Hashish, lsd"*

The wire to the phone I noticed dangled aimlessly, cut off from the outside world. My guard shoved me in the back, making the reply I was about to give pointless, as I now flew past. The long hair carried on his conversation which I gathered from the wire was to no one. I didn't have to keep reminding myself that I was in the nut house. The guard told me as we made our way towards the end of the long room that most of the other inhabitants of my new ward had been locked away. Procedure when a new patient arrived. I looked back towards the long hair, as we now stopped outside a cell that was to be mine. The burly guard grinned as he saw me look down back towards the phone. "Oh don't worry about him, he's the Amsterdam dealer" I got out the slurred words, "Harmless?" The guards grin spread, "Yeah, he's ok, he's only killed about ten" And with that little hindsight he pushed me into the cell and closed me up to think about my location and my new neighbours.

The space was small, dimly lit. A high up set of three bars were the window. There was a wooden chair lying on top of a metal sprung single bed. It seemed very low to the ground. But it was a welcome sight to my weary aching bones. I moved the chair over to the window, setting it just below. Climbing unsteady upon it I realised as my eye levelled with the middle gap in the bars that I was quite high up. I stared at tree tops and black full clouds of rain. I didn't think I had gone upwards on the corridor filled journey, but here I was, high up in my castle tomb. I could hear the dogs again. Every now and again there hunger for some institution blood barked clear their order.

It wasn't long before someone came to my door. There was a spy hole that gave insight into my movement. Thankful when it opened I was relieved to be staring back at the beautiful nurse Silk. She had in her perfect hands a small plastic beaker filled with water. Her other hand, that had been clasped rolled open to reveal on her palm an array of bright red and green tablets.

She asked me so nicely to take my medication that I floated to her, swallowed them as graceful as I could in her presence and floated away again. The door now bolted tight, my mind loosing the light that was fading rapid from the bars. A crow startling me out of my stupor for a moment as it landed briefly upon the ledge n then as quick departed into the sky. My wings had been clipped, burnt off, stamped upon and crushed. I fell onto the metal bed and zonked straight out.

What woke me later came from the noise in the pipes. Not a rhythm that I had heard like codes being sent as I had walked the corridors with Gerard, no, this was an almighty clang. The pipes were smacked hard again, making me now sit up unsteady to listen, steel echoes falling away to silence, making me think back to when I witnessed murder for the very first time as a very young boy.

The axe man hadn't tried to start the trouble; he lived in an old hut out near the back of the mill. I had been on my way to the raft to escape from another of Stan's beatings, crouching when I heard raised voices. The old man who lived alone in the hut, a recluse from the world had obviously gotten for reasons unknown to me, into an argument with this young guy who I knew of from sight walking up past our house now and again on the lane. I had hidden behind a large bush of stinging nettles as the tempers flared. The unbelievable sight of the young lad moving sharp as the old recluse took a sudden swing for him with the axe, the exchange of weapon in the ensuing struggle, the younger guy having more luck with the battle that now raged. The head of the ol guy rolling away severed from the return attack, my shock giving me away. The sudden stare of the killer. He came towards me instantly. I think in the moment he considered killing me as well. Be it with an axe fell, or a quick powerful strangulation. Instead he made me help him dig a hole. The place where it lay had stuck in my mind for a many long night. Years later I still had nightmares, still moved cautiously and respectfully around where I knew the bones laid beneath the now over grown grass. Whenever I neared the spot on the way to the edge of the dense brambles that led to the unknown path, this uneasy feeling of being watched came over me. But with the horror that was Stan in my day to day life, the memory drifted away, seemingly as if it had never occurred at all. I think Stan knew the killer and the victim. Probably even discussed it over cold beers with his rogue pals, maybe the reason that over the passing decade, the killa left me alone. Never, even upon seeing him on the lane did he threaten me again. The day of the killing I had been told with no uncertainty what lay in store if I ever dared to squeal. It was a warning so intense that I always believed I would take him to his grave by my own hand. When I grew old enough to hold the advantage, I was gonna chop him up.

It seems I'd swapped places with the poor old sod whose head now rested for eternity between his feet. The glue clock must have struggled through some hours and my door was slightly opened as the lock clicked clear. No one told me what I was supposed to do, so I just warily popped my head out n looked about to see what was happening. The smell of grub drifted in the air. Tea time was the event. I could see men trudging along down the corridor, mugs in hand to fill up a brew. Just as I thought the cells nearest me had long ago ejected their rumbling bellied inhabitants, the one directly to the right of me spilled out the strangest looking creature. It eyed me for a moment before setting off after the group. I followed.

As we neared the space where a Q was forming in a snaked pattern, the man who lived next to me turned and said, "Hello I'm "Winnie" His dark eyes like pools of oil but it was his mouth I noticed more, all his teeth solid gold. I nodded a nervous acknowledgment n trying to eject my voice from deep inside me got out a solid sounding "Otiss"

There seemed to be a few little cliques forming in the Q but I just slipped in quiet, getting a metal tray of food that I didn't ask about content wize n trotted back towards my cell where I had been informed all meals were to be consumed. I wolfed down the rubbish concoction, the door opening again after about twenty minutes. I was informed to put my tray outside on the floor. Then BANG, I was sealed off again for me to watch the four walls n try to count down the day.

The crumbling wall that peeled in different coloured paint patches held my attention. After staring for hours at one particular spot I raised my weary legs off the edge of the metal bed and reached out to pull away from the wall a piece. To my surprise in the fading light of the evening I could make out in a scratched signature underneath a verse.

Creepier & darker like a thousand curtains closed

Hush in the cave of ice dripping red bold

More layers than a labyrinth

Of a depth that's now being told,

I snapped another piece off the cell wall.

Quieter than the deaths of the people

Untold billions it holds

Pulled as if by a magic serpent

Through a hissing special trick

The hands of the blackest ghost

Red blood congealed they stick

An illusion of the devil

He's so black in body

The last piece fell off the wall of its own ghostly accord, revealing it in its entirety the last stanza.

But the flames are so bright

That the red reflects thee

Not to worry rejected angel

Home at last I scream.

The full stop at the end looked like the poet had continuously stabbed at the wall. Jesus, the shiver it sent down my spine. Where the Hell was I?

That first night in my new long term cell I pulled tight the itchy green blanket right up under my chin. Laid in bed it felt a little safer like that somehow. Protection from the dark fears, for as soon as they flicked off the strip lighting from outside the heavy door, the whispers grew. From under the quarter inch dusty gap in the bottom of the door they spoke. Cries and whimpers, howls at the unseen moon light. The fingers now wedged into my ear drums, still the odd scream getting filtered right down into my brain.

Somewhere someone is flushing their cell bog. Pipes are rattling throughout the whole block wing. I suddenly realise I wake from a quick dream. I had been on the van heading here, the saloon car gone. Keys dangled from big oak trees, instead of conkers as we whizzed past the road side bushes n fields. A moment before waking, the last tree had a small arched door cut into its lower trunk. A massive key hole centres the whole scene, but up in the branches, nooses hung waiting, blowing in the breeze.

"BREAKFAST KITES, get that shirt tucked in, shave, oh he's only fifteen! Well shave his head then". Who the fuck knew who they were talking too? A piece of fatty bacon rash on a cold metal tray materialised. I'd hit the brekki Q without even realising. Even more disturbing was when Iran my hands through my hair n realised I'd been clipped again. The drugs were really screwing with my mind. I'd had a small chat with nurse silk about meds. She had without going into too much detail explained that my swelling tongue was down to the lygactol. The tremor in my legs as I had tried to walk away confident apparent to her wizened ways. My over drooling inquiries hadn't told me much. I hadn't met the patient to the other side of my cell yet, but I did bump into the guy who lived next to him, two down from my peter.

Scot John was about seven foot tall, maybe an inch short of that stature. Covered head to toe it seemed in homemade tattoos that didn't have the crudeness of the prison ink I'd seen on Stan's pal Bricky Barret. A delicate hand the man possessed. A delicate hand that could easily span one handed around any neck. EVEN A BULLS NECK HE LOOKED LIKE HE COULD MAKE APPEAR SCRAWNY.

I noticed on his knuckles he had the words inked DEAR BOSS His nod to the ripper I later found out.

You couldn't just pass him by on the narrow landing that ran outside our cells. He was just too large, plus even though he looked menacing I was glad to meet another fellow in our cloudy pond.

Porridge was off the menu today, just a hand full of cornflakes and a spoonful of milk poured on top. The little tray in Scot John's hand looked like a mouthful would demolish it. And why the hell did I have bacon? I knew his name for I had past his cell where outside you had it scribbled on a card. He also had a red card tucked behind in the metal flap holder.

His first words to me were, "The reason a milk bottle has a sell by date is because of Al Capone. He then tilted back the tray n crunched n swallowed the lot in seconds. Wiping his mouth with his sleeve he went on, "He donated $1 million to schools for milk but said he wanted a sell by date, his only condition, for he had been given spoilt milk at skool as a child and it had made him really sick "He then winked at me n banged up his own door leaving me with the approaching Winnie. I nodded at the strange creature and took a leaf out of John's book n banged my own door up.

I lent my back upon the steel door and looked up towards the high bars. The rain had become intermittent now. I got upon the chair n looked out. Tiny wet squalls on the yard below, shimmering into the morning light. A few drops clung to my bars, some shine off the sun hid behind a drifting cloud. I stayed there for hours staring until it dwindles away to dry floor. Then the pipes made a funny sound, not the radiator pipes but the toilet system. There was a bang on my wall from Winnie's side. I waited, not sure what to do. Then another bang so I climbed back on the chair n shouted "WHAT"

"Empty your pipes "I stared over the horizon wandering what the bleeding loon meant. "The toilet, empty the pipe"

I stepped down from the wobbly chair, studying in depth the toilet. It took a few long minutes and a few more shouts of the same command that were faint on the howling wind, for me to suss it out.

There was besides the old crapper a wooden plunger, its end made of rubber. I suppose it was not thought of as a weapon of such, just something to clear the bog if things got a bit messy. All the pipes were obviously connected so I rammed the plunger down n after a splashy minute the water ran out and back up inside the pipe thus clearing a vocal connection from the cell next door. At the time I didn't know if all the cells were now open to convo. The same strange voice soon echoed up into my cell. I pulled the chair near plonking my arse down n leant forward to reply.

It lasted all of two minutes, just enough time for me to establish that my next door neighbour to my right was Winnie Jah. He only mentioned that he was a pawn broker on the out and that to the other side of me was a very nice but dangerous man called Character. I didn't get to say much for he suddenly remembered the time n said that the medications were due. I then heard him flush the chain n break the connection. I did the same n laid upon my bunk wondering about the man to the left of me.

The door only opened once more that day. Medication was unfortunately delivered by Gerard who gave it his best shot again at trying to wind me up enough to kick off. I don't even know why he bothered cos they were treating me as they pleased, drugging me at will. I could only assume it was for his personal reasons.

The door remained shut solid until the next morning. No mention of dinner or tea time food. I had scratched into the wall with a long overdue cut nail it seemed, sometime throughout the long dark night. The Lowry match stick dog must have been about all I could muster with the medication so strong. Near to the toilet the art stared back. Upon closer inspection, the dogs long tail not some straight dragged line but the words painfully deep, INNOCENTI. The Latin on the gates as I had entered the Faberon grounds seemingly getting into my head.

The rigmarole with the pipes once again soon told me via Winnie that a couple of Brothers called Alan n Tom had kicked off down the block which Winnie ominously called Wa/rd siX.

Apparently they had been put in the same cell together, a mistake by one of the new guards, which had caused them to beat the crap out of each other. Separated for their own good now, the staff not taking any chances, so for the foreseeable future this was how they would remain. All in a normal afternoon's drama here at the Faberon, Winnie delighted in explaining.

Staring from the toilet bowl and then around my cell I could smell the centuries of madness on the hospitals fixtures n fittings. I had hypnotised myself again, my mind heavy laden with the drugs, I couldn't help but just stare blankly at the walls. I could hear Winnie for what was probably hours calling me but I was a piece of stone, another brick in the demented wall.

The evening had me drooling, comatose, lounging awkward on the metal hard bed. A sparrow flew and crashed straight into the bars of my cell today. I saw it happen as I'd continued from the long night before today dreaming now through the light of the morning. I thought I'd pull myself up instead of using the chair. Chin up manoeuvre needed, Granddad Pedley's advice about using strong tree branches as I walked home via the orchard to help build up my shoulder strength. I reached up with a run n a leap at the wall n caught a grip on the bars that yawned now to my view the outside world.

Down on the yard below, the dead bird was on its back. A funny broken necked angle held its shocked gaze back up to my eyes. I pushed mums death image away from rising n hurting. I stared for a while at the creature, thinking that like most of the patients locked away with me, not all flew to freedom.

The barrow man trundled into view and broke the spell. He carefully picked up the fallen angel and put it to one clear corner of his cart. He gazed up and noticed my frozen finger tips holding onto the bird shit caked bars, the top of my head just visible. 'Bury it for me' I shouted down. 'I will find a nice spot' he ventured back. I noticed the pull in my arms fibres, aching now I let go and jumped back to the cells green faded wood floor. Still staring up at the barred window I noticed another bird soar past in the free skies. An inner voice spoke within me. I would be that one day, Years ahead, but one day.

{CHARACTER chapter 42} The quiet one, the one next door to Winnie was some mad loon who was actually quite believable when he recalled how he was the real alive descendent of jack the ripper. He kept an image that took you back to the fog. I'd had a quick glance at him when I had gone for breki.

If you happened to get the chance to peep through on him, he would most of the time reveal a man at ease with his sins. The rumours of his black pipe bubbling away were true. There was a strange smell drifting from inside his pad. Winnie had mentioned about him putting black boot polish all over his cell walls. His hair hung over his darkened eyes like the black marble of new grave headstones. I'm not sure about the rumours about him making medical equipment. He apparently worked a few mornings down the lab with a Dr. Metal tongs that looked like instruments of torture. He was rumoured to say they were tongs for picking up tab ends on his floor. His spine so twisted he needed leverage. Glass vials he had stolen n filled with coloured blue snooker chalk, adding water, making little potions. Smog seemed to follow his movement. The screws just left him alone with his strange requests. It seemed the further you went to the left of my cell the weirder the cell observation became. But that I suppose was before I heard Winnie tell me his tale about Character in the cell the other side of mine. That's who I would learn in depth about first. He wasn't allowed out of his cell at certain times for certain reasons, others seemed to be out n on the landings quite regular. My beady eye at the gap in the iron door would see the zombified shadows shuffling about. Mumbling to the floor or howling up into the Gods.

Medication delivered regular. It had been mentioned through narrative that I tried to recall, which was becoming harder as my ears seemed to be closing as much as my drooping eye lids. There's a meeting again today something about my attitude being bad. Something about my permanent location staying as a patient on the Netherfield... a week had passed n I wondered how drugged I was...

I was informed by Dr Woo that I would be moved cells. A fresh start, 'let's try again shall we." So back to the Netherfield n down from Wa/rd siX I went. I didn't even realise I'd moved up there for a week.

Po Cock brothers, the metal badge fixed to the rubber room door,125, Southwork Bridge Road, London, the address where the bastards made their contraptions of solitude.

I recalled a drugged conversation that I had overheard through the fog. 1958 Sprang to mind, pretty sure it was that date mentioned.

The dreaded padded cell went out of use except at the Faberon. CHLORPROMOZINE rendered them obsolete in that year, which they used alongside the rubber tomb.

A nagging memory of some typing class flashes through my muddled brain. I'm sure I had just signed the bottom of a letter the typing teacher had done for me. Like some standard reply to the outside world that all was well, but I wasn't quite sure as the new drugs that they had been sneaking into my diet infecting n fogging my brain.

That's all I could think about as I was led back down the shit stained demented corridors n back to my peter on the Netherfield ward Nurse Silk was near, I could smell her lavender perfume slightly intoxicating my nostrils over the stench of madness that clung to the fabric of the walls.

Jesus Da I'd love to put the lawn mower over your head, you GRaSs. I'd heard the distant rumble. The grounds were immaculate, a pretence to the crumbling facade within.

A number fifty eight painted on the side of the block wall, all done to completion by the van Goth wannabes. 58 ROOMS OF SHEER MADNESS, an array of multi coloured doors. Distant long remembered howls of insanity, pulsing out from the padded walls. I'd been in another room though, the flash back in the mind a distant remembrance now, duo pulse constant current. The scorches were there on my temples, the mouth a dry river bed.

The mains. The green light. Auto crescendo, output, test ect1, ECT2 Mode. Treat, time.

The rubber mouth piece came horrid in my slava; I knew they had zapped me. Jesus H Christ where the devil WAS I?

Thankfully I was back laid on my bunk. My standard issue pillow filled with heat, for the sun beamed in strong, sinking me backwards into the ocean dream.

Two n a half fathoms down a current of sand washed over my face, the descent had never been so rapid. The blueness of the ocean waves spinning had you caught up in this whirlpool dream. Near the surface I'd noticed in quick bursts through the waves, sea horses spinning, dragon net, all caught up in the tumbling ocean below the deeper darker waves. The sun light here showing but the colours were distinct. Bluey greens washing through my head. The sun fish in my face for a split second n then washed over onto its side n gone. It's basking over for now.

The currents dancing the waves around my tumbling form.

The suddenness of the next descent felt like I'd left my skin behind inside one of the giant waves, crashing me down truly naked past the continental shelf n crushed over a 100 fathoms of weight into my exposed bones. Deep sea squid, giant squid, anglers with their mean faces, the darker currents relating to the depths of terror reached.

I'd been enjoying the dream state, but now I felt a rush backwards, around 200 metres. The tripod fish brought me back to the spy hole in the door, the sea cucumber bringing the clatter of mugs n fawkes. I rose for tea time wondering how I knew all these fish species n depths.

You don't see them until meal times. Suddenly hundreds appear and all of them tame n friendly from morning meds. Like me it seems they live by the glue clocks n slave clocks. The patients shuffle forward. The Q IS FRRIGHTENING. The staff tend to be big fellas usually armed to the teeth with clubs, gas n handcuffs.

Scot John creeping up behind my lug hole, his shadow bent double to come level. "Believe me Otiss, insanity is a terrible sensation. Most schizophrenics have ancestors or relations with mental health disorders". He laughed when he spoke the word disorder.

He seemed the bull goose Looney but I caught sight of another dark shadow that hovered in the air, my other neighbour Character. He just picked up a tray n empty walked back towards his cell. The GOSSIP was instant. I heard around the same time as everyone else.

Positive ED had made a break for it. Rumours aired in certain circles gave Character some part in the situation.

They had both been on the locked logs before dinner call had sounded. Character had let him loose. I think I'd been here about three weeks or a month. I'd realised pretty quick that I was on a rota, one that used horrid methods to pass the time of day or wake you from your drugged slumber. My ice bath drowning three times a week was not the best one to be on. A lot were considered worse. I'd certainly never have to show him the unlocking cuff move.

I'm sure the pigs back at the copshop had forwarded on the info about me freeing the big blue hells angel. I was never going on the log, where I had a chance to escape the grounds. While the gossips flying around the search is under way, the local pig shop is alerted, with a mug shot fax, slowly peeling from out of the yawning printer. At their side

The siren was deafening, even inside the walls. Several of these sirens were scattered around the country side, within a ten mile radius of the Faberon. York was now wide awake, Guy Fawkes spinning in his grave, the flare rising as if in his honour. The staff now all alert within the grounds of the escape attempt in progress.

—

{THE RING KING chapter 43} I was shoved back to my dungeon room, the door crashing heavy with tempers flaring amongst the staff. Things got worse for me when suddenly the door creaked inwards. Gerard removed his long key chain from the lock n let it hang aimlessly for eternity. Dr Woo came into view. He ushered me patiently over to my bunk n sat me down. I listened with a view of his knees in my eye line.

"Young Otiss, I'm afraid that I must inform to you that I need to tend my resignation. I've not mentioned my private business and so it's with mixed emotions that I say I've cracked the Japanese market with a hobby of mine. Gerard from the door frame chimes in.

"Top idea boss, I might even get me some for my wheels ya dig" I decided at this point to inquire. 'What's the biz?'

Dr Woo rose a few inch with pride, I've invented n patented a hub cap wheel design for the Japanese motor market. A ying n yang hub cap set, quite simple but then some are. I was impressed, "So why the heavy heart Dr?"

It turned out by the end of the conversation apparent as to the good hearted Dr's concerns. It seemed as though he had already been hounded out of his position in the hospitals hierarchy. And he was obviously not impressed by the ethics n vision of his predecessor. Luckily the hobby had come to the rescue at the right time for him. He looked down at the faded green wood on the floor n muttered 'they have been trying to get shut of me for years.

The new Dr was called Gaunt. Not the healthiest of news.

Dr Woo made his retreat with the parting gesture of saying he just wanted to explain to all the patients under his care personally. Gerard slamming the door with a horrid screwed up wink, as I wondered about the definition of care.

They found Positive Ed drowned in the underground streams.

The moon was so bright that evening in the cell. Meds delivered to the bidding glue n slave clocks bang on time after a measly salad tea which consisted of nothing more than lettuce leaves mixed with salad cream.

The silver bars shivered faintly with the beam of the moon, the flush of pipes came next. I didn't wait long this time to flush n empty my own, the connection now open, next Winnie's shrill whistle. His gold mouth nearing the toilet bowl, louder the language now. Character had been taken down the block. Winnie filled me right in about the logs.

I heard him scrape his chair to the edge near to his bog to sit and speak to me, his creepy voice coming through now clear.

"Otiss, twisted limbs from a lifetime spent shoved n locked in dark cupboards, their rota worse than your own cold baths.

Hideous deformation, with bones reset to a retarded state. Most of the cupboard monsters, not my phrase for them the guards came up with that one". He hissed the word "wankers" through the pipes n carried on. "They were the quiet ones, the easy ones. Patients that would after a while voluntarily squeeze into their confined spaces. The screamers got a promotion on the rota. These poor creatures would be led early on a morning through the Faberon grounds for a mile at least n chained with feet n hand to large logs. These were felled n stock pilled when they had been chopped to make way for the Directors grand residence.

Brought only back inside the institution building at the late end of the day, rain or shine they sat. Mostly mute from the drugs that they slavered on all day. Character had been from my admission on them".

I got distracted from his info as at the window I suddenly noticed this green wool line drop into view, sideways it swung by on a plunger. I left Winnie's voice at the open bowl a moment n jumped up to the bars on my window to stick my out stretched hand out to catch the swaying line the second time it swung by.

From its angle n without a mirror to see out it was a mystery as to who had sent a message my way. There was a dull mirror on the wall, I'd loosened it n tried it when a line had arrived days earlier but the shine n reflection made it useless. The rizla paper tied to this one now I unpeeled to read in tiny sized handwriting.

ESCAPE CLAWS, A wife who shot dead her husband while hunting told a court in great falls, east Canada, she thought he was a bear.

Tish should have thought of that. I screwed it up tight n swallowed the news. I didn't worry too much who or why it had been sent. It was a mad house after all. Winnie's voice continued as if the pause had never happened. He was on about a bloke called stumpy. He apparently chewed his way clear from the logs about four years back, *eventually breaking through to the bone at the point just above the ankle, a quick snap n he was loose.*

The rumours about character again when stumpy had been found crushed under the wheel of a passing wagon that was delivering supplies from outside. In its self,

"Hang on". I heard a rummage and then the clear strike of a match, he then went on, "in its self not such a suspicious thing, an accident. But stumpy had landed from the third floor rooftop that wound its way from the log area to the guards hut. They observed from above n radioed down to the staff striding around if they sensed trouble or if they decided to pick on you that day. Character again had been in the vicinity but again after blocking him they still couldn't say for sure he had played his part in yet another full moon murder. The tides guide him." Winnie then whistled down the pipes. I was about to ask him how he had ended up in here when instantly the flush went n he closed the connection.

{JESUS WEPT' chapter 44} *A booming voice, it was 11.35 am. He would shout it again on the pm.*

The pipes flushed open again n Winnie started his explanatory talks again. "It's ok Otiss it's just John's screaming, he does it at morning n noon."He lowered his voice n I strained over to hear him whisper like he was in confession.

"It's to do with the bible n Lazarus."

He didn't say any more about John, but went on to his own tale. It had come in strange bursts of conversation and my medication doses made it hard at times to follow.

The fog cleared some Snorkey came all the way to the edge of the grave.

Winnie by holding the pit lamp at a funny angle hit upon his haunted grin. While a purpose worthwhile to Winnie's mind came from these mid night expeditions, Snorkey had no agenda. They had met by chance one wet November night, neither at first daring to question each other, even though they both had a spade to hand. Winnie had hurriedly blurted out his odd method of salvaging his failing rapid family business. He had realised with a little terror, that in Snorkey he had found the perfect body snatching creature.

They rarely removed a body far from the grave site. It wasn't really the bodies that held the interest. It was the treasures. Sludge gathered under foot, making the usual light bodied Winnie drag a stone under each boot heel. It had slowed him nearly to the point of capture. For there were still men employed to deter these heathen acts.

Winnie had seemed to relax into the strange blurted tale, his voice hypnotic through the pipes.

Later sharing the jewelled spoils over much needed single malts, the backroom to Winnie's pawn shop let the early dawn light hit the gems, scattered now into two piles. The one for me, one for you sip of grog routine now out of the way. Snorkey mentioned the other poor sods that had freshly hit the earth, folding the obituary page with a haunted smile. More muttered plans arranged, Winnie heard the shop bell clang and alone he stood again. The stiff corpses finger now in his hand where at the grave it had been stubborn to belong to a new owner. Greased up n now ready to belong, hot tap water filling now the tin sink, the axe saw ready, a prime spot in the shops window already chosen. Business had at last started to look up and Snorkey came cheap. Well better than that, free. The best gems pocketed before the split of shit carrots. Business had to come first before loyalty Otiss. My name seemed to drift strange in the story as it came up the pipes.

I listened in with fresh ears primed now for more details.

Now as Winnie shot past life's normalities, the old bill strolled through their minds as to whom on their patch could be a throwback to the olden day's body snatching in the grave dead of night, fog descending on the scene of crime. Spades against jacks, with Winnie at that moment holding the ace, hoping that Snorkey knew he was the joker in the pack. It was funny what insanity masked.

On the surface, if you cared to look past his strange appearance then on the outside he may have appeared quite shrewd. Oh the funny walls of confinement, brick by brick they stand sealed, cell by cell, as the years roll on crumbling your soul it seemed. He had trailed off again, the toilet bowl becoming silent. He never finished his sentences due to a stress reaction of constantly been told by the review board that he will never ever leave the Faberon.

Id noticed that Gerard would tease him about this, always saying that there was a special spot reserved in the Faberon grounds burial yard Right next to the shed that housed the stinking old toilet blocks. He would also scream at him that he hoped someone dug him up one day n messed about with his ring. Oh the laughter he would walk away with towards the medication room.

Just before Winnie flushed the pipes n broke the connection he came back from his silence n spoke quiet one more time."The wedding ring goes on the left ring finger because it is the only finger with a vein that connects to the heart". That made me think back to home. That's the first finger Stan broke on Tish's hand and I wouldn't say coincidence when I looked down at my missing digit where as a boy he had severed it away with the axe.

Medication kicked in heavy as Winnie flushed n broke the connection.

The bolts of fork lightening were so sharp. They skewered the heavy black clouds, carrying them angrily along until they were solely above my presence. That's when they poked for a burst. Drenched with cold clammy sweat of medication, they let you sweat till the fear hit you, then they the guards would be in. Drugging the food, dosing the drinks, just enough to zombie you until they brought in the needle trays n zapped you into oblivion.

The chain saw exploded into life the next morning. The need for some freshly cut logs for the chained ones I suppose. The cold wet winter had rotted the arse out of the old ones. It had taken a month or so to figure out some of the ways that the institution ran. Like the pulse clock. This was the master clock situated in the Dr Gaunt's office. Every thirty seconds it transmitted a PULSE of electric current to SLAVE clocks, making sure the clocks kept the same time throughout the entire place.

There was also the ELECTRIC SIGNAL, to re-assure the nursing officers that all was well on certain refractory wards. Nurses on duty on those wards were required to signal the officers at certain specified intervals by inserting a key in this devise. When turned, the key made an electrical contact and a buzzer sounded in the nursing office. The rumours of the electric shock therapy scared the bejesus out o me. Especially worrying was the tale about the MAXWELL STIMULATOR. Dr RDH Maxwell was the cruel designer.

Scot John had told me a few days ago about the Amsterdam dealers double fractured jaw. At first this operation held the danger of fractures of the bone from spasms but over the years they had managed to control this. The Amsterdam dealer had obviously not been given this blessing. The staff very random as to who got the full safety treatment

His curiosity had brought the pop group the Beatles into the tale. His take on things had him wondering to me about the reference to the song Maxwell's silver hammer, switching to another song, Yellow submarine, going on to explain that the songs about 'nembutals', which are yellow n sub shaped. He had strolled off singing 'We all live in a yellow submarine'.

It was the same day I'd seen carved on his cell door the words that had confused me on my admission to the Faberon. The swirling iron gates that had held the Latin I knew very little about.

EX HOC METALLO VIRTUTEM. Yet this time underneath was scratched the translation. 'Out of this rough metal, we forge excellence'.

{THEATRE ROYAL chapter 45} *There was information in the late evening about the next day having a play in the recreation hall which was jocularly referred to as the Theatre Royal. It was a rare treat for the imminent departure of the good Dr Woo.*

The inmate actors from another ward where I never got to venture were said to have been rehearsing two plays for our entertainment pleasures. Only one was to be performed. Either way it would be a small break in the constant mental upheaval.

But yet again before that treat I found the night gone again without warning and the morning exercise yard now my domain. I was lent against the fence. The Amsterdam dealer was busy satin the corner nr to me, head down, busy as a bee. I looked away from his disease n lifted my eyes skywards.

God I am so bored, the very soul of my skeleton aches with pity at my lingering torment. Inside this hell hole, with its concrete tomb lid I stay trapped n numb. A feeling when the medication slips past the tongue halter that you are wearing concrete boots to match, dragging around this invisible ball n chain until you move no longer of your own accord.

The free skies hold my attention for a moment but I cannot help stare back at the dealer. He is filling his pockets now with the wraps of yard dust he has made, stuffing his grubby fingers into his mouth, probing for his stash. It wasn't there! It hadn't been for years, the madness holding him in some time n place that to most with sanity on their sides would appear desperate. Yet to him it offered a glimmer of hope. His first name now so lost in time it may well have been burnt in the fire pit of Hell.

Id noticed over the month Scot John winding him up, painting E on pain killer tablets, putting rumours around the wing about this new dance drug, the pill heads, the ones who took meds on top of the already mind bending stated doses were keen to seek this new pleasure. He would leave a few scattered near the cut off phone. The dam dealer collecting them on the sly when he was busy pretending to put in a call to his supplier.

Back now inside the claustrophobic wing with the afternoon sailing away into history, after a heavy stodgy late tea, we were all ready to see the play. The ocean dreams returned as I lay in slumber upon my bunk waiting for the door to creak open. I drifted down with a sea shanty in my watery ear.

'Lo! Death has reared himself a throne

In a strange city lying alone

Far down within the dim west

Where the good and the bad and the worst and the best

Have gone to their eternal rest

There shrines and palaces and towers

Time eaten towers that tremble not!

Resemble nothing that is ours

Around, by lifting winds forgot

Resignedly beneath the sky

The melancholy waters lie.

The commotion woke me.

Then this red glow from up near the high bars of the cell bathed the four walls in a blood bath looking hue. A trickle of sweat ran down my left temple as far as my cheekbone.

Winnie banged the wall n I slid over on stocking feet to the toilet bowl n opened up the connection. This time he was already speaking as it emptied. Such a strange sound as the next verse of my dream came spoken back to me in a hushed tone. How he knew I never found out. Maybe we were all in each other's dreams.

"There open fanes and gaping graves

Yawn level with the luminous waves

But not the riches there that lie

In each idols diamond eye"

He finished the verse n then said.

"The fires raging Otiss"

"Where Win?"

"Not sure at the minute"

Then the strangest thing in my life happened. A large crow flapped to an elegant landing on my ledge.

Character spoke slow and fluent. No doubt in my mind that it was him. Our resident shaman, the Diablo that was my friend had come to call.

"Do not be afraid"

I was, quite hard not to be when a live crow is talking in your cell mate next doors voice. But I was more fascinated than afraid.

"I need to show you"

The wings flapped n he entered through the bars. The next move captured my spiritual side for the rest of my life. The crow screeched n circled near my dull mirror on the wall. Then like a scent on the wind it was gone.

Winnie reaching me with a raised voice, "check the mirror"

I moved cautiously towards it n viewed the reflection. Like a TV show it played back a moment. The chapel of St Faith was there, clear to see. Then I caught the meaning. Gaunt creeping up the middle isle, the striking match, the sudden look around, no guilt on the face just a spreading grin at the flame. I guess he really didn't want the good Dr Woo to have his farewell play. The drugs were fuckin with my mind but I just knew what I'd seen was real.

The play was cancelled. We were all individually summoned to Gaunt's new office domain. The quizzing had begun. Even if the crow hadn't shown me, Gaunt had not been as careful as he hoped.

Later that night, Winnie down the pipes spoke of the faint petrol whiff that had soaked up his snout on his entrance to the office. I realised we didn't add the title Dr now, when we spoke of Gaunt, Doctors in disguise for sure surrounding these wards. It seemed like we were all now destined for the inevitable rendezvous with death, sooner though now than the palm lines suggested.

Id blurted back at Winnie, added my own prosicutrix evidence. The scorched sleeve of his suit jacket I'd clocked hanging on the back of his high backed leather chair. The crow was right in what it had shown. Character was a rare inmate in our cloudy pond.

The chapel of St Faith was a pile of ashes by the morning. Trusted inmates were deployed into the grounds with rakes to level it and quash the remaining stubborn embers. Dr Woo said his quiet goodbyes on the wing. He popped his head round my now opened door n said sayonara.

The next morning I was ripped out of bed n strapped tight into a straight jacket the injection to the neck had my inquiries die down suddenly. To the block first to wait for the daunting trip up to Wa/rd siX. There were certain parts of the hospital corridors that I vaguely remembered from my last week long trip up to the serious punishment block ward. A new corridor showed the posters of the plays we could have seen if Gaunt had not burnt down the chapel of St Faith. It reminded me of my entrance to the Faberon on the first day when those portraits burned their pigment eyes through me. I managed to read a few of the old tattered posters as I swept by.

The feast of reason

It looked like an early production.

The next posters rang a little too close to home.

The Gods are requested not to interfere

I didn't think anyone would at this point never mind the Gods and the short stay in the block was welcome as I was sick to death of the bullshit down on the Netherfield.

The stench as you entered Wa/rd siX knocks you clean of your already wobbly feet. It's a mixture of ether n shit. Add a dose of bleach and a sweat brought on from the withdrawal of many a poor soul before and you get nowhere near the pong.

I believe this time I laid trapped for around ten days. No reason given. Plenty of sharp jabs to continue the darkness. Gerard upping his ras clot bullying, a faint remembrance of Gaunt getting involved when it came to tightening the leather strap restraints on the jacket. I guess I'd wriggled it loose, twisting in agony n frustration through the long day n nights.

Nothing much to report would be scribbled on my file cards with the switch back to the Netherfield ward done in the early morning hours, a final kicking to see you on your way. My cell door opens and closes, the brutes from upstairs slinging me back in like some old rag doll. Slight memories shuffled through my brain. Dr Gaunt was a one off true specimen. I remembered that much. Tall and stooped with grave tomb sized front teeth. I'd recalled him in my face at times, addressing medical terminology that in my drugged stupor was pointless. It was his breath I remembered most, gapping now at the recollection of its disgusting halitosis strength, strange what thoughts held as distant memory's now in my frazzled skull.

A trainee nurse, only a young girl, not nurse Silk, had been by his side most of the time when he spoke to me. It was the casual way she had pulled out of her apron a packet of mints and offered Gaunt one that had stuck most in my dome. He had courteously declined, while she had turned away with a gip and a smile. The same gip I was feeling remembering this nonsense.

{KITES chapter 46} *The white envelope was propped upon my pillow. It strangely scared me as I approached, wandering who had penned contents to me. When I did grasp, I noticed a postcard tucked behind the letter. Its space filled with as much neat small writing as possible. I knew it was Johnny before I even skipped to the end n saw his signature. I opened the letter first and carefully unfolded the two white sheets. The letterhead stated Liberty was in touch. The letter I thought I had typed at the compulsory class had obviously got through. Feeling puzzled I lounged back on my bunk to read. The handwriting was neat, yet slanted.*

The hidden warning was there. In the middle of some great advice it lay. It seemed that Liberty had been warned off the case n me by Yama. So I focused on the rest. Liberty's expensive pen spelt out in deep blue, create your own views. Don't sit and stare at walls. And while sometimes of deep trouble, we have no choice but to stare at those four devils of boredom and blankness. Young Otiss, shine like opened shutters to the sea.

There were other bits, but the drugs from the block had robbed me of concentrated vision. The sigh I released had me knowing I was doomed. There was to be no rescue. No interference from higher up authorities, NOTHING.

To relieve the stress of the letters contents I studied the picture on the front of the postcard. The paradise that was India stared back. The small italic writing stated India's best beaches. It distracted me momentarily before I flipped it again to the writing of Johnny, soon realised I was reading more distress.

Granddad Pedley was dead. I rushed through the small writing, searching for details. Johnny had seen the undertaker outside Huntsman's fold where he had lived. The body wheeled out under the dignified death sheet, the mention of him getting in touch with the firm dealing with the arrangements. He would find out the burial date and attend to pay the respects for the both of us. Granddads stuff would be collected n stored on the Heath. He promised to personally see to that. Old Dolly Blue had gone long term travelling to Southern Ireland. Her old vardo wagon was perfect until my eventual release. Towards the end, mention of a trunk, locked I knew, for I had seen it as a boy, the maritime knots secure n neat.

The cell already claustrophobic, shrunk in on me till I couldn't grasp air to my lungs. Shocking news, delivered as best a good friend could, yet all the more cruel under the circumstances. Gerard at the spy hole, buggin, my mind already starting to fantasise about murdering the bastard any way I could. I measured my breathing into a steady rhythm n dreamed of his demise. I'm forced to now take stemetol capsules four times a day to quieten the nerves, the delivery by Gerard rendering the supposed effect quite useless. The probang he would plunge down my throat with some disipal, which he rarely bothered to give me. It really helps the side effects of the stemetol. Without it my limbs wobble terribly. Also on the rota for me is every fortnight I am dragged naked down to the isolation rooms. An injection of modicate is uncouthly administered, which is specifically designed to curb the symptoms of schizophrenia. Not that I suffer this terrifying affliction, but that small detail is avoided.

The only way out for a section 65 patient like me is if your shrink is convinced you are fit to be discharged. Gaunt was looking more and more unlikely to write anything positive in my file. He stayed in the shadows mostly, or at least that's how it seemed. Coming out of the walls when already under attack he would leap at me

I had studied his grin. The bite marks on my arms seemed to match up. His door seemed permanently closed to our cloudy pond. Gerard rose up the ranks. There was no official pay rise. Yet his power grew. His bullying more blatant on the wing now, but someone was watching, waiting. It seemed I had more than a new friend in the strange and exotic character next door, the moon full like his shadow that seemed to fill with life n jump out n take yours on his 6 moon killin spree.

{YELLOW SUB chapter 47} *The dip in the temperature of the cell seemed to mix with the medicated water. I was away on another ocean dream.*

Henny the 8th flag War ship

Meds heavy again

I saw a timber somewhat Splintered, carved.

1545 somewhere gloomy in the riptide The Mary Rose had entered my dreams.

Human Remains all around the ship with Archers bows, gunner's shoes

OsteoachioloGIST checking the bone puzzles now. Busy Pairing up some thigh bones. Tibea sets all in neat little rows

197 individual bones, 92 complete sets of skeleton, 6 foot tall in the bow of the ship

I had dried right out this time, the ocean gone, tiny fish hopping n jumping on the last Gushes of water that ran from her cannon holes. Then suddenly back deep under, in my face a Snake then a stingray, now a lion fish. Just a flash n change suddenly in front of my bubbling eyes as the Mimic octopus tentacles now wrap around my limbs dragging me through a late diminishing wave n back upwards through the watery swirl.

Then the tannoy breaking through the meds bringing me now sweaty browed back towards facing the cell wall, It's peeling blobs like the capsules they were advertising. Then the needle scratched. They put on a calming song. Morning has broken. Scot John comes out as I get through my door onto the landing. Stretching his giant frame while singing, we all live in a yellow submarine. He turned his head n said "the songs about Nembutals, which are yellow and sub shaped" I hazily recalled the info before, but my throat was so scratchy from the side effects of the cocktails they were whacking into me. So I didn't try to tell him of his repetition. The amount of drugs they were pumping him full off making it no wonder his memory wasn't great.

His stride towards the breki Q left me alone on the landing. Winnie had suffered a bad night n I wasn't surprised to see him refuse to come down. There was going to be trouble ahead. Scot John's tune now accompanying my trip down the metal stairs to get my bowl of porridge like a good little Oliver.

And our friends are all aboard,

Many more of them live next door...

The ward airing court bell rang. Its distinctive tone echoing for a minute after it had switched off. It was used to warn the staff and the patients that it was time to return to the ward. Breakfast had been cancelled and we were quickly banged up. The medication hut was just outside of the Netherfield wards main entrance doors where there would be lunatic fights among the stragglers if they were not prompted to return to their cells quickly enough. The limited staff, at times needed the reminder as well to get these skirmishes under control before they erupted into maniac violence. A lot of the serious patients were medicated at their own cell door, but on occasion even these were sent down the long corridor n through the locked doors to the treatment room hatch. It all depended upon which guards were on. Gerard for example would let well known enemies mingle, hoping for a serious assault to occur, probably taking bets on the outcome.

After all the bodies this time were safely behind their door I heard Gerard's horrible screech. He was bawling out Winnie's name.

"Come on you ring tampering little Jew bastard, get the fuck up n ready to exit your door"

I knew he had been unwell in the night. His constant groans of pain and the weird slavering noises had filtered up from his bunk and travelled to my ear through my own cell window bars. Some obvious nightmare had held him trapped throughout most of last night. But when Gerard was on morning shifts, which he had been all this week, it didn't matter one jot. With Winnie not going down to the medication hatch, he had left himself wide open to Gerard's bullshit torment to begin early. I could hear the squad gathering at the end of the wing, so Gerard already had radioed through for some sly help. He wasn't interested in if Winnie was ill, or even dead. All he wanted was an audience to revel in when he played the big man with one of the weaker members of our cloudy pond.

It was Scot John's voice that first shattered the silence, his booming tone demanding that he be opened up from behind his locked door immediately. He wasn't asking either, he was telling. Missing his porridge could result in pure rage. But there was more to it than that this time. Both Scot John n Character hated bullies and I understood completely their despising of this coward of the species. I had figured out that the staff although trained to stick to hospital protocol, just played it by ear. Scot John certainly got his own way a lot of the time from what I had seen and heard.

The staff usually let him blow off some vocal steam before resorting to jumping him mob handed and sticking needles in his arse as if it was a dartboard. Gerard wanting an excuse to set the mufti squad upon him, shouted to another staff member to open him up. My door bolts and locks surprisingly sprung free too as he now passed my spy hole which I had my eye ball crushed into trying to gain more insight into what was going down. Winnie's door was next to be set free.

As I popped my head out n looked down the wing, one of the new screws, well not new to me, but I had been clued up as to his virginity in the Faberon by seasoned lags, pulled out this bully club n started whacking it quite violently into his other opened palm. The hard slapping noise building like the tension he was forcing into every fresh hit. Winnie entered the scene now and he looked shocking as his usual dark eyes looked as solid a colour as the sludge from the gravesides he used to pilfer. His face looked my way, but through me in a deathly manner towards the new screw. He certainly looked like a maniac this morning, which unnerved me as I had not seen this side to his demeanour.

A hiss shot out from his gold teeth, a face contorted with venom to complete the picture. The atmosphere electric with Scot John stood by his door frame. The no named gunslinger by the saloon doors about to empty his pistol into the card game cheats.

The new screw by now had a puzzled worried look upon his face, checking about himself to find comfort in the backup he had around him. Probably wondering to his self upon why he never put his low grade qualifications to better use. The police force could certainly use some more dummies.

It amazed me where the inmates weapons conjured themselves from, but appear they did as suddenly Scot John's lasso bites into his ankle. The daft fucker should stop struggling with his new entanglement, other officers now running to help. Winnie shrieking like a convicted tragedy, my grubby long nails scratching down my cheek, three bloody lines for the new screw to focus on. He had lost grip on the bully club, it belonged now firmly in Winnie's hand, Gerard now pleading for an end to the commotion as his bullying ideas now looking a bit too much of a level playing field for his liking, now the tools had come out.

Scott John now yanking the rope tight, the poor sod suddenly flipping onto his back with a breaking bone sound. Gerard ordering the needles to be let loose and like javelins to our arses the blackout shots whistled through the air and found their targets. Like a child who chooses not to learn, he becomes later imbecile like. Confused with situations that blatant obvious signs blink nearer and brighter to his now sown shut lids. Blindness from birth would have been kinder. The choice had been mine to get involved. I already felt a close bond to these creatures sharing confined space with me. I think really the shock of the last month or so was starting to creep out of my system. Gerard had wanted me in the mix as well. He had made it clear from day one that he hated me. Incidents like this giving him the official green light to clobber me at will. We unknown to it, move across the building to the other side of the Netherfield. Due to a lack of conscience, the dragging n beating go unnoticed for now, but all three of us were now at the mercy of the dreaded Wa/rd siX.

{THE DEVIL & THE DEEP BLUE chapter 48} *It must have become evening before my glued down lids peeled tackily open. Sleepy hammock day feelings making incarceration for a moment bliss. Inside the mass tablet doses I heard a lull in the keys, a large floating hand that I controlled through the cold block air, stopping it right in front of the screws mouth as he stood outside itching for the violence to start. Then before opening my door, a beautiful silence descended for a split second before the guard came crashing through with my reality. As the shouting started again, a bunch of figures I could make out through the droopy heavy lids of my eyes approached. Dr Gaunt held the large needle this time. The rusty trolley was back, Gerard by its side. They didn't need to restrain me but the straps on the straight jacket were pulled even tighter as the last notch hole strained to its manufactured limits.*

Injection one, came in deep at the crook of my arm. A dreamy feeling begin to come over me again. Injection two was where the nightmare switched places. Gaunt's face manic as he hovered the large needle out in front of my eyes long enough for me to focus on its dripping tip. He then sharply pressed its point into my cheek bone. The upwards angle making it feel to be hitting the back of my green pupil. Then a plunger movement, then a cold liquid feeling, like a heavy tear starting to build at the back. The release of real tears came next, where I just washed away back into the deep frightening Pacific's realm.

Id fallen backwards into the dream. Like when as kids, Johnny would grab my foot into his cupped hands and propel me into a backwards dive into the filthy water of the lake of stars.

Like a submarine,

Down,

Down,

Down,

I am sure I heard the last human words... "periscope, Captain Gaunt please". Then I really was under the heavy pressured waves. Another sudden drop in the ocean floor levels, out of the blue a wave of blonde heavenly hair. She is now mine to hold this mermaid bride. The liquid drugs interfering with the scene when all I want is to hold her tight and feel safe, the mimic octopus here again conning me into thinking I had a love, its changing shape now revealing the demon as a sucker wraps around my ankle n draws me deeper to the ocean bottom. I am now alone and falling deeper into some caught up crushing wave.

A sail fish excited at my flash of presence changes from silver to black, its matador cape the last Isere before the wave releases me from its spinning and I descend some more. Indigo fins of marlin overhead now as I sink down totally encapsulated in my billowing oxygen bubbles. 66 percent of me just went with the flow.

I was way deeper than 21 fathoms. No recreational divers passed this point. Some of the dark horrors down here probably best for them not to see. I liked it at times down here, the medication surely something to do with the strangeness. Yet I knew they had started before then. That thought of home now suddenly yanking me back closer to the surface again, the far off sound from the guards doing the key thing in the cell doors. Bright yellow canoes, their long shapes from below there to see as I looked up towards the surface. The rushing water blinding me again, it was pressuring through my ears at speed, confusing the return. A long time passes, probably a second and I am thrown out tumbling from the cold wave. Back on dry land coughing my guts up on the shore, the guard bangs open the gate at the end of the corridor its vibrations shaking some of the sweaty dream from my brow. I can hear his boot heels approaching to spy in on me. I realise I am still in my block cell up on Wa/rd siX

Peeling paint stares painfully back at me. Why didn't they just come and tell me it was all over, that Judge Yama had died n Moizer had read the trial notes and demanded I be freed immediately. But there was going to be none of that. The guards must have been in my cell as I'd drifted off on the ocean dreams. On a little table made from hardened paper, my bright coloured tablets called out. It had become clear to me that it was less pain to just swallow them without resistance. The probing was horrific if they thought you needed a little persuasion. Waterford finest crystal is what I should be holding in my free hand. I tighten the grip on the light blue plastic, as the standard issue mug raises to my cracking dry lips and I swallow my medicated concoction.

I fought the tablets for a while. Stumbling around the dark cell, bouncing off the walls for a while until the heaviness of the drugs grabbed you. Fatigued, I slumped on the single empty of a mattress cot bed and let my mind think of my bastard father. Stan only had the one Tarot card. The cardboard was battered, fingered by his filthy hands into its grubby state. The hanged man was the picture upon it. The nooses loop punctured through on the card where he sometimes pierced it through the Gorton arrows ancient tip.

Ghosts now already here banging on my wall, there is no midnight curfew to contend with for these mischievous souls. Chains heavy and rattling the still night air, common knowledge that Wa/rd siX was one of the most haunted parts of the Faberon. I would have to just cope, my legs going nowhere even if I could have run away. My locked boots, a security feature of Wa/rd siX clicking in time with Albert's non expensive heels. A tape measure dangles in front of my closed terrified eyes, Pierrepoint's victims closing in all around me, Munche painted mouths of the past so close to my ear, their screams, my friends, for the long night ahead. There was zero escape from the sheer madness. So I just let go and became a part of it.

{THE EYES OF JAH chapter 49} *A week or two later, it was hard to determine the length of time anymore. But whatever the date, after a horrid shivering stay on the block wing, Winnie and I returned to the*

Netherfield ward and back to our cells, albeit a stone lighter in weight and our heads certainly a bit further up our arses!!.Scot John would spend a little more time than the pair of us down there. Presumably for the kick offs I'd heard him involved in on our stay. He had the strength n size to fight back against the system. His tolerance for the drugs now, taking longer for the staff to quieten him down.

Back at my steel door, Bag o bones just looked in my cell spy hole. I knew it was him by his hollowed eye socket that somehow held his pupil in place, he as far as I could gather on the rota for the purging treatments permanently. My random ice bath mornings seemingly calm in comparison.

On the wing, the sparks would fly. Hunger sending some more mad than they already were. Winnie was on it too, his loud sporadic hungered howls coming mostly through the night. They always made me jump out from within my medicated slumber, sometimes cracking my skull into the wall if I had dozed off dribbling by its cold walls. For me, some days, the pain would be so immense that the only way forward, was to go backwards. I would with trepidation, crawl into Stan's savaged mind. Find the real source of terror. It helped somewhat to rationalize the difference between us. Nothing could compare to his abuse, although in a way the years of it, preparing me for this Hell hole.

The demon still loomed large. Mother stared back when I closed my eyes. Cold, dead, finished.

Stan's gaping Fang toothed screams. Mock laughter followed by the cruel harsh tears. The tears were real though. My t shirt would be wet through down its front as I opened my eyes to escape my parents.

Outside the barred cell window, the rain had become intermittent now. Tiny wet squalls on the yard below, shimmering into the dawns first light. A few heavy drops clung to my bars. Some shine off the sun hid glinting promise to the back of a lonely drifting cloud. I stared from my bunk until it dwindled away from view. The long wasted day starts again.

Character had been fairly quiet the few days since had returned down from Wa/rd siX. His killing of Positive Ed had satisfied and dampened down his serial killA tendencies. For now!!!!

It would not be long before the oceans influenced the moon though. Someone might as well start counting down the remaining six months of their lives. He never failed to get a victim. And swimming among our cloudy pond, there were plenty worthy trophies.

No matter how hard the authorities and government tried to stop him. I guess shaman v Regina was never going to happen.

Winnie had continued to tell me little bits about him. But didn't divulge how he had landed here in the first place.

Character had put the staff on edge once again and rightly so. All the preoperational focus from the staff had them running around with their head up their arses, unsure as to even where to begin to put an end to his killing cycle. They were only too aware that the calendar was counting down again to bloodshed. A meeting here, a conference there, Gaunt arriving earlier onto the wing clapping his hands and rubbing the nervous sweat from them." What's on the agenda today" he would pronounce before even saying any other word. Anyone of the lives that trod inside this building had become vulnerable. Character had proved that on many a bloody moon. The nonchalant way he asked his rare questions had most believe he was viewing them as a target. He unnerved people without even doing anything towards them.

Everyone knew he was smart enough to escape, yet chose to stay in this mad house. It was as if it was his own perfect appointed killing ground where he decided to stay and divulge his ritualistic nature. The staff and management knew all this. His files alone were fuel that would blaze bright. The dumb fuckers at the home office wanted results. The ease in which Character kept up his 6 moon killin ritual made for embarrassing headlines. Headlines kept in house. In time I would find out that the outside world knew nothing of the Netherfield ward.

The old establishment needing things dousing, for Character had become a flame, a beacon flashing hatred high above the supposedly tranquilized walls. They wanted him to be an ember, one that had no chance of finding fuel and reigniting.

I had seen with my own eyes his strange shaman majik, when he had shown Gaunt light up the chapel of St Faith. He was certainly the most fascinating member of our cloudy pond. Well one that was alive at least. The ghosts of the Faberon building were legendary.

Dr Woo before he had resigned had told me of the chain rattler. The poor old woman had been chained to the cell wall for no less than 36 years. Dr Woo I recalled making the point that it had not been on his watch as director! After her death she would rattle violently her death chains 36 times at the strike of noon. The noise appearing out of thin air would clink n rattle together. Dr Woo assured me that he had gone down into the basement archives n pulled her case file. She had died on the exact striking of noon.

On occasions in the afternoons, we would, once highly dosed enough to not be too much of a nuisance to the day staff, be allowed to sit in this day room of sorts. It was situated in between the yards locked gate and the servers food hatch. Up a little corridor through some more locked gates. It housed the big brown TV and in the corner a rotting grand piano. I had only been allowed to the room twice since I had arrived. The first time I heard it, I put things down to my heavy medication doses, but on my second visit as I slumped in this high backed peeling leather chair, every now n again the piano would tinkle it's out of tune ivories out of the blue. No one would be sat at the oak stool. No one took much notice of it. The long termers probably use to by now of these weird goings on. Some of the real gone loons would put their arms around some invisible shoulder and belt out a tuneless slave song. Desolation row sprung to my mind, but I kept quiet observing.

The piano ghost, one of the lucky ones now, free of this life time of pains. But looking outside through the barred grills, beyond the worn wire fences to the burial ground, you would find a butcher buried next to a blacksmith, who next to a child killing nanny and so on and so on were stuck in the grounds for eternity.

Rows upon sad rows laid there restless as a severe reminder that for a lot of tortured souls, the Faberon had you forever.

The moon is at its brightest tonight. Dinner was a non event n scoffed already. By tray out, settled upon my bunk I could just lay here staring up through the bars. Like a smart white button pinned up in the marine blue night, its constant fixture in that moment as solid as my innocent bones. It was Scot John who broke the spell of my staring competition. It was nice to hear he had returned. DO LALLY, he had bellowed out into the night. Then silence again. I turned my head away from the bars to ease out the kink in my stressed neck. The newspapers rolled into a bundle were laid upon my table. Winnie as we had come back up the stairs from collecting dinner had stuffed them into my hand, the look on his face a mixture of fevered withdrawal and guilty shame.

I had been determined to read them as soon as I got banged up. I had raced to finish my mushy dinner. The metal trays compartments had spilled into each other making its watery jelly and stewed potatoes mixing nicely together. Some cockroaches ready in the corner of the cell to come n gobble up the juice dripping from my chin. No pudding today, the lazy bastards whoever they were that ran our kitchens useless fat fuckers with big bellied laughs wobbling about in their domain, mocking our starved skinny weak legs.

A drift in the meds had moved a few hours along on the glue clock hands. I slid of the bunk and unfurled them. About four or five front pages stared back with seriously strange headlines dominating the print. I settled back on my bed again and read the first all the way through.

PAWN MAN TRIED TO RUN RINGS ROUND POLICE

I just stared at the bold black lettering. I had through the pipes carefully listened to this strange mans tale. In parts it had made sense. Not the actually crime, more just the way he described things. On other occasions he had drifted off the subject and his obvious madness shined like the washed stolen gems that he had started to speak about. The first line in the article read.

A recluse madman who loved corpses so much he left his pawnshop partially stocked with jewels from the local dead has been found guilty of body tampering and theft.

Winston Jah, son of the late and respected Jamil Jah was found guilty on all charges over the weekend and remanded to a local psychiatric unit for evaluation as to which institution would be best to hold him and try to cure his affliction.

Crowds outside the court were seen to be baying for blood. Relatives of some of the victims had to be forcibly restrained by police as they tried to climb aboard the van taking the prisoner away from the scene.

His life sentence with no hope of ever being freed was passed down by his honour Judge Stricktland.

The quotes that followed from Stricktland were scathing at best.

I skipped the last few and had a good butcher's at the second broadsheets front cover.

POLICE EYE SUSPECT

The photo of an exhibition from the trial made this one look very creepy. A clear liquid in some old glass jar with the exhibit tag tied around its lid with frayed string wasn't too concerning. The severed fingers with wedding and engagement rings told its own story before I even started reading the first bullet headline.

This is where I read more clearly about Snorkey, Winnie's partner in crime. Upon walking into the pig shop n leaving a freshly dug up severed hand on the reception desk, the dirt n jewels spilling onto the counter. The business card of Winnie's late father placed in the snatched limbs fingers. The pigs had already had a tip off from a *distressed widow who was sure n swearing on her grandchildren's lives that she had clocked in Winnie's window her late husband's wedding band. The pigs were just about to make some small inquiries about maybe receiving stolen goods till Snorkey dropped off his business. The large sinks in the back of the shop had been discovered full of floating digits still attached to stubborn rings. Rigamortis well set in tight onto the dearly departed emblems of love. If it had been stubborn to Winnie's frantic yanking at the grave side, then the small hacksaw in the coat pocket had made sure they ended up in the cloth sack and safely back to the shop. He had soaked them in hot water over night in the sink troths, the police had found rows upon rows of decaying fingers on the side, the ones still floating around in the sludgy water still attached to their bands of gold and diamonds. Shelves lined up with glass jars over brimming with fingers n eyes.*

Maybe Snorkey had known of the sly one sided splits when divvying up the spoils, maybe what had forced him to grass up Winnie eventually in the end.

But as I read on it was obvious that Winnie had started getting carried away with the removing of body parts. The fingers I could understand as an occupational hazard, but the police in the reports had mentioned other jars. These had been crammed full of eyes. Totally useless to the salvaging of the business, yet clear as precious diamonds as to Mr Winnie Jah's madness. Even in the flat above the shop, the police had found full on pickled heads, the agonising death faces crushed up against the glass waiting their turn for him to come and start his enucleation.

I emptied my toilet pipes n shouted through to his cell. He was ages before he came to the pipe n cautiously said hello. After a little cajoling he got to the more saddening details of his case.

Snorkey it turned out had hung himself in police custody. I had inquired about his location at this present time making Winnie reveal this twist in the story. Interestingly enough, when the pathologist performed the autopsy, he had found over fifty gold sovereigns in his stomach alongside his last undigested meal of tripe n French red wine. The irony lost on Winnie as I heard him at this

point in the tale swearing n shouting that he was a thieving conning
bastard. It appeared Snorkey had been pocketing a few behind
Winnie's back too.

All that honour amongst thief's bullshit!!It was a sad old tale really.
I had not thought much about the effects of true mental cases and
how their crimes impacted upon a large number of not just the
victims but the families. I'd asked Winnie as gently as possible if he
knew what he had done or the magnitude of his actions. But he
flushed shut the connection and Infolded the papers back into a pile
on the table. The top ones headline had been an old copy of an
obituary page where the police had found it circled in red ink with
fresh prospects.

{WRINKLED MAPS chapter 50} *I awoke freezing with sweat covering
my whole back. Dawn had replaced the dark evening where after
reading the newspapers I must have fallen back into a disturbed
sleep. I had not even managed to crawl under my blankets. Fully
clothed and aching is how I found the new day starting. Recollections
hovering around my sleepy waking head of another ocean dream.
Drawn Deeper again it seemed into the Pacific and its perplexing
mysteries. Yet try as I might to remember details, nothing came and
before I could scratch my brain any longer I found myself down at
the hotplate for breki, back up in my cell licking the tray clean,
putting the tray out on the landing to be collected and now on my
way out down the iron stairs for exercise.*

*At speed without your knowledge was sometimes how time in here
carried on. The cocktail of drugs either speeding incident's together
or the glue clock freezing us all into a howl of trapped madness. Scott
John at the foot of the stairs already speaking as I crouched by him to
head to the exercise door, the info loud and in my ear, some mention
of an Indian mental hospital from the second world war n then I was
out into the quiet of the yard.*

*The gulls are playing in groups, flapping into streams of air,
shooting off at angles, wings taking the rest. The raven draws my*

attention away from looking sky ward, still n watchful she's highly perched on the razor fence. Back down on the floor of the yard, the leaves are restless. More life in them than my own body it seems today. From the dead season perimeter fences tree lined scenery, they had blown close to where I sat with my back crushed into the wire fence. *Unless you withdraw your services from the local peelers within three days of receiving this notice you will undergo the extreme penalty at the hands of the IRA. i.e. DEATH.*

Please yourself now, but failure to carry out the above orders will be frowned upon. Yours faithfully, the firing party.

I stared at the stained crumpled piece of office paper. The Northern wind had flipped it skywards, hurling it towards me where it had held fast against my shin, flapping, waiting to be read.

The type set seemed careless but the contents seriously official along with the threat, yet it didn't seem to be addressed to any one in particular. Circle upon circle the men trotted around the yard, yet from none could I determine who the paper belonged to.

I hadn't moved for long in these circles. I had gotten to know briefly a few who resided near my own cell, but the rest were mysteries. Judging by what I held in my hand someone was or had been in trouble with the Irish. I'd heard enough about them ear wigging on Stan's mate Poidge to know it wasn't something to get on the wrong side of.

But looking around again at the men a little more, I painfully realised that now I lived amongst the craziest bastards ever born of this world. My friend and neighbour liked to pickle body parts for a past time. While to the other side of my cell resided the Authorities worst known serial killA.

Then the wind suddenly tore it from my grasp, sailing it up and over the fence.

Screaming, the guard called for us to get back in n to our cells. Fresh air was over with for today, so I made my way back to my flowery dell and put it out of my mind. The wind would make sure it eventually ended up in the right hands.

You didn't see Gaunt all the time on the Netherfield ward.

But as I'd trudged in from exercise I had noticed him outside cell7. It had stood empty since Positive Ed had been found drowned.

Maybe a new member into our cloudy pond was imminent. Dr Bronze was beside him pretending to show some interest in proceedings. Also Henry star man strange, Gaunt's favourite pet, not just on this particular ward, but the whole of the institute.

She turned the corridors corner and melted my heart like the drugs were melting my brain. The small dab of lavender behind Nurse Silk's ear drifted through the ward so sweet it cancelled out for a moment the usual demented whiffs of madness. I banged up my door and slid down its metal coldness, crouching there for a good few hours, fixated, in love.

I looked up at the sky through the angle of the bars n daydreamed about her perfect beauty. I tried hard to image in my mind the pair of us laid on a blanket in some quiet idyllic lavender field, the sun upon my back as I undressed her beautiful form. Yet the steel hard coldness of the cell door soon shut the image down in my mind. I'm drenched again with the freezing clammy sweat of medication withdrawal. Gaunt had mentioned when he had last addressed me that I would be given different clinical trial drug to see what helped me best.

To me at this present moment, it just felt that time wouldn't move. A sick feeling of oddness wedged in my mind that it may be really stuck within this place. I was already beginning to seriously doubt my sanity. I felt as old now as the last date in March. Wrinkles at the corner of a treasure map I vaguely recalled from my latest dream. I *would at least get a brief respite from these wankers that guarded me as I dropped through oceans. These dreams were becoming constant in my sleep patterns through the quieter nights of late. I think I was nearly sixteen soon. My birth date blocked now from memory. The seasons are now my guide. All I knew was Aquarius ruled my stars, tides, moons, moods and life. The weird lunatic laughter in the wards air rang out, not something that exactly helped you remain sane. There was never silence. Something I was finding hard to get used to. I missed my raft back home. I guess these Ocean dreams were maybe something to do with that fact, compensating me for its removal. The T time meal never materialised and after pacing the cells warn out green wood floor till my stocking feet ached, I slump on my cot bed and doze off.*

I felt I had been born from the ocean. The old clay pot of the Aquarian sign on my shoulder carried the gift of life. The air sign that ruled it lost now as I went under again. The hospital collapsed with a whoosh of the waves from under me. Skool lessons not wasted as I recalled a similar incident happening to Jamaica's pirate capital Port Royal, which in those times was known as the wickedest city in the world. It had sunk Gomorrah like beneath the waves, during the earthquake of 1692. Sinking again in the deepest of sleeps, the Faberon lulled me once more as I followed the beat of the ocean calling. Suddenly the Sail fish catches hold of my sleeve and speeds me at what feels like a hundred miles an hour back to the surface. The ceilings covered in sleepy zzzzzzzz. Caribbean shells lodging in my ears as I groggily wake. Echo's of the oceans sounds too strong to not be real. Confusion as always when I wake back into my cold cell. The pirate treasure map I had surely seen. The loot remains a mystery for now, hidden deep beneath the dreams waves, or up here on the surface ready to be unearthed.

{TAKING THE PLUNGE chapter 51} *A bitterly cold morning was about to get much worse. I was dog tired, not getting back to sleep last night after the ocean dreams brief descent. The first person as I put eye to the spy hole in my door to see if breakfast looked to be*

happening was Nurse Silk. Over her shoulder lay a towel of institutional colour and stiffness, an ominous warning to the threat of the ice cold water drowning they were about to dish out to me and a few other poor souls.

On these days, I would be marched down to the tub room and woken up sharply. I had started to work out some of the routine to the Faberon. What I had seen with my own eyes, what Character, Scott John n Winnie had told me. But it was random at best. Like the meals, like the injections. They just seemed to happen on their time and agenda. I'd resisted the first time I'd had the ice bath. But after the punches to the liver n kidneys, which with your hands cuffed behind your back and you laid over the side of the tub, hurt like fuck, I'd soon given up the useless struggle n let them dip me. I had still been trying to assess the numbing cold tingling panic that much so that I didn't even notice the point where I'd passed out. Claw marks dripping with blood on the back of my neck as they had dragged me back up straight. Nurse silk not involved in the process of helping the dipping party. She was there to dry me off. I suppose in my soppy mind it was worthwhile just to let her rub me down, her hands always lingering that second too long near my groin, maybe just my imagination, but then again maybe not. I would try not to wince as she dabbed the back of my neck. The blood on the towel we both ignored as I got a close up look into her swimming sea blue eyes.

Dried n clothed again. The brute guards would take me back to my cell. Shivering n sneezing I would try to understand why my life seemed to be just routine pain.

There had been a slip of paper under the door yesterday. I had been ordered to attend some education class. No more details than that. No time or date, like most things in here, it would just happen when they decided. As I'd got back up onto my landing, one of the guards had been reassuring Character through his door that his request was being dealt with. Whatever it was, I didn't find out as my door slammed in on me before I could hear any more chat. I heard the guard shout through Characters door as he passed that it was here, then the keys unscrewing the lock in Winnie's door. I had heard no

more sound after that. I only realised picking myself up from the cell
floor with sounds of guards opening doors n shouting hurry up men
its T time, that I had passed out. A total blackout as the concoction of
pills after the return from the bath drowning had sneaked up on me.

Explosive mushy soup on the menu it seems. Fawkes made of plastic.
I'd already eaten some, thrown some and spilled some down my
chest, before Winnie, lagging way behind n still unlocked shouted me
over to my door to show me what he had in his hand. Character had
given his Gee Tar to psychologically boost his confidence in their
friendship. Every one wondered about Characters agenda and
Winnie was no different. His crimes were strange and disturbing,
but Character had the good discipline to assess well the cruel n
wicked from damn right insane souls. And Winnie hadn't technically
killed anyone, so even if he had been on the 6 moon killin list, he
would have come way down the line. It was the sadistics that were
the ones near the top and in very serious and imminent danger from
our in house serial killA.

Headaches from the dry mouth were back again. I would massage
with my hands the back of my aching skull. Mums twisted diamond
rings on my mind, there ugly vulture claw scars were throbbing.
Reminders I didn't need or want in my head. Just like when I would
take a quiet piss in the night, aiming at the edge of the pan so as not
to let my neighbours hear my odd urines rhythm. Stan's water filled
jugs looming wicked in my mind. My own cold water jug in the
corner of my cell was something that if I stared at too long while
daydreaming away my time, could make me shiver uncontrollably at
the memory of his sick twisted games.

Nothing much had happened of any great change for the past few
weeks. The biggest gossip amongst the inmates had been the
anticipation of Characters guitar. I'd heard him early last week
banging on at the interns about his application to have it brought up
from the reception. He had always it appeared, been allowed it in
former prisons that he had been in before landing at the Faberon.
Black like an adder snake was its full bodied wood, with a white
Indian chief in full head gear painted smart on the back. The hospital

had denied the amplifier, which he had caused a minor scene over. The guard giving him that news had been whispered in the ear to that he was next on the list. To which he had run away down the landing screaming that he was a dead man. White as a ghost n puking down his uniform had been enough for Gaunt to stamp the request for some time off away from duties, at least until Character had got past his next six moon killing schedule.

Sweet Jesus dipped in jam! A chord from out of the gloom awakening my suppressed senses, the half hit notes I made out to be D,e,A,f. "Add a tone to that Winnie", I shouted through the vent. My side was flushed open, but I wasn't sure if he had his connection the same. I'd heard the sound through the open bars.

I imagined him, dirty nails way too long to catch the steel strings right. Mouthing songs in silence, with the Indian warrior wishing he was back in his rightful owner's hands. Winnie though now safely guarded by shaman magik.

These drugs, as bad as they were, seemed at times to have their advantages. Even the faint tone of Winnie gently placing his new instrument down onto the wood floor of his cell I could hear astounded with the inner lobes mechanism, still amazing myself as I grew learning more about my own body and its capabilities.

Gerard as if on Q, the gate key that let you onto the Netherfield twisting angrily in its lock. The fucking bullying bastard was on the way down towards our cell block now, with Winnie always his preferred target. Bars n bolt checks would be his excuse to fuck with Winnie's already frayed nerves. Then it would be time for some tranquilizer broth. Only the finest of meals served out to the loonies. I'd dozed again, the morning medication doubled with no explanation.

I had been in and out of consciousness since getting back around six am from the early morning bath drowning. Yet even that seemed very hazy recollections with the double bubble tablet dose.

I woke this time from a dream. Not the oceans. Just a silly boyish dream where I had Nurse Silk across from meat this fancy Italian restaurant which I recalled Liberty recollecting to me one day way back in the pig shop cells.

She had on a tight satin white dress, her hair was tied up. She was sipping champagne n leaning forward laughing as she lit my cigar. Yet it had ended this sweet dream before I had chance to pay the bill. Gerard's screaming demands to get by your doors n ready to move our arses for lunch brought the nightmare life back into a sharp painful vision. My cell wall holding no resemblance to the red velvet patterned wallpaper. Memories now of the back drop to nurse Silks breathtaking look. I close my eyes and try shut off the racket!!! I can feel all the heartbeats beside me. A concrete tomb with a solid beat next door, a skip of a beat from the timid one next to that, then beyond to a lucky one whose heart is just giving in and not caring no more. Then the doors flew open for lunch. The noise of rumbling bellies jingling and rattling down the stairs. A million tablet concoctions jumping around in the gut mix. My eyes wide open n ready for any crazy random attacks. You couldn't be too careful in here. Only the other night when it was late supper, a loon from the landing below mine had ripped a young fruit cakes eyes out in the Q.

The rumoured reason, a glance at his shoes apparently. Probably paranoia due to the cut feet of some men on the ward, their souls slashed to bits. They would open your cell real quiet on a night, like 4am or some God forsaken hour like that when everyone was zonked. Then they would bowl some broken glass underarm towards your bed area hoping that you would spill some fresh blood in the morning light. If you even dared to complain, most didn't, but if you did, you would be marched to your cell where the floor was now swept clean. It was all designed to make you feel even more unhinged and was all part of the therapeutic agenda. I hear down near the food server this cheeky screw shout over to Scot John, "Poets day John "I could see the big fella looking back to the screw with a scowl that left nothing to the imagination. He knew what was coming!

These guards were boring at the best of times and well known for their vocal repetitions. Piss off early tomorrows Saturday.

A few of the arse licker patients had a little chuckle, but besides that I ignored it like most n got my scran n headed back on unsteady feet to my peter. Faster than a bulldog at his bowl, I finished scoffing. The only thing left in the metal tray was the plastic casings from the Mickey Fins. They would leave them in to taunt you, and I'd learned quickly with Winnie's heads up to look out for them n try swerve them in my consumption the best I could, but the odd one would get gulped down no matter how careful.

My cell was spinning, then gone, descending without notice to blackness on the wooden floor. I felt them now, thick the lot of them, yet I'm the clever one under some screw bullies boot Squashed. My brain screaming to be free though, like keystone cops, iQ zilch, silhouetted thugs, yelling at me till they go horse, wanting my hospital number? Did they even give me one? I try a few combinations from out under the boots. No luck, nothing new there!!!

606280 I'm told with a final kick from one heavy footed bastard who's stood nearby supervising. An owl hooting breaks the spell. It's on my ledge like some other big shot supervising this kicking. I make a pathetic attempt through my busted bloody mouth to hoot back at it. Its blinking slow now, not impressed, twisting its head fully around to show off its uniqueness. It gave me a final wink and hopped off the ledge to swoop away into the colt blue skies. The big thug screw caught me staring at it and decided to show off his own unique skills with a full on volley to my head that sent it spinning round nearly as much as that owls.

Dark skies welcomed me back from unconsciousness. I'd been out for hours, .Winnie's voice coming through the window faint, telling me to open the pipes. I got busy with the plunger, soon finding out that I wasn't the only one that lunch time to get a kicking. Some had got it worse. Winnie up the vent spreading the hot gossip about circulation restrictor who was a well established bully amongst the guard who worked down at Wa/rd siX. He had the reputation of a sadistic.

The first few times it happened, the hierarchy in charge of the facility had put it down to over keenness. But it was no accident after those incidents. Winnie's voice hollowed up through the bog pipes filling me in on the latest. The so called over keen daft twat had secured the hands of a chronic after a disturbance that called for a removal from our ward up to the dreaded Wa/rd siX.

A tad over the top had been words used to that effect to smooth over the bad intentions on the ward from some of his pals, who Winnie said had caused for an hour some banging in protest on their doors. The fact still remained though a man had lost his hands. Gaunt briskly striding on and off the wing, soothing individuals at their cell doors, trying to show some kind of fake concern. The surgeons, who had a small theatre next to Wa/rd siX, had removed them both. They could have sewn them back on from where they had nearly been sawn through with the cuffs, but as usual, the easiest way was to just slice them finally off and dump them in a shoe box to later maybe pickle in a experiment jar. The FABERON, you could say was starting to really scare me. The Netherfield ward didn't seem too bad, just dicks like Gerard, bugging the life out of some. But this Wa/rd siX was very worrying. The theatre next door certainly a place I didn't fancy visiting. Rumours that even Gaunt got behind the surgical mask for some cutting from time to time.

{A STITCH IN TIME chapter 52} Trying to get the knack of using these antique machines was hard work. The letter about education class had resulted in me sat in the day room. Things had been moved around to accommodate the class. A few random tables had been thrown together with odd matching stools and these bloody old looking sewing machines. It had taken all morning to get the hang of the floor peddle. The cotton had finally started gripping the line I was trying to hold. It was only the hem of the institutional rough towels that we had been advised to crack on with. I got up to use the toilet at the back of the room, passing Scot John's place on the way. He winked at me and held up these leather patches, like the ones that go on the back of a pair of jeans to show you the make. He had been busy *this morning. He had been in these classes yonks n knew his way round his machine like Rumpelstiltskin. The two patches I managed to read were cool, before the teacher Mrs Tour de force shouted out for me to hurry up with the bathroom break n get my arse back on my stool. One of his patches was stitched real neat saying* **IN HOUSE BLUES***, while the other had been stitched to look like our cell window with bars, the wording said,* **GAOLERS DENIM MADE WITH CONVICTION** *The toilet had been a welcome quiet space for a moment. Lost looking at the wall, trying to think where I was in this mad house, hoping still that someone in authority would just come and tell me I was free to go and it had unfortunately been one big mistake, suddenly Scot John's thunderous shouting broke me out of my whimsical day dreaming. As I made my way back through the door, I was met with a standoff between the teacher n the ScOtish bull goose looney.*

Mrs Tour de force was accusing him off making some remark about her tits. Maybe not much of a matter, but if I told you a little of what Winnie had whispered to me about his case n why among many things he was securely looked away for life, then the implications became more apparent.

Indian tit pouch had been a word I had never heard of before. Winnie trying his best to explain a little about Scot John's case through the pipes one late evening got me to understand a little more. The shocking tale came a little distorted due to Winnie's heavy night time medicated dose. It seems that on the out, John had been a big time tobacco supplier. We're talking container shipments of the stuff. The customs were onto him big time towards the end. His greed had like a lot of men before him, had seen him buying cheap African shit. The sort that was probably twenty percent tobacco leaf and eighty percent bush path twigs ground up.

I'd taken a sip of diesel from my mug. The shit they served you up as a night time bang up brew, and chewed over in my mind the facts so far. I was just about to say to Win down the swirling bog pipes that

*it didn't seem such a big deal to end up in here for life over. Then I
got the full gist of the tale.*

*John's preferred customers, the ones he had been supplying for years,
received one Christmas of late a wrapped normal looking box with a
festive red bow. Inside they had wondered most certainly at the dried
skin pouch, full of the finest quality smoking leaves. They had
probably had a smoke of the stuff. Maybe some had put it back in the
box and kept it safe in their studies. None would have really thought
too in depth about it until the headlines hit the national rags.*

*When the customs had finally busted John, they had raided him at his
offices first which had been located in some old boat yard, but with no
joy on locating him for an arrest at the dock, they had raced to his
residence and busting the door clean off its hinges and running up
the stairs, which I may add was stacked on every step with
dictionaries n encyclopaedia's, they had finally found him smoking a
fag in the bath.*

*It was the search of the house for more contraband that landed the
crazy son of a bitch in here for a full life tariff. The team of officers
had recovered no more boxes of fags. He had kept most stuff at the
boat yard. But not one of them was ready for the sight they found in
the large spare double bedroom.*

*The stink had been held at bay from the door by a series of Moroccan
lamps hanging from the ceiling, burning heavy Frankincense &
Myrrh scented candles.*

*The first agent through the door immediately turned back after
clocking the room's contents, puking all over his stab vest, he stared
ghost like through his superior who had been bringing up the rear
and just ran passed him and out into the residential street to empty
more of his breakfast into the grate by the road.*

*It was the plod in charge of the case who Winnie had read the
statements from. Scot John he said had quite nonchalantly sent them
via a line to Winnie's cell upon his first week arriving up onto the
Netherfield ward.*

Combined, there had been the recovery of 17 woman's corpses. All in varying states of decay, all with some kind of limbs or body parts missing from them. Arranged in very disturbing poses, not in some weird sexual way, they had made the horrendous discovery even more disturbing.

It looked something more like out of a concentration camps surgical experiment lab. Two ladies for example had one a missing right arm, the other the left. One was young, the other old. They had been pushed together sideways on so that they looked like some strange conjoined twin. One half aged with the horror of life. The other froze into youth with the shock of unexpected murder. Others had no heads. Some just torso's, like period Roman statues. A macabre museum, one that only John had been visiting up to now. Much confusion outside the bedroom door for hardened battle scared officers. No rational mind allowing this to be conceived. Yet it was actually in front of you. Grotesqueness and the epitome of sheer brutal madness combined. Something the dead who had torsos remaining had in common, were that like the ripper, they had quite skilfully had their breasts removed. It wasn't till months later, after extensive inquiries about John's life concluded and the trial was set that quite a few associates had come steadily forward to offer statements.

In his many interviews, which he gladly opened up to in detail about his shocking crimes, there was many a mention of the Indian tit pouch. It was noted that disturbingly these facts were always given through a constant stream of smoke swirling from his demanded fags.

When the pile of boxes he had given to his valued customers had been stacked up neat on the interview table, he had howled with laughter for as the statements revealed, some forty minutes nonstop. The breast skin had been cut away in generous circles and left to dry. Then he had stitched them into pouch bags n filled them with his best leaves of tobacco. After days of quizzical looks from the squad interviewing him n been none the wiser as to the reason for this bazaar act, he had lit up a fresh smoke and explained it was an old

Indian Navajo trait. In battle if they captured enemy, the men would be scalped, the woman would be butchered. The tit pouch was made and used in ceremonies to fulfil the ritual of chugging upon the pipe of peace and showing other tribe leaders respect All Warriors had one he had narcissistically commented.

And so the scene as I left the toilet in the sewing class to come back to had what could be called an ugly undertone to Mrs Tour de forces accusations. Scot John had tried to laugh it off, saying he had only been joking, trying to get a laff out of the rest of the class. The teacher called him a twisted fuck and pressed the deafening alarm bell for assistance. Then he bit two ears clean off the first two guards who came rushing in through the door. He managed to push easily passed a third and get down the corridor, where he then flew into a little side room where the guards made a brew n read papers. Sticking the bloodied ears to their recreational dartboard, he was just about to strangle another guard who had rushed towards the gate from the other side after seeing the disturbance. John had moved sharply to the gate himself and as the guard fumbled with the keys he had gripped him with his huge arm n started a death strangle on the poor man. The truncheon blows didn't stop him from turning the guy a funny shade of blue. But the bells had been sounded all over the institute and the sharply trained aim of the mufti squad block officers brought him finally to his knees with heavy blow darts full of all sorts of creepy dreamy drugs.

They left the kicking the absolute shit out of him until they had unceremoniously dragged him off the ward. The class was wrapped up quite quickly and in a matter of ten minutes from me taking a toilet break I was now sat back on my bunk reliving the whole crazy episode.

{THE KNOT TYER chapter 53} *I hadn't been in my cell long before I smelt that sweet lavender perfume of Nurse Silk lingering outside my steel door. This was no surprise.*

Usually after an incident, even though you would have already been given enough drugs to knock out a grizzly bear, the dose doctor would order a top up. On today's menu for me were three little brown tablets. As she unfurled her dainty little freckled hand I inquired as to what they may be. Usually you wouldn't be told. Just given n told to take them. Any resistance n you would be held down n they would be shoved roughly up your deaf n dumb. I almost in my drugged n worn out confused brain thought as she opened her perfect mouth had said "marry me" The word she had actually said when my brain finally registered through the fog was, Mellaril. It was another antipsychotic, which helped Schizophrenics during their visionary episodes.

I knew all the details of the drugs n side effects from Winnie filling me in on our late night chin wags. It was a major tranquilizer in the same family as Thorazine, another drug they had started to pump me full of. In-between all the serious shit going down on the ward, there was still a wry smile from my lips no matter what my unfair predicament.

The Knot Tyer had been busy most of the week. Dr Gaunt had fallen flat on his face twice already, his brogues laces done up like a kipper. Nurse Silk had spent the best part of one of her shifts undoing all the apron strings which they wore as a precaution against our blood splatters, cursing quietly under her silky breath. There wasn't too much to say about the guy. When convict Ed had been transferred from Alabama, he had managed to read on DR Woo's desk the file on the Knot Tyer. Another product of a dysfunk-family, with a Mother tied to the kitchen sink, Mother tied to the bed head posts, Mother tied to the turned off freezing radiator in the cellar. Father tied to his stash of grotty seventies porn mags, rope around the hand and his pathetic knob.

Obviously INFLUENCED? But convict Ed had clocked the case file photos hanging out the side of one of the files, witnessed with his own eyes the Knot Tyer's handy work with the rope around the baby's neck. Obviously Winnie, the great gossip had extracted the info n given me the heads up on another soul in our ever cloudy pond. You wanted to kill them all at the start, but the weekly group togetherness meetings stuffed the message down our throats.

'The insane cannot be blamed', probably one of Dr Gaunt's little quotes from the guide book of the MAD. He did like to bore you to death with those gems from time to time.

He, the Knot Tyer can't have been that insane, for he kept a steady distance from the likes of Character or Scot John. Their laces were safe and knot free, not that they were out of their locked institutional boots for much of the time anyway. A plate of spaghetti for his breakfast, dinner n tea, requested and gladly delivered to hopefully tire him out a bit with his annoying habit at meal times.

That mellaril dose certainly wiped me clean off the planet for a few days. I only really came to in a focused enough state to realise where I was when I heard the shout for breakfast. I knew as I entered the server area that I'd been in a twilight world for days. The blackboard that had info on about days n what grub was likely to be dished up had well changed from the missing meals I knew I'd not eaten it. Sure looked like I had been out from a Monday dinner to this Thursday's breakfast for Christ sakes.

Positive Ed's ghost seemed to stir at the memory I'd had of him. The man in front of me going back up the stairs from collecting breakfast suddenly looked like he had been knocked off his feet. He came crashing past me as he spun n fell forwards. The metal on each rung of the stairs catching his vulnerable shins until the final one at the bottom just for good measure hammered into the front of his bonce. The porridge scented air where his bowl had landed all over the place suddenly to my astonishment appeared to have these hoof like foot prints in them, randomly going back up the next few rungs of the stairs n then they just vanished again. The screws were over quick. Not to help the fallen inmate, more to just get the Q moving again instead of cloggin up the stairs staring at the blood flow which was running fast now from the poor chaps head wound, Nurse Howwell eventually scooping him up n taking him to the nurse's station for some much needed stitches. She was one of the other female nurses on the Netherfield, an older senior nurse who had shown Nurse Silk the ropes when she had joined the staff team. Quolco an institutional joey came quickly with the mop to hand to clear the porridgy floor.

{BLACK PUDDING chapter 54} *It seemed like I had only just put my breakfast tray out on the landing to be collected, when I heard them screaming from below to grab your mugs n get ready for lunch. In fancy script, we clocked that black pudding has been spelt out on the dinner board. As we had trudged n skipped down the metal stairs the rumour had aired that one of the coloured fellas from over on Wa/rd siX had met his fate with the sadistic guards going over the top again. The in house coroner had made sure that by the time the poor chap made it out of the walls of the FABERON, the time of his death would be all wrong to attribute blame to certain shifts on duty. He had died in his cell late at night. That was now the official statement getting wired to the mystery men in suits who dealt with shit like this. When over on Wa/rd siX at night there was no staff with cell keys, only Gaunt in an emergency could unlock those double doors. Trying to believe the guy had killed himself in the night by beating his self to death was quite farfetched. But you certainly did have patients pulling their own eyes out n eating it or cutting their own throats with sharpened stones from out on the yard.*

The fancy writing on the board had taken the tally man some hours. Custard was available to the workers n the mice. I caught out the corner of my eye, for the staff got served first of course if it was something they fancied, the suited figure of the coroner. He was smiling as he got two delicious big scoops of custard for his discreet role in sweeping more dirt under what must have been a very large lumpy rug. Someone even suggested quietly that the poor dead fella had been stuffed inside the server hotplate to throw the inquest off the time he had met his maker.

QUALCOMM Cluny I noticed was still lingering on the ones landing near the phone. He had arrived on these shores a long time gone. He was the most institutionalized person I met. The love of an English rose made the poor fella steal. He had believed that an ice cream would cool her heels. The theft noticed by the stall holder. The arrest on the park green had been utter humiliation to them both and the last time he had seen his sweetheart ever again. When I had encountered him for the first meeting upon which we spoke, he had spotted an opportunity to reveal his terrible plight to a new comer.

Rampton Mental hospital had kept him fully drugged for twenty nine years. No big revelation maybe. There had been longer confinements than that. But for an ice cream!!!!

And the poor old bugger had not even got to eat it or watch his sweet hearts lips enjoy her own.

He would never have gotten it down on paper for you to read at leisure. The tears that filled his eyes were deep filled puddles of regret. I listened so intently to his wasted life as he spoke. So robotic now, he had become an unpaid screw without even realising it. The fat guards lazed back, thinking every inmate had never had a job, never paid a tax. Fuck these silly thick fuckers. A constant battle they waged to strip you of all moral decency. They couldn't see beyond the end of their nosey beaks. Nothing but spies, rubbish ones at that.

I should write it all down. Not let this story languish unheard on the landings. My little chapter lost like the thousands before me. Write one, like this, they wish.

Qualco told me that he had considered advice from the screws to top his self. To go bravely forth to find out if the Angels donned their robes and came ghostly into our world briefly to collect your hand. He would have at least that way been able to sit in the screws office n listen to them continuously rip the piss out of him. Yet he was so far gone, he probably wouldn't have believed it, even after hearing it with his own ears. He felt the screws loved him. Believed he was their friend. It brought another layer of sadness to my world watching him.

I would flatten my left over mash n draw a smiling face in defiance, also hoping it would brighten his day for a second, as Qualco had the job of helping to collect our dirty metal trays from outside the cell doors after meal times.

Nothing of note happened the rest of the day. The glue clocks in full effect. My door opened late in the evening, for I had watched transfixed on the sky changing a darker hue. The crowd was in front of me in no time, the bully squad ready with their trip to the blackness. I stopped noticing the scratch as the needle pierced sharply through my bruised skin. But I could never get passed forgetting. Like a dream within a dream, it became a blissful place to retreat into. The hospital for a while silenced from the screams. The first scene always came along like a dark cloak thrown over my young head. Then the floor would start to bubble, then the green wood gave way and I would be sinking down into the ocean dreams.

{RAPTURE OF THE DEEP chapter 55} *The floor of the ocean misleads in its phrase. Floors are flat and featureless, yet the land beneath me in my dreams had more ups n downs than Winnie's soft whistle when his spade had hit pay dirt on a fresh jewellery filled coffin lid.*

My dreams started this time not with a sudden drop through the water, a shadowy figure beginning at the edge of dry land, walking out slowly, with what looked like the lygactol shuffle from Nurse Silk's tray into the cold sea. I wasn't sure if I was watching myself as this dark figure now moved out towards deep water. Submerging with a gentle slope down the continental shelf to then just vanish completely it seemed.

It must have been me the shadowy figure. I could feel the dark cloak wrapping around my head tighter as the waters volume crushed it into my skull. Then suddenly as if powered by enormous current energy, my shadow would fly straight through the deep open trenches that gapped miles below. Ghost sharks slowly moving out of the way, as the shadow came into their world before an upwards acceleration again.

An ocean dweller passed me on the way up, then bright flashes of light as I disturbed a red Atolla Jellyfish. The anglerfish came to check me out, vibrations causing its sensory studs to tingle with curiosity.

Just before the jolt that took me nearly back to the surface, a common nurse shark and silky shark were unusually circling each other. A severed mariner's foot still laced into his boot came crashing scarily through a deep rolling wave. The nibbled away calf was flapping in the tide as I finally broke surface.

Banging on the wing, some major disturbance had brought me round from dreaming. The deep sea squid facing me I thought for a confused moment. My eyes blinking awake though against the dotty paint of the cell wall. I didn't see anyone much the whole weak end. In fact I had tried to figure out the time I had been away. Yet through the combinations of drugs it was hard to be precise.

I knew March had sunk into April, which in turn had bubbled its way down into May, finally hitting the oceans floor on my last strange dream in June. Life in here moved very slowly in your day to day dealings with time. The glue clocks always in motion. Yet in a rare moment of clarity the months became realised to be speeding along. My head sometimes so full of the flash backs to the trial, it would feel ready to literally explode with pressure. It always sent my mind racing to my so called Father. He was the one who should be locked away in this lunatic asylum. How could he have ever dreamed of such an atrocity?

Every minute of the doomed days dragged along with thoughts of how convincing Stan had described in his statements the murder of his wife!!!!! Not the death of my Mother. Clearly the police had mistaken a crying boy grieving over the loss of his Mother as some devious little bleeder laying on thick the act of deception. Where the fuck had Social services been?

They had been clever over the years my parents. Always making me out to be a liar and a clumsy idiot, that much so that no one even looked into detail as to what the fuck had been going on in that horrible house for years. The pathetic attempts had fallen on deaf ears to reach higher office where maybe someone would have listened and intervened.

I was surprised on the Monday to hear Scot John noisily bound back up onto the Netherfield ward. The black eye must have been a corker punch he had received courtesy of the Wa/rd siX guards, for it still filled the entire side of his face with two painful under the skin bloody lumps meeting to render him one eyed for a while. It didn't seem to have dampened his spirit, for he gave my door a hefty bang as if to say I'm home before they bundled him back into his own peter.

When they let him out much later in the afternoon to receive some eye treatment, he sidled up to the metal dividing us in my door n asked how I was. After I had spoken to him about my latest ocean dream, for I had been disturbed at times by them enough to share my trips with a few members from within our cloudy pond. He had revelled in his thoroughly read knowledge outside my door.

It was the heavy cloak I felt over my head that he shone some light upon for me. 'Luchor pain' was the word that stuck in my mind the most. It was an Irish mythological creature, a form of leprechaun living under the sea, it was he said, able to guide humans beneath the sea either by placing a cloak over their heads or by stuffing herbs into the human's ears. He left me with that little gem to go off n get some treatment from nurse Howwell.

But as I laid upon my bunk thinking about the dark cloak that seemed to accompany my dreams, he came back to my door with nurse Howwell shouting for him to get behind his own.

"Do you know Otiss why they call the prison the Poke?" "Go on" I ventured back from my bunk. "It's derived from old English mate, Pocca, a sack, thus an enclosed space." And with that he banged up to leave me wondering about all he had said in my dreary pokey little new home!

{BUGGIN chapter 56} *It was guard change today, which unfortunately meant Gerard was coming back on the wing. He really was a bastard who abused to the full his shitty guard's position in the FABERON. You could hear him as soon as he turned the key in the wards entry* *door lock."Right you sick men, get this blurd clot mess cleaned up, me not liv in dis shit ole bouy".*

When we were allowed in the day room, he would stride in vexed. He loved messing Winnie's chess game up, knocking all the wood pieces over, then picking up the King and Pawn while bawlin into wins face. "This is me Jah," holding the king piece so close to poor Winnie's face that I thought on a few occasions he was going to ram the crown up his nose. Then holding the pawn piece by his thumb and index finger tips, saying "n this is you"!!

"NOW GET THIS PLACE CLEANED UP YOU LITTLE TIT RAT"!!! Poor Winnie would always be the starting point for Gerard's buggin. Tormenting him to the point where I didn't know how he stood for it. But it was certainly a reminder of my own scared bullied ways around Stan, making my inner body feel uncomfortable. He would use Winnie to syke himself up for bigger fish in our cloudy pond.

The first time he ever proper bugged me came late one stormy night. The storm brewed nasty outside of the cell window. The crack of thunder now up in the air waiting to boom. Scot John shouting out the window, BRONTIDE BRONTIDE BRONTIDE.I had just finished off my training. Character advising me to try to keep some fitness no matter how drugged I felt. The few press ups n sit ups felt good and I had just stripped washed n cooled myself down with splashes from the cold water jug when he came trying my patience.

The lights had gone off in the cell half hour ago. They were controlled from outside the door an around 8 pm they would leave you to whatever natural light you could still see from out through your bars. I had settled tired from the exertion n from the bang up dose onto my bunk, sinking my back right into its digging spring coils. My mind no matter what the tiredness already racing to thoughts of Stan, then the lights started flicking on n off.

"Kites you wanna fight my man?""Wanna fix? Wanna"!!! Had I fallen asleep? Had I started hearing like a lot of the men on my ward, voices in my head? Then the realisation that I was fully awake. There

was a demon at my door for real. The snarling low whisper squeezed its way through the crack in my door again. "Kites you think you could kill a man bouy"?

I could see his red eyes, crooked brilliant white teeth, flashing then gone, reappearing then darkness. I got up from the bunk and walked right up to the flap in the door, looking through the plexi glass the view was normal. Half a metal rail, some strained vision made out the net. The mirror image head on of my own door looking back at me, to whom I wondered at times which one, I was truly behind. Relief sighed in my rising chest. The demon for now had gone.

{FABERON FM chapter 57} It had been right under my nose all along. These drug doses were warping my mind. I'd been picking with my ever growing sharp pointed finger nail at the peeling paint from the cell door. Layers of the caked cracked stuff ready to reveal its former centuries old colours came away with ease.

How many more people had stood here in my cell? Wandering as I was as to who had come before. It was in a strange way fascinating to feel a part of something as old and secret as the FABERON. Thankfully the majority of the population would not have to stare at its glue dripping walls. How much misery could four walls hold? I had been tempted to add my own initials. They at least gave you a small distraction from the minutes that hung like forever in the day. For me, guessing a full name from scratched deep initials had become like one of my favourite TV shows from my childhood. How fucking sad is this place?

I was worried though that if I did add my mark, I would never truly escape this nut bin. Locked in my cell for eternity, you couldn't help but feel the presence of the sad men before my turn.

It was the search out of boredom for more initials in my cell that lead to me coming across the small plug hole. The socket plug had revealed itself as I'd pulled away a small piece of crumbling plaster from under the bunk of my bed. I had been following a scratched initial that was partially hidden behind a different layer of time. Hunched under the bunk in dim light I had thought I was seeing things at first, but after a moment I realised it was a socket. It being situated in my cell was another thing to ponder.

The heavy dosage took me away for the rest of the day n it wasn't until late evening that I got my head together enough to bang Winnie's wall n shout flush the pipes. His familiar voice didn't take long to shout up through the system. I asked him about the plug, which brought a long silence before he told me its usage.

'It's FABERON fm my friend, I will see if I can get you some headphones to tune in. Sundays you should pick up ok'. Then he flushed the connection and left me to wonder.

When the supper time drink of diesel came round, before the night clocky came on for the night n the day staff pissed off to normality, I clock Winnie talkin to the Baron a few cells passed Scot John's home. The Baron I had been told ran the institute's cig currency. They called him Baron Green baki. His joey assistant was a small odd looking bloke called danger mouse. They were the only cell on the entire ward that bunked up together. As I filled my plastic beaker at the door full of the sludgy looking diesel brew, Winnie skipped past winking n banged up.

As my brew turned cold on the side, I heard a bang at the window so I climbed up on my chair to have a deek. Someone had swung me a line from the far left of the cells row.

I jumped down to grab my bog brush n held my arm out stretched into the night catching the line as it came swinging back again. The wool line fell across the out held brush handle, giving me chance to draw it inwards n pull the wool through my bars to see what treasure was attached to its end. A piece of the hospitals cruel equipment is what I thought it was at first as I untangled it from around the string. One of those old style sets of ear phones. Scarily like the ones they use down to administer E c T treatments. Even this pair had pieces of lint stuck near to its ear plugs. I stuck them up my jumper n tucked that into my pants.

Checking through the spy hole I could see old Walter making his rounds, but once he had peeked in on you once that would be it for the night. On the landing, sporadic shattering screams of grief n torment raged through the atmosphere. But that was nothing new n I felt quietly confident to go try out my new source of entertainment. You had to be extra careful though. They were Sneaky bastards who ran this place for real. Dr Gaunt would wear extra soft slippers, so as not to disturb he said. Yet everyone knew it was so he could creep about spying on the patients.

Staff meetings they would be handed out to all on that weeks shift. Gerard never wore them though. He liked to let you know he was on his way, his heavy footfalls scaring some as it grew louder up to your door. Even when I was zonked on the tablets n injections, he would stomp about till I awoke, playing pure bedlam with my beauty sleep. I took a chance.

Crawling under the low bunk I fiddled about poking the metal end into the wall socket. I felt a small jolt of leki as it connected. The wire was white in colour n long enough to enable me to sit on my chair with my back to the judy hole n try have a listen. I pulled over my lugs the white ear compressors. NOTHING!!!!

I tried crawling back under the bunk n aggressively pushing the metal end in some more, but nothing came of it. You could hear a very faint static noise but nothing of value. I then, defeated, lay back down on my bunk to listen to the loony sounds like usual.

With my new ear phones stashed inside the rim of the toilet, I remembered Winnie's words about tuning in Sundays. With it being Tuesday I would just have to be patient n see what came through the ear phones next weak end. Gerard would be on the rest of this week so maybe for the best. A weak end free of his bullshit n only old Walter on the night clocki duties, so I would get chance to listen in and see what this FABERON fm was all about.

{A LULL chapter 58} *The week passed strangely without incident.*
Gerard had his holidays booked for next week n seemed to be in a less
spiteful mood.

The ice bath near downing's were always a great alarming wake up
call, held under, until the dirty reeds from the lake of stars transpired
out of the bath water, hallucinations with the near death drowning
experience bringing back happy memories of my childhood, which
were very few n far apart. I could hear Johnny's laughter as the final
bubbles left my nose n mouth before being yanked back out into the
reality of the clinical white walls of the tub room. My shrivelled
vision once more trying to focus on the only plus side to this
torturous task as I was led over to Nurse Silk to be gently dried off.

There had been a few more caution cards slipped into the metal
holders that were outside everyone's door. Along with the standard
card to say your details n sentence, the caution cards were tucked
besides for the most dangerous, or suicidal patients.

These poor souls were stripped off any personal property and
searched thoroughly morning and night before shift change to the
night clocki. Some nights I would hear sweet surprising music.
Whistlers unknown, beautiful Irish lilts of a sad slow gypsy ballad.
Bad croaking voiced heavy smokers would join in with a hum. The
tin cup drummer would be me, if it was a tin cup, but I made do
tapping gently in my best beat on my plastic, emptied of diesel
beaker, then Winnie would bang the guitar n I would then stop
fighting the 300ml of largactil n drift off holding onto the sad words
of the downtrodden Irish.

On other nights you would hear men being dragged violently from
their pits n thrown along the landing like rag dolls at the mercy of
the brute guards. Patchy, another patient in our cloudy pond and a
friend of the Knot Tyer, would go voluntarily on certain nights of the
week past my door, heading to the aversion therapy shock clinic. It
was with the required co operation of the patient to be wired up to
some electrical jolts n depress the plunger to activate n shock there
selves.

Night and day seemed to hold no difference except the sky was a different shade of colour and the food was in some kind of order, as in breakfast, lunch dinner. It was sometimes the only way to gather your minds attention on just where about the day had caught up with you. The other morning I had slept off deep enough to shake a little of the groggy dead weight my mind held firmly fixed to my skull tripping. I'd noticed the guard's busy outside on the landing, carrying tools back n forth.

The corridor leading off the Netherfield was being stripped of linoleum. It was I gathered from watching two guards carry a large roll on each of their shoulders, getting a new soft carpet, killing two magpies with one rock.

One, the warders issued slippers for creeping n spying would blend into the fabric nicely, making it more or less impossible for you to hazard a guess as to them just rushing open your door. And secondly Dr Gaunt got to over order on the rolls n kit out his little bird watching huts that he had dotted around the grounds. The rumour on the wing that he took some of the more vulnerable patients out there on a pretence of a calming therapeutic walk n did god only knows what horrors to them.

When the guards had finished ripping the old stuff up, we had collided with our lunch time feed. The stains that seeped deep into the fibres wool had stained the bare floor beneath. Long years of spilled blood had left its disturbing mark. Just to leave you in no doubt, Nurse Howwell had passed the dinner Q with a silver rusting trolley, piled high with mouth gags n tongue forceps.

After grub was done n dusted we were shouted, well those that wanted it, for exercise. Inside the FABERON grounds, depending on the way they took you to the yard, you might come across the old black smith anvil. They still sometimes heated up the small furnaces and gave a demo on banging the hammers and tongs, making double leg sets of ball n chain or quick strikes across the broad plate shaping cuffs and screws for the thumb.

There stood nearby quite a beautiful stone grave.

IN MEMORY OF

BENJAMIN LINTON

BLACKSMITH

WHO DIED OCT 10 1842 AGED 80

HIS SLEDGE AND HAMMER

LIE RECLIN'D

HIS BELLOWS TOO HAVE

LOST THEIR WIND

HIS FIRES EXTICT

HIS FORGE DECAYED

HIS VICE ALL IN THE DUST

IS LAID

HIS COAL IS SPENT

HIS IRON GONE

HIS LAST NAIL'S DRIVEN

HIS WORK IS DONE

A former patient of the FABERON, who had been the former cuff n leg iron maker, making all the chains that held you strapped tight against the block walls. He had even made the large sheet metal sign as you entered the block with the cast iron words DESTORATION. Scot John again filling me in on our little trips down to breakfast, giving me the info when I'd asked, that it stood for, PLACE OF CHAINS. Inmates that helped around the institution were given decent burials, while the majority of the others just got a cross. And that was if you had behaved, for some had no marker to their poor lives at all.

Nestling into the solar splendour, my back melting into the yards wire fence I clocked the mesmeric footsteps. Round and round the mulberry bushes ripped out roots. The nameless man sat near me had his nose buried in an old tattered magazine. The sad title read **Stanlow Hall Home for Idiot Children.**

I notice Character staring intently at Gerard. I watched him for a while until he turned to distinctly look my way. His old Gharial teeth shining in the sun as he gave me a reassuring grin. The sky was empty of planes and clouds, yet I could feel another storm brewing. The holler from Gerard to get our arses back in broke the zoned out moment. The hour up before half of it gone, had the men walk robotic like back to the gate, tick with the pencil from Gerard to say you were back inside, a few eyeballs getting sneered at as they passed him, mine I felt for just that second longer than the rest.

A quiet to the ward, afternoon salad slave pickers busy out in the confined veg gardens. Gerard sensing the peace, destroys it with a shattering of his truncheon against the landing rails just to let you know your senses was always going to be in turmoil when he was around.

He sauntered off to the guards supply store to get what must have been his seventh baton this month. Getting back into my peter was a relief. An overwhelming sleepy feeling takes straight over as soon as I hit the bunk to try chill Thoughts about the plug hole beneath my bed, my last conscious thought. Sunday had soon come around. Sunday night around 9pm the line crackled to life.

"Yo Yo Yo Dj waX here listeners, if you missed last weekend's show then I'm afraid to say you missed a gem, but have no fear my dear listeners for tonight we have some great stuff lined up. Straight in with caller 1 on the line, you're live on the show caller the floor is yours". This breathless wheezy voice I hear next, the line quite faint so I press the headphones harder into my lobe.

"Kirby De Lanavolle here, I just wanted to call in n tell you I'm going against science!!"I heard the switch in voices again, Dj waX having a much deeper clearer tone, as he prompts the caller to tell more. "I'm a Breatharian" announces Kirby. An astonished "Come again" from the host.

"Yeah" wheezes Kirby, "I live on nothing but fresh air, I get all the nourishment I need from light, wind, and the vibrations of God."Dj waX hits straight back with an obvious question that if I could I would have asked Kirby myself. "Experts would say that man can at best go without food for 2 month before death would occur."Kirby now obviously enjoying the verbal sparring comes straight back into my head phones with, "anything can feed you if your energy centres are open. I do drink water but not daily."

"Well there you have it listeners," Dj waX' s voice had this incredulous tone to it, "Kirby son we must move on to other callers but thanks for that input, go grab yourself a nice light meal."

The line went dead from my point of view n I wondered looking around the cell just what the hell I'd stumbled upon. It certainly gave me a giggle, something that I'd not felt in a long time. I held my ears pressed tight n hoped more chat came through. The static seemed to buzz for a moment n then I heard the reassuring voice of Dj waX saying loud n clear.

"Ok listeners strap yourselves in we got caller 2 right on the line for you. Caller 2, the mikes all yours"

"Sausages, Sausages, Sausages, Sausages"!!!

I could hear some kind of friction in the back ground, not a fight but some kind of scuffle. Then another voice, female, came on the line. Dj waX in the mix as well now trying to make sense of the call, his voice laughing saying "you telling us what you want for breakfast mate"?, then the female finally getting a proper grip on the phone from her end.

"Ever so sorry about that, I told him not to call in to the show. It's my poor dear husband you see, he was badly struck by lightning at a family barbeque." I heard Dj waX start to say "how awful," when the lady cut back in on the line.

"He spent two days in hospital after a bolt struck a fork he was using to turn over some bangers. He's been in so much shock that all he keeps repeating is the word sausages I'm afraid. The doctors say it will have been like an implosion inside his body."

I heard the host again say without the hint of laughter he had first come across with, that he was "very sorry to hear this."

I couldn't help laugh to myself on the bunk though especially as she ended the call with telling all that it was so ironic because he was a vegetarian n had only been helping out under her moaning to enjoy the party n join in. You could hear the poor bloke in the back ground shouting, sausages, sausages, sausages, when Dj waX cut the line. The line crackled with its faint static n was gone. I kept the headphones on for the next half hour, continuously checking for old Walter creeping around the landing. But he never appeared n the line although a few times seemed to be about to crackle back into life, unfortunately the show never kicked back in and I heard no more that night. I hid my headphones n gave Winnie's wall a bang.

{THE ZIP chapter 59} He hadn't replied late last night. I'd banged a good few times on his wall. You had to be careful with the banging because it could sound like your were trying to break out n it also had a disturbing effect on some of the chronics, who would hear it n copy the noise, only they would just repeat it over n over until they were unlocked by the mufti squad n dragged away for a partial lobotomy. As I had been unlocked for breakfast, I had rushed to Winnie's door to tell him I had heard the show. I found him lounging on his cot with an old newspaper held up in front of him.

All I could see were his long grubby nails n the blazing red inked headlines. It was a copy of the obituary page that the pigs had found in the back of his shop, the large headlines stating

RICH FOLK RINGED FOR DIG!!!

I tapped the metal door n he scrunched the rag into a crinkled ball, probably embarrassed that I'd caught him reading about his own weird crimes. He flew up n out the cell, and we were soon on our way down the metal tier, chatting about the radio show and its odd guests, the rancid smells of breki floating in the disinfected air. Comcolit, an antidepressant preparation of lithium salts were available this morning. You could see the state of the ones that had been on regular doses of the stuff for years. Great big fatties wobbling down the line spilling these extra large jugs of water that they were allowed because of the side effects, the water fountain at the end of the landing had been guzzled dry on more than a few occasions, so the extra jugs had been introduced to keep things sweet on the ward.

The most disturbing thing about being out of your cell n on the Netherfield ward was the corroded wheel chair kept at the end of the corridor, blackened with age it had the imprint of some charred burned body stuck trapped in deathly time to it. When the lygactol got too much for some of the shufflers from the treatment rooms dispense hatch, Gerard with his piss take ways would sing, "When the lygactol kicks in, the wheelin will begin." He tried it in a quick rap like style that always sounded stupid.

Character had told me to ignore him the best I could and that he was from a long line of sadistic idiots who had served in the asylums. It transpired as a family tradition in this particular profession that had run for centuries. Character had said on that occasion that in the 18th century, outsiders would pay a penny to come and watch the patients as a form of entertainment.

The morning sailed away without notice, lunch a distant memory. The tray had gone out but I had been so drowsy with the morning meds I'd not drawn Qualco a face. Apart from the rusty silver trolley being brought to a squeaking halt outside my door after that, I remembered very little of the next few days. I did recall another new drug being spoke of as Gaunt hovered near my cell door clutching bulging bright files. Nurse Silk's beautiful angelic face helping the sting ease off quicker as the injection of Seronace had punctured into my skin n started its mad journey invading my decaying blood.

Lucky for us, Gerard hadn't been on this week. The bully had put in and taken his jollies, a respite that did us all the world of good, probably a lot more for us than him. He sent the usual sunny scenes postcard addressed to Dr Gaunt, who after showing a few of us in the day room that evening, the mention he had given us, stuck it with a red pin to the inmates notice board, which held very little info of use.

Dr Gaunt that particular evening had instructed the delivery of a large brown wooden TV for the day room. Which in itself was named absurdly for we only used it on an early evening. For unknown reasons a top loader video was carried in secure inside this old luggage suitcase. Gaunt got Nurse Howell to dispense some sweeties of the diazepam kind n we were given a film to watch before bed time. This odd black n white short film played out for about half an hour. The title had blazed up on the screen.

THE ZIP

Only the one actor in it, just some odd ball that had woke from bed and wandered into the bathroom and as he pulls the string chord to turn on this naked bulb, sees in the dirty mirror above this grotty sink, this massive zip running the entire length of his stomach in a horizontal zip fashion.

The back of the heads sat in front of me seemed more interesting at times. Eventually the guy built up the courage to pull the zipper down, to which the film ended with all the titles of producer n writer n lighting director flying out in some cheap three D style. The big old brown TV had its plug pulled, the video player was locked back in its suitcase n carted off to wherever they kept it and I found myself wondering again through the distorted drugs swirling my brain, just what the hell this mad house was all about.

{BACK STROKE chapter 60} *I think the zip film sent Dr Gaunt more crazy than usual. For the next night around midnight, he led the charge into my cell with a team of brutes from Wa/rd siX.*

In the hollows of my eyes, where the blackness had started to really show of late, they pushed the injections in at this point. Aiming the long needle upwards, it's piecing of my eyeball the last horror I remembered for a good few days.

When I eventually cleared my eyes enough to see, I realised I was on the block again. Like a hangover where the memories gradually filter back over a period, I laughed out loud thinking that I had come round from the eye ball injection and had been out of my cell a few mornings after, when what had brought me down to the block had occurred. I laughed again uncontrollably in the empty grey walls of the block cell, thinking back to Scot John making himself a kilt out of a pillow slip, using chalk from the dartboard to fashion his own tartan clans design. Then ripping it off in one yank, like a show off, whipping a table cloth from a well laid spread. Winnie like an idiot had mentioned rather loudly that it had been an English man who had invented it. A mistake on the magnitude of say walking into a mafia owned grocers and taking a large dump on the floor n mentioning as you pulled up your pants that it was a message for the cappo di tutti capi!!!!

I'd got crushed under foot in the ensuing commotion, not that I had joined in the kick off John had started making. But I remembered all the alarms ringing in my ears n being bundled to the ground for being near him. Later I learned no more than seven bones had been broken in the scuffles bringing us down to the block. All but two had been the guard's limbs snapping with Scot John's enormous rage.

The hardest thing in the world was, to deal with a time that hangs outside the clock, the wristwatch useless. A broken down time machine, staring inside its mechanisms, not knowing how it had transported me inside here, all the wires tangled, a brain unravelled by a science that wasn't studied. I doubted the Government cared. I'd seen enough white wash n red tape at the trial to believe they had any real answers as to why they let this happen. What the fuck was going

on in the modern world. Why do they keep fuckin up the innocent?
Little ease already confined me, became my room, my world. Alone
with four identical walls, Granddad Pedley's old chats coming back
filtering through in the silence of the dungeon. Like his old pit
tunnels full of danger. I would never forget when I'd mentioned once
some graffiti concerning the government n he had said in a very
serious tone.

"Guy was spot on blow the fuckers to smithereens"

My peter is dull except the faint firework colours under the
institutions boring grey wall. The table n chair of solid paper is
quality, smash able, cost effective. Outside the door it rests, minus
my stone cold numb arse. I can have it back in the darkening
evening. Piles for company, at least I'm not alone. The hung to death
ghosts are stirring. First an icy draft up and around my spine,
followed by a tight but not choking sensation round the throat. Some
of the block cells were the old hanging rooms of old.

The sealed trap door in the centre of the floor starts to gently rise up
an inch. Real late in the night the image of the hangman would
appear. Tape in hand, he would trail it slowly along the floor n tease
it all over my frightened stiff body. When he disappeared, usually
just on the point of a blood curdling shriek, small traces of sand
would be scattered around the cells floor. Floating slowly, dreamily
from the ceiling would be a bunch of white feathers, which upon
landing terrafirma would just vanish into thin air. The sand would
remain and by the time I got released from the block punishments, a
fair size pile of the stuff would have collected in one corner.

That was the last time I went to the block those last months of
summer. The darker nights were drawing in. It was earlier in the day
when the pad switched to a darker shade. Moonlit shadows, rows of
black steel, censor lights from the observation towers shining in
through the bars, highlighting the crudely scratched prison calendars
on the walls of this concrete tomb I inhabited. The birds flew up and
rested on the darkened emptied field's spotlight, the moonbeams
strong enough to outline the structure. The moon shining brighter

over the walls of the asylum, as if all the craziness gathered here powered it on in its intensity as it shone down on our cloudy pond.

They had tried to put me into the block again. Sometimes they went all official n shit, using the official set out protocol, instead of just dragging you down there. An extra shoe lace had been put in an evidence bag along with some left over spaghetti from Thursday's lunch. A breakout was being discussed in front of me I recalled. The three of us locked in Gaunt's office one morning. My clothes barely covering my body as they hung ripped where I had been violently dragged about during the search of my cell. Thankfully they had missed my hidden ear phones.

The absurdity of the allegation was very fitting for this lunatic asylum. It was as if they were determined to send you mad, if you were not already. This extra lace for my shoe had then vaulting me over the walls with ease. Dr Gaunt sat back lounging in his leather backed chair twiddling with it between his fingers. Its length no more than the spine of a mills n boon romance. Gerard moving into the scene with an extra shoe now and as if on Q a few extra bullies enter the fray from where Gaunt pressed this button on his desk phone requesting help. Extra special interest from the squad now it seems, like these trainers could aid an escape and bounce me over the walls and away like a, Tarzan stunt with the string like jungle vines, flying straight through these warped skies hollering my freedom cry.

I'd not gone up to Wa/rd siX, but this was mental war fare at its best. The warnings were intense. It was the not knowing what they were going to do to you down there that got to your already frayed nerves. The night n morning I'd seemed to just be focused on this matter. The drugs could just slaver you out into a long arse daze.

The sun beam had burnt into my neck until it had intensified with heat on the same spot enough to stir me out of day dreaming. I got on my chair n stuck my head as close to the bars as possible n protruded my tongue out to its full length, trying to catch a glimmer of the sun on its tip. I can feel the devil out there. He has come and lodged somewhere deep inside my brain and it's a pain so intense I can't avoid it with all my strength. A critical line on the screen where you view your fading life as it ebbs away.

Scot John on the other hand had ventured up to Wa/rd siX a good few times since. The most bizarre day I had remembered in here started early one morning. I had usually dreamt late in the evenings, yet depending on the breakfast doses of drugs, I had on occasion fallen into the ocean dreams early into day light hours, as was the case on this occasion. I heard the commotion but didn't let it register. The oceans were about to drop again to levels that they had kept secret from man.

I'd had one foot off the bed and didn't notice the regulation boot fill up with cold water. All part of the dream I believed. Yet out of the gloom a familiar voice."Otis, OTISS, we are going to have to move you cells for a while."My reluctant eye flickered open, just the one, which was enough to spot Gaunt hovering by my door.

"Why what's happening DR""Never mind what's happening, just get yourself together we will be back in two minutes for you"

Slosh n bang the sounds I hear as he departs. Only now did I realise the water moving steadily under my door and through the cracks in the wall wasn't from no dream. Large damp patches expanding on the walls. Both my boots now full of cold water.

Loud shouting I hear coming from the other side of my cell door.

"Just remove the towels John" Then I heard my own doors lock n bolts click n slide in to entry mode. On a small wave rode in Dr Gaunt yelling, "RIGHT KITES, GET A MARCH ON"

The landing was completely flooded, with the bizarre site of the hospital staff that was on duty carrying on their duties as normal. Only now they were in bright yellow inflatable canoes. As I was moved into the back of one of these life rafts, I sailed on a steady stream passed John's door, catching sight of him through his opened observation flap.

I knew what he had done. As he had mentioned it a few days ago as he had come over on exercise to say hello n tell me all about his latest book he was reading on Balzac. He must have sealed his cell windows and doors with toothpaste and soap along with ripped up shreds of towels mashed in. Blocked up the plug hole in his sink with wads of soggy paper and held the taps down on full with laggy bands or shoe laces. All these things he will have pilfered over time to pull this trick off. One of the reasons he had drawn me into conversation on the yard that day, asking if I had any spare laces.

The screws only noticed at the ten o clock checks. By that time the water was a couple of feet of the cell roof. The alarm had been raised as a nurse looked in, expecting to see Scot John as he usually would be at this time, laying on his bunk reading a heavy classic book.

What was seen was him singing away while back stroking casually up n down his cell. heard a few lines from the mull of Kintyre being gargled just before the guards, who had by this time had brought metal cutting machinery into the equation, ripped through the door n half drowned poor old Scot John in the remaining depths. I had been propelled along on the remaining tide that swept out of the cell as it had been penetrated. I didn't see him for a long while after that stunt. My new cell for the night was empty. All that water this time did send me into my dreams. The extra dose with a sharp stinging needle to the arse cheek probably helped too.

As I drifted off laid on the bare floor thinking of John being swept away to the chokey blocks, I quickly found myself whooshing down the continental shelf. The cell must have sprung a leak. My ears full of frothy sea bubbles. Yet I didn't stay under the waves long. Or so it seemed. It was the darkened evening that greeted me back into reality. The sea nymphs had been singing sailors lookouts, straight crashing them instead onto hidden rocks.

I'd watched from under the waves the broken vessels horizontal funeral slide majestically past me, losing its ghostly now silhouette as it went deeper than my vision allowed. I'd wanted to descend with the crashed wreck on towards its final destination, along with the other poor souls who now lived trapped in the seas deep grave yard. Spiralled lights were pulling me upwards; something pulled the plug on the ocean n I was back on the floor staring at the cell door. I knew that Gerard was back and on the night clocky job tonight. I could hear him now, as he had been trying to interrupt my brilliant dreams. TAP TAP, those bony knuckles of his rapping on the steel plate.

A stream of dim light from the corridor bored right into my pupil. As he opened the observation flap to now reveal himself, I spotted the black demon snarling n frothing at the mouth. Peeking in at me now, he thought all the power in the world was on his side of the door. The lurid walls seemed to come alive as he whispered his threats of violence n what he was going to do to me.

I shut my eyes again n held my breath a while listening to his mumblings until he got fed up n with a crack of his boot against the door indicating his boredom, he just crept back away into the shadows of the night.

{GYP THE BLOOD chapter 61} After all the water had dried up I was moved back to my own cell. It had taken a few days, yet the change was welcome because anything different in here was a bonus. The boredom was a real killA. Although there is a knife fight due in the morning, I'd heard the threats from out the window between too chronics. Along with a few other select inmates, it seemed I'd been left a ticket for the mid row seats.

It would have never materialised if old Walter had been on the night duty. He would have calmed the pair n got the necessary checks done for weapons. But with Gerard roaming the corridors the sadistic nature of him would have had him winding each individual up at their door, pouring on the pressure for them to slice each other up on exercise. Most bodies the next day would be checked with a pat down to the uniform before entering through the gates to the outside yard. Gerard on purpose letting the two inmates concerned slide past him without one.

Soon two crudely constructed blades were flashing n glinting in the sun light as the tussle got underway. In the arena of paranoia, I took refuge staying close to Character, as the boiling, stinging wonderful sun blinded for moments the action. There were a few slices of flesh before some crowd of inmates started screaming n I could see Gerard making a slow move from the steps to break it up. But before he got half way towards them, a fatal plunge into the younger inmate of the two's inner thigh had him hopping about for a split second before the sheer amount of blood loss covering the floor as it ran down his leg made him pass out. He was pronounced dead on the yard minutes later. The arrival of Dr Gaunt, confirming it as we trudged past, his shaking head of pitiful acting sorrow, cementing the fact that they didn't give a fuck. Back inside the building, Gerard's smirk aimed at a certain number of us as we went past him as we filed back to the cells spoke volumes. He was a real sadistic bastard n proud of it.

Without even realising how quickly time had dragged along, I heard the rumour of Characters next six moon killing. Mr Raw was the name I heard on the blowing wind from outside my barred cell window. He was a strange exotic looking creature. Well versed in the art of killing. Yet he loved cooking ever so slightly his victims flesh. It was rumoured on the Netherfield that he had made the grave mistake of letting his greedy eyes linger just that fraction too long on the slender neck of Character in the dinner Q.

A fatal mistake that now had his name floating around on the wind as bets were placed on the outcome. Mr Raw it seemed was now getting strongly placed by the gamblers amongst us. He was a dead cert for the six moon ritual killings.

Sometimes Character would throw the staff off his scent by talking in whispers to some of the other more, well regarded murderers on the ward. Gyp the blood never said much. Never really needed to once Gerard had let slip his extensive files.

He was the smallest killA amongst us, maybe only four foot n a half. But he had only really been measured up against the disused unclothed snooker table in the day room. His moustache that he waxed into hard points at each end was never out of place. Courtesy of the wax polish for the wards floor that he had his minions steal to keep on his right side. His left side could get rather bloody if you get my drift. Even among these complete psychopaths he was considered by most to be very dangerous. And after hooking up with Character that status was secure and very real. He never spoke to anyone else. The occasional nod he delivered in my direction. Yet I knew it was only forthcoming because Character liked me n knew about my case being a stitch up. Every so often you would catch Character n Gyps heads close together, no doubt whispering about the methods of killing and its pleasures. High on the agenda these last few days no doubt Mr Raw and his ever increasing chance of an untimely demise.

Nearly all the institutions around the country had tried to tame his six moon killin ritual. All had failed. He had originally only been sentenced to 6 moons for an uncharacteristic loss of restraint. Beating a known peado who had been released early n that in Characters mind had started showing signs of relapse. Being a close neighbour he had started keeping tabs on his early morning jaunts. The pretence of grabbing the morning paper, just too convenient as he passed a close by newsagent n headed to one further down the streets, close to a primary skool. Since the first case where the Judge had been sympathetic more towards the peado, giving Character 6 moons to cool off after the arrest for kicking the nonce right in the balls, he had not failed to murder.

The majority were nonces. Character telling me late one night through the darkened bars about his time he had bumped into another nonce hater. He mentioned a scary sounding place called monster mansion, an apparent nick name for Wakefield's gaol. The inmate mentioned went by the name BLUE.

I recalled that night after he had told me, as I drifted off to sleep on my bunk, guitar strings being hit beautifully clear. This was just before he had given Winnie the guitar. The haunting lyrics had given me BLUE's real name as Character sung about

"Ol Bobby Maudsley lives by me

Strangled one, maybe three

Ate out the brains

So forever he remains

Yeah ol Bobby Maudsley lives by me"

Something along those lines like that, as the drugs had been heavy on the brain that night as usual n I had drifted off to Characters hillbilly blues.

Bang on the day of his release he had murdered. I'd already seen with my own eyes his power. Yet he explained quietly one day that he needed to remain. For he had a higher purpose to serve n he was in the right spot. The mental institution had not been as kind on my nerves. It had taken its toll in manners by which at times made me feel uneasy within. The snap in my voice was more constant, even sometimes when talking to Nurse Silk's gentle face. Four walls can play a variety show with your fragile mind. The refreshment drinks of a lygactol cocktail or two would increase the weirdness of it all. I was surprised at times that they didn't stick a plastic straw n a nice slice of fruit in the little plastic beaker. I'd for example a few weeks back had a minor freak out. Down at the nurses' station, I was just being passed my meds through the hatch when I heard behind me, "drink up now Son" Fuck for a minute I had thought Stan was stood behind me. After summoning the courage to turn n face the voice, I just couldn't for a moment determine the difference between Gaunt stood there urging me to hurry up n move along the line n Stan. I swear I could see Da stood there dressed up in Gaunt's clothing, the thoughts that the sly bastard had crept right up on me in the hospital had freaked me out. I certainly didn't remember getting back from the nurse's station. My arms were badly bruised with pin holes though, where the brute guards had come from out of nowhere n made sure I was heavily restrained n knocked out cold.

It didn't take long for Mr Raw to join the illustrious list of six moon ritual victims. It had been crystal to see all week leading up to the eventual full moon, what was about to happen. The ethereal beams shone in through my bars late in the night. The deafening alarm bells not fitting with the chilled light of the moons ambience. All the real loons were screaming out of their cell windows. The night guard had called for backup, which was slow at this late hour to arrive. I'd pulled my body weight up to the bars to look down on the yard. The scene of poor old Walter with a face as pale as the moon high up in the cloudless sky behind him was horrific.

He had two severed arms, still flowing with a fair amount of blood held in both his shaking hands. I think with the darkness as he had reached the yard, he had without really knowing what they were, picked them up. The search lights had kicked in by the time I'd had a deek, making it obvious what he was holding. I felt sorry for old Walter as he was a gentle soul n didn't deserve to find such wicked surprises.

Gyp the blood was the first pulled into Gaunt's office the next morning. Again Character this time making the staff believe others may have really being the culprit. Even though deep down every one knew it was him.

It certainly didn't take long for the alarm bells to be blaring out all over the corridors again. Gyp the blood not taking too kindly to Gaunt's insinuations. You really had to see it to believe the strength of the man. To catch sight of him holding above his head a guard more than twice his own size was incredible. Hurling him into another group as they came running to rescue their colleague was something else as he scattered them all over the corridor as if they weighed zero.

But like any group of bullies with power tripping minds. They soon got the injections into his flailing legs n put him out cold. I had seen the day before from the yard high up on Characters cell window ledge a gathering of Ravens. They stayed there most of the exercise until it was nearly time to come in. As I was walking back towards the gate to re enter the ward, Character had come up behind me n said in a low tone. "Watch for the change" I was just about to reply, as to inquire what he meant when he said, " a group of Ravens is called a unkindness," just at that moment they made a almighty flapping noise with their wings n took off high above the walls n were gone. I was just about to say, did you make them leave, when I thought for a *second they were flying back over the walls, landing again upon Characters ledge. He patted me friendly on the shoulder n said "look again, closer." I strained my eyes to the group gathered up their wondering what the point was, when I realised I was now looking at a group of large crows. Character now with a steady chuckle saying right into my ear lobe, "they call that a murder."*

{NINE LIVES chapter 62} *It was only when I noticed the small group of men being led away after the breakfast Q with the resident priest, who they called stretch, that it dawned on me I was back round to the blessed day of rest. The Reverend's real name was Gully. The cons had given him the nickname stretch because he had given the last rites at so many hangings.*

Breakfast n lunch came n went without much thought. I'd spent the hours watching this butterfly n stupid fly. A strange mixture of Gods bizarre tastes. A bit like the difference between the poor demented souls he had trapped in here n the filthy rich super stars swanking around the world tasting its delights.

The butterfly had appeared on the back of my hand, landing gentle. It wasn't its first visit to my cell. When the moon had last been out, I had stared through nature's lamp light as it had flown gracefully through the middle of my bars.

Permanent fixture she had seemed, as I had laid still watching it, willing it to fly again. It seemed content staring in at my mundane existence, until just as my eyes were shutting heavy with dog tiredness she flew up n back out the gap. A palette of colours on her wings to impress even the great painting masters of old. This time Irish she had stayed longer, but after a brief flutter around the cell bars, her visit had been brief. What did remain was this annoying bastard fly.

The bars were there for it to fit through, but it just buzzed loudly around the room, crashing into the walls n then when it finally did reach the chance of going through the window it would hit the bars n sense freedom but just was too stupid to realise it was right there in front of it. Puking now on the bird shit which was caked on the deep ledges corners, it set off round n round the ceiling again, annoying my already troubled peace. Something as insignificant could snap your temper in here.

There was a change in my medication again at tea time and I didn't hear a peep from the ward till later that night until Winnie's thumping on the wall gave me the reminder to tune in.

The static sounds as I slipped the earphones over my ears was very jumpy, I was almost thinking nothing would come through this time when I heard the crackle n connection pass to a now familiar voice. Dj Wacks was full of life n I huddled down in to my chair and closed my eyes.

"YO YO YO Dj Wacks here, hope you fine listeners are ready for tonight's packed show?"He went straight in with caller 1 Quite a faint voice, it got me pressing the earphones tighter into my head to catch the tale. It sounded a bit tearful already. I listened in n heard a quite bizarre story.

This woman had one day been washing up at her kitchen window, which had looked out onto a quiet road. Her beloved pet cat had been on this piece of grass verge that separated the path from the roadside. So she's telling this tale n I am wondering where she's going when suddenly the tale grows ever so dark. She had seen this saloon car screech to a sudden halt outside. This tall gentleman, dressed as she described as someone fitting a sales mans attire, leapt out the car door, walked to the back of his vehicle n popped the boot. The woman at this point had gone from enjoying the calmness of a lovely sunny day outside, doing her chores n feeling content, to straining close to the window in astonishment as this chap lifted out of the trunk an hammer n proceed to batter to death her cat, which had been lying sleepily on the grass enjoying the warmth of the sun on its fur.

Before she had been able to react, the geezer had thrown the moggy in the boot of his car n sped off.

Dj Wacks chimes in "That is horrendous my dear, I do hope you got his number plate "To which the poor woman, sobbing even louder now says through the tears, that she had thank God. I listened into more, as the perspective from the car driver point of view was put across after the woman herself had got the full picture. It turned out that the guy, who was a car sales man had been after a long hard day at work, been driving at speed home. He had hit a cat in the road and being dreadfully sorry, had gotten out to see if it was dead. The cat lying still on the grass verge had looked to be shallow breathing, so he had done what he thought was the humane thing and put it out of its misery with the hammer, putting it into the boot, thinking he would bury it later that evening. He had told his wife over dinner what had happened, finishing his meal n preparing to go bury the cat at the bottom of his garden. But a loud knock had startled him!!

DJ Wacks jumping back in on the line at this point saying, "What happened next?"The line went a little fuzzy n I started thinking to myself how much I wanted to know what happened next too.

It turned out that the knock was two uniformed police officers, Standing there all serious n asking if he was Mr Farr. He had tried to explain n the police had taken some notes. He had showed them the cat in the boot, again explaining he was going to do the right thing n bury it. The police had realised there was some serious misunderstanding going on. After they had checked around his vehicle, they explained to him that a dead cat was stuck to his grill at the front.

The woman was really sobbing now as she explained the last bit. He had run over a cat, but not her cat that had just been lounging very still sunning itself on the grass verge. He in his rush n confusion had believed the one he had run over was the one he did the mercy killing on.

Dj Wacks interrupting her gently, wanting to know the outcome of the incident. She left the call telling us she hadn't pressed charges. For a moment sadness passed over me. Stan swarming my head with flash backs of his cruelty with animals. Dj Wacks snapping me out of it as his tone returned to normal as he shouted down the line."Ok you crazy bunch of frogs, let's see who we have waiting patiently on line 2."

A real weird voice come creeping next over the airwaves, it was as husky as our very own backi baron. "My partner just died"

"Who we got on the line here caller 2, floors all yours my friend"

"Hi, my names," There was this long pause of silence, making me actually think the show had abruptly ended.

Then caller 2 came back to life. "Would you mind me not saying my name?"DJ Wacks as benevolent as ever piping back in to say "no."

The tale began of another disturbing sad story. I was beginning to think maybe I should pull the plug myself, but the boredom kept me tuned. "It's my Brother I was calling in to talk about, he died recently n I have been feeling rather suicidal since."

I lent from the chair n took a cold sip of the evenings diesel, grimacing as I swallowed its sludgy texture down. There was a sound of cajoling from the host, encouraging the caller to press on to the juicy details of death that fascinates us all. The shocking parts kicked off with the revelation that his Bro had only been released a few years back from this very institution. Before my time, but I am sure a few of the others locked in would be thinking they knew the name he didn't want to give.

The second shock would have made it quite memorable even for in this doolally joint. I listened in as his sibling explained he had died after he had become obsessed with eating rubber gloves. He had not wanted to believe the coroners verdict of misadventure, believing the FABERON to be the catalyst for the problem. He had started the bizarre practise while in here, vomiting up latex gloves on a regular basis, swallowing them at every opportunity he could, so as not to be probed any more.

His Brother, bless him, muddled through the call the best he could, as I tried to keep up. The eventual death had come from him swallowing nine thrown away gloves from a medical bin as he had been on an out patients appointment at the time. His Brother now very vocal on the line stating, "the poor fool even ate the damn swabs as well."

The post mortem had found many more gloves in his gut and abnormally acidic blood. The coroner had gone on to mention that the reason for eating the gloves was cloudy to say the least. Dj Wacks was just in the middle of saying sorry to hear this caller, when you could hear the guy on the line clearly start blowing up a balloon. The host tried to bring him back on speaking but all I heard till his line died was the air filling n his breath heaving n then this almighty bang. The chomping sound wasn't the best news to finish the call with, but that good old D n A never fell far from the tree.

I heard Winnie even through the earphones bang my cell wall, but caller 3 was just being introduced so I ignored him for a moment.

"Yo Yo Yo, who we got now coming live over the FABERON FM airwaves?""Hi my names Peter and I just wanted to share with you all that I just got nicked in Pecs, Hungary."Go on" said the host. "Yeah I decked a cop with a 2 foot salami, AAAAARRRRGGGHHHHH"His shouting went on for over a minute until the line just spluttered out of life n was lost to the silence of the cells four walls.

{BEFORE WE RIDE TO ANCHOR IN BLANKET BAY chapter 63} As my eyes started to rapidly lose focus on the walls, the one eye shut heavy n I blinked the other a few times before I crashed out, drifting off in the hammock of the crescent moon. This time I didn't even notice me dropping through the oceans continental shelf. Seemed like another 300 metres when I encountered this blue whale, who gave me a look from his eye as I passed that sent a message to my brain saying, why can't I go any deeper?

I spun past in the currents, flipping from looking up at the retreating light to downwards towards the dark eerie unknown fathoms. 500 metres since losing sight of the whale and I lost my sight completely.

At this depth no sunlight penetrated. But this time I was going way beyond the last glints of sunlight.

I'd once read in a book Johnny had given me, all about the deepest man had ever ventured under the waves. In the 1960s Don Walsh & Jaques Piccard had managed somehow to travel down to nearly 11 thousand metres. They had only been 22 fathoms from reaching the very limit of the oceans depths, the Mariana trench.

I remembered quite clearly sitting on the raft n thinking of its not many metres of depth below me. Back then even that depth had seemed quite deep. The dream had me heavily under the waves, white translucent fish gathering around me, tickling the soles of my feet as they curiously wondered who I was in their isolated domain. I think what brought me back towards the surface was the crashing noise of the drugs trolley smashing into my cell door.

Pulled out of my skin with the ascent, I hurtled upwards smashing into this sun fish in the rush. It had been munching on a jelly fish as I crashed into its large side, bones flying everywhere from its impacted body. The dream not keeping me there to see much more as it spat me out and back into the frothy waves by the shore. A long thin green glassed bottle threw itself at my head on an incoming wave. I managed to fend off its blow with my arm, grabbing hold of its neck n wading back to this darkened cold beach to catch my breath.

I was awakening from the surrealism of the dream state, with the bolts starting to become real noises as my door was gearing up for unlock, but I was still in that weird space in your mind where the waking from deep sleep is still hazy, still unsure.

The bottle which I'd stabbed into the sand next to where I'd slumped down trying to regain my lost breath was drawing my attention again. In its sandy covered capsule I noticed a rolled up scroll inside.

The next bolt on my door being unlocked made a loud cracking sound. Instantly I smashed the bottles neck on a nearby boulder n quickly unfurled the parchment. In a very old writing style it read in heavy black ink.

OUR DREAMS COME FROM WATER

WATER HAS MEMORY

PAY ATTENTION WATER BEARER

The tide had become rougher as I'd taken my eyes away from its mesmerising waves. I didn't see the one rolling in that smashed me backwards onto my back, the bottle n scroll washing back out to the mysteries it had come from.

I was wet through on my bunk as Nurse Silk finished with the rigmarole of the bolts n keys n showed her pretty face at my opening peter door. She approached me gently with a rather large silver spoon full of thick red syrup. All my eyes could focus on were those beautiful parting pink lips as she told me it was something to help me sleep. Taractan was the word she delivered off her velvet tongue. I gulped down the liquid, trying my hardest to look seductive as my lips retracted from the spoon.

She smiled as I stripped every last drop from the utensil. The sticky liquid had gotten on her finger and as she turned away from me I caught her perfect profile lick n suck n clamp and I had to turn n face the bars n concentrate on the dull sky. The urge to rip her white starched uniform off n clamp my own mouth over what I knew would be her pink perfect erect nipples was getting intense. She sensed the frustration n left saying maybe I should splash my face with the cold water from my jug. Her last look through the spy hole as she locked the door n stood separated from me with inches of hard steel between us got me emptying the entire freezing jug straight over my entire bonce.

"YOU FUCKING BIBLIOCLAST" broke the horny feeling. Scot John's bellow familiar out the window, echoing around the exercise yards walls. I knew what it meant. He had on numerous occasions

filled me in on his own frustrations, which were not of the flesh, but of the missing pages of a book kind.

The culprit who John wanted to rip limb from limb, pulling out his spine, like the culprit did to some of John's treasured books was called Lexi. His real name was Leonard, Scot John giving him his nick name in here. John liked to think he was the Daddy when it came to literature. But lexicon had a bad habit of borrowing his quota of books from the library trolley that came around every month, ripping out the pages on certain important parts, which then when Scot John picked n swapped n ended up with them, all hell would break loose. Especially on a night after the swaps had been done. Lexi would tease John out the cell window, asking if he had got to page so n so yet. John screaming blue murder and yelling about ripping out his spine, as Lexi like a demented nut would just howl with laughter n you would see the pages he had ripped, set alight spiralling down from his bars lighting up the yard below. For a good hour after, all you would hear was John's raging threats and his constant screaming of, you FUCKIN BIBLIOCLAST.

{FABERON GROUNDS chapter 64} The familiar trips out onto the yard were a welcome relief at times to catch some good old fresh air.

But the route some of the yard guards could take, sometimes gave a very disturbing feeling before you got to sit with your back to the fence n dream up into the blue clear skies. Passing through the veg garden, you knew with habitual instinct that the next corner turned had you face to face with the FABERON'S grave yard. A very disturbing reminder, that making it over these walls back to freedom was a gamble that only the institution knew the outcome for certain. Most were unmarked, in sad rows the worn wood crosses lay bent at all angles where the years of weather had shaped them. Passing a section of souls who had obviously done something around the institute while there time here run out. I read a few as the guards halted to light some smokes between themselves.

HERE LIES

JAMES EARL

THE PUGILIST

WHO ON THE

11ᵀᴴ OF APRIL

GAVE IN

I had on this occasion heard of James, the brutes down the block mocking one of the times I'd been dragged down n gave a little resistance to the start of their beatings. I'd remembered them laughing to each other n saying who did I think I was, another James Earl? I had seen his childlike scratches of writing for myself on the block walls. A notorious block brawler who's obvious legend lived on. I nearly did a hop skip n a jump on the next one. Laid into the floor in a large stone slab, I hovered at its edges n looked down to read.

WHOEVER TREADETH ON THIS STONE

I PRAY YOU TREAD MOST NEATLY

FOR UNDERNEATH THIS SAME DO LIE

YOUR HONEST FRIEND

WILL WHEATLY

NOVEMBER 10 1683

Another laid into the ground as well read after Wills.

Underneath this humble stone

Sleeps a skull

Of name unknown

The guards were billowing smoke out their lungs now n setting back off, the ragged line of men behind them starting to move. I read the last one I caught site of before we turned off the track away from the cemetery. The guard at the front turned back to see who was picking up the slack. He clocked me reading at a glance the large upright black marble stone. "An escape attempt Otiss"

I got the gist. The large elaborate slab was there to mark as a warning. It wasn't there to represent a man's memory on earth.

HERE LIES LESTER MOORE

FOUR SLUGS FROM A 44

NO LESS NO MORE

The pink tinge on the horizon looked like smouldering red dabs from an artist's sponge on the palette sky. Vapour trails of fuel hung free in the air, where travellers oblivious to this torment below, happily jetted off to escape their frenzied lives.

Yard time was busy today. Quite a few members of our cloudy pond were out in force. I suppose the pull of the sunshine twisting the arms of the usual reluctant cell dwellers. The Amsterdam dealer was rushing around having rapid conversations with a fair few of the chronics. They didn't have much chance of escaping his lunacy. I could see him fiddling about with these little squares of cardboard, like a master of origami. One minute he would be strutting around the yards perimeter sorting out his fantasy deals, the next sat quietly sifting through the hard grounds dirt. In his own delusional mind he was cutting n sifting the finest opium powder in all of Asia.

It was painful to watch really as his madness not for one minute hiding the reality of it just being fine gravel. Yet he would carry on trying to blag the chronic in his sights that day into a once in a life time deal. He tried me only the once that day. Looking up at his outlined body as the sun blinded me for a moment. The reflection back, my shamrock coloured hard eye staring through him, making him soon pass on to easier blags n sales.

He did have one little mate who lived in his little fantasy world alongside him. Hoover was his name, for obvious reasons. The Amsterdam dealer's confidante, who as the experimentalist for new concoctions spent a great deal more time down the infirmary than up on the Netherfield ward. The Amsterdam dealer had never been a dealer on the outside either. They were ordinary looking, most even seemed genuinely harmless. I watched him set off around the yard again with the fresh wraps he had just made up, like a weary salesman who had pounded the streets all day with no joy, he would suddenly slump n start digging in the dirt again. I'd seen Gerard the wanker wind him up on occasions, with today being no exception.

With a big show telling the dam man in front of all the inmates that he would take his entire stock. The poor bastard would make his way to the wing phone to put in a call to his supplier. Dangling aimlessly the chord to the outside world none of his concern, as he chatted loudly to his man in Cuba. Back fired was the word bandied about the yard though today.

Four bloodied ears were recovered from the in house post box. Not that the post you tried to send went any further than the bin. The art class the evening before had a tad naively turned its attention to Van Gogh n Gauguin. Rumours of madness had been discussed after the brushes and paints had been locked away.

This had resulted in behaviour throughout the night on the wing that can only be described as sheer raving lunacy. But of course our very own bull goose loony Scot John had out done the ones who had sliced off their own ears in salute to the great painting masters.

John had managed to grip one of the child killers on the walk back from the art therapy class. Cutting of his nose n lips for starters with a swiped craft knife and gluing the ears he had hacked off to the wing phone with a stolen prixstick. The later only discovered as the dam dealer finally realised what he had his own ear stuck against, commencing to scream down the entire hall, making even the medication hatch window crack in the din.

On the out, he had overdosed a whole street of college yuppies. Blaggin his deadly wares onto the unsuspecting misadventures of miss spent youth. Thirty three fatal overdoses had seen him quickly locked up n it didn't take long for the police to realise they were dealing with a total fantasists with a penchant for murder.

When he had tried poisoning the entire court room with powders he was slying into the court room carafes of water.

The judge quickly dispensed of his case n sent the nutter here. Character told me that he had been in for around 17 years up to now. And he was still trying to deal his supplies to any one that would listen.

As I got back laid on my bunk after getting in from yard time, I heard the block screws coming to collect John. There seemed to be a peaceful agreement between both parties on this occasion, as I heard no fighting n just his calm sing song whistle fade as they walked him off the ward. There no doubt would be another emergency meeting called to discuss his inner explosive disorder.

Slid into the corner of my cell wall by the door I noticed a postcard lying there waiting to be read. I recognised Johnny's writing.

When I scooped it up I realised with delight there was two postcards for me. The first was from India. It's strange exotic stamp holding my eyes attention for a minute until I drifted into the blue inks message. Johnny had contacted Liberty, but the news wasn't good.

He went on to say that he felt there were restrictions being put onto my case, which were hampering any real chance of appeal. He,

Johnny felt that while Liberty wanted to help, the overall feeling he had got from a visit to his chambers was apprehension to get back involved. He passed on the message from Liberty that I was in his thoughts n that I should keep my chin up, but that was all. The space to write more running out with Johnny signing off saying he would send another card in a few days as he was travelling on. The second post card was full of free space. Its stamp clearly stating it had been fed into a post box in Sri Lanka.

All it said it larger written strokes was,

BOUGHT A GREAT SEA VESSEL

I'VE CALLED IT LADY NAP!!

I was genuinely happy for my one true friend, but I couldn't stop the tears as I laid back on my hard base n starred up through the bars at my nemesis, freedom. Why couldn't I be out there on the open seas, sailing with my best friend?

{EXECUTION LOTTERY chapter 65} *I'd mention birthday's n Christmas n all that celebratory stuff in detail. Yet in here it was tinged with a sadness that should not be attempted by writers.*

I cried n filled my jug the first Christmas that passed in here.

Some of the inmate's I'd gotten close to tried to rally round n cheer up the atmosphere. Even psychopathic killers and the most warped minded of men liked a bit of festive cheer. But these special days passed much the same as the others.

A couple of Quality Street sweets appeared on a line from a random loon who had scoffed all his favourites n sent me the coffee flavoured ones. But the gesture was immense in the reality of the dismal situation. Four boring walls to slaver against n the random acts of the insane to break up the long glue clock days were the agenda. The troubling rumour for most around Christmas Eve was the whispers of the execution lottery.

I wasn't sleeping much that night any way. Above my cell, late at night, dull knife was at it again. I could hear him scraping the odd tools on his floor that he pinched from around the place. They would be confiscated off him in the morning anyway. But that didn't stop his routine. It wasn't like he tried to hide them any way. On this occasion he had gotten his hands on a long piece of metal, like an Ariel. It was Character who had named him.

For even though we were considered loons on our ward, the 1800s committee had decided in their infinite wisdom to allow the usage of metal cutlery when we dined on occasion in the great hall.

Luckily they had realised the missing steak knives that were laid on the directors table were gone n in his possession. Removing them from dull knifes arse where he had carefully wrapped them in cloth n plugged them down the infirmary, before he got any real chance to carve someone up proper. I could hear now above his maniac hands steadily wearing away the floor, trying to shape a satisfactory killing tool.

Scrape, scrape, scrape scrape.

The exertion on the hard floor would be accompanied by a brief pause every few minutes from him. The best one I recalled from his collection had been when he had turned Winnie's stolen Tv glasses into a bladed knuckle ring.

Old Walter the night guard had slid a newspaper a few months back under my door late one night. I'd soon read all about who my new neighbour above was.

On the outside, nr the out skirts of London it had been reported in this news flash on TV of his sudden arrest. The unusual weapon tucked into his waistband had dominated the story. A scarce 6 shot 7mm apache weapon had been removed by armed police, who had pointed about ten guns at his head while he was strip searched on the pavement. The newspaper made it clear as I'd read on, about the said blade having notable wear n tear.

More bodies had been found later. Mutilated beyond recognition, yet revealed by dental records in the autopsies that followed to be the missing persons.

He targeted the homeless, the young runaways who had headed towards the bright lights looking to fill their hollow existences. Filling them instead with holes where he had frenziedly stabbed them in his murderous lust. Instead of bothering me, his monotonous scraping lulled me to sleep. For the rest of the majority of the ward, they were all up worrying about their lotto ticket.

The official line was that if you won, you got a move off the Netherfield and onto a much more relaxed wing in a better part of the hospital. You were told in Gaunt's morning meetings in December that while the Netherfield was a good ward, with the experimentation of psychiatric practises a good thing all round. The lotto winner would benefit even more greatly by moving to what Gaunt called the Aspen lounge ward. Most believed him. A few didn't.

When I wake, I can feel all the cities awaken with me. The fresh coffees served in Paris squares. The Caribbean mans long dreads splashing in the salty bluesy green surf as he wakes the sleep from his eyes. Indian Christians, rising early for thanks and prayers. Then back to the grey rain of the British shores. Ireland close by waking with a show of Emerald beams of sunlight. My bars are frozen like stalagmite formations.

The day dreaming is soon lost to the racket coming from the wing coming to life, Gerard at the end of the wing near the medication hatch, his irritating voice shouting repeatedly this number. I see as I'm making my way down the stairs sniffing the rancid smells of cheap bacon, many men checking their little scraps of paper. The lotto had been called. Luckily I was no winner. And it took the full day to find out who had won.

The reason becoming clear later in the evening when the Dam dealer had his pad searched after supper. He had used his ticket to wrap a gram or two of white powder. It was only flour that one of his customers nicked for him from down the large kitchens, telling them he needed to cut his gear with it being so potent. But his lucky ticket had been stashed in his turn ups on his work dungarees, n had taken a while to find n confirm against the one drawn out of the black cloth bag that morning by a staff member.

The next morning some official looking gentlemen were buzzed onto the ward accompanied by Gaunt, they did a bit of a tour around the Netherfield's facilities before disappearing for ages inside the Dam dealer's cell. His belongings were removed by a smirking Gerard that dinner time and later still in the evening when we had all been told to wait in the Tv lounge, they brought him in to say cheerio.

Oblivious to the rumours, he made a big play of trying to slide on the quiet to a few of us some of his wares."The best, most pure you will ever find my chico"

His leaning over whispers to me as he slid a paper package into the side arm of the chair I was lounging in, my last dealings with the man. At the door he shouted to Winnie, "adios amigo", and he was away n marched quite quickly off the ward. For good measure he made a lunge for the wings phone, its dangling chord to nowhere still irrelevant to his madness. They soon yanked him away and as I watched from the doorway of the lounge door, my eyes with a cold shiver up my spine, focused in on its mesmerising swinging motion back to stillness.

Character who never came down to mingle on evening association whistled through the side of his door as I came back up the stairs to bang up. At his door, I looked through the flap. He was standing bolt upright, an impressive 6 foot 3 at least. His eyes were looking directly at me, centred on the flap. He put his long bony index finger up to the left side of his neck just under his ear n drew it across his throat to just below the ear on the right.

I couldn't help become fearful for a moment, wondering if he had fallen out with me. But it wasn't a threat. It was an omen of what had just taken place over the last few days.

I didn't dream that night. I did lay awake fighting the medications pull towards darkness for a while though. Characters strange gesture was a permanent fixture as I fell away eventually from the lygactol shuffling around my cell to the final heavy slump into somewhere I thought the beds direction was located.

In the morning I woke stiffly, my back feeling in half. I'd missed the bed completely, zonking out on the hard wood floor. Stretching as I went through the motions of hearing the screams for breki n men moving about, I came out of my peter door n straight into the mountain that was Scot John. I was surprised to see him so soon because of the violence he had shown again with the ear slicing incident. But he quickly dismissed it as trivia when I inquired, saying it was only a nonce n even the block screws despised the dirty bastards.

"Death by hanging produced by asphyxia suspending respiration by compressing the larynx by apoplexy pressing upon the veins and preventing return of blood from the head by fracture of the cervical vertebrae." That was quite a mouthful at 7am after kipping on the floor all night drugged out of your mind, but there we had it. "I've not had a library book on medicine or anatomy for over two years young Otis." He was proud of his memory n the things he had read over many years alone in his cell at night.

That was my second omen that not was all it seemed on the lotto Christmas draw. I'd already a few months back asked Character in private about our ward. Was it like the others? Why were they doing some of the things to us they did. Did it go on in other parts of the hospital? That sort of thing, to which he had answered as best he could, without disturbing my already fragile mind, that we were like some kind of un official guinea pig ward. An experiment using the mad, but it was more sinister than that. There were other things they were using the ward patients for.

He had stopped himself from elaborating more. Watch for the signs were his parting words of wisdom that day. They were becoming clearer in my mind, forming a quite disturbing chilling picture. The cloudy pond was starting to look like a deep cesspit of murky horrors.

{GERARD'S BUGGIN chapter 66} *Nurse Fluxatine hovered around a very sleepy looking Dr Gaunt, who leaning on the doorframe near the exercise yards door looked to be just about holding himself up on his feet. He was scratching at his short wispy beard which was in need of a good trim to hide its grey.*

The exertion no doubt from leading the Dam Dealer off the Netherfield had clearly drained the old fool. He clocks me looking at him and his eyes instantly regain some vigour, boring a hole through my retina with his fixed senile stare. It's a stare that disturbs your mind. All I can do is push on n try keep sane.

He's now collared Nurse Silk, bending into her delicate ear, rambling on about how he needs more staff on a night and something about a new order of equipment going missing from the stores. The distant alarms from another part of the hospital go off. Ever so faint you can just hear them. Gaunt's ears pricking up n he's away down the corridor fiddling with his large bunch of keys that he keeps on a chain which annoyingly jangles from his belt. He hasn't been here that long but he hits the gate with the selected key n is through the other side and on his way to the incident as if the gate didn't exist.

Gerard as if on Q, now besides me, ready to start his bullshit. He shadowed me back up the metal stairs as I carried my breakfast tray back to my cell. Its meagre contents soon scattered messily all over the front of my door as I'd nudged it open with my knee trying to enter. His shove into my shoulder blades crushing me into a tangled mess.

He bugged me the entire morning, tapping on my door, staring through the flap not saying a word, just trying to disturb me. He reminded a little of Stan with his pathetic ways. But the one thing he didn't know about me was how I'd learned to live under Stanley's roof. I think that's why he hounded me continuously because I didn't bite as easy as say the Winnies on the ward.

He had been on the Apleton's rum again, the fumes on the light wind sending its spicy smells swirling round my cell. He was back at the corner of the door, whispering through its slits. Always the same threats about did I think I could kill a man. The reference to my Mothers demise hard to keep from setting me off with anger n tears, but I held my own n didn't give him the victory he wanted.

I would pull the itchy green blankets over my head, pretending he wasn't there, hoping that he would bore with not seeing my face n disappear along the tier to bug someone else, but when I pulled my head out to look he would be right there. His patience was growing stronger.

Evening felt unobtainable. I was hoping he was not on tonight's shift, but I'd lost track of who had been on n off. The glue clock seemed in motion tonight, with the slave clocks doing its bidding.

He continued his harassment throughout the day n early evening and as I banged up after supper I prayed inside my head that he was gone for the night. But I was never that lucky.

After the night time games of tapping n flicking about with my lights, Gerard finally got to the point. He opened the cage door, strode to my bunk, carrying with him his pungent smell. A mix of decaying hospital walls, hanging inside his uniform n the cheap grog he swigged blatantly on duty, although behind Gaunt's back for fear of pushing it too far. Grabbing me hard now so that the skin on my chest tangled with my pyjama shirts fibres he yanked me to my feet. He glared at me and I hoped at this point it would just penetrate through my fizog n blind me to his demon plans. But I had to settle instead for just staring back into his watery eyes, trying my best in the panicked moment to gain some insight into what swam in them. The only thing I could say for sure was that it was something very murky n disturbing.

A stand of ensued, for what seemed ages, for he still had to follow some of the FABERON'S policies. Strangulation I was concerned about, his grip now moving past regulation as my mind started blacking out to the point where a grave, untidy, like life, wilted into familiar surroundings.

A loosening of valves as air crept back into the throat, my vision returning a little. Gerard snarling me a grin filled with fried chicken skin wedged in upper teeth. His breath bad enough to hope his hand would pressure my neck again.

Slompin to the wall in a dizzy after effect, I just manage to keep my balance holding onto the bunk bed. Noises from afar I hear, moribund for sure this time, realising from some distance place that now others had joined in the wicked fun. To help me was not their concern, for I knew with the likes of black pudding they could cover over their murderous mistakes.

My eyes burning, hazy stinging vision all I had now. Blinking out rapidly a stream of tears I see Gerard up by the door. He's watching, sweating, this new crowd already starting to concoct oral tracks to cover over their bullying rass clot act.

The liquid cosh being called for, the last bit of info I hear before I feel no more pain for a while. Maybe this time, it was my time to die?

A week or two passed and the only thing that registered deep was the noticeable fresh mound of soil in the grave yard. Gossip as usual from the front of the crowd as we walked one day to exercise, its filtering to the slackers like me at the back soon digested.

The mound looked about the same length of the dam dealer!!!

The big give away was Gerard throwing some tic tacs onto the soil, with the sly comment of deal them you freak, making worrying thoughts as to just where this lotto win took you. But like most things in here, time just forgot, seemingly swallowing whole segments of your life span n just erased the memory.

Today from my starting point of looking, after waking n stretching up for a glimpse through the bars at freedom, the sky seemed split. A distant blue with poking bursts of light pink shining through a few punch clouds directly above their sub metal shapes holding back for now the drizzle of rain.

I had not been so low for a while. Gerard as much as I liked to not admit had started getting to me. The strangulation that night had not been an isolated incident and I was now more apprehensive when falling unconscious to dream. The black demon had been my waking nightmare a fair few times this last week. My usual awakenings now always accompanied with this strange foreboding sweat that clung to every pore of my body.

There had been quite a fuss this morning. Dr Gaunt huddled over near the comfy staff seats with what reminded me of a man who looked dressed similar to mums undertaker. It turned out by lunch the strange suited man was an outside detective, here to discuss a terrible mistake.

A month or so back, one of the long term block patients had been released on compassionate grounds. He had been a friend of Scot John's, but had not handled wing life very well n had spent many years straight down the block in long solitary periods. John had said when he had heard of his friend's release that the guy only had about two more years left before the institution had to automatically release him. The original full term sentence completed.

Now the FABERON'S infirmary wasn't exactly known for dispensing out royal treatment. Tests had been done, swabs taken, bloods retrieved. The outlook had been fatal. A diagnosis with a morbid outlook it seemed. Tests that should have been carried out n samples that should have been sent out to specialist clinics not adhered to.

Misdiagnosed with a deadly disease, he had been quietly let out the front gates n told to go enjoy the few weeks at most he had remaining!!!

Now unknown to the team of shrinks who in here try to probe right through your skull with questions at every opportunity they get. He had very quietly sat n festered an idea of revenge managing to keep it away from the scribbles on the shrinks clip boards n pads. Scot John didn't elaborate on his crimes. But fifteen years in here with two to go gave you a decent idea of the severity.

Now what had caused all the fuss this lunch time, n had Gaunt in meetings all day since his arrival from the big house, was this.

The man, whom remained nameless, had only gone back to his city n murdered the man who had put him away as a crucial witness in his initial case. The irony being that if he had served his full term, those final easy two years, he was determined to put the past to bed n move away for a fresh start. The release on compassionate grounds gave him an entirely different agenda.

But here came the kick in the face that only the likes of this bastard institution could deliver. He was back this morning, sat in the familiarity of his block cell. Tests upon arrest, to check through his palliative care package had revealed he was fine. No sign of any deadly disease.

His fresh trial for murder had been set for in a few month n it looked now highly likely that his soul would rot away its final years under the big crazy roof of the FABERON institute for the criminally insane.

{SPIRITS EVERYWHERE chapter 67} Siberian snow came and wrapped itself around our now frozen cloudy pond. It seemed along with the heavy meds to just freeze over the thoughts for a while, giving a new world of hope to the dismal place. Everything seemed clean n new, without the hated antiseptic stink to the joint.

I'd managed to corner Character again n try prise some more info out of him about the goings on inside this crazy place. .He had stood *quietly for a moment on the corridor, the staff busy with the million demands from the chronics before bang up again.*

Character wore around his neck this little cloth bag, tied secure with this red leather lace. He was fingering the bag as he opened up to me. "Young Otis, this is no game, where we live right now is a very dangerous place indeed. Not above board one bit. It took me a while after living here to figure out that what was happening on the Netherfield wasn't the norm on most wings, and certainly not the agenda of most institutions. It's funded by a special group of men, made up of Broadmoor, Rampton, Ashfield, Stanley royd, X hospital directors.

Old bastards Otiss who are protected by the people who control the Government you see. They know I know Otiss. But I'm luckily a very different species to the ones there use to subduing."

I listened, watching him twiddle with this bag more n more as he explained a few more things. I came away n banged up knowing three clear facts. A private part of the mental hospital was where I for some strange reasons resided, where olden day treatments seemed to be the norm.

The second conclusion this lotto was no lucky win or an escape to an easier ward. It seemed pretty clear from the hints he had issued in our chat that they were hanging inmates as experiments. Something to do with the fact that in Government they were actually thinking of re instating hanging in prisons for certain crimes. The practise in the FABERON to make sure things started off with swift precision when the bill passed in the commons.

And thirdly but by no means the least, what he had hanging around his neck in that cloth bag was called something that he referred to as,' THE LITTLE SMOKE'.

Back in my peter I wondered about this private sector that funded the Netherfield. Our dead eyes were all part of the plan. The outside knew nothing of what was being played out inside these high walls.

*I'd imagined rather naively upon my own arrival here that I would
be led into the safety of a hot shower, fresh clobber, a warm meal n a
handful of valium to ease me into the first nights ordeal.*

*Never in a million years did I think I would go the other route down
a dingy screaming hell hole of a corridor. Ripped off clothes, nearly
drowned to death in an ice cold bath. Straight jacket on n threats of
being kept in its clutches for the next ten years, and an injection up
the arse that sent me to the moon n back.*

Not really the welcome I had in mind.

There were plenty of other things to focus on in here though.

Positive Ed had made a spooky return to the ward.

*He had been one of the first exchange patient's swapped for a British
serial killer with the yanks. The Directors liked the rarity of a foreign
subject in their establishments, as it was something exotic to show off
to visiting guests.*

*While I had been here, Ed had always been flying through plate glass
windows or trying to scale up on to the roof, not to escape, more just
to throw himself to his death. I had to laugh when I remembered him
breaking this large heavy chair over some poor sods back.*

*He had been dragged away to the punishment cells screaming n
crying, apologising over n over saying he thought it was balsa wood.
We had nick named him Spyk because he had this piece of metal stuck
in him that was too dangerous to be removed with surgery.*

*The most bizarre I recalled was when he had dived head first through
the wooden canteen door, looking for matches to set himself ablaze.
The only thing he had on his wall in his cell was the iconic pink
Floyd poster showing the stunt man in the studio parking lot on fire.
There was a very strong smell of gasoline near to where his old cell
had been, and every time any of the patients had tried to strike a
match to light a cig around the ward, it had blown out these last few
days. Tensions were high with the smokers, who were doing their*

nuts trying to get a fix from their tabs. And the Baci baron had started to make threats that no one was buying fresh burn!! He had sent out danger mouse with a full box of matches trying to help them get lit n burn their supplies.

But Ed just kept popping up n blowing shit out.

{BAD SEED chapter 68} *Winnie I had seen this last week setting off every evening after bang up. He had been accepted on to this ancestry course which was run by a local man who came into the institution. Gaunt even though a sadistic, had allowed a few of Dr Woo's policies to remain after his departure.*

And old Winnie had been busy. It had only been on the last day of the week he had been down there that he banged my cell wall n I instinctively now went n emptied the pipes to chat in private.

I didn't dare to dream that I could be shocked any further in my life than I already had been, but Winnie had news for me that shattered n split deep lines of pain right into my very soul. I had while chatting over the time I had known him revealed little bits more of my life, like we all did with the ones we considered friends. I didn't think he would have remembered it all.

Researching away, he had not been too concerned about his own past. Instead the inmates he cared for had been his fascination.

He had found out n told me firstly about Scott John's last name actually being Goose. Our very own bull goose loony was by nature just that. Interesting enough, Winnie seemed very adept at research. Maybe the poor soul had missed his calling in life. A Royal court fool, a man who had entertained the great king Henry the eighth multiplied his seed forward enough to give Scot John his dnA.

Winnie said quietly down the pipes that we had better keep that to ourselves, for our own safety, as calling John a fool was playing with your life.

He was already a poetaster, if he knew he descended from a line of court jesters he would rip limbs off. They always say don't shoot the messenger but on this occasion the saying would mean jack shit. And I had already lost a digit, so didn't fancy loosing anything else, like an arm or leg.

He mentioned a long line of crumb merchants, but I didn't really understand. I think throughout the info his meds kicked in heavy n he lost the thread of what he was trying to say.

We flushed n broke the connection as the late night supper came round.

I got myself a beaker of diesel at the cell door and heard Winnie do the same. About ten minutes later I had banged his wall n we were soon back at the pipes learning very strange things, or I certainly was.

Winnie's loosened tongue now took me right back to the village, recalling my late Mother mentioning the celebrated hanging that had taken place. The killer who had roamed the streets smearing bloody hand prints all over the doors of his victims had come back to haunt me.

It was an urban legend and I couldn't quite remember the year she had said it had happened. I knew it was a long time ago. But what Winnie had worked out was about to blow my mind.

Souls mixing together were nothing new. I had heard old Dolly Blue on many occasions talking about the afterlife and reincarnation before. How the fresh dead would hang about in limbo land waiting to penetrate a new born.

Some did and this is where you got in your own life those weird feelings every now n again of déjà vu. The dark cellar world of Stan must have come from somewhere. Traits in the dnA that were fixed solid, no matter what your own mapped out path of life dictated. We all had them, those urges n out of character moments. Were they really the real us?

As my brew went clap cold on the side I was acquainted with some powerful home truths. I already knew from my skool years that Mischief night on the 4th November was in memory of Guy Fawkes preparing to blow up the houses of parliament. On that night he had been mischievously moving the gun powder into place when he was caught. I realised then in a long time that I was locked up here near York, his birth place. Such a shame those 36 barrels didn't ignite.

Winnie's creepy sounding voice came up through the toilet bowl n gave me more. "Your Grandfather Otis, Stan's Dad, was the hung killA from your village. Your Father, as I have worked out the dates n it fits, was born on the day of his own Dads execution.

It seems from working out where your Grandmother was located, that she moved away from Gallowthorpe, bringing Stan up away from the gossip n stigma. But on other records I found her to be deceased at an early age from what appears to have been a mystery fever, leaving your Dad an orphan at 16.From other records I can see where he moved back to Gallowthorpe around this time n a not long after met and married your Mother."

I thanked Winnie n flushed closed the connection.

Wow, what had I just learned? The cot bed looked so inviting n I slumped heavily onto its lumpy springs n tried to get my head round the news I had just heard. Winnie had said he had some print outs to show me, headlines from way back to confirm his findings to me. I really didn't want to know right now, curling myself foetal into the walls of the mad house n drifting off, thankful at this moment in time for the medication concoctions strength.

I'd plucked up the courage a few days later to read the little green folder Winnie gave me the day after he had told me through the pipes about my family history. Stan's mum, my Grandma, who I had never known, had gone into labour with breaking waters right at the exact time her husband's neck had snapped on the scaffold for his horrendous crimes.

The photo copied headlines I now held in my hands stared back at me as I looked at the large black text

MURDEROUS MISCHIEF NIGHT CHILD BORN WITH TERRIBLE BURDEN AROUND ITS NECK.

But like a lot of shocking headlines, in a village it was tomorrow's fish n chip wrapping paper. It made perfect sense now the reason old Stanley liked to keep up his respectable front in the village. For a split second I almost felt sorry for the poor orphaned bastard, but that feeling soon vanished.

Being dealt a shit hand does not give you the right to carry on in the same vein. I hated him to the core, and would take my revenge if I ever made it back to the village.

{SILVER ACORN chapter 69} *A crowd tip toe past my door. Protected species that move guarded n tense.*

The one we know to be doing 40 life sentences back to back gets the majority of the abuse. We all chorus chant "dirt" as he passes every door, some spit gets through the cracks n as he passes mine I see through the spy flap the dirty bastard licking his lips.

Strange the pecking order status we confuse our cloudy ponds world with. But I am the real rare specimen. Innocenti.

They had eased off me on the early mornings with the freezing bath wake up near drowning. A patient who was on the same rota as me who had been suffering from dissocial personality disorder, which had seen him at a high risk of self harm had been drowned dead by the brutes down in the clinical tub rooms.

Life in here had just chugged along. The glue clocks had been freshly filled and an eternity it seemed of staring into the walls had begun. When I received a slip of paper under my door telling me I was about to have a visit, it seemed to take me a few days staring at it to register the date. Nearly 9 months had passed since the Dam dealer had gone to sort a major shipment with the devil.

I knew my medication had increased dramatically after Winnie had revealed my family tree's not so coincidental horrors. There had been a few melt downs, where the heavily filled needles had finally brought me under control. The doses at bed time increased. And I had stopped fighting the urge to stay on my feet n just instead let the sinking feeling wash over me. There was good news though from reading the official memo that had been slid under my cell door. My one true friend was visiting. Good old Johnny Sand.

Down the block, the cosh had me singing for them to stop. A large empty medicine bottle gets swung. That whooshing sound through the air in my ear before it breaks, tearing into the now blood sticky hair on the side of my head.

Such a sad joke this conviction to deal with in the first place. Always taking my mind straight back to the memories of Stan. In my mind, his horrible words that spat out of his vile mouth return, spinning in neon coloured lights out of the unconsciousness blackness, thankful that under the pressure of heavy waves I wipe them out.

I wondered if I had it in me to kill. Coldly though!! Not sneaky poisons or gutless bullets, real cold steel right up to the hilt. Thrust that bastard Stan straight to Hell. My crime maintaining mapped out fate. We would meet again n I would murder him slowly. The devil my corner man, egging me on to shove Stan's face deep into the flames n laugh as it melted away.

But for now the fog must lift. My first revelation not good as I come round, face down in a pool of my own sick. Snorting up porridge bubbles, my neck stiff n probably minor fractured where over a hundred stones of bully pressure have been kindly applied. The faceless thugs of Wa/rd siX squashing my body into shapes that dared to compromise anatomy. The room, cell, box, call it what you like, remains empty. The door painted the same colour to make you feel the presence of the continuous claustrophobic air where you can't make out the seals.

{CHAMBER OF DEAD ECHOES chapter 70} *They held me down the block a good chunk of time before letting my visit commence. A brain washing operation put into place to make sure I didn't reveal too much of the FABERONS strange goings on.*

I'd had the real giggles the last few days for some unknown reasons. Maybe the trial drugs they were dishing out down here giving off side effects that didn't really fit the depressing situation.

Scot John's quotes coming into my mind. One of his favourites that I had liked n memorised churned over in my mind when my face stopped laughing up at the ceiling enough to think straight.

'Laughter is the primeval attitude towards life- A mode of approach that survives only in Artists & Criminals.' I think it was Wilde.

Constant threats from different guards all the time became the norm. I was told by a visiting Dr Gaunt that he had the power to keep me hidden down here forever. That no one would be able to stop him. I believed him too, as I had heard him through the thick doors talking quite loudly to his assistant about falsifying my files, dosing me beyond human movement and throwing away the key. That's if they decided to keep hold of you.

The busy cemetery a constant reminder of what went on beyond the realms of natural occurring deaths. The small blocks exercise yard that I've never ventured onto is busy today. Through the dirty grills at knee level you can squint through n just make out the legs walking round. Snatches, snippets, sorcery of the upmost evil can be heard. Here's the horror head on.

They would gather in small circles and I figured out that what they were doing was arranging court documents to be sent to each other. Getting their kicks from reading about each other's despicable warped crimes was entertainment for them.

There was only one scratched piece of writing on my block cell wall that I didn't understand the meaning of. I figured it to be Irish, but no matter the guess, couldn't say for sure to be sure what it meant.

The neat indentations of letters must have taken the poor chap a good while.

UAIGNEAS

GAN

CIUNEAS

I missed my Mother terribly at times, her horridness towards me forgotten. I knew if it wasn't for Stan she would have been totally different towards me. The loud banging throughout the corridors shattered the peace. Down here with the cells small n packed together the racket was continuous.

There was one guard who seemed decent enough. Mr Derry was his name. He always seemed to tell the others to leave it now when they were dishing out a kicking. And he had spent a bit of time at my solid door calming me at times when the drugs n stress started really cracking me up.

He had told me when I was calm that John Howard, the Quaker was the inventor of solitary confinement.

When he had left to go off duty n home, I had thought about the man who had dreamed up this box like existence. The poor guy must have either been locked in a cupboard as a child or had grown into an adult with a terrible sadistic streak in his mind for no apparent reason.

{VISIT chapter 71} When I first caught sight of my best friend, his face was deeply tanned. My mind wondered instantly to how I must be presenting myself to him.

While the plentiful sun had left its etchings upon him, I could only imagine his thoughts as he approached me. I had been robbed of any vigour and my face had not only been shrunk, but my very soul. I had stepped through the darkest of tunnels in my mind, pale n hollow, I must have looked a complete shambles of a human being. The glint in his dark brown eyes, were that of a true friend. While I noticed his concern at seeing me, he soon smiled n pushed the obvious comments aside for now. The hug he gave me felt like a new born baby's trip into its Mothers arms for the first time. It had taken nearly 2 years to feel safe for a split second.

Inhaling deeply the outdoor smells he brought with him, just instantly flooded my memory with our childhood together. My words have no structure as I try to tell him it's great to see him again. I'm babbling on, without realising. Again without seeing normal people from the outside, you don't quite want to believe what you now perceive as ordinary. I knew I was hooked on the drugs they had been pumping into me but I didn't realise how bad till in front of him.

Before I could ramble on any more he just said calmly. "Take it easy Otiss, ok, it's me"

Gerard was hovering already near to our visits table. I'd had my final prep talk before entering the visitor's hall. The screws were going to make sure I didn't talk too much anyway. Certainly not about what was going on this side of the fence. But while I was mumbling rubbish they just let me crack on.

After Johnny asked Gerard to fetch me a glass of water, which I could tell from his false smile I was gonna pay for later, my tongue eased a little from the swelling n I managed a more normal greeting of "hello."

Johnny seemed a little reluctant to engage in convo now, lowering his voice as the screws got busy over the far side of the room checking other visiting parties.

"I've had a little prep talk myself Otiss before getting let through to see you. A Dr Gaunt met me by the entrance. He asked me not to pry too much into your time spent in here n to not go on too much about what was happening in the world on the outside, so as not to upset your routine!" A loud voiced guard suddenly shouts, "Coffee time"

So Johnny gets up to go to this little hatch to fetch us some drinks n snacks. All very civil!!!!! I think of how tall he's grown as I watch him from the back walk confidently to fetch our brews. My mind strangely wondering back to my last taste of coffee, which seemed like an eternity back when officer Dick sprayed me through the hatch of the door in the station house.

As Johnny headed back to our table clutchin crisps n brews I smiled at his freedom. The tanned face had filled out n was stress free, although upon closer inspection he couldn't hide in his eyes from me his concern as to my predicament.

I sipped at my brew as he chatted about some of his travels. Keeping the convo nice n relaxed. It appeared that since his last trip to India he had stopped over in Europe, calling in on the city of Paris. Visiting the dizzying heights of the Eiffel tower, which he said he had done at the late evening, giving the lights of the great city sparkling a wonderful panoramic scene. He had also visited the Pere lachaise cemetery where the likes of Balzac n Wilde n the rock star Jim Morrison laid forever serenely in the Poets corner. I made a mental note to tell Scot John.

Other news of his life had me try my damn hardest to keep these drugs from swamping my mind and following what he had to say. I couldn't get enough of hearing about normal life. "Tell me more about India Johnny" "Just a memory"

He smiled that same old smile he had always flashed me as a young kid, when he knew things were extra ruff at home n he had been trying to cheer me up.

Leaning back into the blue fabric of the lounge chairs, he said

"Towards Baga beach the traffic allowed some speed, slowing through choice to marvel at the bustling lives, like a blur as I passed. I'd rented an old trusty Enfield bike from a local man who had woken his youngest son to fill glass bottles with petrol, which he had then filled the tank to full n screwed tight the caps on the remaining bottles, which I placed in my rucksack. Over the main bridge, the road now having some concrete, I zoomed in line with sunny palm fringed coasts. Rising through the red clay gravel now as I turned off to chill at my beach front hut, which was called sea view. Sipping cool king's beer with a soon to be filled rumbling belly, the aroma of Tikka chicken grilled slowly in outside kiln ovens just the best food I've ever tasted. Afterwards, strolling the bike back out again onto the coastal roads, the ferry for the crossing over to Tiracol fort only a few English pence, where I stayed for the night in one of the seven rooms, my room called Wednesday. This was the place where the freedom fighters made their last stance against the invasion from the Portuguese."

I was totally fascinated, but his next bit of news made me feel very alone again. He had accepted a job in a very remote part of India, looking after n maintaining a lighthouse. He could tell by my weak smile I felt hurt. I was pleased for him really yet felt another part of my identity flying away.

"Open your crisps mate"

I'd not touched the bag he had brought with the coffee. I opened them n sat looking at him as I munched away. He had steadily held my gaze waiting for me to finish. As I did, he offered me the last of his bag that he had opened. He widened his eyes, as I was about to decline n took the hint to reach for his bag.

I peered into the opening, casually seeing this silver glint at the bottom poking out through the last few crisps, which were cheese & onion if you are that anxious for details.

I clocked the guard looking off bored at the large wall clock, taking my chance I swallowed the last of the crisps, spoils n all, with a quick tilt of my head back everything slid down in a clunky sharp gulp.

{FECUNDITY chapter 72} *I guess some things were allowed to be handed over on visits n some not. I could see others on visits hugging goodbye to loved ones n the guards staring more urgently at the clock. I drifted back into the conversation, trying to answer Johnny when he had asked if there had been any meetings with some of the hierarchy in the hospital. Had there been any talk of giving me early release."It's about time my friend, your no more crazy than me."*

I was tempted to ask about Stan when the guard in charge of the visits hall shouted TIMES UP!!! "See you later man"

We shook hands like the young men we had become n I watched my best friend disappear with a small crowd of strangers. Alone again I stood.

Gerard straight over, gripping my arm n saying to the visits screw "Straiht down de block wIdis one"

At least with the block, you were left alone for long periods of solitary. This gave me the opportunity to soak up all the words Johnny had spoken, his visit brief but it sure lifted my spirit for a while.

The tomb needed curtains, an inmate before me had scratched a square on the cells back wall that was meant to represent a window. I didn't even have a sharp stone or a metal pin to add a view. I think I would have drawn a scene of a stream and then sobbed enough tears to carry me away from here back to freedom.

I've walked for a thousand miles since Johnny left me after our viz. Shame it's only been up and down these well worn floor boards of my flowery dell.

Catching my eye, for even though you stare constant at the walls, things seem to be right in front of you, yet the obvious can be missed, I see now a fresh bit of scratched wording up near the top of the door. An obviously taller man had let his thoughts go here.

MAYBE THIS WORLD IS ANOTHER PLANETS HELL

For over an hour my eyes just never left the question. The spell broken with loud disturbing yells from the cell next door.

A patient Gerard had laughed about as he put me away behind my own door after my visit, for he knew my neighbour would be disturbing me badly. The poor chap was suffering from dementia praecox paranoid, an archaic term they used in here for a paranoid schizophrenic.

I got all the rest I needed down here. At least twice to my knowledge they had come in mob handed n broke the full needles off in the crook of my arms. I'd had no ocean dreams to drift away down into.

Wa/rd siX seemed to bring back nothing to my mind other than horrid memories of how I had been treated at home, like falling into a swirling dizzying dream where Stan's fanged open mouth met me head on at the start.

It didn't seem too long before my bruises healed n I was back to the familiarity of my cell on the Netherfield. It had been a good few days since Johnny had visited. My system from the drug doses side effects had made my bowels slow to function, but that night the inevitable happened and nature delivered my present.

The old newspaper that had been crumpled in the cell corner now held the shit I didn't want. It got screwed up and shoved out the bars window gap. The yards barrowman would scoop it up with the rest of the shit parcels in the frosty morning.

Shaking out my legs from the cramp that had crept in from crouching so long to get everything out of me, I gingerly picked up the turd that held my prezzie. After washing the silver chain that had attached to its end this Silver acorn with my allowance of fresh water from my jug, I pulled it over my head and felt it nestle nicely into my solar plexus. It was strange how even though the toilet bowl was there I fell in like many of the men who's cells didn't have that facility and threw my shit parcels with the best of them.

The next day after coming back up the iron stairs from breakfast I proudly showed Character, who instantly recognised its symbolism. The blood lines of Ireland that ran through my Mother's side of the family had obviously been on Johnny's mind when he had thought about a gift for me.

"The acorn" Character mused "was the Celtic symbol for life, immortality and fecundity." My baffled look towards the last word made him chuckle quietly n say, "It means invention young Otis."

I smiled inside myself as I banged my own door shut on the wing. I sure was inventing a scheme to get retribution on my so called Father and the plan to get me on track was just about to be set in motion.

{MORIBUND chapter 73} They weighed me this morning, bringing outside to my door these black salter scales.

The food is shit n tastes like crap, but surprisingly my little skinny skool body had started to finally fill out. The weight had gone on steady over the last few years n I had gained a good few stone. Characters advice on exercise had brought firmness to my chest n arms. The sit ups n press ups not easy after the drugs totally kicked in, but there were times when I could press on n build up a small routine. The motivation easy as Stan loomed in my mind as I pushed on sweating away in pain.

Every so often, Character would give me this friendly hug. It generated an unspoken feeling that reminded me I was safe from his killing schedule. We used the good old slang to communicate on association, so as not to let Dr Gaunt suss our plans.

He had been seen on quite a few occasions with his nose buried deep in a book by one of the Kray twins. Good old Reg putting it together in prison with his friend Tully. The sad faced clown on the cover making me laugh as he popped his head out from behind it now n again, inside my head I thought two clowns staring at me. Gaunt desperate for its contents knowledge, trying his hardest to figure out what certain words meant. A vexation to his spirit, for we used many styles of the S ecret Lang uage.

To counter this, and show his power, Gaunt had led his staff around all the cells, replacing the wool blankets of winter with the therapeutic cotton sheets of summer. To twist the knife a little deeper he turned all the radiators to brass monkeys.

The only cell that held any warmth was Winnie's. He had been informed that the reason for this was due to tests being carried out, which had alarmingly indicated he may spontaneously human combust in the near future!!!Even Character would laugh at the mind games and call Winnie to his hatch at his own cell door to warm the frost away.

As I glanced out behind the bars, curious to see what the heavens had leaked upon our fragile world I noticed the thumping rain of the last few days had washed away the bulk of snow that had built up inside the yard. The high walls had lost its icing; the barrow man had finally been able to get back round n collect all the shit parcels. I scratched with a lazy handed motion at my week's long neglect of beard.

Over the past 7 moons I had started sprouting quite thick black stubble, the cheap razors they used in here I'm sure making it grow back at alarming rates.

Another reason though to see Nurse Silk, for she was in charge down the tub room of rendering you smooth n baby chinned like again.

I could hold myself up at the bars now one handed as the strength from the exercises starting to pick up.

Before I jumped back down to ready myself for the door being flung open for lunch, I clocked again the barrow getting slowly pushed by the man, his shovel over his shoulder every now n again quickly flipping to a scrape on the yards floor, clearing up where the scruffs had been busy last night.

What did catch my attention more, as for when you have seen one shit parcel you have seen them all, was this great big smashed up piece of wood. I knew what it had been once. A patient had been making this giant wooden eagle lectern. It had been started so it could be a main piece in the chapel, yet with that burning to the ground it had been decided by the staff to let him keep on carving it in his cell as occupational therapy n all that malarkey. He had finished it the night before last, his last job of finely sanding it smooth complete.

It had been destined to be shipped out to another institutions chapel. The crashing n banging last night above me, which I had ignored, now apparent as I watched the barrow man pick its broken pieces up one by one n pile it into a gargoylish shaped pile on the heap of shit wrapped newspapers that filled half the bottom of the trolley.

"Penny for em"

My stomach made a growl as I mooched down the iron stairs looking for my lunch. Scot John behind me, sensing my head was up in the clouds n asking what was bothering me.

With the emptiness of my gut, I just said, "oh the usual" My weak laugh not fooling him for a second.

For a change out pacing his giant strides to reach the food hot plate first, I filled my tray with slops n got back upstairs to fill my belly n torture my mind some more.

The next few days I seemed to stay with this intense black cloud overhead. The Fab FM had not got connected the last weak end n I'd strangely missed its content in my lug holes. Winnie had said it could be a bit random at times, though it should connect this Sunday if we were lucky.

Something that was constant though was my ocean dreams. I couldn't figure out why they were so intense. The latest one had even ended with me surfacing by my childhood raft.

It had started with a crocodile tear running slowly down my cheek, stopping for a rest on my lips before landing on the faded wood floor of the cell. There had been a bang up all day and as the drowsy afternoon gave way I slid to the ocean floor via the small sad puddle I'd created. Amphibious awakenings as I slept in my slavery pilled world.

The vessel zoomed out of the gloom, Titanic's railings that I floated over, amazing they seem so rust free so deep down here. I'd fallen through the blue surface, down past stars of luminescent plankton to the utter blackness of the deep. Yet this dream like state shone bright the things it wanted me to see.

I clock out of the gloom a binnacle, the compass long gone. A big eye emperor fish swims passed n twigs the gap n starts delving in looking for food I guess. Fiddler crabs clinging onto the barnacled railings lined up seven or eight side by side.

I'm grabbed by a current n pulled in another direction, the great liner lost now to my sight, taken back to its shadowy grave yard where it will rust in peace.

It instantly took me back to my terrible home life. Stan's rizla homework questions seared forever into my mind, the leki meter on £19.12 Stan behind me looking at the opened door, he's clocking the numbers. Hard swipes around the head as I guess wrong a few times. He makes me stand there facing the leki read out until he's satisfied with his tormenting game.

Long days pass that feel like weeks to my aching legs. He kept coming n checking n grunting behind me.

The final swipe came at £4.14 I learned the hard way to remember significant dates in history.

The song he had sung as he left me alone n told me to get up to bed n out his site was, nearer my God, to thee, Stan's horrible voice booming now around the walls of the house as I had limped upstairs on aching legs to finally rest.

Flash backs of reality inside ocean dreaming. I'm not sure if they have increased my medication tenfold this week. With the force of ten Niagara falls I'm catapulted suddenly back near the light. The surface close by, well closer, compared to the depths I had just dropped down to. A second wreck comes into my vision. Again my skool time had given me something useful. I knew what I was looking at here. HMS Pandora proudly showed me her wrecked face. I recalled she had been sunk while trying to navigate a passage through the barrier reef. At the time she was carrying 135 crew & 10 prisoners from HMS Bounty. With 35 lives lost, 4 of them cons.

The skeleton legs swirl below me in the currents. 4 balls n chains still there attached, yet there rusted n rotted in size now n as I drift upwards on mysterious currents they sink back away n are lost to my vision.

The rota for your morning torture was passed around the day room today. A quick glance confirmed I was still on the early morning bath wake ups. Disturbingly though my name appeared at the bottom of the list again with the initials CW next to them, whatever CW stood for, I knew it wouldn't be good news.

I had hoped to get a switch to being taken out n kept on the logs all day, but that hand cuff stunt had scuppered any real chance of it happening. The fresh air I would have liked, yet in all honesty, the freezing drowning near to the point of death were worth it, for I had the five minutes of pleasure to look forward to as Nurse Silk towelled me dry.

Gerard had upped his bullying another notch of late. Talk n whispered rumours of his late night visits to some of the weaker members of our cloudy pond were making their rounds. I could sense Character n Gyp the blood cooking up some scheme, Scot John bellowing quite flippantly out the bars on a late evening about how he fancied ripping the piece of shit limb from limb.

My door had not been missed out. The black demon had really started pushing all the boundaries. I was trying my hardest not to fall into the trap many before me had, which saw men kill inside n end up serving forever.

He had gotten me stitched up over nothing just last night.

A report card had come floating from the other side of my door. It read of bullshit, that I had been seen by Gerard on his last night shift burning my blanket n sailing it out the cell window was just ridiculous.

That no one else had seen this and the more obvious one of my blanket still laying undamaged on my bed didn't matter.

I was led down the NORMAL block after Gaunt had reprimanded me at my door. Gerard the lone guard leading me over there, my relief that it wasn't another trip upstairs to the dreaded Wa/rd siX. He still gave me plenty of verbal shit all the way there just to make up for that fact.

The winter month was still holding on, not quite ready to give up to spring. Down the block the wind that howled away under the lip of the cell door was fast becoming the Euroclydon. Holes in the brick work from the wall had funnels of ice cold air shooting straight through from the outside yards. I didn't have to hand a sufficient spile to block the gaps, so curled up best I could and just shivered my way through the wasted time.

I got to thinking about the latest rumour doing the rounds. The one where Character had been rumoured to be eying up Quolco's poor old neck didn't seem to add up.

The bang of the cell door flying open n large filled needles of drugged out despair soon putting my thinking to nothing but blackness. When I finally came around from unconsciousness, a cell move had occurred. I think they moved you around to just disorientate you more. Moving you about n mixing up the drug doses, along with the glue clocks freshly filled to slow the count had the desired effect. I hadn't lost my senses completely though.

I knew the cell I had been in before was completely bare of scratched names of old.

The one I came around in now had quite distinguished scrapings on the largest part of the worn out bricked over wall. After studying it for an hour, the shudders down my spine didn't ease up.

Another innocent soul it seemed had trod this painful path I myself was on. These stitch ups happening over many centuries, for at the bottom of the poem, the date, scratched deeper into the crumbling plaster said

15ᵗʰ FEB 1796

LOOK AND SEE THROUGH MY WINDOW BEARING INTO MY SOUL

LOOK AND SEE ALL THE TOMMOROWS THAT NOW LAY DEAD AND OLD

IT'S TIME TO SEE THE PROOF THE TIME TO REVEAL THE TRUTH

ITS THE TIME NOW FOR SOME PEACE SURELY MY RELEASE

LOOK AND SEE THROUGH THE SHADOWS AT THE DARKENING GLOOM

LOOK AT ALL THE HOURS SINCE IVE BEEN HOME

IT WONT BE LONG NOW TILL IM NO LONGER ALONE

IT'S TIME FOR A NEW WORLD ITS TIME FOR MY DREAM

HOME WITH YOU MOTHER JUST LIKE THE OLD TIMES USE TO BE

It naturally brought my poor Mothers tragic murder to mind.

The ruined relationship that I could only blame upon Stan caused a rage so deep within me, my whole body scared me. The feelings I had just unbelievably strong n dark when I thought of the hurt I wanted to inflict upon that no good bastard.

{SMOKING KILLS chapter 74} I had missed out on a bit of aggro going down on the wing since my stitch up break down to the block. Scot John had finally snapped n dull knife wasn't feeling too great.

John had been busy down the craft shops that the institution ran once a week. They generally these days labelled him nearly on the same par as the top killA's on the Netherfield. Letting him have a few perks n bending the rules slightly so as to keep him happy, which in turn kept everyone happy. The two guards from when he had kicked off last time on the sewing machine classes were still off sick. Dr Gaunt certainly couldn't afford to lose any more members of staff. Quite a few when the build up for Characters 6 moon killin schedule comes around start turning in sick notes.

John had been busy making his wood sign for his little cell tattoo shop. I'd seen over the last 6 months a few of the chronics sporting rather impressive marked ink. His practise over with the ones not fussed. He had declared just before I had been dragged away from the wing over the burnt blanket that he was setting up shop. Apparently I n a few others were more than welcome to take a seat.

Dull knife had not been able to resist the urge to creep in while Scot John was down the server grabbing lunch one day last week, to sneak in to his cell n swipe all the needles John had been gathering to open up ready to ink.

The places John had stuck these stolen needles when he had found the culprit didn't bear thinking about. Winnie through the pipes my first night back, telling me things that made shudders run through my torso. Good old John could get very creative when it came to the art of violence.

But he didn't have a patch on our most prolific serial killA as Character was about to change my life in here for good. No more buggin for me.

{UP IN SMOKE chapter 75} *I thought I was hearing things as I was just about to bang up. The landing was quiet with most of the screws on the lower landing dealing with a patient who had ripped his own testicles off n was now threatening to eat them. The crazy part being he was in a standoff over some tomato ketchup, demanding it to accompany his sweet meal!!!!*

After a few years in, I had stopped getting curious n gathering with the small crowds to watch the drama unfold. Once you have seen one loon lose the plot you have seen them all.

"What?"

"You heard what I said Kites" I turned to see this pike like eye staring right through me.

I had never seen Character look like this up close and he had never called me by my surname.

"Canteen day" The words slurred out of his crooked side mouth like a bounty hunter in one of those old western films.

My whole body went ice cold. The man was unnerving me for the first time in our dealings with each other. "Listen drop me a packet of burn in my cell canteen day ok"

It wasn't a question, it wasn't an order. Just something I will never ever forget. It was my first contract in the dirty world of murder. I nodded at him. I didn't trust my mouth to get the words out to confirm. Hatred could certainly take over reason.

Character smiling now, the weird look gone thank God. He just rubbed his hands together like a fly n spun away towards his pad.

Just as I entered my own peter, this window shattering sonic boom rang out. Character letting out some frustration, as the moons n tides gathered into their rhythm which guided his murdering sprees.

Later that evening, I heard Winnie shout Character through the bars. Not long after that I saw and smelt the smoke rings of character's little smoke floating up n outside of my barred window. He was communicating with Winnie in his own strange shaman ways.

I had a strong feeling they were discussing me and an even stronger feeling that Gerard was the hunted now.

I smiled up at the bars, one of the smoke rings hovering for an age just in my view. But speak of the devil n he shall appear. My attention now on my door n its spy hole as I heard him whisper through. "Nothing to say Boy"

I had plenty to say, but no point giving the game away.

I was wide awake now and staring right at him as he opened the larger metal flap to show his ugly black face. His lips pressed right up close to the glass n I could see even from laying on the bed the spit that had gathered at each corner of his mouth. He'd been on the rum again, fumes strong soaking through the metal n faintly hitting my nostrils.

The urge to tell him to feck off had long been replaced with the silent standoff. I seemed to figure out his crazy moods the less I spoke. The blank, the diss, the click of his tongue coming back at my wall of silence, all a sure sign I was getting to him. He was losing control of the mind games.

The next bit I'd been practising for a few weeks, waiting for an opportunity just like this. I leaped like a cat onto the floor and steadily started my press up routine.

My eyes in line with his as he watched every dip, knowing after five minutes as I rose without any sign of breathlessness that he was scared.

He tried to pull a face that said he wasn't impressed. But I knew in his tiny mind he was wondering how I was keeping cool n keeping fit. The meds should put a horse on its back after supper. But I'd managed to wedge them up in my upper gums this evening, which on more than one occasion had got me upping my routine. I just turned my back on him n jumped up to hold on vice like at the bars. He watched me for a few minutes, seeing when I'd get down. But he was bored n dejected well before I let the fibres burning in my out stretched arms bring me back to the soles of my bare feet on the faded green wood floor, that smile on my face like a Cheshire cat when I heard him slam the flap back shut n stomp off

I visited the yellow stained pad of the baron the very next morning. Buying the packet of baci seemed innocent enough, yet it was to become an inanimate object of quite some significance.

I had known last night that Gerard wouldn't dare open me up. Others on duty with him had still got some human attributes n were not part of his bully gang.

The morning passed n after a cold lunch it was soon shouted for exercise. The doors clattered open n the boots on iron railings could be heard as patients made their way down to catch some fresh air away from the antiseptic hum of the ward.

Dr Gaunt by the yards door, clip board under one arm, picking with his dirty fingers at a manky tooth, nurse silk behind him, fixing her beautiful long eyelash. Goose bumps ran up my arms as I stepped out into the brightness of the day.

A few punch clouds were up in the sky. I strolled to my favourite spot n slid my back down the wire fence to rest n watch the loons parade around in their mesmerising circle.

My grand night's sleep had me feeling content enough. The rattle from keys not disturbing my peace right now, as the gates were locked n banged up.

Drugged silly limbs tried their best to walk the yard with some sense of normality. But the state that some of the chronics were in would have the scene look like a shambolic line of drunken winos on their way home after an all day session in the boozer.

My mind soon drifted to other business. I stared the distance over the yard n focused on Gerard's horrible bullying mouth. He was busy shouting at some poor old chronic and I kinda tripped out for a moment, watching his mouth open n close seemed to just take me back to Stan's opened fanged hole. I couldn't hear the shouting, just the slow motion of the big gob bastard opening n shutting.

The baki was tucked inside the turn up on my institutional jeans, and as exercise came to a close I drifted back in keeping my eyes off Gerard n headed up the stairs. I quickly slid into Characters immaculate cell, sliding the pouch of tobacco under his neatly made bed sheets that rested on top of his pillow on the cot bed.

It was done, the contract arranged. Back in my own peter, I stared at the blood red Marlboro calendar that Character had given me months ago, the crossed out mass of days ended with today circled n ready to be crossed off in more ways than one. Smoking was dangerous for your health said the warning on the calendar advert, and with my business complete for the day, it was most definitely true. The next 6 moon cycle had arrived.

{NO MATCH FOR A DIABLO chapter 76} *When tea time came and the doors opened to let the crowd down to the server hot plate, I got up from my bunk n closed the door shut again on myself. I had no appetite and couldn't help feeling the apprehension of what was to go down. I didn't know in what way Character was going to even the score for me, my mind over the last few hours running through so many different scenarios.*

I looked through the metal flap that I'd opened on the door before banging myself up. I watched the rippers nephew skulk passed with his tray dripping all over the place. I could hear Gerard bawling out Winnie over something petty, probably trying to prove a stupid point to make him feel superior after losing face to me the night before. I craned my neck to see a little further up the wing, laughing to myself as Winnie flexed a weak bicep muscle behind his back before whizzing past me in a blur n banging his own door to scram his grub.

I let the wry smile stay on my chops a good while as I sat back down on my cot bed n thought how I had sealed the bullying wankers fate with a simple packet of burn. Character had said after our first conversion on the subject, how he would savour the smoke after the foul deed was done. The peace pipe he had said to me, winking n walking away chuckling gently.

I had been through some slow times in this warped space that was the FABERON, but tonight seemed like the glue clocks had been swamped out forever. I was past caring now about the method of Gerard's killin, I just wanted to hear it was done.

He had been dishing out the diesel supper now on his own for about the past four days as his little assistant was ill n down the infirmary. I heard a few doors at a distance open n the usual palava of getting your mug filled up for the nights bang up. I knew every movement on our wing like the timing of things and the noises n what they represented.

I knew Gerard was about one door off Gyp the bloods cell. And that he always quickly refused with a stern No!!!.

Scot John was next, who always filled his beaker right to the point of flowing over. Yet the noises tonight stopped. An eerie quiet swamped the ward. I pushed my ears to the cold metal of the door n strained to catch any sound, yet nothing. Then this almighty scream n then silence again.

The first thing I noticed that made me realise something had actually happened was when the brown sluggish diesel started spreading its way under my door sill n into my cell. I glanced from the floors spreading puddle, back to the blood red calendars circled date and then really freaked out as this green mist started coming through the side of the gaps in the steel cell door. A vapour of smoke and then there he stood in front of me.

Character just smiled those twinkling pike eyes n said, "it's done" and with those simple words he vanished as quickly as he had appeared n exited in this green vapour mist through the open cell bars window. That's when all the alarms blared out.

{CLUEDO chapter 77} The gossip went on all night. Every single one of us from the Netherfield ward had been marched down to the block. Gaunt and some official looking suits, who gathered behind him all very serious looking, began to quiz.

Again I'm pretty sure they knew who had done it. Yet the heads were nearly bleeding, they were getting scratched so much. I had no sympathy with their murder case dilemma.

All I knew was Character had somehow mystified them again.

I didn't know how many other cells he had vaporized under. I knew it must be his little smoke that he carried in that bag around his neck. The bag he guarded with his life.

Not many knew the power of its contents. Certainly Gyp the blood, Scot John, Winnie and myself. But I think quite certainly that's where the list ended.

I had witnessed the crow flapping about, seen Gaunt in the mirror burning the chapel of St Faith to a pile of smouldering ashes. I knew its powers, his powers.

He had shown me the omen only weeks ago with the birds gathering for a murder on his cells window ledge.

But this wasn't my puzzle to solve. The threats of being kept down the block forever were shouted about. Gaunt taking each of us out individually from the block and trying a different tactic as he calmly walked us back through the grounds trying to have this Father n son type chat, hoping to cajole the info out about who could have murdered Gerard.

But it was no good. Most didn't have a clue even if they did want to grass. And the few that did have a good idea were keeping tight lipped.

It was satisfying to listen to Gaunt keep referring to Gerard in the past tense. It was real, he was gone. Dead as a door nail.

They did have a major clue. Qualco's scarf had been found wrapped tight around Gerard's burnt face. The details coming thick n fast on the gossip train.

The full boiling tea urn of diesel had gone over his head. Melting his garrotted face into a death mask no one wanted to mould.

The silence lasted months. They really were starting to have most of us believe we would never get out from the block unless someone squealed.

I heard through my cell door Character speaking through his to Dr Gaunt, the last bit of the faint convo I caught clearly as Character raised his voice as Gaunt started to turn n walk away from the door. "We try to embrace everything, but succeed only in grasping the wind."

There was no option for Gaunt than to attribute Gerard's killin to Qualco. His scarf was the only solid clue they had. And even though to us patients Gerard was a bullying piece of dog shit, to the staff, his colleagues, he was a valued senior member of the team. They were never going to just let it pass. Someone was going to pay.

Gaunt said that the staff had decided that Qualco needed help, not further punishment. A likely story!!! There was a brief memo shoved under each of our block doors. The lotto had been decided early. Christmas had been cancelled due to our insolence and Qualco was the lucky ticket winner.

The silence down here had been to me most welcome. No one spoke, pipes were mused, speech hung library ruled in the air. That coroners van was well down the road to hell with Old Gerard nice n icy. I imagined the black bag zipping up n catching his ruff beard.

The ghouls who do the job even staring in disgusted horror at the mess his face had melted into. We were informed that most of the group initially brought down for the suspicion of Gerard's death would be going back to the Netherfield the next morning. Probably about 2 months had passed in a silence of just staring into space n taking the beatings n needles full of dreamy unconsciousness without much thought.

But I was determined to train myself in my cell now I didn't have that bullying bastard on my case all the time.

I'd started to think of Stan again n how I wanted to torture him to death. I'd had no ocean dreams while down Wa/rd siX and I was strangely missing their mysterious depths. My last night down the block had a surprise.

It must have been around 4 am in the morning, the scratching waking me, the dim light in the block cell made things difficult to see, so I just followed the scratching sound. On the steel door I felt with my out stretched hand in the top corner, the message intended for yours truly. The freezing cold that came off the steel door travelled all the way down my arm n held steady over my heart valves. I think my breathing stopped for a good few seconds as Iran my fingers over the scratched rough words. Gerard was still at it, still buggin. In five

inch high lettering the words I easily made out. BOY

{THE SILENT TAT SHOP chapter 78} Clear to me, the stain. The staff had seen to it that the cleaners had mopped vigorously where the tea urn had spilled over Gerard's head n marked a large circled brown mark all over the landing, but even months later it was visible. I stepped on it as I made my way back to my cell. It was good to be back in my own room. Strange how you start to feel a comfort to something that was once so cold n alien.

Scot John was busy setting up his tat shop, the sign up now above the door. The chairs turned ready to accommodate a willing human canvas. His little ink bottles ready n needles.

There was a calm atmosphere to the Netherfield now. Dr Gaunt had mentioned there would be new staff appointed all in good time, so for now we settled serenely as normal, or as normal as you can on a mental ward.

Breakfast had been late for some reason n as I'd finally managed to join the Q, this familiar now ScOtish accent behind me said, "you should a let mi ink ya young laddi"

Now I had thought of his tats now n again over time in here. He was full of them, with the themes changing depending on his faze at the time. There were many of monsters. Large strange looking things that I could only imagine were from ScOtish folk lore.

Then there were his intellectual ones, again depending on his favourite books he had been reading at the time. I would clock him on association time hovering near the intellects, pulling at his sleeve to memorise the ink running up his arms, before sliding over to casually drop his knowledge into their ears.

It was well known he had covered around 90 percent of his body in ink. It was hard not to read him when you ever viewed him topless by his door. But the tats made me uneasy too. Stan looming large in my mind again scaring me,

The dragon was still alive n as devious as ever.

I didn't dwell on the subject too much, as Stan once in my head could swamp my mind with flash backs and a heavy heart would be my sleeping chamber.

John's latest was still very scabby. Only recently done, his delving into the French poets had made his next choice for him.

Why he did it on his forehead I will never know, but all things considered, it wasn't like the craziest move he had ever pulled.

Lame des poetes.

Those fine words stared back at you every time you had a convo with the man. I told him at lunch, "go on then you can do my back" We said no more on the matter, his nod my confirmation that I'd been booked in.

I found myself that evening all set up n ready for the needle to begin. We had firmly agreed on two things.

Firstly that it was his choice to design what he felt fit. The second that it was not by any nature to be the image of a dragon nor a ship.

Winnie kept watch at the opened door as most patients had gone down to the day room to watch one of Gaunt's weird films. Character had been leaning on the landing railing chatting quietly to Gyp as I'd entered the tat shop.

Old Walter was on tonight and even though they were letting John have his way with the tat shop, we still had to keep it relatively low key n not make a big show of what was being allowed.

I straddled the wood chair that John nodded at, leaning over it so my back was exposed. The first few jabs with the needle startled me a little, but I soon got used to it n closed my eyes in a relaxing way while he got busy.

Ten minutes later Character sauntered in. Soon enough he was swiftly behind me watching John work, whistling shrill n low an admiring sound to the back of my ear. "Looking good young Otiss" I was just turning my head to say thanks when John's large palm gently turned me back away.

Character again chiming in.

"I have a great idea if you can handle another one doing at the same time?" "Trust me from what ol Winnie has been telling me about your strange dreams, you could certainly use what I have in mind"

When he said a chicken and a pig I laughed so hard that John gave my back a five minute breather.

Yet after ten minutes chatting of old Hawaiian sailors, legends, tradition etc.., it started actually to make sense. He wanted to ink one separate on each foot.

Chickens n pigs would always find something to float on and never drown. Character convinced me that I needed a safety net of sorts from the deep ocean dreams that had become all consuming to my sleep.

So I found Scot John busy again on my back while Character sat crossed legged in front of me, ink bottle by his side getting creative on my feet to give me a guardian talisman to save me from sinking n never coming back from my deep dreams.

The feet I have to say hurt a damn site more than my back, but I gritted it out for the full two hours of association.

Winnie busy with the clearing of the ink out of site, John moving his chairs back into their preferred spots, while Character casual as ever stood over by John's window smoking a hit on his small bone pipe, which he kept, tucked away in his shirt breast pocket.

I tentatively pulled on my black vest, just in time as old Walter came pottering past saying come on now men lets be making your way back to your rightful cells. Limping out with my wool socks rubbing the fresh ink n my feet feeling very swelled I got back to my door n banged up.

I was curious as hell to see what John had done. I grabbed my little square dull mirror n positioned my hand holding it at an angle to reflect my back.

The lizard was perched on my shoulder blade, outlined thick, Maori dots detailing its patterns. Reds, yellows n lime green!!!

I never even expected colour, never realised that they had anything other than black ink in the cell. I loved it. And with my socks now off I laid out on my bed on my front and safely fell into an inky black wave of a dream.

{DEATH & RESURRECTION chapter 79} *It was in the breki Q the next morning that I learned of my other tattoos symbolism.*

And hearing it from Characters mouth made it make even more perfect sense. "Young Otiss, its sun seeking habit symbolizes the souls search for awareness. To the Romans, who believed it hibernated, the lizard meant Death & Resurrection.

Just as the lizard is able to drop its tail in order to escape danger, so the lizard totem shows us the principles of letting go & self protection. It's the soul Otiss searching for the light"

I thanked him n he went to pat my back but realised I might be sore so just placed a warm hand over my lizard n the Q moved on towards some grub.

Back in my pad I thought to how Stan had kept me in the dark way to many years n it was time for some pay back.

That night with most of the original patients back in their cells since the murder of Gerard, after lights out, their whistles n hollowing pricked my curiosity n I jumped up to hold onto the bars. Outside, was on fire with falling papers n rags spiralling towards the yard floor where they lit up the evening nicely. A kind of officially send off n good riddance to the worst bully screw the institute had known. I lit up one of my folders that held my ancestry stuff. I'd memorised it totally and watched my own flame spin down on the gentle night time's breeze, thankful to Character for ridding the place of the wanker. I'm sure he was watching from his window, silently taking in the credit.

In the morning, Gaunt come flying onto the wing shouting that if this behaviour didn't cease, that he would have no alternative but to re open ward 27 & 28. Mythical wards, rumours, certainly scary enough to have the majority of the Netherfield pipe down for the foreseeable future.

The wing had a different feel about it now. Everyone seemed to settle into their time better n get on with the little things that made the long days more bearable. A few months or so after the murder of Gerard I got a nice surprise in the mail. Coming back from lunch I found under my cell door a bright coloured post card, Johnny's unmistakable hand writing there as I picked it up n turned it in my hand. The message from Johnny spelled out a nice feeling.

I will never let you crash on the rocks again brother

That's all it said. All it needed to say.

The picture on the front had this dazzling white light house, with its view directed on a choppy blue sea, the foam crashing waves on the rocks not too worrying. Johnny had landed in a nice spot n I was pleased for him. I slept that night dreaming of our occasional summer days splashing n swimming at the lake of stars.

{TIR FO THUINN chapter 80} The land under the waves crept back into my dreaming the very next night. Yet a different ocean floor met me by surprise this time.

I must have gone deeper than over 6000 fathoms. The deepest trench around that mark, yet I stood on an empty bed of sand. Like the dry Aral Sea, which was perfect for no swimmers, I stood without the vast pressure of the water above me.

I felt tired within this dream, as the weirdness of standing so far down the dry earth now hit me. Gushes of water drenching faces of curiously exited explorers, as the surrounding expanse revealed itself for the first time to obviously more than me.

Professionals that had entered these spaces from the clean blue lapping ocean's surface, dripping through the jade green until the darkness of the depths had swept away.

Standing now relatively dry and with unhindered sight, these geek boys were adapting to their good fortune, no equipment necessary now to see the treasures that had mystified them for centuries. Treasures lined out on the wet sand bed as far as the eye could see. Unopened trunks with heavily rusted locks just sat waiting to be bust open.

Yet I felt an unwelcome aspect filter into my dream as I noticed a larger group of men further up the beach looking over n pointing towards me. I was wary of the figures, yet as I moved nearer to them they seemed oblivious to my form.

Slamming axes now replaced the sounds of my cell mechanisms bolts locking loudly into place. It was a free for all.

This retreat I was enjoying, discovering the new world, one without oceans. The wrecks of folklore that had remained hidden stood now proud like fresh relics.

Treasure hunters crowding many areas, excited, maps out, maps getting ripped to shreds with loud yells of excitement, heads together, scanning the expanse for their claim to a nice chunk of gold.

A 200 foot long shadow in the sun met my gaze. A voyage that must have been swept away in rough seas with a terrifying decent all the way to the bottom of these ocean beds. Amazingly a few ragged sopping wet sails, now billowing out the best they could with the fluid inside the cloth still held to the mast.

The periscopes were out at the eyes of men scouring distant horizons that glittered with the booty of long lost pirate's pensions. Thunder clap waves that usually spun my body down here absent, allowing me time to structure my vision.

I followed a speki geek, tape measure trailing behind him as he recorded certain timbers n their lengths, ticking off in a yellow note book certain bits of info. Probably trying to determine what bits belonged to which wrecked ships. To my left, this grand hull, like a great dead whales bones rose from the wet sand, my vision focused on the ugly gash in its side where what looked like a torpedo had entered and foundered the battle ship.

I hadn't even realised that the sun light had vanished. The group had torches lit and I could hear quite easily even from the distance between us that they were discussing my presence. I felt uneasy as they set off at a fast pace towards me. The looks on their faces gave away their intentions.

Like some old style vigilante mob, they were soon surrounding me. I realised I had in my hand a large black rock that I had picked up instinctively to ward off this obvious attack. The gang threw down their lit torches, except two. The darkness now added to the terrifying feeling that I was about to be murdered in cold blood.

Sharp edged axes replaced torches now in most of the group's hands. One of the leaders stepped forward and I caught sight of my face in its polished reflection, his arm now reaching back in a swinging motion, my instinctive duck the last I knew of the scene as the FABERON'S alarm bells rang out.

It must be Monday morning for they test them every single week at ten am, waking up the entire hospital, except a handful of deeply zoned out chronics.

Turning over from a numb arm that I'd been laid on, reality stared blankly in my face. Just the chipped peeling paint of the bare cell wall, the distant noise of keys and other inmates voices complaining of being woken by the alarm tests. I didn't like the feeling that I woke with, those vigilantes all too real in the ocean dreams as I felt the chill from my clammy skin sticking close to the bed sheet. The trap had me again, waking towards my speckled wall, no laze for me today.

Tired from the drugs and deep dreaming, yet this doomed reality claw hammers me back to my true shit existence. This old hotel had that Californian song etched by blunted spoons in its walls. The porter would kick you up your arse as you carried your own bags. The menu was non-existent. I'd never had the freedom of choosing my own food. From home life to here, nearly nineteen years I had gotten by on scraps n disgusting gruel.

I wondered at times if the Queen knew what terrible establishments these were, but of course she did, they had the Tower of London as a tourist attraction didn't they?!!

Headaches coming bad again, the strain of confinement, the pressure of the living concrete tomb, my ulcer stabbing at my sides again, as the stress of Gerard's buggin had taken its toll on my body. Thankfully I was managing to train much better now he was dead.

One thousand sit ups later and the sweat held frozen on my lake smooth stomach. Still though I must put in more effort, a thousand press ups on top and I can take my hands and pray in the indentation between my chest muscles.

The dogs broke my concentration. All of them held close in the pens just behind the perimeters thirty foot first line of defence.

I had thought often of escape. I tampered with the locks, worth a try as Poidge Stone would say to me as a boy.

Oh I was privileged today New clothes for the Emperor, the restraint jacket not a bad fit. A lot better one than last week.

The call for an extra small last week had been a struggle to get on, the brute bastard guards yanking it over my head n fastening its straps to bursting point. Night had crept upon me.

Only one cloud of dark navy I could see in the sky between me n Jesus. The glow from the yards beams lighting up the vision.

Morning appeared as unexpected as night as the rain whipping in through the bars with a wild wind wet all the sills, giving the old stone a darker brown n green colour.

I just managed to add the F to Fuck you in the beans sauce. The tray they had put near me with a few bits of grub on that I had managed to bend over n scoop into my hungry mouth. I was under no illusion I was being punished, but for what I couldn't tell you.

I watched like this for a few long weeks as the walls crumbled in front of my drugged bleary eyes. Another couple of flaky layers peeled off to show dull green with brown to follow then back to green where the system went back to penny pinching in the Annual budget. The old tin pots from the years before would do.

Nobody ever bothered to scrape it all back and start anew.

The very walls held the mentality of the FABERON.

There was to be no fresh start. Just the omnipresent repetition of wasted torturous days, where lives were smothered over n forgot. I was determined to gain my freedom though. To one day be in charge of this pathetic life up to now.

{LIZARD JUMPS chapter 81} *Along with the commando press ups that Character had shown me up against his own cell door to do, I had started adding lizard jumps into my routine.*

They had finally set me free from the straight jacket, with no more reason given to taking me out of it as there had been for putting me into its confinement in the first place. Allowing me to return to my private work out, where after working up a sweat I would cup my hands in the water of the jugs bowl n cool down my blood that was rushing into my head.

The sun's rays burnt through miles of open sky, my bare back soaking up the heat as I stood half stripped in my cell. The Winter beginning to thaw.

The history of torture now and forever my guide to the body's endurance, Aquarian amounts of water cleansing the inner me. Many a time as a youngster I would get from Stan a yard broom to the gizzards, yet no throat punch now could easily dislodge this life. Busting noses for the hell of it eh Dad.

It felt like a young man treading water for fun, swimming near reeds that seemed safe surfaced. Yet darker down in the pond there setting traps for legs to tangle and dance deaths swan song.

Letting them get me, holding out until I could feel the pull of the root, then my twisting retreat away from play. Snapping that deadly grip, floating away free and alive. My face basking in the last hours of the sun, just floating still as the now waters calm surface returns.

The paranoia of the walls could get real heavy at times though. Your mind in a constant battle to believe its own strange conclusions, difficult to listen to most of the time Yet even when you studied and deciphered the contents of the paranoia, rationalized it to the point where you knew it was wrong, it still lingered at the minds table, mocking you right there with the Devil on its side, their bibs tied tight around their necks, ready to catch the spills from your sanity.

I would talk aloud to Mum at times and that was ok. But in here you had to guard well your fragile sanity. So often, men had been lost to the invisible figures. The drug doses made me soppy at times as I fell in n out of love with Nurse Silk a thousand times a day.

I press out more reps on the cell floor. My sweat drips from my forehead onto the green pale wood, like a Chinese water torture of my own agenda. As for little Miss prim n proper, she would sometimes be drawn to my cell door through my grunts of exertion. Or when she was passing to give Winnie his constant medication doses, she would peak in.

I would jump up from my press up or sit up position and just stand there proud of my hardness. My eyes looking directly back on her own as she broke the staring competition to gaze pleasingly all over me. She would open her beautifully formed mouth ever so slightly, just enough for me to see her pink tongue and a little sigh would whisper through the slit of the door and she would be gone. And that sound would lay back down with me on the floor and I would exercise on.

{GESHE chapter 82} I struck lucky with the new staff. They had given old Walter a promotion to day duties n the new night clocky came by my cell late on his first nights shift to introduce himself.

Officer Spring first told me through my door, after politely knocking to let me know he was the other side that he had been chatting to Character n that from what he gathered, I could use a little guidance. He was a Doctor of Buddhist studies, which gave him the title of Geshe.

He had come into the system to try to help the minds of troubled men. Quite how he had met the requirements to work on this particular sadistic ward I knew not.

But whatever the reason he had appeared I was thankful and ready to listen n learn anything he had which could help me become a better man on my release. I told him over the coming weeks, late in the early hours of the new mornings, just how the drugs were affecting my mind. I put my ear close to the door as he spoke in a rather low gentle way.

"Otiss, A true clean high of meditative state shows the mind how altered states of perception are unnecessary. The clean mind reveals the misconception of a drug opening up the mind to greater detail. In fact the body and mind free of interference realises that the substance abuser only closes the possibilities of the mind and its wide range of thinking and feeling.

The only way Otiss to true self knowledge is by letting go of safety and facing the mind head on in clear reality. Only then can the human sense the endless possibilities of the brain and the all important third eye. Trust your gut instincts Otiss n stand up for what you believe in".

I shed a tear after he had left my door. Thinking back on what he had said n thinking about Mum.

It was hard to let go of old thoughts. I had come to realise quite painfully over the last year or two that I had been abused most of my life. But when the new thoughts were also so strong to get out of here, to claim back my life and finally stand up for myself proper, I knew I could do it. I was determined to keep my VIGIL, n up my ANTE.

{DINTS IN THE DOOR chapter 83} *My medication doses had started becoming quotidian like clockwork.*

Except now I had become more devious n determined to not swallow everything they gave. With the injections I had little choice. They still jabbed me at random, always in the groin now or in the foot as my arm veins had collapsed over 6 moons ago. It was easy for them to see I was growing more determined to become strong n fit.

I exercised at random times whenever I could, putting in max effort. I'd scowl in my plexi glass mirror, a silver back hardness glared back. I knew I was becoming hardened beyond ever regaining loving looks, but I didn't care.

I practised smiling but it would still be manic. I would phrase with my mouth pleasant sentences but they would end up in a sneer. It mattered not one dot. . I envisaged encountering Stan and revealing all my pleasant look practising.

Camouflaged with snake skin colours ready for a war he would never see this coming. I visualised his initial kidnap, which would be frightening for us both. Yet I knew I had to train for restraint too. I had planned the mellow torture in my mind over the years with such precision. I couldn't kill him in one punch, in one split second of built up rage exploding right in front of his petrified face.

At times my mind flies out of this coma like feeling, finding a gear that only exists in confinement. Staring at the walls for days on end, the same damn spot my reward for living an honest life.

I've now accepted my dull empty existence, this cesspit box that tries to con me, lie to me, with tormented abuse on a daily basis. I don't fear no more. Something's changed. No warmth from these cold peeling walls, so I fuel heat to my heart with vengeance.

And I am sweating right now thinking of that no good bastard of a Father. Harsh drafts blow through the bars window trying to freeze a creak into my neck, I shadow box away the moment.

The mutts had been given the stick, quieting them down for now, tranquil air, but they would start up yapping again later. There was never a pure silence in here, always some noise going on to disturb the creaking skulls. Like a delayed death strike this sentence. I had wondered many a meal time about poison for Stan's last meal. But it was I knew deep down in my heart going to be brutal his death.

Violence and plenty of it would only suffice. The training so easy while anger engulfs me, which was most of the time. I could find Stan's face anywhere.

Punching the steel plates that held my door together with patch work sincerity, I'd pagger away, as Dad eyes would appear as knuckle dents. His face I would shape with a flying double bare footed kick. I'd broken my hands on purpose as it was the only way to ease some pain.

On the up side, Nurse Silk had bandaged them early the next morning as I was excused from the bath drowning.

She wrapped them like a trainer wraps his fighter's mitts ready for a brawl, as I studied her creamy white thighs lost in my own little fantasy.

{THE PLUG IS PULLED chapter 84} *I had heard him arrive back into his peter and quietly start to strum the two chords on his gee tar that he had memorised from Character.*

A hundred years to rot had been rumoured to be inked in official red on his files now.

His speech which had been going downhill of late anyway certainly worsened after this knock back. We all knew some that would never get out, yet they went through the rigmarole of the hearings hoping n clinging to some remote chance of freedom.

I had shouted him for hours after he arrived back, but he ignored me, sulking in that own little world of his n striving to get right that third chord on his gee tar. I had a strange lingering feeling I had been to the chapel of late, that it was Sunday today.

Not that I remembered anything of a service, yet the trip outside to where it was held in the grounds since the ancient building that was St Faith was no more. Not the large burial ground I was sure, but I had passed a smaller row of worn faded wood crosses. The numbers printed on them mixed up in my memory.

C34690, 2113, and 6119, all for some reason swirling around in the dazed memory bank.

After late dinner, somewhere around six thirty pm, I'd wearily climbed the iron stairs back to my pad to consume the slops.

It was Sunday, as thick lumpy gravy had been ladled over everything, my desert included.

I didn't even notice back in my cell I had a gift. Not until I put my empty tray out on the landing did I notice the ping pong ball hanging from the ceiling on a piece of string.

Puzzled for a while, Character at my door before banging his self up, grinning widely. "It will help your boxing training young Otiss, head movement lad!!"

I gave it a quick flick with a left jab n slanted my head out of its returning way. My mind was on something else as well as training right now. I was waiting for the radio show to kick into life.

Just hearing fresh voices relieved the boredom so much. I laid on my bunk n let my mind run through my routine of training. I was developing fast and at times when I caught my reflection I could see a young Granddad Pedley staring back.

The diesel brews had been cancelled since Gerard's murder. Not permanent, but done with for now. I waited patiently for the night clockie to enter the wing n do his first rounds before contemplating retrieving my ear phones from the rim.

A thousand sit ups later to kill the time, I practised holding my breath for five minutes, the small black spider returning to his larder my guide on time.

I watched a speck of dust for a minute n then blew out the held air.

It was something I had brought into my training routine a while ago n I was started to hold it well.

These were lost years on the agenda for sure but I was determined now to make the time count. No place for soft guts in here and I needed everything to be solid for the day I hoped they let me leave.

Yes in my eyes on close inspection you would be able to see a long term. But no one would see that close and if they did it would be the last thing they ever saw before a painful death.

I heard the familiar bang on the cell wall from Winnie. The show must be on.

I unfurled the head phones n squeezed under the bed to plug the socket to live."YO YO YO, Dj waX here, and what a show we have for you tonight my dear listeners."

I got comfy under my bed sheets n listened in.

"Caller one" I hear this loud clicking sound then this old dear with a strong Chinese accent mingled in with quite good English. "Herlo" More clicking, which I can't quite figure out what its source is then some info.

"I'm hundred n sevorn and I juss gruw new set off teef"

Dj waX didn't hang around with this one. He politely congratulated the old lady showing respect for her age n her new nashers n moved on to caller 2.

"Yo caller 2, what we got to say?"

The static on the line like always buzzed a little and then this clear educated sounding voice came across the air waves.

"Hello, good to be on the show. I would just like to ask your point of view on a little matter that has been concerning me of late"

Dj waX sensing something juicy says, "Go on caller the mikes all yours"

The gent cleared his throat n spoke.

"When your mind is more powerful than the drug, what do you do? Do you turn to the alcohol or do you try something new. When your mind is craving so bad it can feel septic. My question is, do you turn mad or finally accept it?

"Yeah just accept it caller 2.

Although your point of view or question does sway me to believe that you may be one of those lucky humans that teeters on the edge of that thin line between madness n genius.

Are you a star sign Aquarian by any chance? They have a strong tendency to be born that way."

The line went dead, the caller hanging up, not happy with the reply. Dj waX taking it in his stride moved straight on to caller 3.

"I have terrible writers block!!!"

"I'm sorry to hear that caller, what has dried you up"?

Caller 3 didn't really answer back to the host, more an oral airing of his predicament for us to listen in to.

"Have I lost the spark that ignites the end of my pen?

What runs the ink out of my nib, holding back everything now!

Free artistic beliefs left to roam across these chopped trees.

How many pens have been run into retirement? How many wicker baskets filled with screwed up attempts?

Like cold birds that from winter flee.

I need to change my scene, clear my clogged up mind.

Let the poor servant's downstairs ring the bell for a change.

In secret diaries years ago THE INK RUN."

And with that statement he hung up.

"Caller 4"

There must have been some convo between Dj waX n the caller before we got the connection in our ear holes.

"Care to elaborate on that caller 4?"

"Whack on some mental tunes MAN"

"Who do we have on line 4 caller?"

"Swinton Boulevard here, just raided the x wife's medicine cabinet"

"I know who I am voting for, whoever brings down the price of T bags, I am absolutely parched.

Dj waX let his hysterical laughter go on for a few minutes until he cut him off saying "sort your fucking head out Swinton."

"Line 5, I am hoping for a decent topic this time, what you got to say my friend?"

A pleasant sounding chap's voice came in clear to my ear phones.

"May I speak about materialism?" "You may, tell me what's up caller 5"

"People, humans, who for whatever reason, down on their morale I guess. Certainly absent of inner confidence, fuel this materialistic nature that rides high within the very heart of mankind. Examples of importance that reveal more in a gesture than any decent ink man ship.

The man next to me has a more expensive watch, yet just by the way he feels inferior to your naked aura, a sleeve rides up and it's no accident. A pathetic revelation from his actions, thinking he has out done you in some worldly way untrue.

Showing off with a flash of blood diamonds that to this day remain irrelevant to true wealth shows his poor taste. Yet his folly is your gain. My inner belief of time far more priceless than inanimate metals and stones could ever be."

"Thanks for that caller 5, very interesting my man, right listeners let's see where our final few calls can lead us before the break."

"Caller 6 you are on the air"

"Hi I just want to tell you of my friend's terrible experience that's left him quite traumatized.

He was a postman delivering letters on his usual round in a quiet country village when he was forced into the back of his van and abducted by two men. He was tied up and driven around for about an hour before his captors, one of whom was wearing a mask with large floppy ears freed him.

They then set his van on fire n fled leaving him unhurt but very badly shaken. He hasn't worked since, dare not even bring himself to lick a stamp no more, it's just tragic"

"Very worrying, I' am sorry to hear about this caller n please from all of us here at Faberon fm wish him a speedy recovery."

I heard some noise from the landing, even through the lull of the show. Lowering the headphones onto my neck I strained to hear if I needed to be aware of trouble. Things seemed quiet again so I fitted the phones back on my lugs n caught Dj waX introducing caller 7.

"I'm not a sheep man!!!! I'm not the Sheppard either."

Dj waX chiming in with the obvious next question, "well who are you then "The caller straight back at him with this dreamy voice," just a renegade from the flock that's who."

"Renegade my man, just call me renegade."

I was just wondering where the hell this caller was going with his call when I heard the doors bursting open, the heavy steel smashing back against the wall n nearly bouncing back into the squad of thugs who were flying in to get me.

On the other end of the earphones you could hear doors bursting open too, Dj waX screaming to get the fuck back n the line cut off dead as a door nail. The squad of thugs strangled me to near unconsciousness with the ear phone wire as I was dragged around the cell, my head pinging of the walls like a pin ball trapped in the flippers.

Wa/rd siX the destination I was heading in.

Winnie I caught sight of, totally knocked out cold, been dragged along just behind me.

Much larger groups of silhouetted thugs gathering to remove the troublesome from the wing like Gyp, Character n Scot John.

That was the last I ever heard of the radio show. It was to be the last different voices of the outside world I heard for the next 7 years.

{A LONG YEAR chapter 85} It was a long punishment this time. The directors of the asylum had gone n flipped out thinking that an outside source had been able to penetrate our ears. They were more worried that patients may have been able to transfer their voice the other way n let out the horrors that were blatantly going on in here out to the wider world n cause some God awful scandal that would rock the government.

The injections now were sending me on sleeps that I never believed I would wake from. Just random visits by brutes who shaved me roughly n sheared my hair out of the tangled dread mess it became.

Probably a year passed before I even received a breath again of fresh air. This small cage made of barbed wire, large enough for maybe three men at a push was where I was led.

Character a welcome surprise as I entered.

The guards left us alone n after two minutes of silence he hugged me n asked if I was ok. He looked remarkably fresh, considering our location. Like a magician he pulled this old large coin from behind his ear n placed it in my palm. "Break it" I feebly twisted it n looked back at him.

He pulled the same coin from behind his ear again n holding it between his two thumbs n two index fingers broke it clean in half.

The guards were coming back n shouting already that time was up n it was time to get back in the hole. Character gave me one half of the ripped coin n smiled. His pike eyes glinting back at me "You keep on trying" I shoved the full n half coin in my sock n shuffled back inside.

I got my next bit of fresh air a few months later with Dr Gaunt bringing me on one of his therapeutic walks through the grounds trying to quiz me about the radio show n if anyone had reached the old outside world. We stopped near this large oak tree, not too far from the one I had seen upon entering the building that led to the Netherfield ward. The name to me forgotten which I had seen carved in its trunk, the feeling of being here forever not quite so faded.

On this big oak tree another carved name that Dr Gaunt clocked me staring at. Telling me to sit down a minute, he paced around in front of me, giving me another of his boring lectures.

"You see that name Otiss carved there? Well that is Mr Meek. Or should I say was!!

He gave this creepy laugh, cleared his throat and went on.

He was most certainly one of our most troublesome patients that ever stayed with us here at the institution. We tried everything to calm the man down Otiss, but to no avail.

He ended up too much for the system, a failure really on the FABERONS part. 45 years he spent chained to that large oak.

There was no other way to secure his madness. The rages he had so out of this world. The strength of ten men Otiss, but ten mad men, so it was like fighting a 100.

You are sat on his bones lad!!

A fitting resting place we felt."

{A FAREWELL GIFT chapter 86} *Let me describe the scene from the magpie up on the turret. My sad little face held up to the bars with my white knuckles gripping on for dear life.*

A lost young soul in a lost old world of madness is what she sees from her vantage point. The last autumn leaves began this day to release and descend to the hardening ground. Faster over the coming weeks my view from my cell would change with the new temperate season due.

Every year just before Christmas, to my eye out the bars looking I would get to see this magnificent red bricked chimney. It hid well by the foliage through the summer season, yet now the cold of an arctic winter was on the wind, it held forth in my view over the fortified walls.

I was hoping that the lotto would be forgotten this year. Too many rumours by inmates, confirmed it was nothing like the move the staff tried to make you believe.

There was no better ward. Probably there were slightly more relaxed wards around the place, but nothing that any one from the Netherfield would ever see. Certainly nothing like the bullshit they were trying to put across about winning this lotto n going to a much better place. I never even understood their need to lie about the Aspen. They were getting away blatantly with so much anyway. It was almost as if it was some sick game to play with your mind.

It was nearly Yuletide again. The soil over mum would have penetrated her coffins wood box by now.

These horrible thoughts of dirt filling her mouth n ears. Her eyes shut, yet the worms wiggling in with the mud would be at them.

Stupid I know. She would have rotted away a long time ago.

The earth cruel to dead bodies, as their images soon appears unrecognisable.

I try to stay positive in the face of all this adversity.

Even the clanging and banging of the wing opening up for the morning gruel is a sweet melody. My mood for the day shall be uplifting. At least until a sudden injection knocks me off my already unsteady feet.

I fall into my press ups on arrival back in the cell.

The gruel demolished n fuelling my training. My illegal banana that Character somehow gets for me and leaves on the window ledge I scoff next.

There's therapy class today.

I get unlocked again and slide around outside my door on the messy spilling bastards drops of porridge.

Outside Scot John's I grin to myself as I see his tray shining bright, licked clean with national pride.

I'm pulled aside n notified I won't be going on therapy today.

No reason given.

I don't mind, it gives me a break from the chronics that I would have to sit n listen to. Their disgusting crimes aired quite freely in these classes, enough to make me puke on occasion after enduring the morning chit chat.

The lotto's notice has been pinned to the board. The tickets would be drawn very soon!!

I'm just chilling on my bunk reading a book on antiques that John lends out if you are cool enough to be his friend, when suddenly my doors open and with raised voices I am being told I am moving cells!!!

I go along without much struggle. They tell me not to pack my gear it's just for the morning while the therapy class is in session.

A few cells up above our landing are where I'm led. I had not been up on this level. Two guards hold me slightly by the arms as we make our way towards the last cell in the row of three. There are some other doors on the far side, but they are bolted shut beyond any look of ever being opened.

As I pass the last heavy bolted door, a scream n banging ring out n make me jump out of my skin. The guards grip me more tightly n move me to the end where they want me. Some poor creature from the bolted doors other side cries out, "help me, please help me, somebody pleeesssseee"

The guards don't even notice the pleas.

The door that's to be mine is unlocked n it's a bare cell with no window, just this strange white plinth rising from the cell floor. Sat on top of this is a large mahogany box with a handle poking out from the side of it.

An alien looking thing if ever I saw one.

That's all there is.

The guard closest to me tells me he will bring a chair for me to sit at the wheel!!

"The wheel" I inquire.

"Yeah the crank wheel Kites, you have to turn it ten thousand times before lunch or you stay in this cell for the rest of the week."

I was told that I had it easy, that the screws on it were not that tight. A piece of piss apparently, he commented before slamming the door on me.

I looked the thing over for a few minutes then gave its handle a grip n spun it round. "One" I said out loud to no one in particular. It was going to be a long morning.

By the time I had gotten into half an hour my forearms were burning like pokers in the flames. I took a rest trying to figure out how long I had left n trying to calculate how many spins I could maintain in certain portions of time.

Not long after I had settled into a steady rhythm, one of Gerard's bully mates who was on this week's shift showed up. Most had kept a low profile since his killin, yet there was one who had always given him the most back up with his sadistic ways, n the bastard was at my door right now.

He tried to whack me up the first morning I was in the crank cell. Probably believing I was isolated enough up here n vulnerable enough to give the bully's guts some nerve. Flying in all tough looking through the door, his figure huge in his oversized uniform, it was he who got the shock though.

I had changed again in the year since that fucker had been part of the bully crew. My jaw plates where I had spent years tensing my teeth together had a hardened steeliness to them. My chin had widened nicely n wasn't something weak you were going to break with your best punch.

Jesus I even had this thick growth of black hair coveting my entire shoulders like an animal cape, a beast not to fuck with.

But he gave it his best shot. I followed the arc of his swing as he threw his punch. I didn't even bother showing him my reflex powers. I let him connect right on the button, his face a picture n worth the pain just to see the shock. It freaks a man out when he suddenly realises he's messing with something he doesn't understand. He made a pathetic statement saying that was for Gerard!!

Like I gave a hoot as he noticeably shrunk in stature n left the cell mumbling to the floor all dejected.

I carried on getting the hang of the cranks wheels momentum, feeling that this so called punishment was becoming use full to the strength gains in my already powerful arms.

Thankfully I hit my target on the old archaic machine.

I struggled to hold my tray from lunch out in front of my arms as I headed back to my peter. Smiling inside knowing they were giving me all I needed to become what I wanted to be.

Winnie hadn't been as vocal for a long time. The beatings he had received after the radio show was busted seriously dinted his confidence. He had withdrawn more, studying mostly these days his ancestry stuff n keeping to himself. Every now n again I would bang his cell wall n he would come to the pipes n we would have a natter about the goings on around the place.

I had told him my ocean dreams had become less of late.

The sea Gods calmer yet never redundant, as now and again ferocious bubbles popped on the surface of my dreams. Yet since the total empty ocean had revealed itself n the strange crowd, I hadn't been swept down even a fathom of late.

A few nights later a surprise bang on my wall from old Winnie interrupted my shadow boxing against the cell wall.

He had a gift for me.

Or so I found out after we had emptied the pipes connection n nattered on for a while. He seemed very down on himself, afraid even, from the vibes I was picking up from his voice. I asked what the sudden gift was all about n he just repeated over n over down the pipes that it was something he felt I should have, something he wanted me to own.

He told me to get ready to catch a line at the barred window. So I flushed the connection as my curiosity got the better of me. As to what this gift could be I had no idea, dragging my chair sharpish over below the window, getting my bog brush ready to catch the line being hurled. My outstretched arm felt the biting winter cold but I didn't have to wait long, Winnie an old hand by now flying his target straight into my clutches.

I shouted cheers n got down.

The wool of his bed blanket was wrapped around the end of my stick, the piece of screwed up paper wrapped around at the end like a spider had weaved his best pattern secure. I spent a few minutes unravelling it all n finally opened the paper.

It dazzled me at first. Something with such light n beauty, in amongst the drabness of the cell so out of place. I twirled it in my fingers and a strobe shot out of it in electric green n silver. Its diamond qualities had caught a reflection from the outside beam of the arc lights that swept across the yard at random times.

I didn't know much about jewels, but at a guess I would say it was a full 3 carrot stone at least of immense clarity. It was set in this gypsy style that I had seen on old Dolly blues hand before. She had worn the fancy ring of her deceased husband Uriah, as a tribute to his style n wealth.

Ten claws held this stone I was holding into place, a magnificent setting for such a diamond.

I flushed my pipes out n banged Winnie's wall. He didn't take long this time to connect. "What's going on mate?"

I could see him mentally through the wall deliberating before speaking back to me. Finally his cleared throat the first sound I hear, then, "It's a gift, it belonged to my Dad Jamal."

"Cool my friend", I ventured back, "but why give it to me?"

The pause, I later that night was to realise, an indication as to why he was giving up something so precious.

He had left the toilet pipes connection open, yet he had not said another word for hours.

I had fought off the medications tablets concoction this evening, trying my hardest to train my chest with some push ups. I had almost given up on hearing back from Winnie that night. The diamond I had hung tied to a piece of the line he had sent me. Around my neck it sat just above the silver acorn.

The night clocki had done his last check ages ago n it must have been the early hours into the next day. I had done enough on my chest, as much as my aching arms could do. It was just about time to climb into my pit when I heard him at the pipes again.

I cocked my ear down towards the bowl n heard him say, "Otiss, this is a message from Character, its important mate that you look".

"Look at what" I ventured back bemused.

"Into your water in your jug "And with that crazy talk he was off, flushing the connection closed.

I stood in the middle of the cell, the dark sky held a streak of yellow behind its navy cloak. The wing was fairly silent at this hour of the night. I stared over at my wooden stand in the corner that held my water jug. I had emptied some of it over the course of the evening, cooling my head n neck as I had finished each set of press ups. Around half remained in the jug.

I moved close, peering down its open neck n stared into the waters reflection.

I watched my eyes blinking back at me for a while n then just as I was about to shout Winnie asking what the hell he was on about, something happened.

{NO.1 BOX chapter 87} The water stirred and at the same time I got this ringing in my ears that became painful. Then not actually

Characters voice, but this overwhelming strong sense that his thoughts were inside my own.

Without actually hearing the noise of words I followed Characters guidance as he explained just what it was I was seeing.

Down in the jugs water, a scene, just like the time he had shown me the one before in the mirror of my cell.

Here was Dr Gaunt, creeping about just the same as he had been when he burnt down the chapel of St Faith. This time he was near his desk, a large black box sat imposing on its surface. The water rippled again in the jug and I now had a more close up view on what was written upon it in white painted official looking letters.

On its side just below the lid on the front it said, No 1 BOX.

Also laid out on the desks top was a white cloth bag, with this large card that held a list of the box's contents.

The revelation clear now as to what I was actually focusing on. The very top of the card gave clear instructions as to what its contents use were for. Execution box!!!

There were 4 ropes, a block n fall, 2 straps n the sand bag. Then I read further down the list.

1 measuring rod, a piece of chalk, a pack of thread, copper wire and the most scariest item, the hood.

Characters voice, again without words, just clearly there as if my own thoughts telling me to look some more into the water.

It's rippling washing away now the scene of the hang mans tool box.

Now it zoomed out to show Gaunt laughing n talking to a figure I couldn't quite make out. The Drs Hand was inside the cloth bag up to his suit sleeve, pulling back now n holding a ticket in his hand to see who had won the lotto.

The water in the jug rippled n seemed to change a few colours before settling back on the vision. Now I could see quite clear that the name Alan & Tom was written upon the Winning ticket.

I remembered the pair mentioned from when I had first entered the asylum.

But here was the sly bastard Dr up to his tricks again. The last rippling from the jugs contents showed the reason Winnie had gone quiet n the reason I was wearing his Dads diamond ring around my neck.

Gaunt laughing louder now, and the mysterious figure in the office is pouring out over in the corner two glasses of fine looking malt.

Before I see them chink the glass together in celebration, the vision focuses on Dr Gaunt ripping up Alan & Tom's ticket, its fallen pieces floating towards the heavy thick carpeted floor.

There's a new ticket being waved about n more laughter.

Poor old Winnie's name clear as this diamond he gave.

There was no luck in here. No equal chance given. They just did what they damn well wanted n it seemed it had been decided by the faceless men in power that it was time to hang old Mr Winnie Jah.

{*LORD OF THE WINDOW chapter 88*} Of course the official word would be therapeutic!!!But a select few knew just where Winnie was heading.

They quietly came for him the next evening. He had refused to come and talk to me at the pipes or window. Yet he banged my wall in his old familiar style n I took it to be his farewell gesture.

When I say quietly, it was with an almighty crash of his door being opened aggressively when I see him for the last time. They led him away quietly along the landing clutching his ancestry files tight in *one hand, his bag over his sad shoulder he held in the other I studied his profile as he passed. He never glanced off to the side to wink or nothing, just a face set dead ahead, knowing these were some of his last steps as a living man.*

Next day was solemn. Scott John explained to me about how the French dealt with their mob of crims. French slang had been his thing this week, reading up on certain stuff he could get his hands on from the library.

Apparently LORD OF THE WINDOW was the dreadful name that convicts give poetically for the guillotine.

He went on to say he had a great idea for some new tattoo.

I'd seen him the day before Winnie went off the wing.

He had been pointing at Dr Gaunt's head on the landing, mumbling the word Tronche over n over. I had then noticed him pointing with his tattooed finger at his own skull, repeating the word Sorbonne.

He got around to telling me what the hell it all meant. A lingo used by thieves, invented to satisfy the need to consider the human head under two aspects.

Firstly the Sorbonne is the head of the living man, his brain, his power of advising n directing. Tronche, a contemptuous word designed to show the uselessness of a head parted from its body by the executioner.

I got the gist of his pointing. Gaunt was a dead head. I told John that I had read somewhere that strangulation was the bully way of killing. After parting n getting back to our cells, I am sure just like me, a few of the men were wondering how poor old Winnie's neck had faired against the hangman's stiff rope.

I woke that night hearing banging against the wall. I knew it couldn't be him. I flushed the pipes out of habit more than anything n spoke though, "WINNIE", nothing, just the silence of the cell, distant groaning, the usual chronics having bad dreams n wide awake nightmares, but no Winnie at the other side.

I pulled the string from around my neck and put the ring over my finger. I loved to look at it in the dark. I waited for the light from the yards search tower to hit the right spot, holding the stone so that it caught at the right angle to shoot of its dazzling beams that only diamond can.

As I was about to pull it off my finger and put it safer back around my neck it moved. Just slightly at first, to the point I thought I was just tired n over thinking, but then it spun around on my finger the whole way. Four times it span before it stayed where I had placed it. Old Winnie was here alright, or somewhere in this life that is just a brief split in the sky to another world's dimensions.

{SLOW BURNER chapter 89} The band in the day room was growing. Now when the piano keys tinkled with its unseen player, Winnie's mischief on the guitar would blend in. He was still no better in death, yet his echoed strings were a small comfort to his friends who missed him. Just knowing he was fine on the other side was consolation for our grief.

It did get me to thinking more deeply though as to just how n what you took through to the other side. Was he playing from a far, or projecting a memory of sounds as such into our living world?

The time for me to train was right now. There were no radio distractions and no Winnie to chat with through the long evenings, even my ocean dreams seemed to have more or less dried up. The Geshe night clocki was a God send, his wisdom talking through the Gaps in the doors late on a night invaluable.

My training becoming much more than the physical, I was preparing for all out war upon release.

If it ever came!! I was still very dubious about ever getting out of here, but Character kept saying he had seen the future and that I was in it, as free as a bird.

So I pushed on, training like the mad man they said I was.

I would dip my head towards the water jug when it was full to the brim, placing my face into the cold water, my eyes open as my mouth n nose submerged under. Then in my head I would start the count.

It took a while, practising every other night, but I was soon able to hold my breath for a good five minutes easy.

Floor hand stands were soon to become my favourite exercise. My tip toes of my bare feet resting up against the cold steel of the cell door. Steady with the balance n then down with my arms. Commando press ups until I shook with fatigue. My shoulders bulking out with great power inside them, then I would get a quick rinse at the jug. Cold splashes onto my fizog. Sit ups while reading my book.

Invigorated stretches now, not those old tired dog stretches of some.

I was to become what you might call a slow burner. I learned to not be like Stan with that quick temper of his. It was never an option on becoming a vigilant man.

The fuse needed to be more than long. It needed to be never ending. You didn't light the fuse either. You lit the fire inside until it raged, then you burnt the fuckers you had your eye on.

I remember back as a kid once hearing him from upstairs as he shouted at mum below in the lounge.

"What a horrible little creature, I have committed a terrible sin bringing forth that into this world."

Such a memory brought a great feeling of sadness to my spirit. What was worse it got me thinking to the sister I had never had.

Shannon was here name. Not that she had ever got the chance to hear any one call her by it.

Stan had been adamant that she would not see her first breath.

Around four or five months into the birth, I hauntingly recalled this dirty looking tramp call at the house, claiming to be a Dr.

He had the Gladstone bag n bowler hat, but that was about as far as it went to being decent.

My Mothers lump had disappeared the next morning as I had gone out the door for skool.

When I returned that day I had walked in on Stan in full flow screaming he didn't want the fucking thing n that it would have turned out a slag like its Mother!!

He had gone drinking for weeks after that day sleeping in the shed n not speaking to a soul until he decided it was past.

I had thought of her before in here. One of the early ocean dreams floated me out from a cavernous spot slowly heading deeper to the source of a river, where I had drifted off under emerald waves.

I had told Character about it at the time. He had mused about it then told me the great Irish river started about 16 miles away in an underground cave. The Shannon pot had been the word that made me think of my poor dead sister.

And that was just one of many things that motivated the training until I was ready to commit my own moral crime.

Taking that bastard out forever, and a Amen to that I thought as I grinned n thought of Jesus spitting straight into the Roman guards face in defiance of wrong full arrest.

Gaunt went and put his foot down again in a show of strength.

The silent tat shop was to permanently close. But it was to needle out one last masterpiece before it did.

Gaunt had the backing of the directors to come in and pull the wood sign which had been so lovingly carved down from above John's door.

Character was to be the last client. There was to be a select few invites to watch.

As the sewing needle dipped back n forth from the ink bottle to his open shirted chest, he told the gathered crowd as Scot John carried on jabbing away at his skin.

"Because the Holy man is clear as to the end and beginning, as to the way in which each of the six stages completes itself in its own time, he mounts on them toward Heaven as though on six dragons"

The wooden tat shop sign was to be pulled down the very next morning by old Walter. They sent him knowing the men on the ward respected him in a way n that there wouldn't be as much bother. He was the most harmless looking guard so I guess it made sense. Scot John tore the sign down himself n snapped it in half over his broad knee, handing it's two pieces to old Walter without any more violence. Character now the proud owner of six swirling black dragons circling around his heart.

{PILE OF CALENDERS chapter 90} *I scribbled a love note to Nurse Silk last night. I had screwed about ten attempts up n burnt them out of the cells window. This one I liked n had thought about giving her it all night.*

In the harsh light of morning though I flushed it away embarrassed at my soft side getting the better of me again.

With Gerard off my back, I had settled into a brutal regime of my own accord. A thousand sit ups here, a thousand press ups there. In the early days I had kept tally, yet now I had stopped counting. I had stopped counting when it started to really hurt many moons ago. Counting was a waste of time. I had no limits. Why would I restrict myself to a number? I wasn't training for some championship belt. I was contorting myself into an ugly mass of vengeance which I was going to see laid at my Fathers door.

Golden sparks flew through the night air. My hand speed was as quick as those belt holders. My solitary practice in these lost years you could say ready even now. But I was fine tuning this killing machine. There was never a time when I didn't think I could learn no more.

The slow wheel of justice reminiscent of the old broken miller's wheel that just had a trickle of water to torture me Chinese style.

This political wheel oiled by lab monkeys. I wasn't bothered now. I wanted the long length of time. I needed the decade they had spoke about in Yama's court room to fine tune the vigil. Upping the Ante Dad.

My growing shadow starting to unnerve me with its similarities to the wanker as I came looking for him in my cell every night.

I would find him too, but I had stopped hurting myself to some extent. My hands hardened n solid, yet I would be breaking every bone in them smashing his face when the time came.

The winter I didn't even notice pass by except for a few strolls in the spring months on the yard that reminded me of the seasons passing.

Nothing could stop time. Not even these glue filled clocks that they tried to con you into following blindly.

Scot John had done ten years today. That was a lot of time spent looking at these dull walls.

Yet in his inevitable style, he came strolling into my cell on morning unlock as if he hadn't a care in the world. I mentioned it was some kind of anniversary, to which he just smiled n closed my door nearly *shut, with the pair of us on the inside. He had been on a language voyage he said over his shoulder to me, devouring all the books the library offered.*

He spent five minutes scratching with a homemade shank something into my door. His back so broad I couldn't even make out a clue as to what it may be.

The screws were calling for the stragglers to grab their last chance for breakfast. I grabbed my mug to fill with sweet tea n tapped John on the back to say I needed to pass.

He had finished any way n as he moved aside I caught sight of his handy work.

He left me reading it with a cheerful, "One for each year"

I didn't understand all the words, yet Identified enough to know he had written the words in different languages to say insane. Starting with,

INSANO

FOU

HULLU

NEBUN

GILA

DEMENT

ALIENE

MESCHUGE

ELNEBAJOS

I guessed it would be something to memorise as I sat behind this steel blockage to real life.

Silent man came into my life without much bluster. Winnie's cell had stood empty. The new patient uttered no sound.

I had read on my way to lunch the other day the marker card upon his door. I feel I shall die upon the spot if I reveal its horrid secrets.

The red card like Scot John's was tucked in tight and new behind his details. Thankfully there was no Religious card, so I would be spared the charade of praying with such a heathen every other Sunday.

Only once did Incuriously look in on him. He had eyes like old Winnie, as black as northern coal. But that's where the similarities ended. I had stared hard at him through the glass panelled flap. I made him eventually feel the need to move to the side of the door out of sight, the best place for him. And quiet like a mouse he remained, unspoken to n as if it was just an empty cell still, which suited me fine.

Like the new night clocki had begun to school me. I had taken his advice on excluding all outside noise, except maybe the pleasant noise of the bird's song from upon my ledge.

The Kingdom is anew. Ruins underground whose vaults have lain undisturbed are now mine to dwell inside. I was beginning to sooth the turmoil, closing off any negative chatter, replacing all my thoughts with sweet revenge.

I am changing for the better every day, every second. The world around me has become new. I am not seeing the blank walls these days. I'm more with nature.

A thousand lives I feel I have lived before this one. All that preparation to finally kill off the bad blood that has ruined my veins, my enlightened souls flame was going to burn out Stan's DnA forever.

Sometimes it was hard to let go of old thoughts. But I knew I was on a path that had light along the way. I was not going to complain about my cards dealt in this life. I was going to play my hand and if I had to cheat to beat old Stanley, then so be it, I would.

I had tried the coin many times.

Frustrating for sure, I had hung by the bars holding on with just my finger tips, strengthening the grip until it was like an Eagles claw.

Never mind one missed calendar that Character had given me every year without fail, Seven now lay collected upon my wood table. The warning on them about the dangers of smoking still the message, but it had done his victims over the long years past no good.

It was like being a youth again, where the details of the wasted hours n weeks n months too monotonous to mention in full. When I stared out of the window for say half an hour, my mind would shut down the FABERON, and a near decade of staring would stare back at me through the same old views.

Silenced screaming and moaning that held the air that surrounded this space would be placed on mute in my brain. The messages directed with little electrodes to the ear not getting through now.

Faraway the reason for being here drifted on a shushed breeze.

There had never been much of a view, yet I did have the pleasure of seeing the odd tree top in the distance when the seasons were right. It was from this view point that I trained my thoughts.

A stately home I resided in. A prisoner from some long forgotten war kept politically for a trade with some other poor soul, who held sway with certain high officials.

The scenario changed over time to suit my moods. My favourite was the idea that I had sacrificed my entire life which had been full of riches and privilege to become a hermit, high up in my castle, training my mind and body for the afterlife, letting go of the Worlds destructive materialism, which in turn enabled me to focus on the important factors in life.

But it couldn't ever completely shut out the horrors of life inside such a demented hole. My arms would tire, even with the growing strength I was training into them. I would lose my grip on the bars slipping back into the harsh reality. My feet grounded back into the cell of the ward.

This crumbling fucking mental case institution that went by the name of the FABERON had me trapped. I would stare up at the bars set high into the concrete and feel an overwhelming sense of doom. The out of sight tree tops back then didn't hold the roots to a free dream. Their swaying gnarled branches tickled down into the graveyards here of the lucky dead.

Think of a little old lady sitting quiet in her bungalow, knitting a winter scarf in red and white, suddenly a lorry carrying boxes of fireworks crashes through her garden wall, bursting into flames and setting off all bangers n rockets.

Well that's how the sound of the wing would come back into my gentle ear lobe after hanging up at those bars dreaming. You kind of got use to the dreadful din. There was never a complete lull in the madness. Screams were trapped deep into these tortured halls.

{SNAPPED chapter 91} The rumours on who Character was viewing for his ritual moon killing this time seemed a step too far even for this place. Yet it made perfect sense and I hoped it would become true in the next week or so.

I myself had received another letter from my old friend Liberty. Enclosed on his expensive paper, the neat slanted writing brought forth more surprising news regarding my freedom's bid to get out of here. There had been some meetings he stated. Things seemed after all these years to be looking like I may just not have been training for the hell of it. There had he wrote, been even talk of eventual release. Yet he had gone on to state that it wasn't going to be plane sailing n he still had many minds to convince. There had been the usual greetings n advice too.

He hadn't forgotten me. On the contrary, he had thought of my plight often.

The best news inside this white envelope had been the statement written into the letter quite matter of fact that Judge Yama was dead. He had gone blind n stepped into the road on some foreign holiday, killing him instantly. I myself would have written this in ten foot high letters on the institutions wall, but the news was the same either way. The old bastard was dead, flattened like a foul bird on a country road. The ache in my cheeks from grinning was going to be there a good while over this wonderful news.

Liberty did not quite say as much, yet reading between the lines of the letter, it looked now with that old buzzard out of the picture, he could start trying to break me legally out of this hole.

I put the letter with his other. I had re read the warning in the first about Yama scaring him away from helping me in the early years. Yet knowing that he was 4 foot under now gave me hope, real hope that this maybe soon could be over.

I ripped the coin in half the very next night.

As if on Q, Character burst out in song. He had claimed back his instrument when Winnie had departed the Netherfield ward. I had heard Winnie try to get the hang of this certain tune, yet even after a year of trying he hadn't managed to hit the right chords or get the entire words right.

Old Bobby Maudsley lives near me floated through the insane air.

I finally heard the last verse as Characters soothing voice penetrated my cells space.

Killed a man, killed three, yeah old Bobby Maudsley lives near me.

He had told me about his acquaintance with the man when he had been in the normal prison system years before he had taken refuge in the asylum. Character had mentioned how he had been in a particular place nicknamed monster mansion, where he had come across the cannibal that was bobby M, living on the same unit that housed the most dangerous in the system.

The only decent bloke in that place he had told me one day out on the yard was the legend that was Mr blue.

I listened to the song and thought about the six black dragons circling Characters heart.

Stan's tattoo had always haunted my vision. I could see now in front of my eyes my small child like arm reaching out all those years ago, so afraid of the monster.

I was about to turn the tables n change all that. The monster may still be alive. But not for long once I strolled out of these gates.

{A SURPRISE RETURN chapter 92} *Nurse Silk filled the wards many flower vases this fine morning. They kept them filled fresh with species that grew in the asylum gardens. It helped keep the terrible stench at bay from the seeping filth that penetrated from under the cell doors.*

Dr Gaunt always wore a flower in his lapel. Along with the snuff he would snort from this little silver delicate trinket box he kept inside his suit jacket, there were no flies on him.

Yet there had been a creature keeping a watchful eye on his habits. The rumours had been kept to a minimum to decrease the risk of a tip off.

Sweat had poured out of me last night, even cooling myself at the barred window while the place slept off its troubles, brought forth nothing but ill effects. Like a fever brewing on my brow, I had still been trying to work out what nasty way Character would be able to inflict his killing habit. I knew the target, as did Scot John n Gyp the blood, but that was it. The whole damn place was in for a shock alright the next time the alarms rang out in distress.

Could the faint cheering from the blocks wing be a sign that the rumour had broke? I noticed up outside the bars a smoke ring on the wind.

Smoke ring number one was the silent flow of character I thought to myself. A second one sailed by. Smoke ring two the unsuspecting victim.

They both collided n swirled, vanishing forever.

I had a strong internal gut feeling that something had happened. My mind racing through scenarios as to which part of the hospital owed him his last stance. I could have done right now with good old Winnie, he would have been busy twirling a line to the next block and beyond.

An expert tuned in via the pipes gathering news of death.

There had been a killing that much I was sure of, Character the guilty laughing party. But without Winnie, I would like the rest have to wait for news to filter down before knowing the full pictures true horror n delights.

Breakfast was usually around seven am. So the screams must have been first heard around half six.

It kind of took the edge of the joy for me to be honest. The poor girl didn't deserve to be the one who found him.

I clocked her through the doors flap window, running franticly onto the wing, tripping over n knocking one of the vases full of water n flowers flying from where she had only positioned them the previous day.

It took a good ten minutes for the other guards on early shift to prompt the info out of her.

Her serene stroll through the grounds which she took most mornings unless she had a rare day off had become a horror scene.

She was housed not far from Gaunt's residence in the grounds, in a lodge house dedicated for the residence of the female members of staff.

Obvious to all staring at her, she had become witness to some horrific incident. Her clean white starched uniform was saturated in bright blood, her dainty knees covered in grass n mud. Her hair that had become loose from her bonnet tumbled over her weeping face, covering most of her beautiful eyes.

I nearly tested my strength right there n then. I was certain I could break through this steel door. Go console her, hug her even tell her of my love. But I stayed put, listening n watching to suss out as much as I could, hoping to confirm the rumours.

The whole place ten minutes later went into a meltdown that I had not witnessed in many confined years here.

Dr Gaunt was dead!!!

Murdered in cold blood in the grounds and hung by a tree naked as the day he was born, just waiting for some poor soul to find.

Character didn't care for my crush on Nurse Silk. He considered it a weakness. Viewing all the staff the same whatever level they were on.

It was an Us& them attitude that he remained solid about his entire life. So even though I don't think he would have planned on her being the one to find the mutilated corpse, it certainly wouldn't have caused him any lost sleep.

I felt sorry for her, yet the elation of this particular six moon killin had me on such a high that I soon forgot her distress and celebrated like everyone else.

They shut the whole wing down for more than a week. No one was taken away though.

It didn't come to that this time.

Character made a full confession.

He didn't explain how he had gotten into the grounds. But from an interview he conducted, they were in no doubt about his guilty involvement. Details of certain wounds that only on autopsy had been revealed, he had reeled off the top of his head, with that grin of his, constant throughout.

They transferred him to a more maximum secure facility, something that the Home Office had built with the intention of housing the worst of the worst. He left without any fuss.

My cell door he visited n that pike looking eye stared through at me. It had unnerved and been the last thing many men would see before their painful deaths, yet to me it held a sparkle that filled me with ease. In his honour, I carved on my cell wall,

221,500

He had once told me that he had counted those seconds down, waiting for the moon to be at its perigee.

What surprised me even more was the next week. Dr Woo was back, looking all very Japanese in his dress sense. He had been recalled back to take charge n steady the ship after a most brutal murder of a medical director there had ever been. He kept a very low profile around the hospital though.

Only coming on to the ward if there was an emergency, preferring the sanctuary of his newly furnished feng shui office.

{A BUSINESS FRONT chapter 93} *I had a letter from liberty stating his intensions to be present at the meeting about my possible release.*

Months of quiet boredom had passed since Gaunt had been buried on his request in his will inside the grounds. A strange request for sure. One the Authorities n directors of the asylum granted though. I had refused to attend the patient's requested attendance at the ceremony, visiting the block for a quarter of the year as punishment.

It was upon that return to my normal cell that I got news from Liberty about his impending visit. I had been busy with business just in case I did get set free in the near future.

Johnny had asked me about investing. He had been steadily putting away cash from his long term employment over the years. I wasn't stupid or naive. I knew he had a few scams going on here n there. He had always been a clever kid.

He had mentioned in a letter about where I had thought about living when I got my freedom back. I knew for a fact I wasn't going back to the house where Mum had been murdered. That was a certainty.

My few belongings, mainly Granddad Pedley's trunk was stored safe in old Dolly Blues vardo still, but I didn't fancy no cramped space after all these years with my nose more or less up against the wall.

I knew with what my plans were on the outside that I was going to need a cover for my activities. I had the money from Granddads estate. So over a little time, something I also had plenty of, we sorted out n finalised a deal on an old red brick building in the middle of the village lane. It had lay empty ever since we were kids, yet boarded up solid, stopping us exploring.

I had not taken long to be convinced that this was the perfect spot. Johnny doing all the paper work n meetings as he had taken a visit back home to see his family.

To me I wasn't even sure about buying a property in the village. Yet the more I thought through the proposal, the more it became clear that this is just where I needed to be on my release. Right slap bang in the midst of my Fathers patch. We finalised the deal through the post with me signing the documents with a flourish of my pen.

I had a sleeping partner who had both eyes wide open when it came to our business venture. I left it to my best friend to sort the refurbishment out. He in turn left it to a trusted friend of his to renovate the place to our requirements.

He wrote me asking about a name for the place. I didn't hesitate. It was the first thought that came into my mind. And so after a lot of hard work n a good chunk of my inheritance spent,

THE VILLAGE EYE

Opened for business and it was going to be filled to the brim with customers from the very first night I launched it. A nice little boozer slap bang in the middle of the village crawl.

After so many cruel years of torment I actually started to see some light at the end of the tunnel. The official letters back from Liberty had stated that things were looking promising.

I had never imagined things in here turning around. Yet with the killings that Character had carried out, there was a glimmer of hope strong enough that I could actually start to believe it.

After last night's fitful sleep, I recalled when he did return with an answer, it consisted of a peculiar liquid warble. Probably produced by the way he touched his tongue to the roof of his narrow mouth. I had tossed n turned all night long, hoping to fall back into one of the ocean dreams that I had been missing so much. Nothing had happened, so I had laid a wake most of the night turning over the meetings major points.

It had taken nearly another year for the letter Liberty wrote telling me of the progress to materialise into action. Yet I wasn't dreaming. I had yesterday sat by his suited side n listened to the arguments to release or keep me inside this institution.

They didn't give much away. The chair person, often looked throughout the three hours vacant eyed, like he had heavier worries on his rotten mind than any other mortal man.

This was my life they were fuckin with again. Liberty on more than one occasion sensing an outburst from me n giving me a sharp heel to the shin under the table to quell my anger, letting his eloquent words stating my injustice do the talking for us both.

It was a long night, Jesus it was a torturous week. The longest yet in nearly a decade but the official word came back.

It had become something that had totally messed up my thoughts.

Over the years you kind of forgot the outside world. It became like places far away n exotic. You knew they existed but you never truly believed you would see them with your own eyes.

I'd primed my body to return for Stan. Maybe a million press ups, who knew. I had certainly stopped counting after Gerard was dead.

It appeared I was to be released. No supervision, no apology, no compensation for a lost youth. I had the strangest feelings that I didn't want to go now. Funny what a human body can adjust to. Get used, get ill, get well and get even.

I was on my way home soon Da, for a nice little catch up for old time sake.

I had lay here every night on my bunk, a few nights short of a decade.

Out of my young head there has been enough thought of wild despair, at times a complete abandonment to grief. Not pretty to see. This impotent rage that has suffocated me many times, yet also built me into this killing machine of dark vengeance.

Oh the bitterness n scorn of it all. No contest at the start against a young boy. Yet I managed to up that ante and keep up the vigil.

I have passed through every possible mood of suffering. Scot John's Wordsworth poem that he once read to me, seemingly now very fitting for my long spell away.

'Suffering is permanent, obscure, and dark And has the nature of infinity'

With hardihood I kept on the path to avenge my Mother's death. I had to believe all these years in my beating heart that if it had not been for Stan, she would have loved and cared for me better.

{A SOLDIER'S FAREWELL chapter 94} *There was no big fuss the day it happened. You would assume after such a journey there would be some great big brass band playing you out. But I have to say it was real quiet.*

Good old Scot John was by his door as I passed with my small cloth bag of belongings.

As I pass his door he says. "Go on give me your best punch to the gut"

I knock the wind right out of him with a swift left hook right up into his rib cage.

But he laughs it off n gives me a bear hug that if it hadn't been for the training over the years would have crushed me dead.

Next up I pass Gyp. He gives a heartfelt handshake, his first in twenty years.

It's old Walter walking me off the Netherfield and I am so glad of that. There not all monsters who work these strange professions locking men away for a living.

She's been on my mind the whole time. Since the very first day she gave me my meds.

They had been weaning me off the heavy stuff all this last year. I was still rattling like some maracas when I walked, but I had been advised on getting clear of most my medication. Some they had said would remain with me my whole life.

I got to the other side of the gates n she was there. Walter at his discrete best saying, catch up with me n look sharp about it.

I stood in front of her, nearly a free man. There were no words from me. Just my best smile that said thank you without noise.

She took my hands in her own n bowed forward and gave me the sweetest kiss on my lips. The taste I had dreamed about confirmed.

I walked on with dignity in my stride and as I was just about to turn the corner Nurse Silk called my name.

"Otiss, my names Ruthi"

I pulled the twine from around my neck n untied the diamond ring. She hesitated to take it as I held it out on my palm, eventually though with a smile and a bright blush from her cheeks, she picked it up n clutched it tightly in her palm.

"It's beautiful" she sighed, and with that she was gone back through the doors n out of my life forever. I caught up with Walter as we had a few more doors to get through before I was finally out.

That corridor was still the same, still slippery under foot. Gaunt's portrait had been added to the long line of eyes that stared at me the whole way to the end.

Dr Woo popped his head out from his office to give me some personal advice that I will just keep to myself. After five minutes, he let go of shaking my hand n shouted for Walter to turn the key in the big door.

I had a good spring in my step as we descended the steps, my mind surprised as I hear the sound of gravel crunching under my foot for the first time in ten long years.

The fountain was still there, still trickling water down its green moulding sides. That trapped in time man howling, I now realised was no God or mythical poet. It had been a mirror of me for ten long years.

Walter walked close to me, heading down the long drive to the gates where I recalled that Latin lettering soldered onto its front.

Things had changed down here at the end over the passing wasted years. The open gate had been replaced with a sturdy looking fortress type door way. Thick smart red new bricks either side Circumferences the entire grounds from what I could see.

The mechanism clicked and the whirl of heavy metal being put into slow movement started.

Just a slit of free light to begin I see as I stand there a little unsteady. All the hours since I have been home hovered in front of my eyes.

My eyes instinctively shoot out a glance to Walter who is stood off just to my right. I half expect the violence and hatred that he never showed to surface now. To grab my arm and say

Oh no you don't, you are never leaving here sonny!!!

But he sensed my troubled glance and put a reassuring hand on the small of my back n shoved me gently forward through the now opened space of the gate house. The heavy doors access clicked into reverse. Those levers operating with a whirring noise, the last trapped thought in my ear.

I don't look back. I just wait until I hear that satisfying clunk as it's fully shut. The sun is warming the whole of my face as I just keep my eyes shut for a second gathering my thoughts, savouring the moment, breathing one last long sigh from out through my nose, I'm free.

{32 MILE STROLL chapter 95} *When I open them the first thing I see is this stray dog. He is running down the other side of the roads path. Sniffing, busy, then bolting off to sniff similar things.*

He gets my feet moving one in front of the other. I had decided I was going to walk home. Everything amazed me. It was like being re born.

I was surrounded by open green fields that had by the looks of it recently been swamped by heavy rain. The skies were still. A few clouds floated aimlessly above. Nothing black looking to dampen my mood.

Inside hedgerows I heard all manner of creature's stir. I was totally tuned in. The first ten mile of open road side I didn't even notice pass.

Not the distance.

Everything I observed inside my now non blinkered view.

I rested on one of those old stone carvings that marked the miles between certain points. Leeds 21 it said, the little arrow weathered giving me the heads up on which way to continue.

There was the odd vehicle that passed me. I kept eye contact to a minimum, just letting them pass without turning. New models that from the back looked very high tech.

Away for a full decade n there was no doubt going to have been some major changes. You don't see them as you are living outside. They are much subtler to the mind. The little change I had in my pockets was jingling n strange. I kept dipping my fingers in to the trouser pockets they had provided on release, feeling the cold coins.

My half ripped ones. Mine n the one Character had given me secure n safe in my back pocket. I had kept the silver acorn around my neck.

There were bits of the journey I hazily remembered from that trip in the car from court. Those words of Yama still easy to conjure into my mind, but I wasn't worried now, I had beaten the old cantankerous bastard.

It must have been late evening when I decided to have a brief rest.

There hadn't been a sign for a long way n I was unsure if I had missed a turn. There had been a fork road a few mile's back, but the stone marker showing the way had been smashed, so I had taken a coin n flipped. Tails I hoped was the right way to proceed.

I probably if I had wanted to could have walked the whole way home by now. But I had enjoyed a steady pace, taking in all the beauty of this world.

I found an old corrugated out building, quite near to the side of the road. I had initially passed it by n carried on, yet a half mile further I had thought with the weather looking like a change was coming for the worst I would retrace my steps n take some refuge for a hour n assess the situation.

Heavy sleep had taken me through a combination of exhaustion n excitement. It had been a long strange day. My senses had been on over load. I had thought shutting my eyes for ten as I had crept into the corner of the structure n sat on my arse hugging my knees, would do me n I would be off again.

The pitch black that greeted me made me realise I had been out for hours. So deciding to stay in my spot I fell back into a rather peaceful sleep.

Being a free man will have that effect upon your soul.

A bright morning greeted me. I wasn't exactly sure upon the time, yet with the cocks crowing just outside of the old barn I took it a sign for early dawn.

I trod on.

There was no urgency to hit the village outskirts. I had always thought back in my cell that I would rush the journey, eager to get my hands on Stan. But the last few months had changed the plans in my mind.

I was going to settle a few old scores first before I went after that bully of a Father.

So I found myself ambling on, content with my pace. I took another rest when I reached the mile marker that said I was a few miles from Scroftune.

On this quiet green there sat an old tramp, his layers of bulky clothing making him appear rather large. As I stood in front of his begging cap, which was sadly only filled with a few crinkly leaves, he lifted his weary head and with the saddest of eyes pleaded without words to me his message of despair.

I wasn't going to give him the ripped coins in my back pocket, but I did drop into the cloth cap with a nice sounding rattle, the entire contents of my use full coins. It wasn't much, probably be wasted on spirits, but the right gesture I felt as I wished him all the best n trundled on.

There had always been an intention in the back of my mind, even as a kid, to make some use someday of the old red brick building. It had always seemed to blend into the background of the village lane unnoticed. It had at one time been an old plumber's yard, then a front to a garden centre. But as I had got to around the age of 9, it had become permanently closed. Boarded up tight, with only a slight inkling of what lay behind if you pressed your youth full nosey eye right up to the slight cracks in the bolted down panels.

As I had become a little older, it just faded into the lanes structure. It had a small green to the side of it, which Stan had delighted in telling me, trying to scare me, that it had been an old graveyard from way back. There were some old stones scattered around, though Stan had said the real old grave markers were at the back of the property.

And for some strange reason as a kid, I had just never ventured around there. I was always in a rush when I passed the building, either on my way to Mr Longbottom's shop or in a daze from a beating and scurrying quickly to get to the sanctuary of the raft.

My biggest worry when I had realised in the FABERON that I would be returning to the village n would need some kind of front to my activities was that someone would see the potential I had all those years back n purchase it from under my nose.

Johnny had always liked the building too. So it had been no surprise when he had put forward it as a suggestion for business. I had sent him a private letter out from the institution. My infatuation with Nurse Silk had its benefits. I trusted her to do the right thing. Just before the tribunal to release me which had consisted of a Doctor and a lay person, a member of the public from the nearest village to the institution, along with Director Woo, I had received a postcard from London. Johnny had sent a coded message via a friend of his. My requests for the building were being carried out.

We had developed a secret slang between us as kids at skool. I had burnt the postcard, sailing its ashes down onto the dark yard.

The chimney stacks of the North got sucked into my tight lungs as a young un. Seeing the village plumes of smoke rising as I came over that last hill was a sight to behold. For over Ten year's I'd been priming my body to solidness to return for Stan.

Maybe a million sit ups!!I'd stopped counting completely after the murder of Gaunt.

I felt strong as I steadily descended the other side of acropolis hill. The house was about a ten minute stroll away. Urges strong to just go straight through the door with my booting foot, Kill him right there on the front room floor.

But that was not my trained mind. That was the foolish actions of an amateur. I was a trained killing machine. Restraint just one of the many attributes I possessed.

I searched out the public footpath that took me on a journey onwards, over near to the back of the railway lines. I was heading over the common, Dolly Blues vardo wagon my first port of call.

{PICK A KEY chapter 96} *Johnny had given me a list of instruction.*

Where the key was to enter the locked Vardo, where the keys were to Granddad Pedley's trunk etc..Where the stash of money was from the remaining bundle I had been left, after the purchase of the Village Eye.

I heard the factories whistles blaring out to tell the workers lunch break was over. The long path that I had walked down towards the edge of the common ended.

Just the vast sweeping gradual rise of bright heather mounds. A few shire horses loose n grazing and minding their own business.

To the right, proud with its bright yellow and green panels the wagon not more than fifty paces away.

The key was hooked by some twine onto this old copper kettle that hung beneath the wagons belly. I opened the door as quick as Gaunt going through the gates. Even though I was free, my mind kept switching back to the inside of the FABERON.

All reference point of thoughts having nothing to go off except the institution after a decade buried in its concrete tomb. The door creaked open n the light from outside shone the scene through to me.

I'd noticed the gold leaf on the doors, hammered in with patience n love for the old craft. To the right was a fire place surround in red and gold which had green tiles on the inner part where the grand black stove sat. Above on the mantle some figurines of ballet dancers and an old pipe carved with a dog's head for the bowl.

There was an oak floor with a beautiful Indian rug upon it, which led my eye to these wooden built in cabinets for storage with the bed built into the top of that. It sheets of lace n woollen bright blankets a most welcome sight after the barn last night. There was a little port hole style window above the bed, with a few wooden shelves either side full of crown derby plates.

To the left, a small chaise lounge, so you could stare directly into the flames of the fire. Some black painted milk urns with these delicate painted red yellow n white flowers running down the sides. From the drabness of my old cell, it was just a wash of bright happy colours. My cheeks grow as I smile into a grin as I hear the horses neighing content outside the door. I shut the door for a moment, more out of habit than anything.

Behind the door I notice a large ornament in black marble. The stance of a fighting man with his bare knuckles raised stares back.

I sat my arse down on the edge of the bed for a moment.

I must have dozed off on the bed for a few hours, waking in the late evening hungry and confused again. I remember Johnny saying the trunk of my Granddads was here. The only place it could be is in the space below the bed.

It took a while to drag it out of its tight confined space. Its rope wrapped. Secure as hell.

I finally get a loosening on a knot n start to unravel it away from its body. With all the ship rope off, which I throw outside the door for now, I reach behind the crown derby plate that showed a scene of fox hunting n grab a bunch of old metal looking keys.

I try the padlock with a random key. Nothing happened. I try the next one that has a distinct pattern to its teeth. Nothing again happens. On the third try, I pick a key that has these carved notches in the handle.

Sprung, the latch clicked clear. I popped the heavy lid back n peered inside to my Granddads world God bless him.

Up inside the inside of the trunks lid were pasted in some great old fairground posters. They were faded as hell and just as I was wishing how much he hadn't stuck them down I noticed propped up in one corner of the trunk a roll of them.

As I unfurled the first, I realised with delight that these fair posters were actually advertising his fights on the booths.

I spent the next hour sat crossed legged reading through his opponents who he had beaten to a pulp. Fascinating names with stage name monikers like, the fighting sailor, the Nottingham slasher, the Gas man, the star of the north, the Nailer.

I'd gone back out n got the kettle from under the wagon, broken some wood from the nearest tree n got the stove lit n some hot sweet tea on the go.

There was some old navy kit bag in the trunk, which I found was where Johnny had put my wad. I didn't count it. Just stuffed the bundles back in n pulled it shut. I would count it later.

There seemed a good sum left after the eye purchase. I had spent a King's ransom on a special gift for myself too. Well half the money towards it.

Under the bag I had picked up from the bottom left side something that was very familiar. I stared at the silver photo frames. Old BUCKHORSE stared back, which was like looking in the mirror now at my own face. It wasn't just the face though that I had inherited. The massive shoulders, the iron spine that held my back as straight as a rod, the glare that when I wanted could turn a man to quickly look away n not be so foolish as to dare look into my eye. You didn't want to see what lurked their swimming in the dark pupil of green n orange fleck.

An old pair of clog heeled pit boots sat in the other corner of the trunk. It wasn't till after I had drunk my first cup of cha n was pouring another that I got an inclination to examine them closer.

Inside the left one, an old Rolex watch, the date 1915 on the back and the words BEST SON made me think it had been his Fathers. My Great Grandfather, a name he had never mentioned.

I knew it was an officer's watch from the First World War or what most called a trench watch. Old Winnie had schooled me well on the jewellery trade.

I slipped it on to my wrist, its rose gold shining nicely in the open stove fire's glow.

On the other pit boot, tied into the top of the laces was a solid gold boxing ring. Two gloves touching each other. It only fit my wedding finger, so I left it on there for now.

Closing shut the lid of the trunk I got to thinking about my missing finger n Mums sad end.

The horses woke me.

Out of the porthole window the evening was just losing its last light. The thoughts of Mum had sent me into a trance where I had eventually fallen away into dreamland.

I lit the candles that were on the mantle. The glow of the inside of the Vardo was lovely n chilled.

The boxing ring I must have taken off in my sleep. I noticed in horror that I had rammed it onto the stump where Stan all those years ago had cut through my finger with the axe. A small circle of blood was on the bed sheets where I had curled up n drifted to sleep. I didn't need reminders to get my temper rising on Stan. His day was about to come. The tables turned now n we would see how he fared as the weaker fighter.

I checked the horses were ok, which they were, pulling the door's shut but not turning the key. I couldn't bear to bang myself up like that now.

I flipped the lid open again and delved into the last bits I'd not looked at inside the trunk. Two fine wooden boxes. A fine pair of 17th century duelling pistols glinted back from their silver handles. The whole set was intact. Use full for sure.

In the other box a man stopper pistol of the finest condition.

An old Ghurkha knife was inside this leather satchel along some bits n pieces & photos of what looked like a young Granddad in Africa in the War. This tattered old manual amused me, on the front it said, bomb throwing practices, another handy piece for my upcoming exploits.

I had seen enough. I settled down on the rug in front of the fire which was still throwing out solid heat n slept.

{FOOTSTEPS OF YOUTH chapter 97} Rain against the porthole window disturbed me into waking, the wagon cold now with the fire died right out.

Minutes later I had a fresh brew sorted n I was ready after placing my belongings safely away to go check out the eye.

Passing a couple of folk as I made my way to the lane, they faintly seemed to recognised me, just not sure enough on passing to stop n ask.

Looking over the small metal railing that below held the water that lead under the road, a million thoughts seemed to hit me suddenly. When dusk came one night soon I would go check out my raft, but not until I had a little cover from the darkness and a few days shut away to think.

The village Eye pub wasn't five minutes along the lane from the raft. This was no coincidence when picking out this location.

Johnny had done well. The image I had last of this building was a ruin of old red crumbling bricks n boarded up windows.

What now stood in front of me as I viewed it about twenty feet away on the other side of the lanes road was a beautiful looking sight. Smart brick work which looked newly pointed with these dark black metal pipes running down from the roof. There was a brand new wrought iron sign swinging ever so gently in the breeze. Its VILLAGE EYE sign writing in the middle looked perfect.

Fresh gravel ran from the edge of the street path to the arched doors, which Johnny had left as the originals, only now they had been sanded n varnished with a blue. This was where the stone stairs led up into the first floor bar area. As I looked up at the large sliding doors set high into the side of the building I felt proud.

I could keep a good eye on things from up there.

Johnny had left all the keys I needed to get access in the vardo. So without any more hesitation I unlocked my pub n climbed the stairs to have a gander at the bar n to see if my special requirements had been carried out to my liking.

{V ROOM chapter 98} *Gleaming was the bar. Fully stocked with all the things I had requested.*

On a small side table where I had told Johnny to put me a comfy chair that was right next to the sliding door that looked out over the lane, he had placed a bottle of antique whiskey.

A small white card lay propped against it. I took a pew n ripped it open.

Dearest Otiss,

I hope this note finds you well my oldest friend?

I know that you will find everything to your satisfaction, as I have followed your requests to the letter.

Don't worry, all the private requests I carried out myself.

Enjoy your freedom and do what you have got to do.

Love Johnny x

Over in the corner of the bar there was a small free standing wood burner, logs n kindle n matches at its clawed feet.

I got the blaze going easy n burnt the card, watching it disappear through the glass panel in the door.

There was a special small silver key on the bunch I had. The door in question was through a normal door that led to a few small stairs that would take you up to my private quarters. Nothing too fancy, just a bedroom en suite n a study that held a decent library.

In the bedroom, what looked like two windows either side of the wooden bed frame was where my secretiveness began.

They both had full length rich red drapes, yet the one to the left overlooking the back gardens was fully drawn. The other curtain was pulled back n held by a gold hook, revealing the outside to anyone who may care to venture a peek.

Pulling the drawn drape to one side I turned my attention to what looked like a very high tech looking door.

I moved over to study the rows upon rows of books on my book case shelves.

Running my finger along until I found the one I was looking for.

The rather large red leather volume had upon its side written.

The complete plays of Bernard Shaw

I slid the book out to reveal a coded panel that lit up when you turned the right key in it. Inserted the correct one from the small bunch n punched in my 7 code system.

Instantly, without any noise the panel slid back n I strode over n stepped on through. The two wooden boxes of granddads I had brought along in the leather satchel would fit nicely into this room. They certainly wouldn't be the only fire power in here. But it was my swords gleaming upon the wall that caught my attention the most.

The ancient samurai that I had asked Johnny to purchase in this Japanese auction sale was the finest looking piece of steel ever to behold my eye.

The 13th Century precious swordsmith Go Yoshihiro was the one I had heard from Johnny was coming up in a catalogue auction in Koyoto. He was regarded as the best student of the legendary maker Masamune.

Go Yoshihiro died very young, only 27 years of age. So he hadn't made many swords before he passed on. His work even getting confused with his own master, as it was that good a standard. Johnny had put half the money up, giving me ownership of the full sword as a welcome present home.

This fine sword was staring back at me from my own wall. Its fine blackened handle with two cut circles in. The blackness seemed to travel continuous all the way to the sharp tip, with Gleaming silver edges framing its contrast.

There is a saying in Japan. One never sees a ghost or a Go. It is that rare.

But so is my intended business. I must slay these cowards with mastery at hand.

I had named the secret room the V room. For vigilante, simplicity at its finest, yet in my mind I always referred to it as the plotting room. I stayed a few nights, reading cool books that Scot John had gotten my interest with and practising with the Go sword, its beautifully crafted structure swishing majestically through the air with a sweet sounding silent menace. It wasn't long until the official opening night which had all been arranged.

I had gotten bored already with comfort. Don't get me wrong it was nice to wiggle your warm toes at the end of fresh bed linen.

The first bath had been amazing. An array of scented salts I had let flow into the fully running hot taps. Fire vapours up my snout, Eucalyptus stinging my eyes as it all vaporised together in the steam. It sizzled away all the bad karma from my skin, yet as I watched the steam rising to the ceiling he got me again.

Stan, looming as large as he had ever been, invading my mind with his cruel bad memories. As a kid, my fortnightly bath would always be interrupted. The bastard would let me get settled. A few minutes relaxing then BANG, he would be through the door, bursting in to whip my wet skin with electrical cord.   That thought did it for me. It was time to go have a peep at the old man.

The lane hadn't changed too much in ten years. The old haunted fish & chip shop had finally been pulled down. Some housing development signs stood showing these rather smart looking properties that were to be built up soon.

The goggle box video rental store had become a newsagent's, but in general things were how I remembered them as a kid.

The wooden stile that took you over the fields was still there. A little more weathered, with the graffiti we had daubed as kids faded into just unrecognisable paint blobs.

Already in a foul mood thinking of my journey towards Stan, it got me thinking to the chap who years ago had ruined our ball game, where the ball we use to leave at each end of the field by the stile. The *one he had for no reason but spite stabbed to deflation just to ruin our playful fun. A visit on the cards I believe was due to him too.*

Day light was dropping, enough for the street lamps on the lane to start flickering on to guide the path. Large puddles here and there on the path and road side, the gutters busy with rushing draining water.

I nearly let the glare of the isolated old red phone box draw me inside. A strange urge to call the houses land line, hoping that Mum would answer n tell me I had been in a dreadful nightmare.

To hear her voice, but I knew she wasn't there. But that old bastard would be. Not that he ever answered the phone.

I could see as I had moved behind the booth, leaning on the tree that as a kid would be my leg up point to jump over into the orchard, the heavy drapes were fully closed. Not changed or washed in a decade from the cut of them. Filthy old Stan hadn't gone and got domesticated in a hurry.

I decided after half hour just staring at the window to move closer.

Not the ginnel, too close and risky for now, so I made my way around the side of the green, along the small Clogger Street which brought me up beside the old garage, trapped memories suddenly of the car boot came ripping through my mind. I push them away n hop over the high fence into Mrs Burnley's over grown garden, avoiding the crunching gravel of Stan's garden path.

Outside Mrs B's old boarded up door, I silently say a small quick prayer. I would be adding her revenge to Stan's suffering when the time came. But this was just a creeping mission, viewing the prey, weighing up the victim.

It felt good thinking of him in those terms.

For so many years he had scared the absolute shit out of me.

I hit the latch quietly on the gate n stepped across the yard to have a peep through the kitchen window.

I had promised myself not to get drawn into the bad memories. But it wasn't as simple as that.

Traumatic events as a child impacted on my adult brain. And as much as I had strengthened my mind and body, his abuse and its severity got into my head.

Through the chink in the back kitchen curtain window, a faint light from the stairs hallway gave me enough insight into how much he had gone to the dogs since me and Mum had disappeared.

I put the ketchup scene out of my mind.

The whole kitchen looked a shit hole. It looked like the after math of some large party, where the cleaning up had just been forgotten. Without Mum and me skivvying for him, he had just let things go.

Then suddenly I clocked him.

Stumbling into the kitchen, the light blaring on, making me hunch down n hold my breath, watching him fling open the disgustingly filthy fridge n pull apart a single can from a pack of four. Dad had become much weaker. I just could not believe looking at him, that this weak old bastard had once held the strength to ruin n abuse my childhood.

Too much abuse can never be fully forgotten. The tear rolling down my cheek caught me by surprise. I was a massive bloke, but still a kid at heart when it came to viewing this monster.

I almost felt sorry for him as I watched him hunched up coughing his guts out in between swigs of his cheap tinny. But I soon caught a hold of that weak emotion, sailing it down somewhere deep in my body.

I'd seen enough for now as he flicked the light of n left my beady eye unknowingly staring through at him.

I had come prepared for one thing before I left the village eye. The metal coat hanger I let slide from inside my coats cuff.

Worth a shot I thought as I waited a few minutes for him to predictably slump back into that old ragged shaman chair.

After enough safe time, I got to work.

I had already unravelled the coat hangers shape before I left. It was now just two straight lines folded together. I unfurled the two bits giving me a decent length n curved a little hook into one end of it. I lifted quietly the letter box n went fishing.

It took me 30 seconds to feel the weight catch upon the hook, drawing back through the box my catch. Mums old set of slaughter bungalow keys jangled quietly as I slipped them of the end, pocketed them deep into my dark over coat, folded the metal n disappeared back through Mrs B's gate n quietly slipped away along Clogger Street, the raft now my next port of call.

Matricide was still hard to contemplate. Stitching me up for it, how could he stoop so low?

But he had, and planned it to perfection, just like I had planned his horrible death to cause him the maximum amount of pain.

How had those twelve puppeteer led idiots on the jury got it so wrong? One of the names at the top of my hit list was now dead.

And I hoped the judge was rotting in the cold ground with the whole weight of Hell bearing down on his splintered fragile coffin box lid.

Yet there were plenty more names on that list, all with imminent visits due to them all. My thoughts of revenge consume me and I realise without noticing the journey that I am stood by the old rag mills gates.

The mill had been shut for years. Johnny telling me on the visit about its closure and the workers left jobless in the villages.

Sneakin past the guard had always been the best part.

They had kept a man on though. Tea leaves eyeing the metal machinery left behind for scrap or the mountains of lead that clung to the wide roof. It had always been a difficult path to get towards the raft, even as a kid. I slid in the shadows passed the dozing guard, who seemed to jolt a memory in my mind as I passed him, head down sleeping on his folded arms on the desk.

At that point I didn't give it any more thought, yet logged it in my brain for later. Something about him didn't sit well with me.

The brambles were thick and grown to high levels. My kid footprint lost in the decade of growth.

But I soon found the old familiar path.

The waterfall still fell heavy n fast, still had that much needed curtain of privacy.

I pushed the nettles back with a pulled down coat sleeve. Johnny's message was faint, weather beaten, yet still profound.

I felt like the soldier now.

I waded through the heavy mixture of long wet grass n reeds, towards the other side of the entrances pillar.

I reached my hand around my back n slid out from my belt Granddads Ghurkha knife and in line with Johnny's message on the other side I carved deep now my own.

Scot John's T.S Elliot quote that he had mentioned often had always stuck in my mind. I let the blades tip start to carve

THE PURPOSE OF LITERATURE

IS TO TURN

BLOOD INTO INK

And oh boy how fitting that saying was going to be ringing true for those bullying bastards. The raft was going to be busy for sure. The river taking away the spilled bad blood under my vigilante watch, salack soaked for miles.

Navigating the tow path n its obstacles I now found myself back on my safe spot. I stared into the cool waters and it was as if I had reversed a decade in a split second of staring.

My reflection transported all my childhood scars n bruises straight back at me. The small pile of books I had left on the raft were now rotten, which again as I flicked through them got me straight to thinking about Stan.

He had when taking a bath had in the corner a small collection of pulp fiction horrors. His deep sea diver helmet lamp would hold a red bulb, casting a bloody hue over the pages as he soaked away reading. I ripped the sleeve in the old army jacket, trying it on for fun, my massive arms not even flexing to expand the fabric to its bursting point.

Sat on the raft I swayed on steady currents, quietly smiling to myself. I was no longer hiding, well not out of fear. Below me in time would be rapscallion bones that if studied carefully would show they had met a most vicious death.

{TICKING AWAY NICELY chapter 99} I stayed in the back ground mostly.

A young girl Stef who Johnny had trusted all his life had been put in charge as manager. She had worked in the business all her adult life n needed no telling on any pub related matters.

On the first night though, it was like fate just decided to send me my first victim Or at least the first warning beating I was to issue of many!!!

Opening night had been a great success. This place was perfect for a busy pub to thrive. Slap bang in the middle of the village pub run, where piss artists on their way from one end of the village lane to the other just couldn't give up the chance to pop in n top themselves up with ale.

I knew the pub was a great idea. The people around this village, like most were predictable when it came to being near some true horror. The large barn door set into the side of the building allowed me to watch the punters coming staggering down the lane. I say staggering, but they were mainly just merry. To me I hated any piss artist drinker, which unfortunately was how I viewed most people out supping.

Back inside the bar area I seen a few careless wankers have a sly look my way n then turn into the group they were with n I could just tell the convos were momentarily halted to give my decades absence a thought. Gossips at best, which I took note of mentally but generally ignored.

Others though who out of curiosity had come into see how I looked now after such a long period of time had passed, were decent enough to offer a welcome back turn of phrase. Most just commented on how lovely the village eye looked n wished me success with it.

Not one of them mentioned my Mother or Stan. It was exactly what Intended, a plausible front to my real activities around the village.

I'd been in the small back kitchen making a sandwich when I heard voices raising just that octave higher than fun n banter. I came back through and went to sit in my comfy chair, except now I was on the edge of its seat, leaning forward, my arms n chest tensed, my ear cocked in the direction of loud voices.

I pretty much knew most of the crowd in the group causing the commotion, some good, with a few bad, all had a slot in my mind for some shit reason or another. None had been on my radar. Certainly none were upon the rafts list.

I clocked out of the corner of my eye down on the path side outside the pubs entrance this shaking disturbed looking kid. He so reminded me of myself all those years ago when I would have had too much stick in the house n would be legging it to the safety of the raft.

Under the light of the orange street lamps glow I could see him tapping his feet nervously, with sudden shudders running through his upper body, coming that hard I could see them clear from up here. My other eye caught the movement of the step Dad, making a sudden exit down the stairs to the street level.

Stef distracting me as she passed saying the lager was empty n she was just quickly going to change a barrel. When I looked back out the window the kid was not in sight.

I didn't really expect to turn my full attention to the step Dad. The kid was in the back of my mind, but for now the vibe inside the bar took precedence.

A few hours later, I was readying to tell Stef n give the nod to shut the bar. The woman who had been in the group had gone a while back. Just the step Dad remained with a few mates. Racing down fresh pints to make another trip to the bar before the bell was struck for time gent's please.

Now I couldn't hear the words that were coming from his mouth. But the institution had taught me well. Lip reading or reading backwards and certainly reading upside down had all been mastered.

I clearly thought at first that I was just listening to drunken boasting. You know that lad banter bullshit. Keep up the hard man image n all that.

They were all laughing now, splurting froth out of their mouths from their pints. I moved close.

Leaning on the bar next to them I hear. "Yeah the daft little fucker had put the salt in the sugar pot & the sugar in the salt shaker"

"How many times"?

The question from one of the divs in the group rapidly answered with a swelling of this beast of a step Dads chest.

"Plenty""Cracked the little stupid confused bastard in the mouth, but then I thought about the grassing little turd, so I gave him it in the kidneys good style."

I gave Stef the nod n she shouted, "TIME PLEASE."

They flew over to the bar, desperate to get a last pint in. I wasn't interested in listening to their orders. I let Stef serve them the slops with a smile, while I moved back over to chill in my chair.

I didn't even notice that a short time later I had drifted with bad intentions upstairs. Inside the Vroom I could see the sharpened tools staring back at me.

Not time for that yet I thought to myself. The warning would be the best place to start with this abusing old fecker.

I went back into the bar, paid Stef from the till n told her I would see the stragglers out. We bid each other a goodnight.

I turned to face the group that were left, "Come on now gents lets be having your glasses off please"

I got back. "Alright mate, just finish these pints off ok?

It wasn't ok, I wanted them out. They tried drinking off slowly, still trying to make some statement of power to me.

Soon they left, my constant staring at them making them leave liquid in the pots that they banged on the bar, muttering crap, feeling big in a group yet bumping into each other as they made their way down the stairs to the street. The drunken pricks didn't realise how vulnerable they really were.

The step Dad was the last out the door as I was about to lock up.

"Night mate, I'm off home to fuck mi sexy wife mate yeah I'm off to"

I cut him short. "Night piss head," n banged the door in his face.

I flew up the stairs n sat in my chair.

Luckily for me the group had split off, Step Daddy was alone n stumbling up the lane. I left it two minutes n then set off.

He never even heard me come up behind him. The garrotte around his neck before his brain registered what was happening. I held it a while. I wasn't trying to kill him with strangulation.

Winnie's murder flashed in my head as I let loose with a sharp raised knee right into his kidney area. I let the garrotte go loose n he crumbled into the path.

The shadows hid my reflection. I had the bally on any way.

I let him catch a few intakes of badly needed breath. Just as he was about to predictably ask what he had done, I volley off a nice left foot right into his bollox.

The tape went over his mouth easy. I didn't want too much racket from his gob at this time of night.

I had his full attention.

The big silhouetted redeemer gave him a warning. I told him straight that if he ever laid a finger on the boy again I would kill him in the most horrific way. I gave him a few extreme examples.

His eyes, staring up at me full of tears were getting the message.

BOOT.

His arms had not been fast enough to protect his mouth from my final kick of the night. I knew most of his teeth had shattered with the steel in my toe capped boot.

I pulled the black masking tape away with a satisfying rip. Some teeth were stuck to it. Most just fell out onto the path.

"Not a fuckin finger remember"

I just left him there, crawling about in a daze, trying to pick up his teeth with one hand while trying with the other to hold in the loose ones.

I couldn't resist making him look at me one last time. Balaclava eyes upon him as I framed a square with my fingers n said "say cheese" clicking with my mouth a few times to mimic a camera.

I kept that shattered mouth photo in my mind as I headed quickly back to the eye.

Back in my chair I screwed the lid off the power whisky n poured myself just one small nip. "Cheers Stanley" I said to the empty bar, lifting my lips to the glass. Just the one nip, I was no alki bastard like my Father.

I got busy over the next few months around the place. I had been up on the roof, painting a large eye onto the gable end. From there you could see right the way down to the end of the back gardens. Stan had been right. The old graves were situated at the bottom. I hadn't mended their weather toppled appearance. I just let it be.

I had read in the deeds to the place that the ground had been a sacred patch since the year 1741.

I tended the grounds, no hypnotic strokes like the beaten men I had encountered a decade ago in the grounds of the FABERON. My work was done with a swift hand to its toil.

I had put trellis along the brick work, growing up red n white roses to contrast each other. Everything was looking good, with time becoming a pleasant partner by my side now.

I spent most of my time those first few months in the Vroom though, its solitude a perfect place to train for my revenge. Father I am sure would have heard by now somehow that I was free. Living and working not more than a steady ten minute stroll from his very front door. I was hoping that the fucker would grow some balls n come confront me, but who was I kidding. Bullies don't confront real men.

I was hoping his dead body would fit nicely into one of the old graves out back, day dreaming these wonderful thoughts as I tended my garden plants.

The peeping in on him hadn't stopped. I had even seen him outside of the house, down at the back of Iron Street, not two minutes away from his house. Doddering about, up to what I couldn't guess. He looked frail now, pathetic. The urge to just run up n twist his neck to an angle that death agreed made a great look. But I could bide my time. Others needed their medicine first.

It was approaching bonfire night and I had this wicked idea to scare this certain individual on my radar to jelly with it. Iron fisted deliverance, with a nice little twist for the remembrance of guy Fawkes.

{ST PAUL'S chapter 100} Bonny night was close, chubbing from the local kids I watched from out the side barn window of the eye.

But first I had a gift that had been delivered n installed to view. The leaves of the cemetery trees loosened by the onset of Winter blew towards me as I made my way up the winding lane. Light footed I dodged them, unlike the problems in my youth.

I can see the steeple of the church, my destination today. I had thought about lighting a candle inside for many years while locked away.

Yet now back on the village lane for months, I had become scared to go. But it was Mums birthday today and I was giving her the best present I could think of. I had called at the church Vicars residence about three weeks ago.

Over sweet tea he had told me how he was new to the parish. Not the one who had interned my blessed poor Mother, he had though remembered the murder. He had lived in another village, looking after a different church but the local papers had carried the story.

He gave me all the help he could. Nipping out to his office to make enquiries on my behalf when I had shockingly but then again not surprisingly been told that my Mother had no headstone.

There had been an inquiry from a certain Mr Pedley.

Good old Granddad trying to do the right thing. But he informed me that old gentleman had passed away himself before arranging any order and so the plot remained unmarked. Stan the bastard just didn't even bother keeping up the grieving pretence once Mums body hit the cold earth.

My blood had boiled so much that I snapped the handle of the fine china cup the vicar had given to me.

He had brushed off my apologies, sensing my disappointment and anger.

He had helped me that day draw out the plans for a long overdue fitting tribute. I know she had been cruel to me, but I just kept on clinging to that belief that if it hadn't been for the influence of Stan, she would have loved me. I had to keep believing that.

The moss had covered over many names. Mums neighbours hide their souls behind spreading green ivy. Some old tree roots have erupted from the ground. They look like gnarled limbs in the distance, creeping out from their nearby tombs.

I stop in my tracks. I'm not ready even now to see Mum.

Her Tombstone I have been informed earlier in the day has been fitted to her plot.

I pick a spot to sit a moment to contemplate the nearby majestic old tombs. Their blackened stone silhouetted strange shapes before my eyes. My tablet doses have been sporadic since I came out.

The Drs I have visited once n said what he wanted to hear. I still feel strange at times. A decade of psycho drugs will do that to you.

Buffeted by the winds of time, there are many bones all around. I hate crowds, unless their resting deep below. So many lives not lived. So many children that God must really want to take. I can feel the millions of parental tears that have wept hard at these spots.

Broken tombs near me too, vandals of today's youth? Or maybe just chipped corroded time?

I fear this place yet start to find some strange comfort. My soul hovering here and breathing real time above these deep dug holes.

I try to push quickly away the thought of all those empty eye sockets, their once lovely colours now gone forever into the soils decay.

I find some bravery n move with this map of the bone yard to where my Mothers bones lay.

I have a strange thought about hoping they had straightened her up from the crumbled awkward form I had last seen of her, the memory that had fuelled my desire to get free and seek her revenge. The earlier bright winter's sun had dropped below gathering clouds as my body now shivers inside my overcoat. I can see the spot where I need to stand n pay my respects. The order of grey marble stands out amongst the entire row of black headstones. I read her neighbour's names as I pace slowly down towards her.

Like a little miniature row of a street, you get no say who will be your life long eternal neighbour.

I see an old boxer's name, a bit of a local hero to some. I'm glad Mum isn't too close to that one.

My relief as I stand staring at the one right next to hers.

She is the last in the row. I have to grin. I believe it's the medication. I'm stupidly thinking she would have been quite happy to be semidetached in her plot.

A good neighbour she certainly got. And I guess you cannot ask for more than that in the afterlife.

The old farmer on the lane had always said a cheerful hello to me when I had passed his gates. A pig farmer who had grafted hard all his life n loved his family well. He had the respect of the entire village. Mum when she was decent with me always spoke highly of him, telling me to study hard n work hard n become a decent man like Mr Illingworth.

I stared at his simple black stone. In gold leaf lettering, besides the details of his name n passing n birth, there was a quite short but fitting quote as a tribute to how he had lived his life.

LIFES WORK WELL DONE

LIFES CROWN WELL WON

THEN COMES REST

My mothers, I had been in a quandary over for some time. I had written on a sheet of paper a few different things.

I wanted in large neon lights, the words, MURDERED BY HER HUSBAND, but obviously I couldn't n wouldn't put that.

I had written many quotes, Scot John's poetry from my time inside coming to mind, yet I rejected most. I eventually settled on a simple thing.

TRISH KITES, nee PEDLEY.

CRUELLY TAKEN FROM THIS LIFE

GOD REST HER SOUL ETERNAL

That was it. I'd wanted to put more, but just couldn't justify the things I was writing down.

I had one more stop before getting back to the warmth of the village eye. Along with the enquiries to the parish priest about my Mother, I had also inquired about Mrs B.

I knew she had no family. And as I suspected, the information back revealed she too lay without a marker to show she had lived once.

I had paid for this rectifying at the same time as sorting my Mothers headstone.

It was a fair way from Mums. I checked the map again.

It seemed like they had placed her in an older part of the cemetery, Just about fitted her in to this corner plot where there was a small space. I had again gone with simplicity.

HERE LIES

EVA BURNLEY

GOD REST HER SOUL

I had paid my own tribute in my own way. The black square headstone had a four inch thick white band along its top.

It had supposed to be in remembrance of her Guinness which she loved so much, but as I moved away after silently saying God bless I got to thinking I had made a terrible mistake. I realised that I was thinking of how that cruel bastard Stan had killed her with the funnel. I could alter it, but no, she had loved that drink, one of life's true pleasures for her. Oh that bastard was going to pay alright. The sooner I cleared up the village bullies n got around to torturing him the better.

{WARNING BEATINGS chapter 101} Downstairs in the eyes bar area is a small kitchen that I used for making grub. I didn't eat much these days as I didn't want the extra weight that could come from the tablet medication side effects to ruin my shape.

In general I was solid muscle, eating only bananas, nuts, steaks and my favourite, pineapple. I drunk only water, with my celebration nip of power whisky only passing my lips, after I felt I had dealt satisfactorily with a bully from around the village.

Some fireworks had been going off early this week. Just young kids giddy about the holiday coming up.

In my mind all the noises of banging in the air n most people distracted looking up at the array of wonderful colours was to my advantage. My next target was never going to enjoy bonfire night ever again.

Inside the V room I awoke. A sudden nap had overtaken me. A painful reminder and habit now from the afternoon lock ups at the FABERON.

On the red carpeted floor I notice I have left out two long barrelled parabellum revolvers. I place them both back away inside the gun cabinet fitted to the wall. I wouldn't need those quite yet. Not tonight.

The morning I had spent outside in the back garden. Drilling two small holes into the end of the shank that I felt needed ripping through this bully bastards guts who I was about to go after. It released oxygen into the wound upon entry and made certain the death.

I was careful though, restrained. I knew the police wouldn't tolerate straight up mutilated bodies turning up all over the streets. I knew if I went too far with the beatings then they would have no choice about poking their nosey pig beaks into things.

But that's where the raft was going to fit in.

I had thought for many years in the FABERON laid upon my bunk just what an ideal place it was to sink a body of a dead bully under.

And that's just what Intended to do.

Some of these fuckers deserved more than just a severe beating n I was back now in the village for one reason only and that was to dispense some rough justice.

I decided to drag this one out a little for two reasons. Firstly it amused me to prolong this coward's fear factor and also the bonfire night holidays had given me an idea of where to start with frightening this scum bag.

I visited a local charity shop just up into the town centre. I went all hood up n scarf round most of my face, just shuffling about as if I was on the verge of tramp hood.

I bought some old geezer looking clothes with a grunt at the till as I paid, coming away with a pair of pants n large hooded coat.

I hadn't given much hope to the selfish wanker picking the two kids up from skool. Just like Stan had always left me to fend for myself too n from my own skool years on the lane, this dude was no better.

He would be well into an afternoon session in the pub by now. Stood with that fat belly n cheap cigar, he would lord it by the bar trying to convince the piss heads around him that he was superior.

I had noticed the pattern. The two young boys jumping up at the pub windows where cruel harsh burnt out faces of life stared back at them. That is if they even noticed at all.

The fat Dad eventually coming to the entrance n telling them he would be along in a while n to go get their arses home to mum.

He wasn't too busy to pick his pint up though. Supping away right through the afternoon, he would then take a taxi home for dinner. The schedule never changed.

The fat greedy fucker only had this luxury of time because he had been left a garage when his Father had died.

He had been quite young n the staff had all stayed on n the place more or less ticked over without the son having to learn much, except going in n sticking his fat fingers into the till n pulling out greasy wads of cash.

These warning beatings were not really that personal to me. Not in the sense that they had affected me directly. No, what these were about were the reminders of how Stan had been.

I mean what the Hell was wrong with society. Are we all going to sit about and do nothing!! Just lay there all comfy knowing there's a cruelty next door. A blatant abuse over the road, yet we feel it's not quite our business to intervene. A death on the news that we sit in shock staring at the screen saying, "oh how awful"

No, my work on the street was justified in my mind. I wasn't going to sit back n do nothing. Quite the opposite, I was going to turn the tables right on these yellow bellied scumbags.

My target wasn't just a bully indoors to his wife n kids. He treated the staff at the garage like his personal joeys. People in the street he would look down his nose at. So many things I had seen n heard that put him on a collision course with yours truly.

The reason I had picked this time of year was because this was when he did his best to con the village into thinking he was really a decent sort. He sponsored the village green bonfire night show. Supplying all the necessary cash to make sure the fireworks display lasted at least ten minutes.

Pie n peas n large slabs of parkin cake would be delivered. His staff from the garage would be brought in to dish it out to the hungry kids on demand.

But I knew the real man. Not this false bullshit.

His ritual lighting of the first large rocket with the tip of his cigar would start proceedings. He had shown enough decency to the crowd, which he hoped kept him in good stead for the rest of the year.

In between the village green n his favourite watering hole, he had to pass over this small foot bridge that was over a stream that run from further up in the village, its waters passing around my raft at a certain point.

Now I knew from tailing him the last few days that he ignored this young kid who had decided this spot for his guy Fawkes might rake him in a few coins over the bonny week.

Last night after watching the bully ignore the kids "penny for the guy" for the third time, I waited half an hour n then gave the young lad a fiver n said go try up the lane by the working men's club, where he would earn a few quid from the drunks passing the doorway.

I knew as the fireworks started hitting the sky that it wouldn't be long before he was going to saunter over the bridge to head for the navigation inn.

The large rocket sailed into the night sky. By my timing he would be about ten minutes away.

The bridge wasn't used much. Most people stuck to the road side instead of getting their feet muddy crossing the field. The bully didn't care about the state of his footwear.

Clothes maketh the man alright.

My target like clockwork, when it came to matters of importance, like sinking fresh pints of ale

I held still, a dummy on the floor, harmless.

I was as still as I had been when the other night I had looked through his homes window. Watching the real persona at work, with Daddy giving both the kids severe beatings right there on the front room floor. The glimpses I got through the not quite shut curtains confirmed the village gossip rumours I had been hearing.

A belt buckle dangling had them both scurrying across the floor looking for sanctuary. Which they hadn't found in time!

It had been hard not to just put the window through right there n then. Strangle the bastard with that belt. But I didn't want the kids to see what I had in mind. They had seen enough shit, so I waited for the night now here to dish out some justice.

I had my head turned facing the entrance to the foot bridge. The large hood on the coat covered the stocking face. I had stuffed a few newspapers around my cuffs in the jacket n out the legs of my baggy trousers.

I knew all the bully would see when he stepped foot onto the bridge would be the abandoned guy.

I clocked the glow of the circular red glow.

Cigar smoke mixing in the air with the mist from burnt out fireworks.

As he approached me, his pace slowed, unsure for a moment of the body leaning up on the bridges railing. Then he remembered it was the boy's guy n brazenly went to take a kick at its form.

I couldn't see his face clear because of the stocking mask, but it must have been a great picture of confusion as he hit solid leg.

"PENNY FOR THE GUY" I shouted making him jump back even further.

I rose steadily, letting my size n height creep up on him.

I smashed him in the face with all the force of a hurricane ripping up a flimsy fence, the cigars red hot ashes exploding like a little firework right into his face. I'd had quite enough of this overgrown bully boy.

The years hadn't been kind, A heavy drinker who in reality was just a fat bastard, the sixteen stone braggin to the divs in the pub not going to help right now. Half of it blubber belly anyway, wobbling about slowing him down.

He tried to cry, "Do you know who I am?" That old chestnut, which got me to pull down the hood on the coat so he could see the distorted face squashed behind the stocking mask.

The plea of please came next. But I was having none of that. His dentist appointment coming early this year as I socked him a tremendous left to the mouth, relieving him of his two upper front teeth.

I picked up the stub of cigar from the floor n stuck it into the bloody gap laughing at him now. The worried to death look on his face priceless.

I had deliberately started with the bare fist, which he stupidly must have believed was the limit of my rage. I see a little more of the whites of his eyes as the knife plunged into that whale blubber stomach. A gasp blew out of his mouth that would have put a ninety year olds candles straight out.

In front of me I bend down n scoop his knocked out front teeth onto the tip of the blade, its dark congealing blood holding them steady at the end. Grabbing his throat in a death grip with my left hand, I hold the knife tip right out in front of his eyeball. His jaw is shaking, I can smell hot piss. He hasn't even moved the cigar stub he is so rooted to the spot in fear.

I left his eye intact. This was just psychological war fare at its best. I returned the knife to my belt, he was lucky I had changed my preference regarding my weapon of choice. I had taken just a normal knife out, not the one I had modified. After flicking the teeth clear from the tip, the water below is where I put them.

I led him into the darkness of the middle of the field, away from the lights near the path that took people towards the lights of the navigation inn.

I lit up a few sparklers, tickling his nose deep enough to get some nice scorching smells going from his hair nostrils frazzling.

When I stuck the two bangers in his ear lugholes, he made a move to flee. Such a smooth manoeuvre my knife made from my belt to his thigh n back to the belt amazed even me. My practise had become so natural. It certainly stopped him in his tracks.

I lit the bangers simultaneously, their short fuse not giving him much chance to prepare for the explosion. The daze it left him in was as still as the guy he had first encountered about half an hour ago.

He was kinda unconscious and didn't even register more fear for my finale.

The Catherine wheel I pinned deep into his nose, pushing the long nail right down deep into his snout. I set it going n walked away. The village eye was calling me home, my power whiskey certainly earned this evening.

Another bully boy dealt with.

Guy was right, blow these fuckers to smithereens.

I would keep a vigil on this one. Remind him again if I felt he didn't correct his behaviour. But I had a feeling he would.

Back in the pub I owned, I sat warming myself in my comfy chair, the free standing stove chucking out some lovely heat.

Imagined the Catherine wheel still spinning n scorching the wanker's face.

I picked up a book of red leather bind I had been reading before I ventured out earlier this evening. Seán O'Casey, the author.

Sipping the power whiskey I picked back up on a very fitting passage.

'The hall way of every man's life is paced with pictures; pictures gay and pictures gloomy, all useful, for if we be wise, we can learn from them a richer and braver way to live'

{THE PLAGUE REMAINS chapter 102} *I wouldn't mark the red paint to the doors. They got no clue as to going onto the list. Why should I give them a heads up? The surprise was all part of the fear n fun.*

The worst bully from the bus had always been in the back of my mind. Even before the events that landed me inside the FABERON'S walls for a decade. I had always had the intention of giving him a taste of his own medicine. It seemed to becoming a factor in many that had bothered me as a youth. Major piss heads the lot of them, which only made the retribution easier than ever to drop on their unsuspecting souls.

It again didn't take long to suss out this clowns boring regime.

Christmas had passed quietly enough. The village eye takings a most welcome boost to my savings account. I hadn't celebrated much, but I was happy n free.

Fresh flowers& wreaths had been put upon the graves of the souls I cared for.

Stan I noticed didn't bother with a festive tree. My spying on him had become boring. I was ready now to grab him. But there was an order of fuckers to deal with first, so I bided my time.

The bus boy bully had stayed a single bloke. I hadn't come across any people in his life, which was in my favour, witness wise.

Up to now I had gotten away relatively scot free, in the sense of any one even remotely suspecting I could be in any way, shape or form responsible for the few beatings that had occurred.

There had been a piece in the local rag about the bonfire chap getting stabbed up. He had been found unconscious still bleeding quite bad on the field. Severe burns n trauma had also been mentioned along with the great news that he may have gone blind. I had read with joy my copy before burning it on the fire in the eye.

The police were clueless.

The other guy who got a clout after leaving the village eye had not a clue what happened to him. Well that's what the small piece in the paper had said along with the Police saying they were making routine enquiries but I had heard zilch n wasn't overly worried.

Plus I had been extremely clean at these scenes of crime. Living besides Character for all those years had schooled me well.

Plus these fuckers didn't want any major inquiries into why they had suddenly become targeted victims. Heavens forbid the police started snooping into their own lives n crimes. The fuckin domestic violence team would have a field day.

These bullies after the initial shock and pain subsided on their sad arses, would realise they had gotten away lightly considering the amount of abuse they had dished out to others over the years. And to think most of it was upon their so called loved ones too. Jesus, I'm surprised I didn't murder the lot of them.

With my Bus bully I decided on a long play, building up to fray his nerves nicely. The letter I penned upon Granddad Pedley's trunk one night as I visited the Vardo to make sure all was safe.

I had removed the kit bag full of money the first week of arriving home, keeping it now in the V room, where it was much more secure.

Off the top of my head I penned.

I WILL TAKE YOU TO THE GRAVE A BROKEN BONED SMASHED TO A PULP EMPTIED OF BLOOD

AND FROZEN IN HORROR AS TO THE REALISATION OF MY RAGE YOU SO STUPIDLY UNLEASHED.

I KNOW YOUR SECRETS

I WATCH YOU

GO TO THE POLICE AND IWILL SEND THE PIG BASTARDS MY DETAILED REPORT.

YOUR MOVE COWARD

I wrote it out without much attention to punctuation or grammatical correctness. I didn't want him even trying to figure out where the hell it had come from. I refrained from mentioning the skool bus. It was funny how it got me thinking way back.

The guy had made my life hell every morning as I tried to make it up the lane or back down it to the house. The orchard had helped by way of cutting out much of the openness of the journey. But those jeers he would scream out the window, I could hear them now. I could feel the tenseness that I had carried inside my skool uniform. It wasn't so bad I guess. Thinking back now as I felt, it almost seemed silly. But those little shits on the bus didn't have a clue as to the horrors of my home life. Mr big mouth, the one who orchestrated his little bunch of sheep followers, at that time in my life, just added a stress I didn't need.

So I was going to add some stress right now to his life, which upon peeping in on it looked like it didn't need any more sadness. Well tough tit.

I was on my way with the letter to slip it in the dead of night under his front door.

I waited a good few days before I went and had another stare at him.

Around eleven at night I closed in on his back window.

He lived just near Balloon Street, which was a quiet place at the best of times, so I had no bother with any one seeing me about.

I had taken precautions anyhow, dressed in my new army fatigues. The stuck on beard n glasses making me look odd, yet if a description came in about a stranger, it wasn't going to throw up any thoughts to my clean shaven look.

I caught him reading the letter.

Sat all hunched up on his tattered sofa. The letter so close to his nose he must have needed glasses badly. Crumpled paper gave the clue as to just how many times he had read over n over this warning.

I smiled to myself thinking how much it was worrying him. He certainly looked like he hadn't slept in days.

I banged the window which made him jump about a foot into the air. He didn't head over to see what was out there.

I slipped back into some bushes, covering myself nicely.

Minutes later his scared cautious face appeared at the window. He looked like a mole peering out into blackness.

The small pebble I threw landed right where his nose was pressed. I nearly howled with laughter at the face he pulled in fear n shock, falling back n then yanking the curtains closed.

I hear another bolt slide across his front door.

I left it that night, chuckling to myself on the way home, thinking how that security bolt made him feel a little safer. He just didn't realise what he was dealing with.

I'm sure the warning letter would be getting read a good few more times before I went back.

What really got to boiling my blood with this one was the fact he used the club next door to Stan's humble abode. My surveillances on *him gave me the insight that he used the club maybe two to three times a week.*

Always up the car parks back steps was his preferred route. Parking his old banger near to where the bowling green captain parked his old jag.

The warning letter had just been for starters. He had the whole entire menu to get through first before I would be done with him.

On the Tuesday evening, the skies dark n cold, he came ambling out of his house, heading around the back to where he parked his car under this old sycamore tree.

The crumpled fiver, just noticeable enough for him to swoop down to the street path, picking it up, thinking it was his lucky day.

As he unfurled it, making sure it was real money; I see from the hedge that I'm camouflaged into his eyes give off a vague look of surprise.

The warning was clear, written in black marker pen, scribbled in untraceable handwriting.

YOUR DEAD

He wasn't scared enough to drop the diver note back to the ground. Hurriedly stuffing it into trouser pocket, he now quickened his step to get to the car.

I let him drive away.

Friday night I got close again. Switching locations, this time I met him at his watering hole.

When the bus bully closed his car door, the cold night was just attempting a freeze. The warm flickers like fire from the electrified windows of the opened pub hurried him towards its doors.

I waited in the cold for three hours patiently.

The writing had to be quite large. The bully also didn't care about drink driving, another thing I despised.

Here he comes. His breath billowed into the still night air with the back draft of reeking ale.

When he finally got his arse squeezed into the driver's seat n popped on the head beams, he clocked the message. I'd scraped it deep n large into the bonnet of the car.

I caught the disturbed bewildered look of a piss artist thinking he's seeing things. He wasn't.

He was just reaching for the door handle to take a better look at the writing the right way up when the brick came sailing through the air, shattering the right side of the windscreen. It was stuck half hanging out, it's surrounding glass a large sphere of shattered patterns.

I waited a few seconds, hiding back in the shadows. Just giving him enough time see the next brick flying straight through the screen this time.

He ducked, and a good job too, for I had aimed it at his skull.

I let him read the white painted words, printed on the house bricks side.

BULLY

HA HA

He could sense the laughter outside of the vehicle now. For a second he forgot his bullying yellow streak of piss that ran throughout his entire body, getting out of the car with a bit of rage I detected.

Yet when he heard my

"Over here"

He sensed the darkened danger in front of him and retreated to the relative safety of what he believed was his vehicle.

I let him leave again.

The gear box he must have come near to breaking as he panicked n grinded through the gears before he found reverse n pulled back a good distance before hitting first n zooming out of the car park.

The next night though I came away from the village eye, staying out in the midnight hour just long enough to fire bomb his car to a burning melting mess.

The silencer on the gun I had brought out to test worked perfect. I had fired right into the corner of the glass, destroying a hole large enough to pour through the funnel the petrol I had brought along for the job.

The match I dropped through lit the car up very quickly.

My sprint home though had me tucked up in bed dozing before I heard the fire engine thundering up the lane toward the scene. It would be put down to kids, vandals, that sort of thing. But the bus bully knew.

He didn't venture out for over a week. I had kept up my vigil on him.

Yet the pull of addiction towards the ale had him the next Thursday get ready n ironically jump on the bus to hop off outside the club.

I'd had enough now. It was time to really hurt him.

After he had had his belly full of grog, I let him get twenty paces in front of me. I then materialised out from the shadows n let the steel tip of my iron mortuary sword drag a little on the path.

He was scared, I knew he had heard the scraping metal, yet he didn't want to look around n confirm it.

I started with a few missiles, a decent shot with the coin as the wind on my side, swerving it along seemingly to ring his ear with a new kind of change.

A couple of stones later had the piss artist looking back and muttering crap to his self.

Rain was crying above, falling in large droplets from the navy dark sky. The cold miserable weather held the streets eerily quiet, which suited me fine.

I pulled up my coat zip, securing my hood tight and jogged to the other side of the road. Sprinting now n quickly passed him, eyes dead ahead, arms pumping like pistons inside the jacket, I duck in on the other side, his side? No my side!!!!

He was approaching now with caution, not knowing if he should stay in the wet shadows or try to stay more under the street lamps glowing false safety. I cared neither way.

Grabbing him, snatching him, destroying him, could be done at any time.

He even heard me step out n scrape the blade along the floor again before I put it to his throat. He seized up on me that much I actually believed he had died of a heart attack right there on the spot.

The slash I gave him across that big mouth of his got him moving again. Bleeding all over the pavement yet he just remained silent.

I left it at that. The late night rain would take care of the majority of the blood stains

I'd wanted to take his head clean off but didn't want the attention. I had bigger fish to fry. He had his gaping slash over his entire mouth as a reminder of his gob.

For the ones on my raft list, well they were going to see the executioner. They were going to be in doubt what so ever that karma had caught up with them fully and it wanted its pound of flesh.

I could still taste the air loaded with that rusty blood scent.

On the walk back to the eye for my ritual drink of power whisky I believed on this occasion that I had done the right thing by not warranting his death. He would be another to keep a vigil upon. I would make sure no more gossip of his bullying ways reached my ears. Anymore and he could join the ones that had a destiny with the raft, his body under the road rotting in the cold waters for eternity.

Before I went back inside the eye for my drink I went through the back gardens. I had lit a smallish bonfire before I had left. It's burnt down wood still throwing off a foot of flame as I now threw my coat n gloves into its red n orange glowing centre, staring at the fibres as they started to burn n smoke. I watched for a good ten minutes, satisfied that the garments were now destroyed. Maybe only small traces of blood had splashed upon my coat as I had slashed his mouth. But chances were what got you pinched and I couldn't be having that.

That postman of mine was certainly always jolly. His whistling n cheerful greetings on a morning were welcome. I guess all those fresh mornings and lazy deserved afternoons could do that to a man. He even delivered packages out of his own free time on Sunday mornings till around ten am.

He slid into my hand this fine morning a small wrapped brown package, bidding me a good day n roaming off to find other letterboxes.

I usually opened the eye on a Sunday tea time till eleven.

But last night after seeing Stef out I had said I would be closed for a rest the next day.

So I found myself wondering around the building, putting up a few pictures here n there, cleaning the weapons in the Vroom, just generally pottering about at a nice steady pace feeling rather content with my current situation.

The great white would be no match for me. The day is mine and only I could dampen its mood.

I had placed the package from the postman on the table by my comfy chair. I had starred over at it a few times as I had gone about my choirs. The bottle of power whisky had stared back from next to it. I put its hypnotic trance like calling out of my mind and went to hang another print in the Vroom.

There had been a few nice things in Granddads leather satchel that after reading through them I thought would be nice to frame, so I could read them frequently as I passed my walls each day. Call it inspiration. Call it sentimental.

THE SNIPER'S RIFLE

IS AN EXTENSION

OF HIS EYE

HE KILLS WITH

INJURIOUS VISION.

Something from his war days Imagined.

I had placed it in a tortuous shell frame.

I read it again, only this time I was looking down the barrel at it from my 12 bore Manstopper pistol.

I had cleaned it earlier along with one of my real favourite guns. My Luparas gleamed now, the deadly Sicilian shot gun was a real gem in my collection.

Johnny had put most of it together for me upon my request. Character schooling me well on the best selection to maintain in my cabinet for all eventualities.

His list had become my list, which in turn had become Johnny's list. And here we were now, fully locked n loaded.

I cleaned a finger print off the glass of another small piece from out of Granddad's satchel.

I had framed this in silver and put it on my bed side reading table. It read.

HOW GREAT IS THE POWER

OF MANS THOUGHTS & FEELINGS

TO EITHER BUILD OR

DESTROY HIMSELF

It was written upon a piece of fine cloth. The words embroidered upon it in tiny pearls.

I placed the blindfold around my head and pulled it tight across my now darkened vision.

The lamps chilled bathe of light gone for now.

Knowing its ambience is there though helps my sword play.

I had purchased a few fine swords, yet my hands always reached for the Go samurai blade.

For the next hour I fell into the rhythm of swishing still air into a million little pieces.

The hot shower cleared the sweat I had built up from my practice. I was back down in the bar area, robe on, slippers. My package I decided needed opening.

The familiar business card stared back at me from within the ripped brown paper. The gift was an elegant gold pen.

Written along its length, Liberty had gotten engraved a most fitting quote.

After years at the side of the great poetaster Scot John I knew it to be one of the fine Irish masters.

BETWEEN MY FINGER AND MY THUMB

THE SQUAT PEN RESTS; SNUG AS A GUN

It was from within a poem that Heaney penned called digging.

{UNDER THE RAFT chapter 103} I had already in mind, my next target, but fate being the way she is sent me in a different direction for now.

After the lazy Sunday, I had risen early and written a short note back to Liberty. My travels down the lane to the village post office gave me an insight into a man I didn't really have my eye upon that much. But I did now.

The snaking Q was taking a while to lead me any closer to the post office counter where I needed to be to get my letter stamped.

Quite by chance I noticed her bruises through her wrinkled stocking leg.

A keen eye needed to clock this. She caught my stare, both of us embarrassed now. I knew of her husband from a kid.

Old Mr Expo had always been known for his no nonsense attitude. Thrashing his kids legs in public. A bit too liberal, the way he would use the old style corporal punishment methods to keep his brood in line.

I really didn't contemplate dealing with him. I genuinely believed he would have stopped his antics by now. Jesus he must have been fifty. I remember Stan once going on a rant about him after he had got *home from the pub. He had bumped into him at the bar n their chat had wound old Stan up. So we got to hear all about it when he rolled in drunk. Most of the village tolerated old Expo because he had won some crappy medal in the War. But he wasn't convincing the likes of Stan, who said it was either an iron cross or the firing squad. And that it wasn't bravery, cos no one wanted to be shot by their own side.*

I had remembered old Expo's wife, who they called Easter, always asking if I was ok if she spotted me upon the lane. She herself always seemed to be bruised up or have her arm in a sling or a pot on her ankle.

I didn't give it much thought back then, but staring at her ugly black bruises in the post office Q right now got my cogs turning. It made sense now why the old girls bruises never seemed to heal.

I posted my letter back to Liberty, wishing him well n stating if he ever wanted a drink to look me up at the village eye.

Over the next few weeks I started my surveillance on old man Expo. His kids had left home early and who could blame them for wanting to get out as soon as they could.

I think the thing with Expo, the thing that made him tick all wrong was the harsh reality of his failed military career. He must have thought that old bit of tin pot medal was going to get him some cushy office role, bossing folk around.

But that hadn't happened. The system had let him down, his country also. He told any one that would listen, that he nearly died for their freedom.

He didn't understand he was just expendable cannon fodder. He in his mind really believed he was some real life action figure.

And so the rage had surfaced upon his poor kid's n wife. They had taken the flack over all these years.

And from what I had gathered, the old poor cow was still taking his shit as the years only made his anger worse it seemed.

Snapping point came when she turned up at the bus stop outside the eye, her left arm cradled in a heavy white sling.

I had nipped out down onto the street path n inquired.

Her bullshit story about falling as the dog had pulled too hard on its lead fooled no one, least of all me.

That night I had carried in my bag two full bottles of cold water.

The hammer which rested besides them I tried to ignore for now.

Since she had gone in the sling, old Expo had walked the dog late at night.

Lazy bastard that he was only gave it a quick trip onto this playing field near the house they lived in.

The old girl would usually walk the hound a good mile at least.

The nights had been freezing the paths like ice rinks all week. The weather forecast I had checked on the bars small radio.

I knew he would pass this certain area every night with the dog, so here I spilled out the contents of the two bottles.

The night time freeze would do the rest.

I'd say around ten pm was when he gave the dog its brief walk. At around eight I went back to the spot n poured another fresh bottle.

Not many used this path, so I was hoping with a bit of luck he was going to take a nice fall.

My chosen area had a nice coating of ice. The fresh water with the temp how it was would just freeze nice before he came along.

I sat down hidden n waited.

It was like a kid's game this to me.

I did sometimes catch myself thinking I was being a little childish. Killing him violently very quickly was easy to do.

I wanted to string out the terror on them.

Things worked out better than I could have hoped for.

The other thing I had placed on the path, besides the water, had been a nice pork pie for the mutt. I had placed it just at the edge of the circle of ice.

Well I spotted him walking, the dog already pulling a little, its nose well ahead n already frothing its jowls after picking up the scent of the fresh meat.

I had wanted a decent fall, a shattered arm, a bang to the back of the head. What I got in delight was an almighty crash to the ground from him as the dog neared the ice, smelling the meat strong now, its bolt towards it pulling him along with the lead, which he managed to let go of. But it had come too late. His feet were a good way onto the slippery patch before he realised he was falling. The slamming sound as he knocked the wind right out from his back made such a noise on the breaking thin sheet of ice that I couldn't stop the grin from spreading all over my face.

I called the ambulance without giving my name from the red call box nearby.

I would call the hospital pretending to be his worried son in the morning from the same booth.

Delightful news, as I put the receiver down with a satisfying click.

The young nurse I had spoken to confirming that he would be laid in his hospital bed for a good month.

Spine damaged, surgery needed, plenty bed rest.

Perfect.

The old girl would get some peace at home for a while at least.

I left it a week before I paid a visit to his bed side.

I arrived in disguise, giving his sons name at the desk.

I woke him by flicking a few picked grapes from the bunch I had brought. His eyes blinking all confused from sleep n the confusion of the figure before him. My hand caught over his mouth as I leant forward to level my mouth with his ear.

I won't repeat the threat.

It kinda sickened me to be threatening a man who was in my opinion old. But he had to learn.

I left him to chew over my words.

If I had to see him again, he knew he was a dead man.

That night Is nook out late after the village eye was well closed. Preparation was crucial here.

I made my way to the raft. The waterfall splattered into my face.

I secured the boulders with the thick rope, perfect as anchors. The hooks I had taken from a visit up to the slaughter bungalow gleamed they were that sharp down here under the road.

On the way out after sorting what I thought may become necessary by the raft. I got that strange familiar feeling as I passed the sleepy guard again. The familiarity of his body language I just couldn't shake.

I had to figure out my suspicions.

I moved well away from the side of the factory where the path led towards the raft. Over near his porta cabin office I let loose with the ball point hammer, sailing it straight through the meshed window.

In the light of the doorway I nearly gave myself away, my voice nearly betraying me as astonishment as to whom I was looking at.

officer Dick, as slow and clumsy looking as ever peered out into the yards dark night, flicking on a flash light n feebly shouting "who's there" in that annoying bastard voice of his.

A voice I hadn't heard for well over ten years since he had smugly walked the stations corridors blatantly giving his lies and helping to bury me.

He had aged terribly. Probably the guilt I hoped. But I doubted it.

A man who can lie under oath like that to secure the final nail in a wrongful convictions coffin had no conscience.

I had thought about him a fair bit.

He was certainly on the rafts list. But I didn't think I would drop on him in this situation.

My mind filling with disturbing thoughts about what I wanted to do with him. Did I really care if I got caught? As long as I showed these gutless bastards retribution, it seemed the only thing worth worrying about.

I had my plan B

Me & Johnny speaking on the phone booths from time to time, the call costing only 50p as I sussed that if you angled the coin in at a certain point n just before it dropped you banged the casing on the bottom part of the booth, the coin came back out in the return slot but the 50p registered still as credit. So I would push in n bang out until my coin registered for me a good few quid, making the call affordable. I put officer Dick on hold for now, he was going nowhere.

Inquiries made revealed he had been sacked from the force three years ago. He had rose to sergeant seven years ago, a coincidence with giving evidence against me something I didn't miss.

Little wanker thought he could rise up the ladder off my back did he?

I was going to snap every rung in his spineless back!!!

The next month took up all my free time. Surveillance upon a few needed serious concentration. I would get around to the lying rat Dick very soon.

{DONE & DUSTED chapter 104} I had got it wrong. I really did believe the threat I had served into old Expo's ear had filtered down n made sense to his brain. But even I could get it wrong n misjudge a man's stupidity.

Revolting beastly behaviour had continued. He had been out of hospital on crutches no more than a few days.

I was going to leave him alone for a while but the bar had been quiet so I had nipped out n had a peep through the back windows of his house.

What I see is sickening.

Poor old girl was shaking like a leaf in this patterned wool chair. Old Expo stood by the side of her. One of his crutches seemingly froze in time as he held it above her frail figure menacingly.

Blood was flowing quite freely down her head from a blow on the top of her dome.

That was it for me in my mind. No more warnings ever were coming from my mouth.

I was about to up the ante in a big way.

I rushed back to the eye to retrieve a weapon from the Vroom cabinet.

I waited for hours outside, hoping he would step outside for any reason so I could grab him without his wife seeing what was going down.

My break came as I checked my watch, reading one am on the illuminated dials.

The back door opened and he came out a foot from the door and lit up a small pipe. I let him get the bowl a blaze. Call it his last pleasure on this mortal coil.

Lead piping connected sweetly just above the back of his ear. He sunk into my arms with a slight moaning sound. I threw him over my shoulder in a fire mans lift, pushed the door quietly back shut n set off.

It wasn't a long trip. Only once did I panic when I spotted a late night car cruising my way. I threw him over a garden hedge n ducked in by the gate until it passed.

Soon I was at the entrance of the mill.

I didn't take him my usual route as his weight was making me that bit too slow n I didn't want to risk a confrontation right at this minute with the guard Dick. So I threw his body over the small railings that were on the path side.

He made a terrible thud as he landed on the grass verge below.

Quite sure he was well unconscious still, I made my own way around past the sleeping guard.

He had come around a little bit old Expo by the time I made it through the undergrowths path to him.

Crawling maybe a foot no more I soon put my boot on his neck n told him to start praying.

I cuffed him round the ear with the claw part of the hammer, ripping the ear more or less clean off.

His praying grew a little too loud at this point.

I caught site in the shadows our forms merging. The lower crumpled half never me.

I slid the old hammer away up my cuff. Dealers n cheats in Vegas would have raised an admiring eyebrow from such a smooth sleeve trick.

Whimpers coming from his mouth now, put the complaint in elsewhere mush. I wasn't listening.

He had on this big coat, like I mean big as in at least three times too big for his frame. I suppose it made him feel the big man. Beating up his wife all these decades, he certainly needed something to make up for the spineless bastard he really was.

I dragged him through the curtain of water to the rafts side, shocking freezing water from the sheer drop banged in to his face waking him fully now which is where I wanted him to be, so he could face his karma with a clear view.

I clipped him sweet again just above the temple area. I didn't want to kill yet, just knock him out so I could carry him over the smashed up tow path. I hoisted him up onto my back in the fire mans lift, letting my feet sink into the cold water, finding their grip on the metal rope.

After carefully edging across the gap I slung him back onto the floor n smothered his face with a cloth full of smelling salts. He woke up quick, dazed for a second, so then I got to work proper.

I pierced the first hook straight through his foot. The next one went through his knee cap, he didn't make a sound.

The tongue I had just before ripped out of his mouth with a Stanley blade, tossing it onto the narrow towpath that ran alongside the stream.

I ripped his other ear off with a fine slicing motion with the blade. The tears streaming down his face hard now.

The large boulder I had already prepared. Wrapped in heavy fishing net, secured with good strength rope, it awaited his neck.

I booted him hard into his mid section, knocking all the silent pleading out of him for a moment. It settled him enough for me to place the rope around him.

Snaking around his body a good two foot of it waited for its deployment to the depths. I shouted to him "On your feet soldier."

I gave him a side chop with my hand straightened right up under his noses septum bone, just hard enough to jerk his head back so he was looking forward into my eyes.

I held the white feather out in my fingers to show him what I truly thought.

As Infixed the silencer to the gun he turned away, showing his big coated back to me. Too yellow to face it head on.

I wasn't going to mess about n turn him back around.

The bullet I let loose blew the back out of the coat. His small frame soon came to light, falling to his knees before slumping completely over onto his stomach, his arms n hands all crushed underneath him as he had instinctively grabbed at the wound as the bullet tore straight through him.

That big coat would have made a grand lining for his coffin, but he was going deep into his watery grave, stripped as naked as the day he was born.

After I had sunk him, securing the rope that held him tight to a hook that I had hammered into the underside of the rafts planks, I now sat bobbing on the gentle currents for a while.

Those years of practise holding my breath in the top of the jugs water working perfect for me as I held my breath easy while dealing underneath the raft to secure these scum bags.

The blood on the towpath needed swilling away, which would be done before I headed home. His pile of clothing that would be burnt was in a small crumpled heap near the dark red puddle of blood. It would be ashes by the time I left.

I sat thinking about him under there, just below me. There were empty hooks that I had gotten ready for others. I had been so busy of late I never thought back much to the FABERON, to my strange ocean emptying dreams. They had seized to materialise in my sleep since I had become free. I strangely missed them.

{GOAL chapter 105} *One of those simple things as a kid, an unwritten rule amongst the village gangs, which that football had represented was trust.*

After sipping my power whisky late last night after I had got back from dealing with old Expo, I did start to wonder what was driving me.

I could have left these other people's lives n business well alone, just dealt with Stan, but I felt compelled to interfere, to stand up for the weak in society, for the ones suffering behind their own front doors.

It had to be done.

Many talked about it. But I knew I was quite alone out there on these dark nights dishing out real justice.

Describe the tongue of the woodpecker?

You can't can you?

Just like I can't explain the joy I feel when I raise a fresh glass n toast the demise of this scum.

As a youth just getting out to the open fields every now n again cleared my mind of Stan's bad shit for a little while. I didn't get chance much, but now n again.

I remember one of the public footpaths had a little sign next to a little knoll of overgrown grass, where this leather brown football rested from its recent game by the foot of the stile.

Every one of the kids who used the ball had signed it over the years in different coloured pens, stickers were on it too.

At the very end of the path, maybe a half mile away, another stile, with another sign carried the rules of the ball just the same as the other sign stated.

The gist of the rules were that anyone could pick the ball up, using it for a kick about as you made your way over the fields track. Then you put it back at the other post.

Simple really, as when groups or individuals would cross paths they would have a little three a side game n then one of the bunch would keep the ball n make sure it got left for others.

Every kid had a ball, so no one got the urge to nick it. I didn't own a football, yet I still followed the rules not wanting to spoil it for the other village kids.

The target I had on my radar next was all down to a memory I remembered all too well.

I had been on my way to the raft.

Stan had belted me with these new windscreen wipers he was fitting to the car down by the garage. He had asked me to come down n help him but all he had done was stood me in the cobwebbed corner of the dark garage for half an hour and then whacked me around the face with the wipers, saying I was a good for nothing little shit.

I had run of thinking the raft was where I needed to be for a while, yet I had taken a little detour over the first stile by the fields, grabbing the ball n doing some tricks that I was trying to master like the great George best.

Near the middle of the path, I noticed this tall stranger walking slowly in my direction. As I got around twenty feet from him he shouted for me to kick him the ball.

Warily I did, although his demeanour made me think as soon as the ball I booted to him landed at his feet, I had made a mistake.

Shockingly he pulled out the largest hunting knife I had ever seen in my life, slowly drawing it from out under his lumber jacket coat.

He did a few impressive kick ups with the ball until on about number twenty from my count he missed a knee n dropped the continuation.

That was the moment he stabbed the ball so hard it totally deflated like a pancake in a split second. He threw it back towards my feet like how you would throw a gentle frizbee.

I had already started running back in the direction I had travelled at this point.

His boots hard noise on the ground behind me all I could hear as he closed in on me.

The next thing I knew I was face down in the dirt path from a trip he had caused me to have.

Glaring down at me, the tip of that knife rested on my nose, he threatened to deflate my face. Told me he should puncture all the wind out of me.

He didn't physically touch me, but he stood over me a good ten minutes, which seemed like hours, just repeating his threats n pointed that lethal looking blade.

I knew even on that day why he had done it.

He burst that ball because of what it represented. Someone like him couldn't comprehend why people were happy to leave it at either end. But his threats towards me I didn't comprehend as to the reason why he felt the need to scare the life out of me.

It had taken quite some time for me to trace his abode. I had it firmly memorised n was heading there right now with my own pointy tool.

The details are irrelevant as to how I now had him down besides the raft. Let's just say I had learned a trick or two from old Stanley when it came to the finer points of rendering a body unconscious.

He was still tall, yet all these years later I was now the bigger man by a good six stone, and my weight was solid weight, not the scraggy skin that was hanging of his bean pole frame.

It had taken me less than half an hour to land at his door, knock him out n bring him down here.

I had waited all day reading in my bedroom back in the village eye, just waiting for a little evening darkness to give me a little cover, enjoying the writing skills of the author Breandan Behan's first novel, Borstal boy.

I shone the snake torch into his eyes like a Dr examining you. He had awoken very confused.

Looking around under the road, trying to figure out where the hell he was n why. We were on the far side of the tow path.

The black masking tape I had wound around his head until the roll had run out.

Poked eye holes the only thing he had to see out from.

His head kind of looked like some old football, down here in the dim light. That sewing class way back in the FABERON was going to come in handy on this one.

I gave him a good solid beating all over his body while I had his mouth all wrapped up n him silent screaming. The muffles of pain were never going to be heard.

I noticed his eyes on occasion darting to look at the old leather ball that I had brought down weeks ago. It rested on the tow path next to another ready set boulder wrapped in thick fishing net. The rope n hooks ready next to it.

I let him bleed for a while.

He must have believed at this point that I had finished and I was just letting him soak up the beating.

I picked the football up n bounced it off his head catching it back in my hands.

After a few times doing this I asked him if he remembered the threats he had given towards me all those years ago.

You see the thing is with these ding bats is they never in a million years envision this day coming.

Yet those long lonely years sat in my cell had given me a tremendous time to think back on all the bullies in my life.

When I started cutting the tape from his face with my blade, I am sure I heard him start to say, oh thank you.

Fool he was.

When I had ripped it all off, except the bit securing his big mouth, I booted him in the face saying "you like football mate?"

It registered then in his eyes just who he had in front of him.

The tape around his mouth got busy as his pleading started to increase.

When I carved the first piece of flesh away from his cheek he nearly lost consciousness, so I splashed his face by cupping my hand into the stream n scooping it up into his face to shock him back to reality.

The piece I cut from his forehead must have really hurt.

His other cheek came next then both his ears I sliced off.

He was in and out of consciousness around this time. A decent amount of blood loss he had spilled onto the towpath floor. The grey shirt he had on was just crimson now.

I sat cross legged in front of him n got to stitching the panels of flesh onto the football.

I used a large sewing needle n decent thick thread.

After half an hour I had all the skin n ears on. He was awake staring at me with wide eyes. God only knows what thoughts were now running through his mind. He certainly knew this was just no ordinary beating on the cards.

His blood loss by my reckoning would put his lights out for good quite soon. So I got to finishing up.

I did a few kick ups with the ball, laughing as I managed about ten before I lost it n it sailed into the stream with a heavy plop.

I grabbed a large tree branch that I had carved as a nice stick n retrieved it.

I lunged at him next n rested the tip of my blade against his nose. Only this time, unlike his veiled threats, I carried through n with a nice side swipe cut the tip of his beak clean off.

I had left the needle threaded with a good long piece of thread.

I stitched the ball secure to his lips, the zig zag thread I just left dangling with the needle still attached after I tied the knot.

I then stabbed him straight through the jugular.

It took a while to clean all the mess up n get him secured under the raft. It had been very quick the way he bled out.

I was that tired after this one I just lay upon its wooden boards n let the gentle swell bob me to a deep sleep.

My boots removed and socks gave a lovely cooling feel to my feet as I dangled them off the end of the raft to cool myself down from all the excitement. I was soon away to the dream world state.

{THE BLOOD GUTTER chapter 106} *I'm happy like a pig in shit.*

There is a near quarter of power whiskey drained from the bottle.

A good few name's on the list now ticked off.

There wasn't an actual physical list. It was just set as stone in my mind. No trace of evidence was ever going to be found.

The next few months I had a rest from my blood thirsty activities.

I certainly kept my vigil, the ante again soon to be upped.

February came and went with thoughts on Valentines about Nurse Silk.

We had not contacted each other since I had kissed her hot lips.

For the best really, for I didn't think she would understand quite as well as I did, my need for such retribution out here if I tried to even explain.

March & April calmed the coldness from the past month's weather.

A not so welcome change, as the dark nights were becoming a little lighter, but it just meant I had to hit the streets a little later in the evening. *The cold didn't bother me after a decade freezing internally in the asylum.*

A shower and a shave on the cards this morning, before a walk by the river path up to the lake of stars, where I wanted to check a few things out.

I had chilled, after habitually waking early with the dawn. I had read and finished at leisure the great book Moby Dick.

The writer Herman Melville had intrigued me enough to read another of his earlier works that sat upon my book shelf.

There was this great passage in it that I must have read over n over about ten times while I chilled out all toasty in bed.

The book was titled White jacket and it had certainly struck a chord with my nocturnal activities. The opened book lay on the blankets of the bed, which I read again one last time before preparing to ready myself to leave the pub.

Nature has not implanted any power in man that was not meant to be exercised at times, though too often our powers have been abused.

The privilege, inborn and alien like, that everyman has of dying himself, and inflicting death upon another, was not given to us without purpose.

These are the last resources of an insulted and unendurable existence.

Most definitely a novel only a fool would boycott his entire life. I guess reading certain books when it was too late to act upon their knowledge gained was one of life's true sad encounters.

I had gotten rid yesterday of a few tools that I had started to take a fondness too on some of my unrecorded escapades.

Some tools I only used the once. My favourites I tried to break down but never could.

Like old Granddads ghost was too strong in the very fibre of them to let go.

I did worry slightly that my downfall could come from these sentimental attachments, but it would take a clever man to catch me on the street holding one, with certainty in my mind that not a living soul besides Johnny knew of my Vroom.

I guess the Go samurai sword was clean of activity right now. But that was certainly going to change.

After this next target I would bring it out to play.

This guy was quite near the top of my list when it came to how much I wanted to scare the shit out of him before a brutal death became of his cowardly bones. From time to time when I had passed the graveyards in the FABERON it had occurred to me of this poor old guy's unwanted resting place.

That old tramp from the village who I had stumbled across that day fighting with that young bloke was finally about to get some revenge, courtesy of yours truly.

I would have had the bloke on the list any way, just for the fact he murdered the harmless old fool. OK, you could say it was self defence, but that old guy even though he had swung that axe was no threat. It wasn't like the young guy had been confronted by Conan the Barbarian. He could have taken the axe, set it down n given him a crack round the ear. But he had decided on murder.

But that participation he made me do of burying the old tramp that day, the threats of murdering my old Granddad if I ever told of what I had seen.

I had never forgotten. The hate he had directed towards me after the burial had been so intense I had realised when I got back to the house that I had wet myself with fear.

Well this time when we had our reunion, there was going to be fluid spilled. But I was not going to be satisfied with him pissing his pants in sheer panic.

No.

What I wanted was complete blood loss. His 21 grams he could slowly leak after the blood had drained out.

He will surely see I have grown since our last meet. See how he handles the threats this time. I'll tell you some real shit. Killing is easy up close and personal. The ones who have fucked with my nerves will have time with me.

The sleep had been dreamless again. An invigorated awakening after my cold shower after been so absorbed into my literature had me springing out to the early morning mist.

Out in the back garden of the eye the axe caved the first log with such ferocity that the handle snapped itself clean in half.

I finished off with the hatchet a few more logs that I was splitting up small enough to feed the wood burner in the bar area. The broken handle could go on the blaze too.

Half hour later, my coffee drank, I was ready to go and capture the axe man.

I had a good place in mind to keep him throughout the day until night fall would cover our presence as I moved him in the shadows in the direction of the road. I might even keep him a few days until his time was truly up. I was about to scare him to jelly.

The small motor I had bought I paid in full, no questions asked. The dealer couldn't believe his luck getting a cash sale so early in the day.

All I wanted to know was if it started first time, ran ok and had a decent size boot.

I got an automatic as I had never driven before and thought after my test, which had consisted of reading a few books on how to drive and putting my common sense into gear, that it would be easier. I mean how hard could it be? You turned the wheel in the direction you wanted to go, kept to a reasonable speed n used your senses!!!

Everything was to my satisfaction, and we spat in our palms n shook hands as I counted out the wad on the car bonnet.

I'd used a dealership a good distance from the village.

I drove without incident a good few miles and parked up a few houses away from where my target lived.

Only two latches away from popping his gate and knocking his door, I patiently waited for the street to become totally empty. Not many people were about and it didn't take long before I spotted my chance to nab him.

I didn't want to arouse suspicion bundling him into the car by walking him up the street, so I pulled forward and parked the back of the cars boot level with his front garden gate.

I got out and walked the tidy garden path. My knock an average sound, I didn't need to bray on the door n make him wary as he opened up.

After five reasonable taps with my knuckles on the red gloss painted door it swung open. The little bottle of spray I had already in my hand, it was filled with a remarkable liquid that Character had schooled me on to mix to perfection for just such an occasion.

His mouth was open to get out the greeting of can I help you, when I caught him with three jets of the stuff right into the back of his tonsils.

He was a sleep on the hall floor before I put the spray bottle back inside my jacket pocket.

I went into overdrive, yet remained calm.

He fit perfect into the boot, covering him with an old blanket from out of Dolly's vardo.

Job done and I was off down the road with my pray.

I pushed away hard the thought that as I was driving I was no better than Stan. Like all those trips to the Dr's he had forced me to take in the dark boots confined space.

I soon shook of the thoughts. My work here was justified. I wasn't like Stan, this had purpose. This was right.

I heard a few muffled shouts coming through the cars boot area. He had awoken.

The spray mixture I had used at the door would only lead to a man's brain to black out for five minutes at the most.

I had secured his mouth well with masking tape at the doorway before dragging him low down the path to the awaiting open boot.

I ignored his muffled pleas.

The old mill ground was quite a large area if you walked its full circumference. It was around the very back of the buildings where the old tramp had lived in his little hut. His dead body not buried too far from that dwelling.

I had parked the car up right around the back. A forest of thick trees darkened this quiet dirt track lane where I killed the engine n got to popping the boot.

His eyes blinked surprise as the light hit them when the boot rose, but he didn't see the bright sky for long. The spray caught him again, this time directed at an angle right up his nose.

As I carried him to where he had made me dig that hole all those years back I had a horrible flash back in my mind as to the exact moment that head severed n fell with a thud to the ground.

Those eyes of the killer as he heard me as I'd hid. That stare he had given me as he had walked my way, Jesus it ran a shiver right cold down my spine.

As I had him within ten feet of the hole I dropped him off my shoulder n started dragging him by his hair towards the overgrown spot. This time as he came around he looked up from the floor the entire length of the spade, where I rested at its handle to greet him. Screams that went unheard came next. I told him he needed to man up.

The slice into his shin must have smarted just a bit.

He passed out again for thirty seconds from the sheer shock of the blow. His shin bone split right through, the foot only hanging on by a few fibres.

I had intended in my planning while I had practised with my favourite blade in the plotting room to just bury him alive.

But as I had thought of putting him in the same hole as the old tramp, it seemed unbefitting to the old man's memory. So I went with plan B.

Which when I contemplated the horror factor was worse luck for my target.

I secured his hands with rope from a bag I had fetched on my other shoulder. It had the things I needed.

I told him just to fuck with his mind that he was going in that hole as well.

But I was going to let him slowly bleed nearly to death first before burying him alive.

It certainly got his full attention.

I didn't care about asking him why or what or whatever the fuck had gone on all those years back.

He knew who I was, knew why I was here in front of him. When you dance with the devil you don't wait for the song to stop.

When I cut hard through his wrist with the edge of the spade he cried out that much that he nearly blew the tape free from over his mouth.

Half a roll later he was silent again muffling away his whimpers.

I let him watch me start the unearthing of his murderous secret. A few spades deep into the hole I told him I would finish off with him asleep. That the spray I used on him only lasted five minutes. That by the time I had dug down n thrown him in n stated filling over his body with cold soil he would just be coming around.

The thought of him waking like that had the desired effect. The hot circular stain in the crotch of his pants quite satisfying for me to see appear.

I sprayed his nose n eyes n ears and he fell away into blackness.

Confused he would most certainly be as he awoke.

Rattling around in the car boot again, I was on my way driving him to his next little destination to scare him n hurt some more.

I knew when I had coat hanger lifted the keys through Stan's letter box that I would use the slaughter bungalow to scare the shit out of one of my targets on my list. When I had gathered the hooks for the body securing from there the place had given even me the creeps, so I knew it was a great location to torture a lucky scum bag on my list.

The place like the old mill had been shut down years ago.

Nothing had been reinvented as a working structure. It's boarded up doors n windows looked likely to remain forever that way, except for my little break in.

I had cut two holes at either side of the property as I had been out walking the other day. The lake of stars backed onto the very far end of the giant car parks fence where the freezer trucks use to be loaded with meat. That's where I intended to exit later.

I pulled the car over directly next to where I had cut a section big enough at the point of where I wanted to enter the grounds.

There was no fear of people about up here. Nothing maybe except a solitary dog walker, but I hadn't seen a soul.

I got the axe man out of the boot, giving him a nice punch right into his rib section before I dragged him out onto the path. Quickly I locked the car up n pulled him down by his hair n dragged him through the gap I had sliced with metal pliers the other day.

I didn't need to put the man stopper pistol right into his back n tell him to get marching over the car park. But I thought it added to the drama.

The loading bays that backed onto the killing rooms, where they use to slaughter the animals and then carry them out to the back of the freezer trucks my destination to start the fun n games.

The door I had already crow barred open a while ago when retrieving the hooks late one night, I had wedged it shut, easy to gain entry again when the time was right, which was now.

We were soon in the building. This is when I pulled the hood over his head. I marched him about for a few minutes, making him lose all sense of direction.

When I pulled the hood back his eyes bulged out of his head as he clocked the scene. A split second before he had been nose touching this giant plastic curtain. As I swept it aside n pushed him through and the whimpers coming from him told me he had now got the gist of my intensions.

The bright hooks had lost most of their metal shine as they hung in rows from the ceiling. They certainly hadn't lost any of their menace.

There were old sets of overalls, with these belts of chain mail hanging around them.

Discarded knives that looked more the size of swords were scattered around the floor.

The place should have been snapped up by some B movie film company. There horror films location certainly found. It was perfect.

I hung him a full 24 hours.

The hooks imbedded into both his shoulder blades had held fast nicely. Steady blood had run from his torso making its way finally to the blood gutter set into the flooring.

He must have surely thought his demise would happen in this location, but I had other plans of fear for him to enjoy.

I got bored punching away at him as he swayed about all half unconscious, a few ribs certainly broken clean in two as I had let go some proper venomous clouts that old Granddad would have admired.

I cut him down n let him think for a while that the bullet was coming to end it all. I slowly let him watch me load bullets into the pistol.

After blindfolding him again I pointed the nozzle at his temple until he screamed for help behind the muffled masking tape.

I put the gun down n sprayed his nostrils again with the knock out mixture.

Straight to sleep he went for five minutes.

On my shoulders n on towards the car park I made tracks. I was heading over the back fields to the lake of stars. The raft was waiting.

There was another way to end up by the raft, but only if you were unfortunate enough to fall down this large waterfall that leaked the overflow from the lake of stars.

If you went in the water at that entry point you would tumble down a sheer drop to be met by icy cold water crushing n holding you under as you franticly fought your way to the surface.

We were both going over the edge.

I knew I could hold my breath to the point panic wouldn't over take me.

For the poor axe man, well his lungs were going to fill quite a bit as we swirled about down there.

The water from this water fall led from a fast paced stream down another smaller less frightening drop which eventually settled n floated you right by the entrance to the raft.

We were both now stood on the precipice as I yanked off his hood, which I had only put on for a bit of dramatics.

I didn't give him time to take in what he was facing I just held my hand up for him to see we were roped together n leaped off.

I cannot tell you what he made of the journey. Sheer panic all the way I would imagine. But for me it had a weird sleepy feel off my ocean dreams.

Twigs were in a downpour dream Old bike wheel swirled in a churned up flash of wave.

I caught sight as we spun under the pressure his mouth blowing out streams of bubbles. A bad move I thought as I stayed calm n held my breath.

By the time we had gotten through the descents and were just about floating toward the last part where we would go under the curtain of water n disappear under the road, I had to keep his head held above the water mark or he would have been gone before I got him to the raft.

When about ten feet away from the raft, he had come around enough to know he was still of this world, I pulled him under again n swam along until I had the rafts underbelly just above my head.

My knife severed the tie I had made to him and now with both free hands I secured him to the hook I had left waiting.

When I surfaced I was exhausted, yet elated.

I held on to the side planks of the raft n just retrieved my breathing until it was completely under control.

That few minutes I had spent recovering I knew full well that below me, struggling for his freedom and trying to hold onto that final breath before his lungs filled with a gush of dirty lake water the axe man was no more.

After I had changed at the side of the tow path into fresh dry threads I had walked out of the mill through the undergrowth path, passing the empty guards box of dick, he wouldn't start his shift until this evening.

Turning out onto the village lane, I casually walked away.

I peered down when I got level with the small iron fence that looked down from the road side. The curtain of water that rained down below arrived at this point via a quick running narrow stream to the left side of the railings.

It's flow of water directed downwards at this point as this particular vein of current finished its journey. It travelled the length of the railings, just below the pathway. It had been blocked off with large boulders when the mill had been built as it would have carried on right through the main entrance.

 The lake of stars had a few branches of water running from its source. This particular one had always pleased me. I had always even as a young kid been thank full for its coverage into the rafts entrance. It was perfect for me how they had blocked the waters pathway. How it fell away as it smashed back on itself from the boulders gave me forever the cloak of secrecy I always needed.

I had driven a good few miles outside the village of Gallowthorpe n then smothered the entire contents of a petrol can over the interior n struck a match. I didn't need the car no more n wanted rid of any traces of the axe mans presence from the boot.

The walk back didn't take long. I kept my head down n hood up on my tracksuit top, encountering no one for prying conversation.

Back in the village eye that evening I watched a couple over in the corner clicking two champagne flutes together celebrating something nice. I raised my half full glass of power whisky in their direction n as I smiled at them in my mind I silently toasted my latest tick on the list. Bon voyage wanker.

{QUICK ONES chapter 107} I got busy in the last week of May. Something that wasn't on my radar had caught my attention as I had casually read the local paper one bright spring morning.

The headlines in a small piece that the paper didn't seem to warrant a front page cover story, read.

MAN SHOT HIMSELF

AN ECCENTRIC RECLUSE WHO SHOT HIMSELF BECAUSE HE FEARED A ROBBER WHO ATTACKED HIM IN HIS OWN HOME WOULD RETURN.

I read the piece through a few times as I sipped my freshly squeezed pineapple.

The more I read the more anger rose deep inside me. From what I could make of this tragic story, this poor guy had been minding his own business sat outside his garage, playing quiet guitar blues n smoking a ciggie.

Some little oink had strolled past n demanded a smoke.

When the poor old guy had refused, which in my mind was his damn prerogative to do so, this little viscous bastard had cracked him a good one over the head with a steel pipe.

The kid had rightly so gotten a few years in gaol. But he had been due out shortly. The poor old guy had been that worried that he was going to return n finish him off had only gone and blown his brains out with a shot gun. The tragedy at the end of the piece in the paper being that the gun he had used had belonged to his Late Dad, who had killed himself with the same gun years ago.

Before May became June I had found out through a contact just when the little bastard was getting out.

On the day at the prison gate he had no one there for him as he strolled out all cocky with this bulky plastic bag over his shoulder.

But unbeknown to the little rat, he did have someone there to watch him leave n regain his freedom.

I thought in my mind as I watched him and let him get about twenty metres in front of me that he better enjoy every damn step of this short lived feeling.

His karma had arrived as I fingered the handle of the Ghurkha knife in my coat pocket.

Not yet though I thought, as I let him carry on his journey for now.

In the early morning light I crept along the paths with the odd cat looking for mice.

Outside this little creeps council flat he had fastened to the gate a tattered old union jack.

He had been free 24 hours.

I pulled the knots from the corner of the flag and untied it from the posts.

I wasn't messing about on this one. He was already interfering with my priorities on my list.

I ripped up the union jack to use as a butchers apron.

Three times my knuckles went tap on the door before I see the hall light flick on and through the frosted half glass of the door his figure approach. He certainly wasn't expecting visitors at this time of night.

I had heard the old church bells from up at St Pauls strike one am as I had left the village eye.

A bleary eyed toe rag pulled the door open, a safety chain his only protection. The shoulder barge interrupted the cocky little bastards greeting of, "Yeah can I help ya mate"

As I moved through into the doorway he was already scurrying back along the hallway floor. His eyes so confused as to what the hell he had in front of him.

I hadn't worn my bally. There was no need to cover my identity.

As I pulled the gun out he went to scream. The flying kick into his head broke his jaw on both sides of his face, the pit boots steel toe cap catching him perfect for such a fracture to occur.

The whimpers came now as he froze watching me screw on the silencer.

I could have attached it beforehand but I liked the tension it built up.

The fear factor cranked right up to the max.

I squeezed off two perfect shots.

Both eye orb holes the target.

Instantly blood splatters on the red white n blue of the apron.

I watched the brains n blood drip down this old white mucky looking radiator on the wall for a minute.

The life of him well spent.

Silencer quickly unscrewed n returned to the inner jacket pocket, the pistol next found its way back into the belt around my waist.

It was time to leave.

I didn't really celebrate this killing.

I was glad I had given him a taste of fear n ended him so he could never inflict a death again on an innocent.

I left the top screwed tight on the power whisky bottle.

The beginning week of June was a strange time for me.

I could sense things building inside of myself.

I was beginning to sense that I was losing my track of thoughts for a while.

A few rumours I picked up around the village n on its outskirts had me come knocking on a few more doors before I made my final preparations to grab a hold of officer Dick.

In bed over the week I had random flash backs to my midnight actions. Bang, the gun smoked a powder burn into his cheek as I angled the nozzle n blew his cowardly brains out.

The faces of terror haunting me all through the early mornings, my sheets upon waking like a dog bed all messed up from tossing n turning.

Like, the one last night isn't worth a mention, his desperate pleadings gave my stomach a bad turn, the pathetic begging of a grown man enough to give you the fever.

I cannot even bring myself to write of Thursday night' target, for as I dished out my own retribution for his crime I seemed to have Stan on my mind way too much n became a monster I wish not to recall upon the page. I actually felt I had gone too far with that one.

I expected the police to crash down my door any minute, but nothing. I hear sirens from time to time, speeding too late to save any of them.

But apart from a card being left behind the bar, which Stef had given to me as she had started work one night, not a peep of the old bill sniffing.

I had propped the card behind a bottle of rum on the back of the mirrored bar shelf.

It had the usual crap on it. Call this number if you think you may be able to help with enquiries.

The last guy had lived just outside of the village. I felt I could if I wished just go from one village to another to deal with all types of sickening individuals.

But for the most part I was going to stick to the list.

I had intended to kill Paddy Stone. Stan's old pal. He had always unnerved me as a youth and I knew I had always got it worse off Stan when he had made a visit to the house.

Yet when I had peeped in on him, I found this pathetic looking creature in a filthy chair zoned out with his eyes on the empty TV screen. His shaking was so bad that it was clear to me that he had some terrible affliction like Parkinson's disease.

He looked like he had suffered a stroke too. His once strong brutal face was all lopsided n slaver ran freely down his lips onto his shirt. I still thought about slitting his throat as I spent a good half hour at the window watching him. In the end I thought better of it and left fate to suffer his days away for him.

{officer DICK chapter 108} So many thoughts had disturbed my mind when it came to thinking of a fitting end to officer Dick's life.

I knew in the court room a decade ago that I was surely going down, yet the way he had lied to help secure my fate, I could never forgive.

I'm not sure why he had seemingly gone from a decent promotion riding on the back of my conviction to sitting guarding old metal at an empty factory.

His down fall fitting, but he was about to really fall from grace.

The urge to make him have a slow pain filled death had been very appealing.

A convo Character had once had with me around the time he murdered Gerard stuck in my mind as an option.

He had been casually leaning against my cell door when he spoke about using his apache blades tip, his favourite weapon on the outside he mused. He really had wished he had had it to carve the skin off Gerard.

The gist of the story had been that if you coated the blade with shit then when the culprit got the stabbing a nasty infection would set in. When I had said about dipping my blade into the toilet pan when I eventually got released, Character had given me this dark stare and explained that you didn't want your own dnA upon it.

Don't coat the whole blade he had said. Just the tip needed dipping. Old dog shit off the fields he had chuckled as he left me wondering just what stuff he had gotten up to out there on the streets.

It had remained a strong contender for giving Dick some slow pain. But after the few months of upping the ante with the other scum bags from the village, I decided that he needed a real show piece to his death. I was about to make a massive statement just like he had done.

Difference being mine wasn't going to be with a pen. The sword I'm afraid would be more powerful in this instance.

I had sheltered from a shower in the phone box, my collars turned up as I huddled down in the booth chatting to Johnny. The fifty pence's banged in n back out.

He had been on my case a good while now about getting out of the village, leaving the eye in Stef's capable hands and taking a flight out to the light house.

India certainly appealed to me as I had more or less cleared up my list.

Up to now the police had not realised my activities. They certainly knew there was something very disturbing going on in the village. This last half of a year had seen some strange beatings n a few murders.

But like most places these things happened from time to time. Most of the victims had a list as long as your arm when it came to being hated for some reason or another.

On the TV, the local news stations had mentioned the ones that had been killed. But the reporting had been scaled down so as not to cause panic in the area.

The worst one had been the young lad shot on his door step, which the news reporter had mentioned in her piece that it was more than likely drug related.

The kid had apparently owed people in prison for stuff n maybe associates had come a calling looking for pay back. It certainly suited me how they thought.

The bodies I had stuffed under the raft had only gone onto a missing person's list. So I wasn't overly worried.

But I knew when I did Dick n Stan the heat could be on. There was a link. But one of their bodies was not going to surface.

I had hung up the phone to Johnny with the promise of coming out to stay for a few months by the end of June. I certainly had earned a vacation in the sun and I missed my best friend. So my mind was made up.

{THE SCALES chapter 109} My Columbian civil guard 45 felt nice n heavy in my hand.

I had been in the Vroom all morning cleaning the collection.

I knew I was taking out the Go samurai tonight.

On the reading table in my bedroom I had earlier read about this character in mythological history. It had seemed fitting to how I was viewing myself these days.

The mirror in the small bathroom was smashed though, as brushing my teeth the other night I had caught my reflection n seen the face of Stan n just let fly with this left straight jab causing a spider web of slivers.

The green leather bound book had revealed to me about the execution of the bully in a scene of mythological drama. According to Tertullian, walking amongst the corpses strewn in the gladiator arena is a remarkable character. His nose not of human form, more a large bird's beak, dressed in tightly fitted attire with leather shoes, pointed at the toes. In his hand he holds a large handled hammer.

He represents the ferryman Charon who transports the dead across the river Styx to the underworld. He is a figure based on the Etruscan God of death also called Charon, alongside the God Mercury in his role of accompanying human souls. With the burning point of his staff he jabs the victims flesh to make sure they are really dead. Then Charon takes possession of each body, hitting it to the head a massive blow with his hammer. After that ritual the bodies were dragged out of the arena by coliseum staff with large hooks.

It was fascinating stuff to read especially after what I had been dealing with of late.

I paid Stef up for the weekly wages I owed her. After closing that night and seeing her to the door on the street level I told her off my plans to leave for India for a few months and that I needed her to oversee the running of the place, which she more or less did now anyway.

Thank full when she told me it would be a pleasure, I gave her a fifty quid bonus n said I would be shut for the rest of the week n that she should use her own set of keys for the bar n to start from then. I had told her I had sorted the suppliers out for deliveries to continue and she had money in a float to see her right for paying her wages n the bills.

I would be in touch via letter to say that I had settled in ok and when I was likely to return.

An hour later I had the bar lights shut off mostly. A few lamps I left on for my return gave off a calm feeling before things turned nasty.

I had all I needed from within the Vroom and the doors were now shut tight again. Stef was no snoop. I was sure of that fact, but she only had keys to the bar area. My upstairs quarters were locked and only I had the key.

Even getting into the bedroom there was not much chance of finding the weapons room.

The only thing that I did out of sync as I left the eye was this time I sipped just the one single power whisky before I left. I set the empty tumbler down on the table to use later when I got back in after finishing my business on the street.

I let the sting in my gums intensify a while before I let the last drop swim scorching down my throat.

I popped on the hobnailed boots at the door. coming out of the back entrance of the eye, I booted this pile of house bricks I had stacked a while ago next to the low wall sending them flying all over the path. I was getting in the mood for grabbing the lying bastard.

I turned out onto the deserted lane n headed upwards until I was opposite the mills entrance. I stayed in the shadows a while just looking over the lanes road, watching n waiting for movements. At this hour there was nothing. All was still n calm so I crossed the road n entered into the grounds.

The security box that Dick was in was over to the right hand side set back into the darkness. I'd watched him many times over the past month. He had outside the door these green wellington boots that he would put on if it was bad weather n the grounds were rather muddy.

Over a month ago when I had just been observing him I had dropped some pieces of rough sharp glass into the tops. I had waited until I heard this yelp, laughing to myself as I headed to the raft to check on the bodies.

I had typed out on another occasion an Osman warning n when he had been doing his rounds I had snuck into the cabin n slipped it inside his lunch box. He had come out when he got back after half an hour with this half bitten sandwich in one hand n my note in the other. He scoffed the rest of the sarnie at the door nervously looking out into the darkness. He could have seen me if he had looked properly. But he was scared already.

By the time he appeared with a flash light he was jumping at shadows on the real dark corners. Before he fully got around, he would grab his hand to his heart n I could hear the daft bastard say,

"oh my god I thought there was someone there". There certainly was, yours truly. But that had been my fun n games.

As it stood tonight with me properly ready at the gate, he was bang in trouble. I wasn't going to be invisible tonight. It was so dark by his cabin that as I had stood with my face not a metre from his little metal grill window he hadn't noticed me yet. Munching on crisp packet after crisp packet he was oblivious of the danger right outside his door.

I moved away n got myself behind one of those dark corners that he nervously hated turning n waited. By my timings he would patrol in five minutes.

It reeked of piss where I was near to this hedge. He stopped here frequent to take a leak. I held steady n after a short while I heard the low whistle of a cautious man. He did the usual freak out at the turn n I waited until he was static relieving himself before I let him catch sight of my hooded presence.

He lent forward as if he was about to keel over, peering hard into the black night. A face before him he knew for certain now as I pushed my head forward and said, "GRASS"

The temple tickler came fast. A punch I had mastered against the steel door of my cell. He spat his front row of teeth out like a man spitting pips from a blood orange. Quick bursts of the knock out spray put paid to any signs of yelling for help. I had him.

I didn't want to risk been seen in the streets carrying him with the fire mans lift method, so I got a good grip of him around the shoulders as if he were drunk and walked right out of the mill n up the lane.

I played along, chatting to him as if we were two drunken pals on a night out, swaying a little myself at times to keep up the pretence. A good few miles I carried him like this until I got to my location.

Fate on my side as a week ago I had checked this place out, thinking that the climb would be impossible but a stroke of luck had seen scaffolding set against the building on one side rising right to the roof. Some guttering repairs I found as I casually asked this old workman on the street if they were putting on a new roof.

I had been lucky too on the journey tonight. Only one other person on the late night streets n he was more pissed than we were pretending to be.

I got a "good night I see" out of him to which I just started singing football songs.

Obviously not his team as he skulked off the opposite way without another peep.

I had to be careful though as I neared the court. For opposite was the pig shop and I certainly couldn't afford any of those nosey bastards to inquire how drunk we were.

I had become adept at blending in, staying close to the walls as I neared the back of the building to gather myself for a moment before heading to the side to climb.

I had sprayed Dick four times on the journey up to now, giving him a final one for the journey over my shoulder up to the crowns roof. I didn't need him waking while I was on the scaffolding n ladders.

I had given myself a five minutes breather before the climb though.

Thinking back as I leaned against the back of the courts brickwork how I had felt so trapped all those years ago. It was time to make a statement showing I was truly free.

Up on the roof I stared out over the skyline of the surrounding buildings. I didn't quite realise how high up it was until looking down.

The task getting up was relatively easy. My strength was unquestionably freakish. My training in the FABERON had not been in vain.

officer Dick had not woken. He was groggily coming around as I had let him fall to the flat roof floor once had got him over lip at the very top.

There was another level to the height of the building. A vertical front to the whole building in fancy sand stone where at the very pinnacle stood this large stone statue of the lady of justice holding this wrought iron set of scales. I would be going up to that bit in a moment but first I needed a few things to take with me.

With the hands bound solid in a good old fashioned sheep shank knot, he was going nowhere. If he had known my intentions at that point I would dare to say jumping off to a splattered death on the path below would have been preferable.

Full roll of heavy duty masking tape was wound tight around his mouth. The blood from his teeth flying out had more or less stopped running down his chin now.

I had never seen a man look more scared than when he fully regained his wits n laid looking up at me.

I told him just to nod or shake his head as I asked a few questions. I got him to nod in shame when I had asked him why he had lied. Was it because of the detective in charge McDermott.

I knew they had all lied. They knew deep down that they were sending an innocent young man to jail or worse, an asylum for many a long year.

But they didn't give a toss.

My suspicions were spot on when his head went nodding n shaking telling me I was right when I thought that Stan had something over one of the cops in the case.

Even when I stabbed dick in the leg, missing on purpose his femoral artery, which if it had been severed would have bled him to death in seconds.

He didn't know the answer to just what it had been that old Stanley had as blackmail.

When I pulled the tape away from his mouth he must have thought I was going to let him speak.

Before he even engaged his brain to order his words to leave I had sliced through the tongue with my Stanley blade n slashed it clean off.

I held it in my hand, all weird n warm n wet.

I threw it at him, hitting him on the right cheek.

He would have screamed. Oh the irony!!!!

Now I knew quite well that there was going to be a major inquiry about this particular killing. But on my side was the fact that Dick had been a long serving pig. He had at least a thousand enemies.

Yes my name would appear somewhere down the line. But by then I was hoping I would be done with Stan and away to the sun.

Even in the back of my mind if I had to face the music for all this vigilante activity, I was strangely ok with it. Whatever my destiny, I would face it like a man.

They could even put me back in the FABERON, where my name would become so lost they might as well burn my birth certificate in the fire pits of hell.

When I pulled from behind my back the Go Yoshihiro samurai, old officer Dick literally shit his pants.

I told him how disgusted I was in his weak behaviour. The stench didn't bother me.

When you have breathed in an asylums smelling decay for a decade a turd is like a red rose.

Little cuts I started with. Just the tip of the blade so sharp it drew deep blood from the slightest touch, even through his clothing.

The stab wound had caused him already considerable blood loss, yet these little nicks on his arms n chest were stingers for sure.

When I stopped and told him I was going to take him up to the statue for a closer look, he stupidly believed he was going over the side.

I had no intention of taking all of him up there.

I stripped his lower half, cutting away with the sword until I was confronted with his little shrivelled dick.

He was certainly named true.

As he stared up at the stars in the dark night sky I told him to look at me.

As he lifted his chin up to see, I went into a low crouch with the sword and from my hip sliced an arc with the blade taking his balls n dick clean off.

It was a beautiful moment.

I had to bring him around with this adrenaline shot that I had prepared earlier. I didn't want him to miss the grand finale.

Through tearful scared eyes he watched me go retrieve his tackle from over by the wall.

I scooped it all together and cat like climbed the tiled V shaped front to the building, up towards the statue.

As I flung the gruesome bloody organ into the scales I thought, yeah, justice is a load of bollox..!!!!!

The town hall clock nearby struck 3 am, booming its bells into the silent night, informing me it was time to nearly get down.

I slid down the tiles in a crouch and went to grab him, pulling him to his feet by his scraggy hair. As I dragged him limp up toward the statue so he could see where his manhood had ended up. He stared down at the scales full of his tackle n just sobbed this pathetic sound through the tape.

I guess that is where all that lying will get you in the end.

No point delaying the death strike any longer.

He had certainly suffered terribly.

Go Yoshihiro made the sword for this exact purpose as I spun showing off and cleanly removed Dicks head from his shoulders.

It tumbled towards the level where I had tortured him.

I grabbed for his body before it collapsed n pushed it in the same direction.

I got down myself and booted the head over towards the body, covering it with some sheets that had been left up there from the workmen. It would maybe delay the find for a little while.

The climb down and the walk back to the village eye just like always seemed as if I was in some kind of dream state. Stan always did say I was a sleep walker.

Back in the peace of the pub, I fell into my comfy chair and poured out a stiff measure. I toasted the silence with thoughts of me as a child. Proud that revenge was a good thing.

The time had come to face my demon.

Stan was the last name I needed to tick of my list n then I was flying away, hoping that the heat would have died down if I ever did decide to return.

I was going to enjoy trouncing his head. Probably start with a game he knew only too well.

Sucking the eye ball, only this time I was going to suck it clean out of his head n spit it straight into his horrible face.

Yeah dad I thought as I savoured another sip of the power malt. Iv' saved the true sickness just for you.

{MELLOW TORTURE chapter 110} I sat musing, looking out on the lane from up at the large window in the bar area. The storm had surprised me.

It had glued me to my comfy chair for a good hour watching its natural aggression. The last blossoms from spring had ripped away from branches. The lane carpeted with rain flattened petals.

It had been relatively empty of human form, just an old tramp looking fella huddled up in bulky clothes, treddin the path to nowhere.

I should make that end of the world is upon us sandwich board to let them see something solid declaring it. Why didn't they dream?

Real dreaming, not day dreaming!!

I had all my gear needed packed and waiting in Granddad's bag by the door. Flames were on their last legs now in the stove fire. I was going to have a last check around the place n set off for home!!!

Two items came in the post today. A sunny palm fringed beach had been the chosen postcard. That Indian stamp telling me Johnny was trying to tell me to hurry up n board a flight. I'd never been on a plane before and it scared me a little trying to figure out just how they stay up there in the sky.

All those jets I had watched from the ground of the exercise yard. It was time to spread my wings.

The other thing had been a crisp white envelope. I knew from the writing addressing it to me that it was Liberty. That slanted pen of his unmistakable.

He had mentioned previously about making a trip to see me. To catch up n see how I was getting on.

But if my memory served me correct, he had said he would be here around the last few days in the month.

I was sure I would be gone by then as I only needed a few days with old Stanley n then straight onto that flight. Liberty would understand if I missed him. I'm sure we would be able to meet up later down the line.

I propped the envelope unopened with the postcard behind the rum bottle on the back of the mirrored bar.

I would read it after I got back from seeing Father.

The old house felt strangely quiet, all the times I had heard it filled with anger.

I was on the other side of Mrs B's attic wall. I'd already removed a few bricks n had my ear fully through into Stan's domain.

I'd broken in via Mrs B's back door, nice n quiet with a jemmy bar, the place just as chaotic as I'd remembered.

It was obvious looking at the large damp patched walls n rotting floor boards why no one had bothered buying the place.

I carefully removed brick after brick quietly stacking them up in a neat pile, the hole now big enough to climb through.

It took me back as I stood in the darkness. A few cracked tiles beamed in a little bit of the fading days light.

I switched on the torch n sat down to listen. If I pricked my ear to its finest tuning I was sure I could hear splashing n singing.

I crept over towards the attic lid. The floor boards still missing in places with their zig zag pattern under my feet.

I'd switched the torch off n removed my boots near the dismantled bricked wall.

Creeping along I got my ear to the wooden hatch n listened again.

"I hear the train a comin It's rollin round the bend

And I aint seen the sunshine Since, I don't know when."

Wow, a blast from the past alright. I'd figured he was laid in his bath still privately acting like a lord with not a care in the world.

That Cash song sending a shiver right through me as I thought back to him always locking me in the boot of the car, scaring me to death with his tuneless voice.

I got ready to enter the scene.

As I lifted the lid, there was a little creak but he didn't hear it as he was belting out his hero's tune.

He had skipped a verse. I knew that Folsom prison blues song like the back of my hand.

As I peeped through the gap as I lifted the lid enough to see the landing carpet his raspy old voice sung.

"When I was just a baby My mama told me Son

Always be a good boy Don't ever play with guns

But I shot a man in Reno Just to watch him die"

He pulled the plug on the bath at this point, just repeating the last line he had sung.

"Just to watch him die, Just to watch him die, Just to watch him die."

His voice was booming now as he howled like a cats chorus thinking he could hold the note like Cash.

I spotted him, towel around the waist heading out the door n onto the landing. I let him get half way n then I thundered through the gap, landing behind him.

As he spun his towel flew off.

Not the greatest of sites in the world. But I didn't mind starting with a little humour.

As I said "Hello Dad" he just froze. His mouth opened n shut a few times trying to get a sound out, but nothing came.

"Mum was right about your pathetic gift from nature"

My words making his hands grab for the fallen towel, holding it back now against his nakedness.

I had adapted the spray bottle to fire its liquid a greater distance. The shot I sent out catching him flush in the face. As he collapsed I went to put the plug back into the bath water that was draining.

Still half a full tub was in, plenty for my intended purpose.

His body looked a little like the Boston strangler had placed him in the tub at one of his famous crime scenes. One of his legs hung out over the side, his head all bent up against the wall at a strange angle.

I cupped a handful of water n splattered his face.

Shaking his head he came too.

I was sat over on the toilet seat now staring at him with the most contemptuous look.

I'd not secured him yet.

The gun trained on him in my hand would suffice to keep him under control for now.

He stared at the end of the dark barrel for a long while, probably expecting me to pull the trigger and repay him for a childhood from hell.

I moved in on him n cuffed a hand to the large taps. "I won't be long Dad, just nipping down stairs"

He never said anything. He could have shouted for help but no one would hear him. If he did start playing up I wasn't going to bother with the masking tape, I'd slit his tongue as fast as you could say, jack flash.

I ignored looking in on my old bedroom. No need to cause myself any unnecessary flashbacks of pain n anguish.

The cold was still in those stone steps though as I flew down the stairs and went right into the kitchen. It was time to stick the kettle on.

Down in the kitchen, I again avoided looking over at the cellar door. I hadn't quite realised how emotionally charged I would feel back in this address.

I stared at the daisy badge on the old cooker as the steam started rising in the kettle. I was soon on my way back up the stairs.

His wrists had red welts on them where he had tried to free himself. He didn't try to look guilty for trying, almost a look of defiance which I soon wiped off his face. Cactus spikes nicely stuck in his eye as I smashed the full plant pot at him. It had grown since he had rubbed it in my hair all those years ago.

It settled the old bastard down again. His blinking eye more than likely blinded a little.

I'd left the kettle just outside the door on the landing.

"Fancy a brew Stanley" He wasn't stupid, he knew what was coming.

I wanted to pour it straight over his head, but I made do with following the faint red scars that Mum had caught him with from the top of the stairs. It seemed like a million years ago.

That thin old skin started bubbling away again nicely. What a stink.

I'd put the salt and vinegar in my coat pocket while down in the kitchen. I threw it smashing it against the baths panel side, it mixed nice into the water, giving an extra sting. I left him to soak n have a think about the prodigal sons return.

This was just what Stan needed, a damn good scare, get that mean old heart of his to pump that black old devils blood around his body.

I pulled Stan's Navajo blanket out from his wardrobe. It was still funny being in his bedroom, still strangely scary, even though I had him cuffed naked in the cold bath water. His skin must have been in agony.

The heavy blanket I carried back through to the bathroom throwing it over him.

Its thickness was so itchy it could only add to his discomfort as I told him to get some rest.

I was going down stairs for a smoke out of his tin. That particular piece of news would have confused him for sure. But I had decided to try his weed, see what all the fuss was about. Mellow torture him for days.

{STAN'S IN THE BAG chapter 111} *There was only one small radiator in the front room. It certainly wasn't switched on as I entered the freezing domain. Old Stan's fireplace was cold n sooty too.*

The only sign of heat came from a small flicker of light coming off this near burnt down candle.

In the hash tray next to it a docked out near full size spliff. He must have been having a toke on it before heading up to climbin his bath.

His Shaman chair was turned to closely face the switched off TV set. As I lowered myself into it, even through my thick wool coat I had belted tight around me, that coldness, like a mortuary slab was there.

So this was his all powerful throne was it I thought. The amounts of times I had curled up scared trying to hide somewhere in that room while he lorded it over me was overwhelming.

I picked up the spliff, lit it from the candle flame n took a deep long drag.

With it finished n crushed into the hashtray to stub its last flame out, I settled a little into the coldness of the chair. My focus laser like as all I could focus on was the ancient tip of the Gorton arrow up on the mantelpiece.

Daylights upon my knee creeping colours up my leg as I realised waking that I have been out of it all night long.

The draws crumbling real nice, a rumour confirmed.

The hurricane had passed. I really was safe now.

I remembered drifting off with my head in the clouds. Yet this laser like focus upon my thoughts had remained throughout.

I had woken throughout the night n smoked about four more of Stan's joints that he had pre rolled and put in his tin for himself later.

I had amused myself burning with the lighters flame the edge of this quite large lump of dark brown resin. Its stream of smoke I had held under my nose, inhaling its pure substance.

I had never been a smoker but I knew all about it from being Stan's lad. The last I recalled from last night after I had finished off all the ones he had made to smoke was that tip of the arrow. Its ancientness making me fly backward in time, questioning why the Government didn't just bring back hanging for the truly disturbed in society.

Even further back I had gone in my mind. The ducking stool needed to stay redundant.

But why were we in Britain just treating these vile offenders with kid gloves. Compulsory castration no good, it needed enforcing as a rule, not an option.

Proven cases of child abuse needed jumping on early. Fuck waiting for the murders of innocent kids. Get those bully adults early as we can see them coming a mile off, so why the leniency in courtrooms? The old chopping block is too good for these liberal nonce loving judges.

All the heavy fumes inhaled from the weed certainly bringing all this political stuff to the forefront of my mind late last night. But right now I had my own kangaroo court in session.

Through in the kitchen I got a coffee on the go n made myself some current T cakes smothered in butter n jam. I think I had what Stan use to refer to as the munchies.

Before I went up to see how he had faired through the night. I flicked though the stack of records below the stereo he had always had in the kitchen. I found a vinyl to set on the needle playing.

As I ambled steady up the stairs, munching on my breakfast, the music kicked in. Its volume I had set so Stan would hear it up in the bathroom. Jimmy Cliff's beautiful clear voice accompanied me along the landing.

Many rivers to cross filled the house.

Stan was staring straight at the door as I entered, his shivering like a junkie on the third day of its cluck quite apparent in his shrivelling limbs.

"You like this song Dad"

It wasn't really a question, more a playful joke to myself for I knew when this was over he would be under the road.

I had the claw hammer stuck in my belt, behind my back.

I drew it out real slow n walked towards him with it outstretched above my head, like a zombie homing in on its prey.

I just paused with it hovering menacingly above my head.

He was watching me intently now, waiting to see what part I would choose to smash.

I froze for about a minute, enjoying the build up it was causing him. I could see the fear written all over his face.

I turned and walked out without doing a thing.

Back in the kitchen I scratched the needle on the record player along until I found a lyric I wanted, I then raced back up to the bathroom door.

'The harder they come The harder they fall

Is all I know Yes it is.'

I then ran at him n smashed the claw part of the hammer right into his shin. The volume of the record drowned out most of the yelling that came from him as he looked at the white bone revealed in his leg.

A nice thick pool of blood had spurted up against the white tiles of the bath side, giving a nice horror feel to the scene. The cold bath water tinged now as if he had taken a nip from a great white.

"Enjoying your soak Dad"

My laughing all he heard as I headed out n down the landing to my old room. There was something I needed to fetch to the party.

In the tin on top of my old wardrobe, the darts were a little more rusted since I last felt them in my leg.

Stan's body azoic looking as I leaned against the bathroom door frame viewing him for a moment.

I'm a better aim, the first dart catching him in the cheek. Its weight making it hang limp against his face where it had stuck in nice n deep.

It more or less woke him.

The second one I threw certainly did. It pierced straight through his left bollock.

Now I had his full attention again. I poured some glue out of this old glass marmalade jar that had been on the shelf next to the darts.

His shin had steadily lost blood all night n I wanted to slow the flow down to just a trickle now.

It was time to get him out of the bath n a little more comfortable.

I slipped on my brass pair of cestus n gave him a combination crack so hard he went unconscious before he felt me unlock him n drag him onto the bath room floor.

I figured it would be easier getting him where I wanted him next while he was totally out cold.

I had already stripped the beds duvet in his room.

Years back it wouldn't have held his weight but he was a shadow of his former self n the sheets would hold just fine.

I got him bent into the right shape to squash him inside the duvet n tied the end together with some rope I had brought along.

I gripped the end and climbed up the ladder that I had fetched from his bedroom, banging Stan's head off each rung as I rose myself to the top n went through the attic lid.

I had left the claw hammer in my belt and a bag of nine inch nails I had placed by the lid before entering the scene.

I held the sack of shit with one arm, quite a strain but manageable.

I then nailed him to the heavy wood surround of the attics entrance. Ten nails in n I let the weight fall from my grip. It held just fine. Stan now in his little cotton ball prison, swaying gently at the end of the rope.

By the time I climbed down the bag had stopped swaying, the effort and the weed from last night now beginning to make me feel like having forty winks. As I had climbed down the gap squeezing past him, I caught him a beauty with the elbow to the ribs. Well I thought it was his ribs until I saw the red blood dot grow into a hanky size circle.

That hulk weed he had spread into those four pre rolled joints sure fucked up a man's judgment.

His nose breaking had been the crack I heard.

I didn't wake until dinner time. A little groggy upon coming around I felt, but a fresh spliff should see me right to continue.

I wondered into my old bedroom to look out the window. The gnarled old fruit on the trees was rotting I noticed. Although I couldn't stare out long as the slashes of sunlight squinted my eyes shut as they hurt from its glare. It got me back walking the dark landing again.

I needed a piss. Coming out the bathroom the chain flushing had started to stir him in his bag a little. I eased him back into his slumber with combination punches to what I believed his ears n throat, it startled him awake to shout out to me to stop. The leap which came next with my knee connecting sweetly with his head put him back out good n proper.

I moved off back down the landing and re entered the room where I had elected to sleep, the door latch clicking quietly back shut into its mechanism.

The paraphernalia from Stan's smoking tin magnetizing to try roll up one of my own.

The first attempt looked like the ones I had seen him roll after a full day at it. It wasn't ascetically pleasing but it would do the job for now.

I rooted out a few different clippers from this shoe box he kept with all his papers in n lighters. He kept his weed bag n lump of resin only in the tin.

I sparked it up n went a lookin for him like he use to come a searchin for me as a child.

I had smoked a good half of it before I flicked the red clipper into life again n burnt a small hole in the fibres of the sheet. I let the flame die before the diameter in the bag got no bigger than an old half penny piece.

The weed had chilled me out a lot over the last day or so, but not to any extent where I didn't still want to murder him. I knew his paranoia was ripe. Old age had done him no favours in the brain department.

Years of neglect, where he just never figured out the cool things about weed, it had always been a way to dampen his shine, just another release like the whisky to get him to the darkness as quickly as possible, a craving, not a pleasure. Every toke I inhaled on the last half of the spliff I blew the smoke inside the burnt hole I had created.

"Let's get proper stoned hey Dad"

No reply. Just a slight sway came from the bags own natural movement. My very own experiment to do what I wanted with, and right now it was time to really bond.

Blow backs now whistling through the air into the bags small hole. I had seen him give Mum them nuff times as a kid. She would be sat away from him while he lounged in that shaman chair of his. Hunched up toking away in silence he would suddenly jump up n take the joint the other way lit into his mouth.

He would blow a thick line of hatred right into her face as she moved her head from side to side trying to escape the dense clouds. It was a familiar scene from our home life back then. It started me drifting off again into memories of childhood.

I was always sent to bed early, a dead certainty for me. I would then shuffle to the top of the cold stone stairs, freezing my arse off, listening to the shouting. Always accusations against Mum n me and it never mattered that it was usually him in the wrong. We would be copping the brunt of it for sure. Listening most nights to Mum telling him to calm down n that it was all in his head and to stop smoking such potent strains like the hulk.

All these memories made my sickening assault upon him seem therapeutic. I whispered through into the bag.

"You awake Da"

I heard him groaning n seemingly in quite a bad way.

I went to my canvas bag I had propped in the bathroom sink n retrieved a needle. A shot of this n he would be back in reality for some more fun.

When I was satisfied he was back in the room with me, I asked him if he remembered this game.

He fell deadly silent wondering what I had remembered and just what I was going to do with him.

I pushed the rizla packet through the hole and asked him if he could see what I was holding. It took him a good minute to focus his one good eye n say he did.

"Do you know what Lapidation means Dad"?

I was just mocking him n his stupid ways of old. He really thought he was schooling me in the right fashion asking me all those tricky questions from the back of his empty rizla packets.

He certainly didn't get my question right. He never even had a stab at an uneducated guess.

With my mouth up close to the bag, barely a whisper from me he got the answer. "Stoned to death"

It hissed out of my mouth with such venom he started to make these pathetic sounds. Daring him to make one more pathetic whimper he shut up n got a hold of himself.

With the last drag of the joint I held it to the fibres near the small hole I had already made. Semi circle motion with my hand I enlarged the gap n let Dad have a better view out onto the landing.

I sprayed a small tin of lighter fluid through, making sure I caught him in his eye where all the cactus needles had done there damage.

I certainly didn't want him totally blinded in both eyes. I wanted the bastard to see what was coming. I struck a match. I had the lighters but this was more dramatic.

I held it between my finger and thumb until its wood became nearly totally charred black.

He expected at any moment for me to toss it through n set him alight.

I let it burn down n fade. Then I walked away down the landing. I could feel his eyes on my back.

As I turned the corner out of sight he must have breathed a small temporary sigh of relief. I waited 3 seconds n appeared again then walked back towards the bag with this hatchet in my hand.

The bag started moving, as though he thought he might be able to escape my approach. I gripped the bag with both my arms wide n outstretched and then like a Carney kid at the back of a waltzer chair I spun the bag around so I had the lump that was his hairy old back facing me.

I sunk that hatchet into the right shoulder blade the best I could place it. He howled like a wounded animal caught in a trappers set.

I swung the bag back round to face me, peeping through, enjoying what I saw. A screwed up face of pain n anguish stared back.

I had a little stoned rant while I had his attention. I told him all about the word Assassin.

For 200 years a murderous sect of religious fanatics terrorised the Middle East. They killed under the influence of pot. Notorious through their Arabic name, Hashshishin, they were wiped out in the 13th Century by the Mongols. The Anglicised version of the name lives on.

"You won't learn that off the back of a rizla packet Dad"

I had learned it from the one and only Scot John.

I left him swaying about in the bag to ponder that bit of new info, but before I stepped off down the landing, I spun the bag again n gave the handle of the hatchet a good grip n pressured my fist forward into it.

He was still howling at the shock of the pain as I reached the top of the stairs n crossed the little thresh hold n went back into the spare front bedroom.

The lump of resin must have been a good ounce in size n weight.

I'd decided to mix things up a bit n try something I had seen old Poidge Stone make.

It had been on one of many all day sessions when I had watched him make what he called a DALIK.

I had brought to the room from my last trip to the bathroom the nearly used toilet roll.

I now pulled the last few remaining sheets off it.

I dabbed away a little of the blood from my knuckles where the cestus had caught my skin.

I reckoned about 15 decent size spliffs should do the trick.

By spliff three I was rolling like an old master.

There was more resin burned from off the lump into every one than there was tobacco going in.

I'd poked through the tube with the tip of a screw driver randomly. Inserting the white cones, like arms coming out from the tubes body, the Dalik started to take on its form.

When I had them all inserted, I removed each one again n lit them all one by one taking a quick drag to get them burning nice n bright. I then placed them back in their slots.

The evening light from outside the window was still enough to see without turning on any lights or lamps. Yet dim enough to show the desired effect. The room glowing with these 15 tips alight.

Mouth open to the max, I took a huge gulp of resin filled air which swirled fast down my throat burning n sending my head into space. The full toke from the entire thing would blow any mans mind.

I came around laid on my back staring up at the ceiling. I was so chilled I could have just lain there all night long. But I had work to do.

I switched on the lamp in the corner. My attention on two things straight away, one being the short arms of the Dalik as I had sucked it down in size. It had taken a good hour to get through it. Secondly some of old Granddads magazines from his war days were scattered around by my feet.

I had totally forgotten about reading them for a moment. Forgotten even that had brought them in my bag with me.

The latch clicked as I opened the door and the landing sounded deserted. No noise at all penetrated my ears.

I certainly didn't want him dead just yet.

My memory was coming in random waves to me.

I had considered after smoking the majority of the Dalik to try out some techniques that I had read upon. I had found some old manuals of Granddads which referred to the K G B methods of torture. A small drilling to the back of Stan's head and then over a period of time, small pieces removed off the brain. Complete loss of control, his eyes or what remained of them would cease to function then speech would deteriorate and so on and so on.

Maybe I did not possess the patience to apply such techniques.

The urge to just pull it all out in one swift move, laughing to myself now, thinking it would not be much as Stan had to have the thickest grey matter on the planet.

I returned from the kitchen, scent spray in hand. Three quick squirts into the burnt fibre hole, Stan out for the count, I made sure it caught him in the eyes all the same.

This spray was for my own purpose, as he had been in the cotton ball prison now for a fair block of time.

Aromas had never been his strong point, the brown, yellow, red stains mixing his worst whiff. Fresh air circulating now as I rose up the ladders to do a little repair job as I felt the nails were coming a little loose with all the blows he had received.

Night fall was here. My vantage point if I decided to move him now.

The claw hammer made the descent with me, a nice quick crack around his shins. Wanting him awake now I'd decided on my next move. In front of the bag I asked him if he was ready.

I loved the mind games, the doubt and suspension of it all, the great unknown. There was no point delaying his death much longer. For some time now the swaying bag had ceased any significant movement.

Splatters of his blood still soaked through the wooden floor boards. The stains downstairs on the kitchen ceiling directly below where I had him captured, encompassed the look of a rising sun as the flow had become real heavy from that latest hatchet blow.

Stan had tried to make some feeble attempt at begging for mercy the last time my elbow had connected with his skull. Complaints again going unanswered, riddles would have to suffice for him.

Probably all the communication problems I had occurred as a kid stemming from his gibberish. He was certainly trying to rant now the cheeky fuqua.

The stew I had emptied from a tin into a pan was bubbling away nicely down stairs. The rest of the lump of resin I had crushed up n stirred in when I had gone for the spray.

I had enjoyed the smoke, even more so now the effects were beginning to wear off a little. A peace closing in on me with a feeling of euphoria as I understood it was nearly all over.

More mellow torture coming Stan's way.

Roll UP roll UP. Who the hell was I talking to?

A private screening of something the censors would never allow, sat in the front row, my seat reserved for years.

As I stood at the top of the ladder ready to cut him down from the hanging bag, I noticed for the first time some old names scratched into the beams above. It showed the first occupier of the house to have carved their mark in 1827.

Stan's not so fluent chisel mark dented into the wood, showed the 80s nightmare that I had somehow survived.

I slashed the rope holding him n listened to his form crumble heavy into the landing floorboards. It bothered me not a jot that he hadn't been awake for the drop.

He was so in n out of consciousness now that I had to keep checking to see he didn't cheat me out of his last breath, for I had to savour that moment fully aware of its passing. His black out this time had gone on way too long. Medically he was way past treatment.

I jumped down from about the fifth rung, landing nicely on his knee, that horrific cracking sound music to my ears.

I wished I could have introduced Stan to some of my friends from the institution. Now that would have been fun. Scot John here with me muzzled, peckish for a bite into Dads leg.

We would have drawn vampires on the bathroom wall in his blood.

Winnie digging him back up the very night he had been laid to rest, not giving him any peace in the quietness of the grave.

God only knows what Character would have done to him.

I had been more than certain that after I had smoked the Dalik I had seen a slight green mist floating up by the top of the window which I had left slightly open.

I had thought nothing of it, quite forgetting about it until I had thought a little more of my strange companions that had lived side by side with for a decade. I fingered out of habit the half ripped coin that I carried for luck.

I ripped him out from the confines of the bag, grabbing his hair tight in my grip.

Dragging him along the landing until I reached the top of the stairs, the door to my bedroom where that old war blanket had been not getting a thought now. I yanked him to his feet. He was too weak to even attempt to fight back now.

The shove into his back sent him sailing through the air. He didn't land on any of the stone steps, except the very bottom one. It must have broken some bones for sure.

I sauntered down and stepped over him, like Mum had done when going to the slaughter bungalow. Again I had to push hard away the thoughts that she hated me so much, replacing them with conviction that she had had no choice in the matter when it came to the reflection of her love towards me.

I took the pan of bubbling stew off away from the heat of the stove. It was well hot, not that burning Stan's mouth would matter right now.

I went to fetch him.

Booting him in the ribs so hard that he spun n made some progress on the floor to the spot where I wanted him in the kitchen. A few more boots n he was out from the space at the bottom of the stairs n over by the stereo.

I stepped towards the front room. The heavy drapes were still pulled tight, its tomb like presence very fitting to my feelings of hate right now.

I picked up the shaman chair and carried it through to the kitchen.

Once I had him picked up n sat into it, I went back into the front room to get Mums Wedding ring. The bastard had only gone and had it hung through the shaft of the Gorton arrow.

I snapped it clean in half n pulled the ring back off, placing it now onto my little finger.

I shallow stabbed him to the knee cap with the arrows tip as I re entered the kitchen. He gave a yelp but I soon stopped it with a punch into his mouth.

I spoon fed him the boiling weed laced stew. I had intended making it last a little longer this torture, but I'd just not been able to hold back.

The point of stoning him now quite pointless, but I carried on shoving it down his throat until he was spewing n coughing it all back up violently.

"Good boy Dad"

I scratched away a lash that needed catchin in my eye. As I did, Mums ring again glinted n caught my attention.

I was quite certain that the eye of Stan's I had caught when launching the cactus pot at him was more or less blind.

I made certain it was now as I slowly extended my little finger until it was deep in his orb socket. The words obey on her band disappearing now as the pupil finally gave in and sunk.

It gave off such a stink I gave him a spray around the face with some polish from under the sink.

He hadn't said much while it happened which surprised me. Maybe the painkiller effect from the weed had kicked in fast.

It surprised me when he started babbling away about his childhood. I had to listen real careful to pick up the gist of what he was saying.

It sounded like bragging to me.

"I killed her"

The low groans of agony that were running through his body were making it difficult to catch his words structure.

But he had defiantly repeated a few times in a row the same sentence until I knew he meant what he wanted me to hear.

The laughing came from deep down in his chest. Small blobs of blood had started to be spat out now.

He was certainly on his last legs.

"You killed her" came next, n then more laughter, which I stopped with a hard slap to his face.

"You are just the same as fuckin me"

He really spat that out with some spite. Snot and slaver running freely down his face. Tears would have been there too if he had had possessed a heart.

"I killed my own Mother & so did you"

I'd had enough of his ramblings. It was possible that he had murdered his own Mother years back. But he wasn't going to put into my head any longer that I had played a part in my own dear Mums tragic murder.

"Let's get the washing up done eh Dad"

It was one of the things that had hurt me most as a kid along with what he had done with those jugs n cotton threaded needles. I had most certainly entertained the idea of cutting off his tackle.

I pulled him out of the chair over towards the kitchens large butler sink. He looked me in the face and told me he had poisoned his own Mother.

The clear water was in the sink to show him what I had in store for him. I didn't need to hide the danger in murky water like he had done all those years ago.

It was his hands I had thought to shove into the sharp broken glass that waited menacingly at the bottom. Yet after his latest outburst about poison I just shoved his head down into it all.

The water clouding up with blood red swirls.

I held him a while, dragging him about making sure the whole of his face caught on shards of broken spikes.

When I pulled him back out n let him drop backwards onto the tiled floor, I knew I was on the verge of snuffing him out permanent.

I set a light to the shaman chair n once satisfied it was burning well I threw it tumbling down the cellar stairs.

It painfully flashed back in my mind Mums body going the same route to her death. The worn upturned seat lay exactly where her broken bones had all those years ago.

It was time to end this nightmare.

I pulled him along the floor over to the cellar doorway, yanking him to his feet facing the top of the stairs. I jabbed him to the neck with the last of my rejuvenating laden needles.

The full dose brought him around just enough to see his own end coming. I grabbed the back of his hair tight n forced him to look down at the flames licking n curling around the chair arms.

I whispered in his ear.

"In the moment between the breathing in and breathing out is hidden all the mysteries"

I then sliced the Ghurkha knife hard into the front of his throat.

Stan's last breath I savoured with the intensity of the moment. A pop of air gulped inwards then turned back knowing its usefulness had expired. Just the whistle of ghosts now as I let him fall.

{THE BITTER END chapter 112} My intention for a good while had been to scrape him up from his killed position, throw his arse into the boot of his car n drive him through the mill gates n wedge him with the rest of the scum under the raft. But after looking down on his fallen beaten body at the bottom of those stairs for a long while, I knew it was fitting to leave him right there, right where he had left my Mother.

He didn't even deserve a grave. Not even a watery one.

As I had stared down at his broken distinguished life form, this passage from the Bible that I had heard Scot John frequently say out loud as he had rushed around the circular perimeter of the asylums yard, came to mind.

I was done now for good with this vigilante business. If I didn't stop now I could just end up going on forever.

The verse I recalled I spoke out loud down at Stan's corpse.

"Father, forgive them, for they know not what they do.

And I heard his voice inside me, and he took the sword from my hand.

Again my plans seem to change as I neared the end. I had intended to burn the house to the ground. Destroy all the evil that had lurked in its four corners. My prerogative as a free man to do as I damn well pleased, making me ditch that idea and just tidy up a little around the areas where I had been mellow torturing the horrible beast these last few days.

I left his body n the small chair fire burning. It would extinguish itself out before long. I shut the cellar door n moved on upstairs.

I threw the bag n rope into the wicker wash basket in the corner of Stan's bedroom. I felt a little disorientated.

The blood splatters I just left on the floor n walls like some strange tribal art.

I was going to walk out the back door n post the key after locking up but again I changed my mind as I was wondering around.

Back in the attic, I leant forward into the hatch n pulled up the ladders, throwing them once through the gap onto a few of the zig zag floor boards.

I jammed the hatch lid back into place as firmly as I could n went on through the hole back into Mrs B's.

I placed from the neat pile I had left, the bricks back into the empty space. Not a great job but something that if looked at from the door way wouldn't be obvious.

I then slowly worked my way back down her rotting stairs n crouched out again through the panel I had loosened in the back door.

I gave it a shove back into place n piled some old chimney pots that had weeds coming out of the top against it n crept away down the path on to Clogger Street.

It didn't take me long to slink along the lane hiding in the shadows n hedges, getting back to the village eye's safety in no time. I went around the back, passed the old graves n entered my abode.

It was a great feeling as I slumped exhausted into my comfy chair. I had finally beaten the bastard at his own game, yet I felt I certainly held the moral high ground if you compared murder and its finer details of madness.

The cap seemed to screw itself from the bottle of power whisky. Half a glass full had me pause to admire in the lamp light its liquid warm colours before taking another serious slug.

That one drained, I poured a refill a little more near the rim this time and settled back into my chair. I had heard on arriving back the church bell tolling 8pm.

Probably a good hour I just sat still sipping on the glass contents, feeling all smug for a change.

I eventually lit the free standing stove, a few nice logs soon catching a warm glow, heat now not just from the spirits returning into my body. I hadn't realised just how zoned out I had become over at Stan's house.

The last day had become very cold with the atmosphere of impending death creating a freezing presence to my bones n mind.

On my third glass of power I went up behind the bar n stared at my face in the large ornate mirror. I suppose I did have the look of Stan. But I looked more like old Granddad Pedley in that fine photo he had always shown me as a boy. That fairground booth where I inherited my solid fists was no place for the weak.

As I stared hard at my reflection, giving in finally to a small crooked smile, I realised it had only taken what seemed like a life time of hardship to reveal it.

I grabbed some writing paper & a pen from under the bar and went back to my seat.

I think the drinking was already affecting me as I decided to draft a letter. I realised as I began that the pen I had picked up had been the one Liberty had sent me ages ago as a gift.

The blue ink started to run out of the expensive nib. I had in my mind a confession. Scot John's tattooed knuckles my starting point. I had lived near the rippers descendent in the FABERON.

So I played up to that.

Dear Boss

I hear you are having trouble finding out my true intentions.

Here's a clue. Watery graves far away from the streets you search.

A swift revenge that your corrupt system sweeps under its filthy littered rug is what I am here to correct.

I've been keeping a vigil, upping the ante.

You have members on the list.

Disgust runs from upon high in your ivory tower of so called justice.

Adding pips to your epaulets with lies, while I add notches to my favourite killing knifes handle.

There's a surprise in store.

But you won't find me for I live in the shadows.

Watch your backs.

See you very soon. Jack x

I read it back to myself aloud, laughing as I poured out the last bottom drops from the now empty whiskey bottle. It took me about ten minutes staring at its ink, before I got up a little unsteady on my feet and went over to the stove fire to burn it. Within five seconds it had vanished.

The pigs were just going to have to figure it all out without any clues from old jack.

Over on the wall, just off from the fire was a square pillar. I had hung my map of the world on it in a nice silver frame when I had first moved into the eye. Its circular globe seemed accessible now, unlike when I had dreamed about it in the asylum as just some flat fantasy.

The beauty of failure is you can always turn it around if you dig deep n grit those teeth with steely determination. I had proven my point with the system. I had survived.

I came too in the chair, jolted awake from a drunken sweet slumber with a horrid nightmare running rampant throughout my lucid mind. Those torches were back, that olden day scene of a vigilante mob outside the building, screaming for my blood. Pitchforks n shovels raised angrily above crazy dark faces wanting to crush my head in with their tools.

Some had my hooks from under the raft in their hand like claws. Faces I had killed in the background, pushing forward through the *disturbance to just stare up at the village eye window where my chair faced out.*

I had woken as the doors and windows were getting smashed, thunderous footsteps on their way up the stairs to murder me for my crimes.

Jesus, the sweat on my back held me stuck to the chair back for a moment before I peeled away n went looking for another bottle behind the bar.

I selected the old navy rum this time. A few toasts to good old Granddad Pedley were in order before I slept it all off n disappeared in the morning to board my flight.

Maybe half way down the bottle my head seemed to gather a headache tight on the skull for sure. It was time to call it a night. I was in a bit of a state.

The bar area lights behind the mirror I had flipped off on the switch. The lamp's plug I had pulled out from the wall socket.

Only the dying embers in the stove held any colours except the black of night now. I was just about to fold in the wood shutters on the large window, when I noticed a movement that didn't fit the quietness of the lane at this late hour.

A disturbance going on for sure as I stood as close to the glass as I could to try get a better view.

The sketch was one I know recognised as a familiar scene.

Some guy who I couldn't quite make out identity wise was busy shoving this petite female about.

I had already decided to go down to the street n get him off her.

When he dragged her down into the dirt of the roadside curb I didn't bother wasting time by going for a weapon from the V room. I still had a few things in my pockets from arriving back from Stan's. I could always tear him apart with my bare hands if need be.

Down on the lamp lit street, a quiet now met my view.

I could still see the two figures, except one was far up the lane now where I had seen the bullying taking place.

I walked quickly in that direction and as I neared within twenty feet, the woman who I could now make out to be this slim blonde, turned when she heard my footsteps, gathering up her skirt in both hands. She gave out a small scream before fleeing off at speed into the night.

Perhaps in the mind she feared the return of the abuser, mistaking my presence for his.

Satisfied that she was heading away from danger I turned and went after the man.

He had cheekily been lighting a cigar as I swiftly passed the village eye n caught up to him a little further down the lane. He wasn't too far from the beginning of the old mills grounds.

I already had the garrotte out from my jeans pocket.

Before he got his Cuban lit properly I had snuffed him out. A large thud as he hit the pavement. The lights down this end of the lane spaced out very thinly, his features right now I couldn't make out.

After carrying him on my shoulder at a joggers pace to the metal railings, I threw him over quickly and wondered just how I had ended up dealing with this type of shit when I was half an hour ago getting ready for some serious sleep before my big day of travel.

They say practice makes perfect and it's true. It didn't take me long to have the hooks prepared n the boulders wrapped around a leg. I hadn't planned on getting wet but I knew I could finish up here quick n get my arse home to dry n get that sleep I so badly needed. My head was pounding.

Five minutes submerged and I was satisfied I had him lined up secure with the rest of the bunch.

The only sign I had been on the streets would have been a set of wet footprints leading away from the rafts tow path edge. But I had ditched my wet boots at the sheer curtain of water, making my way back to the eye bare foot.

I drank a swift glug straight out of the brandy bottle when I got back n was soon tucked up in the warm blankets of my bed.

I woke up confused to a light I certainly didn't need. Its unforgiving pain as I blinked towards the bedroom window severe.

I had well n truly plastered myself last night. Certainly more lucid dreams had accompanied me in the dark hours. I think even a certain scene from the days of the oceans emptying had crept in washing over me. My blankets certainly told the tale of a night of extreme tossing n turning.

That whiskey & brandy mix had certainly delivered the bastard behind the eyes of a hangover.

Over ten minutes with my feet ready to climb out of the bed, I finally made it onto the bedroom floor. Steady walk to the bathroom, a little cool splash of tap water into my cupped hands hit the spot as it washed over my face.

Two minutes repeating this n I was ready to walk the small stairs back down to the bar area.

I was getting this awful feeling. A flash back suddenly of last night's disturbance. Upon waking it had totally slipped my mind, the fog in my brain not useful right then to think of anything much.

I got some beer towels from off the bar and soaked them in the ice bucket. Wrapping them around my head gave some relief. The headache was fully back n banging my brain like a prize fighter slugs his opponent's chin.

I stared over at the two empty bottles on the table. Surprised, as I knew I had finished the power one. But I didn't realise I had smashed the brandy as well.

Twenty minutes or so later, I hadn't moved from the chair.

I had to get myself together as I had a flight to catch.

The nagging doubt of last night's unwanted drama after I had got home unsettling for sure n it just kept on at me. I had a great instinct and something was bothering me but I just couldn't put my finger on it.

I went to re soak the beer towels. They were certainly helping to ease the pain of the head ache.

As I threw them in the bucket I picked up the letter that had come the other day with Johnny's postcard.

I had intended to open it late last night as I relaxed after ridding the world of Stan, but that couple on the lane had interrupted me.

I tore open the envelope n scanned quickly down the writing.

I read it again.

My mind not working right with the haze of booze I'd consumed. I took the gist of it to mean he may arrive early. I guess when I had told him about my plans to visit India he had taken action to catch me before I left.

I tucked the blue paper back into the white envelope and returned it behind the bottle on the bar.

I guess he had become delayed. Maybe a case had come up.

With the beer towels firmly wrapped around my skull again I got as busy as my fragile body would allow. There wasn't much to do. I had sorted everything days ago.

But I wanted one last trip to the raft. My curiosity of last night's coward had me intrigued.

I waited until the workers had made their way off to their jobs, leaving the lane relatively empty. My thoughts as I strolled along the quiet lane had me still not quite believing that Stan was no more. He had held such a strong influence upon my life that it still seemed plausible for him to just appear out of nowhere and get me.

Childhood mental scars so deep that I wasn't sure if they would ever end the torment of fear he could instil in me if I thought about him. I knew he was dead alright, yet he haunted my mind with a thought of if I went back to the house to check his body it would be gone. That he had somehow come back from the dead to finish me off this time, like he had always intended.

I shook off the doubt. I knew I had sliced very deep into his neck. My only regret was that I couldn't kill him over n over again in different scenarios.

As I closed in on the mill stone wall that held the gated entrance my mind switched again back to the curious case of last night.

It had been quite a blur as to just what I had done. I wasn't even too sure what injuries I had inflicted upon the woman beater or just how I had killed him. The garrotte I'm sure was his demise as I turned left and entered the factory grounds.

I had trodden this wild path now since a very young lad.

I wasn't too sure if really all these bodies secured floating underneath my raft had become something of a symbol to me, just temporary representatives to appease my pains before I beat my psychological demons enough to go after the real threatening force that had always been my Father.

I read at the entrance the graffiti both me and Johnny had done over different periods of our lives. I was looking forward very much to seeing my best friend again. The more I had thought about India, the less nervous of the long flight I had become. I was ready to flee this village and I didn't even care if I never came back.

Slipping through the sheer curtain of water, I lost some of the daylight and looked on down the darkened tunnel.

The first thing I noticed at the beginning of the tow path before it broke away was this shoe. It was laying on its side right next to my boots that I had left behind.

A smart black looking thing, yet when I picked it up I noticed all the laces were congealed with dark blood.

I had certainly been sloppy last night in my dealings with the bully. Usually I would not leave the eye without some plan on my target, but this had come out of the blue and I had dealt with it the best I could to say I had been three sheets to the wind.

I went through the palava to get across the gap I had smashed away years ago. On the other side of the tow path I sat myself hunched on one of the boulders, readying myself to dive down n see what victim was now down there with my other bunch.

I sat staring along the tunnel down towards the waterfall falling with its back drop of daylight shining through it.

I snapped out of it when a thought hit me as to how much time I had already had wasted from my life just sat staring at nothing in particular, like those four walls of my cell, ever current, lurking in my mind.

I snapped out of my day dream n stripped down to my shorts, folding neatly my clothing onto another boulder, which I had decided to launch in and sink when I was heading away. No need to leave them there wrapped in the heavy fishing net. Hooks nailed deep into their stone core with rope and hooks trailing around the path. They could definitely sink without trace.

I dived in but instead of heading downwards I shallow dived and no sooner had I hit the water I surfaced by the side of the raft. Climbing aboard I steadied the planks slight movement before gathering n throwing to the towpath my few bits of personal belongings.

I wrapped all the books inside the old army coat n peeled up Granddads faded old photo n slipped that inside a dust jacket of Oscar Wilde's classic, picture of Dorian Grey. I then threw under arm and landed them safely by the boulder where my clothes were folded up.

Sat on the raft, I swayed on slight currents, smiling gently to myself. Those rapscallion bones below me that maybe in time one day would be studied with shocking revelations to their demise.

The heavy boulders I had used though as a kedge well secure to keep the bodies out of sight forever maybe. But I did slightly worry about development concerning the mill and maybe one day all this would be uncovered.

I had tuned into the radio n local news channels concerning officer Dick. The workers on the roof obviously for now not back to work up on that level just yet.

I would be far away by the time that piece of shit was found.

I laughed out loud again wondering if they would mention on the news about me leaving his wedding tackle in the scales. I doubted it. I mean who would dare say such a thing!!

The next time I dived into water after this descent would be to splash about in the green seas of India.

I didn't bother gathering my breath. I was not going to be down there too long. Just a quick curious check was all. I stepped off the rafts end plank feet first and plunged straight down with my arms tucked into my sides. My eyes firmly shut until the silt from the streams bed had cleared away I now looked through the shallow dug avenue.

Without eyes something very familiar stared back.

Down here enough light penetrated to know I was not mistaken. The stream so clear now that there could be no mistake as I stared at Liberty, furnished with all the fittings of death.

It couldn't have been Liberty pulling the woman about on the path. Panic hit me. The scene could just not be real down here.

Had he also been on the lane last night? I focused in on the steel grey hair cut now waving around in the waters slight current. Then I noticed everything.

The fat cigar stuck in his dark suits jacket pocket, right next to the silk hanky with the L K initials.

I swam a little closer to him, feeling like I was about to throw up.

One of the sharp hooks had penetrated through his large hands palm, the very same palm that he had enclosed around my teenage mitts over a decade ago.

I was wiling my eyes to be lying to me. For this to be some disturbed dream I had yet to wake from.

But this was no fuckin dream. It was a real wide awake nightmare and I could not believe I was one of the main protagonists in it.

His hand that was skewered to the hook was floating up by his face. The rope tight n leading up to a well screwed in hook under the rafts planks.

It was all wrinkled with the overnight submersion.

What had I done to his eyes?

Where were they?

As I held him close to me hoping for a miracle that would breath life back into him, a few of his distinct business cards that he must have had in a pocket came loose n floated past me to the surface.

I followed their direction and hit the surface with an almighty breath of air releasing a powerful cry.

Just what the Hell had I done last night?

I held the side of the raft shaking and crying.

One of the business cards floated near me just off to the left.

I grabbed it n flipped it to the side where he had his slogans.

Through the tears I read,

'Money really is spreading disease

Please always wash your hands

After a grubby deal'

I didn't want to hear the ticking of the clock no more.

Back stroke manoeuvre, I made my way to the tow paths edge.

Climbing out and securing both my ankles with the two boulders that I had left, in a matter of less than two minutes I was on the edge and saying my final goodbye to the piece of shit that was me.

I had also with me a set of handcuffs. With one hand secured I placed the other into the clasp n locked it up.

I swallowed the key, even though I knew how to free myself.

The point was now I didn't want to. With a hefty lift I scooped both boulders into the cradle of my arms.

I shuffled forward until both my big toes were right on the edge of the path.

I took a deep breath n closed my eyes.

Blowing all the air out of my lungs before inching towards the plunge, I was soon at the bottom.

Through the silt I nodded a final farewell over at my friend Liberty as fizzing large bubbles burst out in front of me with my final scream.

Those ocean dreams all real now as I faded away into the watery blackness. The rush backwards a familiar feeling as my body seemingly propelled upwards to what I believed was the light of heaven.

Coming around spluttering on the towpath I really did start to believe that it had all been some strange dream. Yet when I finally stopped coughing up what seemed like half the contents of the stream, I noticed my hands still cuffed. My ankles still wrapped all up in the rope yet the boulders were gone and the end rope was all frayed where it had been sliced free.

It came as a distant laugh at first, but as I turned my head to look around, I found the source.

Character was sat on the edge, his legs dangling in over the side. He stopped chuckling for a moment and spoke.

"We all make mistakes in this cruel world we inhabit.

I've been watching you ever since that day you walked onto the Netherfield ward.

And I have continued to watch you at work out here.

Impressed enough I have been that I've decided to show you the bigger picture when it comes to vigilante business.

I'm very sorry about your friend

But you I'm afraid are nowhere ready for retirement.

Your only just getting started Young Otiss"

He stared at me with that serious pike eye of his

"Follow me"

And with that he turned his back to me and I marvelled as these giant black wings seemed to effortlessly grow out from both his shoulder blades.

It was time for my flight.

THIS IS THE END

BEAUTIFUL FRIEND

THIS IS THE END

MY ONLY FRIEND THE END

OF OUR ELABORATE PLANS
THE END

OF EVERYTHING THAT STANDS
THE END

NO SAFETY OR SUPRISE, THE
END

I'LL NEVER LOOK INTO YOUR
EYES...AGAIN

BOOKS ALSO AVAILABLE BY DALE
BRENDAN HYDE

THE WHISKEY POOL

THE GODS R WATCHING

STITCHED

New Novel Coming Soon

'The Death Row Thrift Shop'

By Dale Brendan Hyde

'Even the executed leave things behind ...

Accreditation for use of quotes & samples of lyrics or poetry used in this novel are as follows. John Steinbeck, Mark Twain, Virgil, Johnny Cash, Jimmy Cliff, Jim Morrison, The Beatles & many of my own creation...

I must mention and say a heartfelt thanks to anyone who in any way has helped me over the years within the long process of completing this debut novel. Your feedback and support certainly helped ne focus at times when the end never seemed in sight.

I would also like to mention that I have numerous projects that I will be working on once this novel is safely secure on the bookshelves.

This debut novel is dedicated to my Mother & Father and my beautiful young sister & older brother and my only Son Dylan.

LOVE YOU ALWAYS.